The street was empty, no cars passed, no pedestrians were on the sidewalk. When he stepped out of the shadowed doorway, the sun smote him like a golden fist. He took his jacket off and hung it over his arm, and then his necktie, but he still ran with sweat. The office buildings stared blank-eyed from their tiered windows; the gray factories were silent. Mark looked about numbly, trying to understand what had happened, trying to make sense of the unbelievable situation. Five minutes ago it had been midwinter, with the icy streets filled with hurrying people. Now it was . . . what?

In the distance the humming, rising drone of an engine could be heard, getting louder, going along a nearby street. He hurried to the corner and reached it just in time to see the car roar across the intersection a block away. It was just that, a car, and it had been going too fast for him to see who was in it. He jumped back at a sudden shrill scream, almost at his feet, and a large seagull hurled itself into the air and flapped away. It had been tearing at a man's body that lay crumpled in the gutter. Mark had seen enough corpses in Korea to recognize another one, to remember the never-forgotten smell of corrupted flesh. How was it possible for the corpse to remain here so long, days at least? What had happened to the city?

EDITED BY
CHARLES
WAUGH
&
MARTIN H.
GREENBERG

A TOM DOHERTY ASSOCIATES BOOK

This is a work of fiction. All the characters and events portrayed in this book are fictional, and any resemblance to real people or incidents is purely coincidental.

TIME WARS

First printing: November 1986

A TOR Book

Published by Tom Doherty Associates, Inc.
49 West 24 Street
New York, N.Y. 10010

Cover art by John Pound

ISBN: 0-812-53048-9
CAN. ED.: 0-812-53049-7

Printed in the United States

0 9 8 7 6 5 4 3 2 1

ACKNOWLEDGMENTS

Contents

INTRODUCTION

Poul Anderson

Unless humanity someday, somehow, is transformed into some kind of glorified ant, we will have conflict among us as long as our species endures. Whether or not it will always lead to wars, or even to private violence, is a question to which I have no answer. Nor does anybody else. We do not understand ourselves well enough. Maybe, at last, our descendants will; or maybe not. Meanwhile we live in a world of mysteries, with the human heart perhaps the deepest of them.

Given this, it is not unreasonable for science fiction writers to project organized conflict—war, under one name or another—and crime indefinitely far into the future and indefinitely far across the cosmos. At least, it is not unreasonable in your and my part of Earth; where Communism prevails, optimism in science fiction is compulsory. However, for us, too, the mood can be hopeful. We can tell tales of right triumphing over evil, or, at any rate, the survival of some order and decency.

These are not pure daydreams. They happen in real life: for example, when Allied armies cleanse Europe of the Nazis, or simply when your neighborhood policeman goes on patrol. The stories in this book reflect the good as well as the grim side of things.

Do they, though, have any other claim to being more than sheer fantasy? After all, they involve travel faster than light, travel through time, and travel between entire universes, each one of which is considered impossible by the majority of living scientists.

Let me offer a twofold reply. First, every fiction, to the extent that it concerns imaginary people and events, is fantasy. Of course, if it has any merit, it tells us something about reality; but I just claimed that that is what the stories on hand do.

Second, are these different kinds of travel necessarily impossible?

I hasten to say that in all probability they are—as far as our present-day knowledge goes. And it does go quite far. Our nuclear devices, scientific and industrial as well as military, would not work if we didn't design them according to Einstein's principles of relativity. We have now actually measured, on an aircraft circling the globe, the contraction of time rate with speed which he predicted. Ironically, the wave-mechanical uncertainty which he denied is in everyday use, in such items as the tunnel diode. A complete catalogue of our information would be long indeed. Some physicists believe we are on the verge of a formulation that will forever sum up the basic laws of nature.

I doubt this most profoundly. My skepticism does not arise merely from the fact that, in principle, we can never be certain that we have written the ultimate equations. Rather, it is that even a layman like me can see riddles and paradoxes everywhere around us.

Never mind technical details. Either you know something about Schrödinger's cat, Bell's theorem, Kerr metric space warps, Tipler machines, Everett's many-worlds interpretation, and like matters—or you do not. If not, don't take my word, but look them up. You can find several excellent, fascinating popular books on these subjects: for instance, *The Dancing Wu Li Masters* by Gary Zukav.

The point here is simply that I think, in entire seriousness, we are an enormous way from knowing everything there is to be known; and so we can legitimately speculate about the unknown, provided only that we recognize this as speculation and nothing else.

Undoubtedly, as science learns more, all our science fiction will turn out to have been mistaken, as much of it already has. Homer, likewise, told stories about a far west in which we can no longer believe. Yet in his day that was a little-explored realm where Scylla, Charybdis, the Sirens, and the Cyclops might very well exist. And we still read the *Odyssey* with pleasure and enlightenment.

I do not venture to compare any modern writer of any kind to Homer; but I do invite you to enjoy these stories in that same spirit.

SCIENCE FICTION is a field characterized by prolificity, and it is not unusual for writers to produce large numbers of stories under several names. But Randall Garrett (1927–) is exceptional, even by the standards of sf. He churned out enormous amounts of saleable copy in a variety of genres from the early fifties. In the late fifties and early sixties he seemed to take over *Astounding/Analog*, frequently having several stories in the same issue. Among his many names, the most important are David Gordon, Darrel T. Langart, Mark Phillips, and Robert Randall, the last two used for collaborations. Much of this production was very good, particularly those featured "Lord Darcy" stories that combined systematic magic with the detective story. *The Best of Randall Garrett*, containing a portion of his finest work, was long overdue when finally published in 1982.

The following story is about another man who has become a legend, though not in his own time.

FROST AND THUNDER

Randall Garrett

Ulglossen was dabbling in polydimensional energy flows again.

Do not try to understand Ulglossen. Ulglossen's time was—is—will be—three million years after Homo sapiens sapiens *ruled Earth, and Ulglossen's species is no more to be understood by us than we could be understood by* Australopithecus.

To say, then, that Ulglossen built a "time machine" is as erroneous—and as truthful—as saying that a big industrial computer of the late 20th Century is a device for counting with pebbles.

Doing polydimensional vector analysis mentally was, for Ulglossen, too simple and automatic to be called child's play. Actually constructing the mechanism was somewhat more difficult, but Ulglossen went about it with the same toilsome joy that a racing buff goes about rebuilding his Ferrari. When it was finished, Ulglossen viewed it with the equivalent of pride.

In doing the mental math, Ulglossen had rounded off at the nineteenth decimal place, for no greater accuracy than that was needed. But, as a result, Ulglossen's "machine" caused slight eddy currents in the time flow as it passed. The resulting effect was much the same as that of an automobile going down a freeway and passing a wadded ball of paper. The paper is picked up and carried a few yards down the freeway before it falls out of the eddy currents and is dropped again.

Ulglossen was not unaware of that fact; it was simply that Ulglossen ignored it.

The device, you see, was merely a side effect of Ulglossen's real work, which was the study of the attenuation of the universal gravitational constant over a period of millions of millennia. Ulglossen happened to be on Earth, and had some experiments to perform in the very early pre-Cambrian. Ulglossen went back to do so.

I'll try to tell this the best I can. I don't expect you to believe it because, in the first place, I haven't a shred of proof, and, in the second place, I wouldn't believe it myself if I hadn't actually experienced it.

Sure, I *might* have dreamed it. But it was too solid, too detailed, too logical, too *real* to have been a dream. So it happened, and I'm stuck with it.

It begins, I suppose, when I got the letter from Sten Örnfeld. I've known Sten for years. We've fought together in some pretty odd places, argued with each other about the damndest things, and once even quarreled over the same woman. (He won.) He's a good drinking buddy, and he'll back a friend in a pinch. What more do you want?

A few years back, Sten and I got interested in what was then the relatively new sport of combat pistol, down in southern California. It's a game that requires fast draw, fast shooting, fast reloading, and accuracy to make points. One of the rules is that you *must* use full-charge service cartridges. No half-charge wadcutters allowed.

We both enjoyed it.

Then, I didn't see Sten for some time. I didn't think much about it. Sten does a lot of traveling, but, basically, he's a Swede, and he has to go home every so often. I'm only half Swede, and I was born in the United States. Sweden is a lovely country, but it just isn't home to me.

Anyway, I got this letter addressed to me, Theodore Sorenson, with a Stockholm postmark. Sten, so he claimed, had introduced combat pistol shooting to Sweden, and had built a range on his property. He was holding a match in September, and would I come? There would be plenty of *akvavit*.

He hadn't needed to add that last, but it helped. I made plane reservations and other arrangements.

You would not believe how hard it is to get a handgun into Sweden legally. (I don't know how hard it would be to do it illegally; I've never tried.) Even though Sten Örnfeld had all kinds of connections in high places and has filed a declaration of intent or something, informing the government of his shooting match, and had gotten the government's permission, it was rough sledding. I had to produce all kinds of papers identifying the weapon, and papers showing that I had never been convicted of a felony, and on and on. Fortunately, Sten's letter had warned me about all that. Still, just filling out papers and signing my name must have used up a good liter of ink.

Eventually, they decided I could take my .45 Colt Commander into Sweden. Provided, of course, that I brought it back out again; I couldn't sell it, give it away, or, presumably, lose it, under dire penalties.

Mine isn't an ordinary, off-the-shelf Colt Commander. I had it rebuilt by Pachmayr of Los Angeles. It has a 4½-inch barrel, a BoMar adjustable combat rear sight, a precision-fit slide with a special micro barrel-bushing, a special trigger assembly that lets me fire the first shot double action, and a lot of other extra goodies. It's hard-chromed all over, which means it can stand up to a lot of weather without rusting. In a machine rest, I can get a three-inch group at a hundred yards with a hundred shots. When Frank Pachmayr finishes with a Colt Commander, you can damn well bet you've got one of the finest, hardest-hitting handguns in the world.

So I had no intention of selling, giving away, or losing that weapon.

Sten Örnfeld met me at Arlanda Airport and helped me get through the paperwork. My Swedish is as good as his, just as his English is as good as mine—but he knows the ins-and-outs of the local ways better than I do. Then we got in his plane, and he flew me to his little place in the woods.

Not so little, and more of a forest than woods. It was on the Österdalälven—the Österdal River—on the western slope of the Kjölen, that great ridge of mountains whose peaks separate Norway from Sweden. It was some miles northeast of a little town called Älvadalen, well away from everything.

Sten landed us in a little clearing, and said: "Theodore, we are here."

Sten always called me Theodore, another reason why he was a friend. I have never liked "Ted." My mother was an O'Malley, with red-auburn hair; my father was a blond Swede. Mine came out flaming red-orange. So I was "Ted the Red" —and worse—in school. Like the guy named Sue, it taught me to fight, but I hated it.

Of course, if Sten was speaking Swedish at the time, it came out something like "Taydor" but I didn't mind that.

He showed me through his house, an old-fashioned, sturdy place with the typical high-pitched, snow-shedding roof.

"You're the first one in," he told me. "Sit down and have a little *akvavit*. Unless you're hungry?"

I wasn't; I'd eaten pretty well on the plane. We had *akvavit* and coffee, and some *rågkakor* his mother had sent him.

"Tonight," he said, "I'll fix up the spices and the orange rind and the almonds and the raisins, and let 'em soak in the booze overnight for hot *glögg* tomorrow. And I've fixed it up for some people to drive up from Älvadalen with a *julskinka* we'll serve fourteen weeks early."

"So I'm the only one here so far?" I said.

"First arrival," he said. "Which poses a problem."

I sipped more *akvavit*. "Which is?"

"I *think*—I say I *think*—you're going to outshoot the whole lot of 'em. Now, I've got this special course laid out, and a lot of 'friend-and-foe' pop-up targets. I was going to let each of you guys run it cold. But there are some of these hard-nosed skvareheads who'd secretly think I took you over the course early so you'd be prepared. They wouldn't say anything, but they'd think it."

"So what do you figure on doing?"

"Well, I haven't set the pop-ups yet; I was going to set 'em in the morning. Instead, I'm going to take all of you over the course before the targets are set, then set 'em up while you guys watch each other here." He roared with laughter. "That will keep you all honest!"

Sten isn't your big Swede; he's a little guy, five-six or so, and I stand six-four. I must outweigh him by thirty-six kilos.

I could probably whip him in a fight, but I would be in damn sad condition for a while afterward. I have seen what has happened to a couple of large galoots who thought he'd be an easy pushover. He was standing over them, begging them to get up for more fun, but they couldn't hear him.

"Hey!" he said. "How about checking me out on that fancy piece of artillery, now that we've managed to get it into the country?"

I was willing. I showed him the Pachmayr conversion of the Colt Commander, and he was fascinated. His final comment was: "God*dam*, what a gun!"

When we were glowing nicely warm inside from the *akvavit*, and I could taste caraway clear back to my tonsils, Sten put the bottle away. "Got to keep the shootin' eye clear and the shootin' hand steady for tomorrow," he said. "Besides, I've got to do the *glögg* fixin's."

"Need any help?"

"Nope."

"Is there anyplace I could go hose a few rounds through the tube, just to get the feel in this climate?"

"Sure. There's a dead pine about eighty yards due south. I'm going to cut it down for winter fuel later, but I've put a few slugs in it, myself. Make damn heavy logs, I'll bet." He laughed again. Then: "Hey, you got a name for that blaster of yours yet?"

"No. Not yet." Sten had a habit of naming his weapons, but I'd never gone in for the custom much.

"Shame. Good gun should have a name. Never mind; you'll think of one. It's beginning to get late. Dark in an hour and a half. Dress warm. Good shooting."

Dressing warm was no problem. I was ready for it; I knew that the weather can get pretty chilly in the highlands of Sweden in September. Walking from Sten's little plane hangar to his lodge had told me that I wasn't properly dressed for afternoon; I knew good and well that the clothes I was wearing wouldn't be warm enough for dusk.

"What's the forecast for tomorrow, Sten?" I yelled at him in the kitchen.

"Cold and clear!" he yelled back. "Below freezing!"

"I should have known! You call me out of warm California so I can freeze my ass off trying to fire a handgun in Sweden!"

"Damn right! You got to have *some* sort of handicap! Shut up and go shoot!"

It really wasn't cold enough yet, but I decided I'd have a little practice in full insulation. I put on my Scandinavian net long johns, and an aluminized close-weave over that. I get my outdoor clothing from Herter's, in Minnesota; there's no one like them for quality and price. I wore a Guide Association Chamois Cloth tan shirt, Down Arctic pants, and Yukon Leather Pac boots. Over that went the Hudson Bay Down Arctic parka with the frost-free, fur-trimmed hood.

For gloves, I had two choices: the pigskin shooting gloves or the Hudson Bay buckskin one-finger mittens. I shoved the mittens in my parka pocket and put on the shooting gloves. *Try 'em both,* I told myself.

I'd had the parka specially cut for quick-draw work, with an opening on the right side for the pistol and holster. Before I sealed up the parka, I put on the gunbelt, a special job made for me by Don Hume, of Miami, Oklahoma. It has quick-release leather pockets, five of them, for holding extra magazines. The holster is a quick-draw job made for my sidearm. When Don Hume says, "Whatever the need," he means it.

"Carry on, bartender!" I yelled from the door. "I am off to the wars!"

"Be sure that old dead pine doesn't beat you to the draw!" he yelled back.

It was cold outside, but there wasn't much wind. I saw the dead pine, and headed for it.

Night comes on slowly in the north, but it comes early east of the Kjölen. Those mountains make for a high horizon.

Sven had, indeed, used that pine for target practice; he'd painted a six-inch white circle on it. I went up to the pine, then turned to pace off twenty-five yards.

I was at twenty paces when the wind hit.

I don't know how to describe what happened. It was like a wind, and yet it wasn't. It was as if everything whirled around, and *then* the wind came.

And I was in the middle of the goddamdest blizzard I had seen since the time I nearly froze to death in Nebraska.

I stood still. Only a damn fool wanders around when he can't see where he's going. I knew I was only fifty yards from Sten's lodge, and I trusted the insulated clothing I was wearing. I wouldn't freeze, and I could wait out the storm until I got my bearings.

I put out my arms and turned slowly. My right hand touched a tree. I hadn't remembered a tree that near, but it gave me an anchor. I stepped over and stood the leeward side of it, away from the wind.

In those two steps, I noticed something impossible to believe.

The snow around my ankles was four inches deep.

There had been no snow on the ground when I started out.

And I don't believe there has *ever* been a storm which could deposit four inches of snow in less than two seconds.

I just stood there, wondering what the hell had happened. I couldn't see more than a couple of yards in front of me, and the dim light didn't help much. I waited. The howling of that sudden wind was far too loud for my voice to be heard over fifty yards. Sten would never hear me.

But he would know I was out in this mess, and he would know I would keep my head. I could wait. For a while, at least.

I looked at my watch to check the time. Very good. Then I leaned back against the relatively warm tree to wait.

My hands began to get cold. I stripped off the shooting gloves and put on the one-finger mittens. Better.

As sometimes happens in a snowstorm, the wind died down abruptly. It became a gentle breeze. Overhead, the clouds had cleared, and there came almost a dead calm as the last few snowflakes drifted down. My watch told me it had been twenty-seven minutes since the storm had started.

The sun glittered off the fresh snow.

The sun?

By now, it should have been close to the peaks of the Kjölen. It wasn't. It was almost overhead.

I looked carefully around. I should have been able to see the dead pine, and I certainly should have been able to see Sven's lodge.

I could see neither. Around me was nothing but forest. Only the distant crest of the Kjölen looked the same.

The whole thing was impossible, and I knew it. I also knew that I was seeing what I was seeing.

My mother, bless her, had told me stories when I was a kid—old Irish stories about the Folk of Faerie and the Hollow Hills.

"If you're invited beneath a Hollow Hill by the Faerie Folk, don't ever touch a drop of their drink or a bite of their food, or when you come out after the night, a hundred years will have passed."

Throw out that hypothesis. I hadn't been invited beneath any Hollow Hill, much less taken a drink or eaten a bite.

Unless Sten—

Oh, hell, *no!* That was silly.

But certainly *something* had gone wrong with time. Or with my mind. The sun was in the wrong place.

If you can't trust your own mind, what can you trust? As old Whatsisname—Descartes—said: *Cogito ergo sum.*

I think; therefore, I am.

I decided, therefore, that not only I *was*, but I was sane.

I had read about cryogenic experiments. Theoretically, if an organism is frozen properly, it can stay in a state of suspended animation for an indefinite time. Suppose that had happened to me. Suppose a sudden blizzard had frozen me stiff, and I had thawed out years later, without realizing that time had passed.

It didn't seem likely. Surely I would have been found by Sten. Or, if not, I'd have waked up flat on my back instead of standing up. No. Not likely.

But I decided to check it out. It would take a long time for Sten's lodge to deteriorate to the point where there were no traces left.

I walked over to where the lodge should have been, trudging through the ankle-deep snow. I'm a pretty good judge of distance and direction, and I checked the whole area where the lodge should have been.

Nothing. Pine needles under the snow; nothing under the pine needles but dirt. Nothing.

There was an old, broken tree stump about where Sten's living room should have been. I brushed the snow off it and sat down.

I don't think I thought for several minutes. Then I noticed that I was beginning to get a little chilled. Get some exercise and build a fire. I went out and gathered what broken bits of pine branches I could find, and built a small campfire near the stump. No rubbing two sticks together; my butane lighter still worked.

I sat there for an hour in a pale blue funk, wondering what had happened.

I know it was an hour, because I looked at my watch again. That was when I heard a quiet noise behind me.

I jerked my head around and looked. My hand went to my right hip. But I didn't draw.

Standing not ten paces from me were seven men.

They were quiet and unmoving, like frozen statues except for their eyes, which regarded me with interest, curiosity, and caution.

They were heavily clad in dark furs, like Eskimos wearing black bearskins. Each one carried a long spear and a roundshield.

They weren't Eskimos. Eskimos don't have blue eyes and blond hair. Those blue eyes regarded me with suspicion.

I lifted my hands carefully, showing them empty. I couldn't figure out the spears, but I didn't want to get in a hassle with the locals.

"Good afternoon, gentlemen," I said in Swedish. I kept my voice low and controlled. "Would you care to share the fire with me?"

There was a pause while all of them looked blank. Then one of them stepped forward and said something in an equally low and controlled voice. I couldn't understand a word of it.

Still, it sounded damned familiar.

I can speak—besides English—Swedish, Norwegian, Icelandic, and Danish very well. I speak German with a weird accent, but I can make myself understood easily. Afrikaans is a language I can almost understand, but not quite. This was like that.

"I don't understand," I said.

The man who had stepped out—obviously the leader—turned and said something to the man next to him. The second man answered. Their voices were low and so soft I couldn't get the drift. I figured the second man was second in command.

The leader turned to me again and spoke in a louder voice, very slowly, syllable by syllable.

It took me a few seconds to get it.

I don't know if I can explain it to you. Look; suppose you were in that same situation, and some fur-clad character had come up to you and said: "*hwahn-thah-tah-pree-lah-wee-thiz-show-rez-so-tah-theh-drocht-ahv-mahrch-ath-peersed-tow-theh-row-tah. . .*"

You might feel a little left out of it, right?

Then, suddenly, it comes to you that what he is doing is too-carefully pronouncing Chaucer's *"Whan that Aprillë with his shourës sootë/The droghte of Marche hath percëd to the rootë . . ."*

And then you have to translate that into modern English as: "When April, with his showers sweet, the drought of March has pierced to the root . . ."

It was like that to me. I got it, partly, but it was older than any Northman's tongue I had ever heard. It was more inflected and had more syllables per word than any I knew. It made Icelandic seem modern.

What he had said was: "You say you do not understand?"

I tried to copy his usage and inflection. It came out something like: "Yah. Me no understand."

I won't try to give you any more of my linguistic troubles. I'll just say that the conversation took a little longer than it should have.

"You must understand a little," he said.

"Yah. A little. Not well. I am sorry."

"Who are you, and what do you do here?"

"I called Theodore." But I pronounced it "Taydor."

"What do you do here?" he repeated. Those spears weren't pointed at me, but they were at the ready. I didn't like the looks of the chipped flint points.

"I lost," I said. "I have hunger and suffer from cold."

"Where do you come from?"

"America. Across the western sea."

They looked at each other. Then the leader looked back at me. "You are alone?"

"I am alone." It was a dangerous admission to make. A lone man is easier prey than one who has friends. But I figured a bluff of having friends around wouldn't work, and I didn't want to be caught out as a liar right off the bat. Besides, if worse came to worst, I figured I could gun the seven of them down before they could touch me. But I didn't want to do that. Not unless they attacked me without provocation.

The spears remained at the ready, but the men seemed to relax a little.

"What is your station?" the leader asked.

It took me a second. He was asking my rank in life. Was I a thrall or a freeman or a noble?

"I am a freeman and a warrior," I answered honestly. The time I'd spent in the service ought to count for something. "But I have, as you see, no spear and no shield."

"Then how do we know you are a warrior? How did you lose your spear and shield?"

"I did not lose them. I have come in peace."

That flabbergasted them. There was a lot of low talk among them. I sat quietly.

I was taking the tide as it ran. I still had no idea of what had happened to me, but I was damned if I'd be a stupid tourist in someone else's country.

Finally, the leader said: "Tay'or, you will come with us. We will give you food and drink and we will talk over your oddness."

"I will come," I said. I stood up.

They gripped their spears more tightly, and their eyes widened.

I knew why. It was something none of us had realized while I was seated. I was bigger than any of them. Not a one of them was taller than Sten Örnfeld. But they looked just as tough.

I folded my hands on my chest. "I go where you lead."

They didn't all lead. The head cheese and his lieutenant went ahead; the other five were behind me, spears still at the ready.

It was about twenty minutes' walk, which made sense. The fire I had started had attracted their attention, and the wisp of smoke had led them to me. It had just taken them a little time to decide to investigate.

We ended up at a collection of log cabins. I was marched straight to the largest one and led inside, past a curtain of bearskin. I had to duck my head to get through the doorway. Just inside, the leader stopped and said: "You are in the mead-hall of Vigalaf Wolfslayer. Conduct yourself accordingly."

There was a fire in the middle of the earth-floored room, just below a hole in the roof which was supposed to let the smoke out. Maybe eighty percent of it went out, but the other twenty percent filled the air. Underneath the smell of pine smoke was an odor of rancid fat and cooked meat.

By the fire stood a man with a great gray-blond beard, and

long hair to match. He was a giant of a man, compared to the others; he must have stood a full five-eight.

I took him to be Vigalaf Wolfslayer, and, as it turned out, I was right. He said two words: "Explain, Hrotokar."

Hrotokar was the leader of the squad who'd found me. He told his story straight, emphasizing the fact that I had given no trouble.

Vigalaf looked at me for the first time. "Doff your hood in my presence, Giant Tay'or," he said—not arrogantly, but merely as a statement of his due. I peeled back the hood of my parka.

"Truly, not one of *Them*, then," he said. "The Eaters-of-Men have no such hair, nor such eyes. Are you truly one of us, Giant?"

"A distant relative, Vigalaf Wolfslayer," I said. I thought I was telling the truth, but God knows how distant the relationship was.

"You will call me Father Wolfslayer," he said. Again, no arrogance—just his due.

"I ask pardon, Father Wolfslayer," I said. "I am not familiar with your customs. Forgive me if I err."

He nodded and eased himself down on a pile of furs near the fire. "Sit," he said.

I sat. My escort did not. Evidently, they knew his order had not been addressed to them. There were no furs for me, so I planted my rump on the bare earth of the floor, crossing my legs.

"Bring him mead," he said.

By this time, my eyes had grown accustomed to the gloom in the windowless mead-hall. I saw that there were other people back in the dark corners, all wearing furs. In spite of the fire, there was still a chill; most of the heat was going out the roof hole.

From one dark corner, there was a gurgling noise. Then a figure stepped forward, bearing a horn of mead. I mean it. An honest-to-God cow's horn, ten inches long, full of liquid.

I've done a lot of drinking in a lot of places, but the one drink I'd never tried until that moment was mead. I knew it was made from honey, so I had, somewhere in the back of my mind, the notion that it was sweet, like port or sweet sherry.

No such thing. This stuff tasted like flat beer. It had a certain amount of authority, however.

Before I drank, I thought I ought to say something. I lifted the horn and said: "I thank you for your hospitality, Father Wolfslayer." I drank.

It was evidently the right thing to say. I saw his beard and mustache curl in a smile. "Truly," he said again, "not one of *Them*."

I took the bit in my teeth. "Forgive my ignorance, Father Wolfslayer, but you speak of *Them*. Who are *They?*"

His shaggy gray eyebrows lifted. "You know not? Truly, you are from afar. *They* are the demons, the Evil Ones, the Eaters-of-Men. *They* are from the Far North, and they come to slay and to eat. *They* speak as do animals. *They* are Giants!" He paused. "Not so great as you, but Giants, nonetheless." Another pause. "And they wear frost about them instead of furs, as decent folk do."

I couldn't make any sense out of that, but I filed it away for later reference.

"I know nothing of them, Father Wolfslayer," I said. "They are certainly no friends nor kin of mine."

An enemy of these people, obviously. But the "demon" bit, and the "evil" and the "eaters-of-men" I figured as just so much propaganda.

"You speak well, Giant Tay'or," Vigalaf said. He raised a hand. "Bring him food."

The same person came out from the shadows, bearing a wooden bowl in one hand. This time, I looked more closely at who was serving me.

Me, I wear a beard. It's as red as the rest of my hair. I think shaving is a bore. The rest of the men there wore beards, too. My server was either a beardless boy or a woman. A people who use flint points on their spears find shaving more than a bore; they find it impossible. Besides, the lines around her eyes showed more character than a kid ever had. With those heavy furs on, it was hard to tell anything about her figure, but my instincts told me, more than anything else, that this was no teenage lad.

The glint in her eyes as they met mine confirmed my assessment of the situation. There was a slight smile on her lips as she handed me the bowl.

I automatically took it with my right hand. Then she held

out her closed left hand toward mine. I opened my left hand, palm up. She dropped three nuts into it and turned away, going back to her dark corner.

I just sat there for a few seconds. The bowl contained some sort of porridge with a few chunks of meat in it. But there were no utensils to eat it with. And what about those nuts in my other hand?

I could feel every eye in the place on me. This was a test of some kind, but I didn't know what. What the hell should I do next?

Think, Sorenson! Think!

The mead-hall was utterly silent except for the crackling of the fire.

I don't know what sort of logic I used. All I knew was that if I failed this test I had better have my right hand free.

I closed my left hand on the nuts, put the bowl in my lap, and said: "Thank you again, Father Wolfslayer."

There was no answer. Carefully, I began to pick up the lumpy porridge with the thumb and first two fingers of my right hand, conveying the stuff to my mouth. No reaction from the audience. I ate it all. Then I put the bowl on the ground near me. Still no reaction.

It was those damn three nuts, then.

What was I supposed to do with them? Eat them? Give them? Shove them up my nose? What?

I opened my hand slowly and looked at them. They were some kind of walnut, I guessed, but the shell on them was a lot thicker and harder than the walnuts I was used to.

I wiped my right hand off on my pantsleg. I didn't want a slick hand if I had to grab for my gun. Then I lifted my head slowly and looked at the Wolfslayer, holding his eyes.

He nodded silently and gestured with one hand.

The broad-shouldered blonde woman brought me a flat rock, laying it on the ground in front of me before she retreated to her corner.

I got it then. Every man in the place—and the woman, too—carried a little stone-headed mallet cinched at the waist.

Well, what the hell. A chance is a chance.

Frank Pachmayr will supply you, if you want them, with magazines that have a quarter-inch of rubber on the bottom, which, according to some, makes it easier to slam the magazine home on the reload. I never cared for them. Mine are steel on the bottom—no rubber. A personal idiosyncrasy.

At that moment, I thanked God for my idiosyncrasy.

I put the three walnuts on the flat rock, and drew my weapon.

A gun should never be used that way. But, then, a gun should never be used in any way unless there's need for it. It saved my life that time. I took it out, grabbed it near the muzzle, and carefully cracked nuts with the butt.

Call it instinct, call it intuition, call it what you will. It was the right thing to do. I found out later that the terrible Eaters-of-Men carried large stone axes, but not small ones. If they ever ate nuts, they cracked them by grabbing the nearest rock and slamming them. No delicacy.

The nuts, by the way, were very bitter.

As I ate the last one, there was a deep sigh that sounded all through the mead-hall. Wolfslayer said: "Giant Tay'or, will you be our guest?"

Searching back in my memory for what little I knew about the ancient history of the Northmen, I said: "I have no guest-gift for my host, Father Wolfslayer."

"Your guest-gift will be your strength, if you will give it. Will you fight against *Them* when the Demons come again?"

That was a tough one. I only knew one side of the quarrel. But, what the hell, a man who can't choose sides, even if he's wrong, isn't worth a damn. "I have no spear or shield, Father Wolfslayer," I said. And realized I was hedging.

"They will be provided."

"Then I will fight for you."

"Then you are my guest!" Suddenly, he came out with a barrel-roll laugh. "Mead! Mead for all! Come, Giant, sit by me! Here is a skin!"

The party began.

After about the fourth horn of mead, the Wolfslayer leaned over and said: "Where did you come by such a strange mallet?"

"It was made by a friend in a distant country," I said. "It was made for my hands alone." I didn't want the old boy to ask to handle my Colt.

His bushy eyebrows went up again. "Of course. Are not all such, in all places?"

"Of course, Father Wolfslayer." More information. The nutcrackers were personal gear. Fine.

That night, I slept under a bearskin, still wearing my insulated outdoor clothing. I hadn't bathed, but nobody else around there had, either. You could tell.

When I woke up, I was sweating, but my nose was cold. Around me, I could hear thunderous snores, but somebody was moving around, too. I opened one eye a crack. I should have known. The men were still sleeping; the women were preparing breakfast. Women's lib had evidently not reached these people. Which reminded me—

Just who the hell *were* these people?

I was sleeping on my left side (a holstered .45 makes a very lumpy mattress), with my right hand on the butt of my pistol. I kept my eyes closed and checked for hangover. Nope. Whoever their brewmaster was, he made a good brew.

This was the first opportunity that I had had to really think since the squad of seven had found me in the forest. Since then, I had merely been doing my best to stay alive.

I realized that I had accepted one thing: Like Twain's Connecticut Yankee or de Camp's Martin Padway, I had slipped back in time. How far? I didn't know. I still don't. I probably never will. These people weren't Christians, by a long shot, and they'd never heard of Him; I'd got that much in my conversations the previous night.

They'd never heard of Rome, either, but that didn't mean anything. There were a lot of things they might not have heard of, way up here. Like Egypt.

Still, I think I must have been at least fifteen hundred years in my own past, and probably more. Their use of stone instead of metal certainly argued for great antiquity, and they didn't act at all like the bloodthirsty Vikings history records so vividly.

They were a hunting-and-gathering culture, with emphasis on hunting in the winter. Bear seemed to be their big game during the cold months. A hibernating bear, if you can find one, is fairly easy to kill if you can get it before it wakes up. The meat is good, and the skins are useful.

Snores were changing to snorts and snuffles; the men were waking up. I sat up and yawned prodigiously. Almost immediately, the broad-shouldered blonde of the night before was kneeling in front of me with a wooden bowl full of meat chunks and a horn of warm mead. She was really smiling this time, showing teeth. I noticed that the left upper lateral incisor was crooked. Charming. If only she'd had a bath.

"What's your name?" I asked, after thanking her for the food. As I said, I won't go into my linguistic difficulties. She didn't understand me at first, and we had to work it out.

"Brahenagenunda Vigalaf Wolfslayer's Daughter," she told me. "But you should not thank me for the food; you should thank Father Wolfslayer, for the food is his."

"I shall thank *him* for the food," I said. "I am thanking *you* for the preparing of it." After all, if she was the Wolfslayer's daughter, I was talking to a princess.

She blushed. "Excuse me. I must serve the others."

It occurred to me then that since everyone addressed the old man as "Father" maybe everyone called themselves his sons and daughters, whether they were biologically his children or not. I found out later that only his true children took the Wolfslayer's name. Brahenagenunda was his daughter, all right.

I saw a couple of the men going out, and I had a hunch I knew where they were going, so I followed them. I was right: they headed for the woods. When I returned. I felt much more comfortable. Snow is a poor substitute for toilet tissue, but it's better than nothing.

The cold was not too bitter. About minus two Celsius, I figured. The people from the other, smaller log cabins were going about their business, their breath, like mine, making white plumes in the air, as if everyone were puffing cigarettes. I was glad I'd never had the habit of smoking; I had the feeling tobacco would be hard to come by here-and-now.

Squad Leader Hrotokar was waiting for me just outside Vigalaf's mead-hall. "Hail, Tay'or."

"Hail, Hrotokar."

"We go to seek the bear, my men and I. Will you come?" Another test, I decided. "I will come."

"There is spear and shield for you." Then he looked me over and became less formal. "Are you sure those funny clothes you're wearing will keep you warm enough?"

"They'll be fine," I assured him. I wasn't going to tell him that they were probably far better than the stuff he was wearing.

"Well, they'll have to do, I guess," he said. "I've got an extra jacket and trousers, but I doubt they'd fit."

"I think you're right. How do we go about this bear hunt?"

Primarily, it turned out, what we did was look for tiny wisps of vapor coming out of a crack in the snow. It indicated that a bear was holed away underneath, breathing slowly and shallowly in hibernation. Then we checked to see if the bear was a female with cubs. We only killed males.

I won't bother telling about that day's hunt, because that's all we did—hunt. Didn't find a damned thing. But Hrotokar and I got to know each other pretty well. Unlike most hunts, we could talk; there's not much danger of waking up a hibernating bear.

The thing was, I wasn't able to get in any practice with spear and shield that day. There's a Greek friend of mine in San José who is a nut on spear-and-shield work in the manner of the ancient Greek *hoplites*. He and a bunch of his buddies worked out the technique, and practiced it, using blunt, padded spears. I practiced with them, and got pretty good at it, but trying it for real is very different indeed. I've had lots of practice with bayonet-and-rifle, too, but I've never had to use it in combat. Or against a bear, even a sleeping one.

The sun shone most of the day, but the clouds came in in the afternoon, and it was snowing again by the time we reached the settlement.

We came in empty-handed, and so did all of the other squads but one. They had a bear, which caused great rejoicing and happiness throughout the community. (I never actually counted them, but I'd estimate there were between fifty-five and sixty people in the whole settlement.) One of the other squads had seen a deer, but that was the one that got away.

During the winter, most of the gathering done by the women is for firewood. Fallen branches, twigs, anything that will burn. If they find an occasional dead tree, or one that has fallen over, they mark the spot and tell the men about it. Then both sexes form a work party to bring it in.

I was not the guest of honor that night in the mead-hall. A guy named Woritegeren, who had killed the bear, got all the kudos—which he deserved. Father Wolfslayer stood up and made a speech about his bravery and prowess, and then a little guy with a limp—a bard, I guess—made up a chant about Woritegeren that made it sound as if he'd slain a two-ton Kodiak all by himself.

Then Father Wolfslayer shouted: "Mead! Bring mead!"

A woman came from the shadows and brought Woritigeren his horn of mead, but it wasn't Brahenagenunda. This one was older and a good deal more worn looking.

Another woman, even older, came out and whispered into Vigalaf Wolfslayer's ear. He scowled.

There was tension in the air; I could tell that. The mead for the hero was supposed to be served by the Wolfslayer's youngest and prettiest daughter, and that hadn't been done.

Technically, Woritigeren had been given a social putdown.

Vigalaf Wolfslayer rose with majestic dignity. "Woritigeren Hero," he said, looking at the hunter, who was still holding his mead-horn untasted, "neither I nor my women meant insult here. I have just been told that Vigalaf's Daughter Brahenagenunda has not returned from her wood-gathering. The sun had gone to his rest, and the blizzard is over all." He turned to the little guy with the limp. "Make us a prayer to the All-Father, Song Chanter."

He made us a prayer. I didn't understand a word of it; it was in a language even older than the one they spoke. But it had a solemnity and dignity that made it a prayer.

One thing. I almost got caught out. I started to bow my head, but I saw what the others were doing in time, and looked upward, out the smoke-hole, toward the sky. I guess they believed in looking God in the face when they talked to Him.

When it was over, the Wolfslayer said: "It is her Wyrd. We shall look for her in the morning."

He was right, of course. I wanted to charge out right then and start searching, but in a blizzard, without lights, it would have been senseless. He—and we—had done all that was possible for the time being.

Wolfslayer lifted his mead-horn. "Now, Woritigeren Hero, to your honor."

And the party was on again.

It may seem heartless, the way they behaved. Here was a woman—girl, really; she was only sixteen—out in the dark and the freezing cold, alone and without help, while her friends and relatives were having a merry time and getting all boozed up. But these were a practical people. When nothing can be done, do something else. She couldn't be rescued yet, so get on with the original schedule. When the time came, things would be done.

In the morning, the sky was clear again. The squads went out, this time both hunting and searching. Deer, bear, or dear Brahenagenunda, whatever we could find.

We found nothing. The snow had covered everything. It was six inches deep on the level, and deeper in the drifts. She might have been lying under the snow somewhere, but you can't search every snowdrift.

There was no party in the mead-hall that evening. Neither game nor maid had been found. It was a gloomy night. I slept only because I was exhausted.

The next morning, I went out again with Hrotokar's squad. The gloom was still with us. We didn't talk much.

It was about noon when we came across the Death Sign.

That's what Hrotokar called it.

"The Demons," he said very softly. "*They* are here."

I saw what he was pointing at. It was a human skull—the upper part, with the jawbone missing—impaled on a stake about thirty yards away.

"What does it mean?" I asked.

"War," he said simply. "*They*, too, want the bear and the deer. *They* come from the North, with their clothing of frost. This is our hunting country, but *They* want to take it from us. Drive us away or kill us. Come, let us see."

He gave orders to the rest of the squad to be on the lookout, in case this was a trap of some kind. We went up to the Death Sign without seeing or hearing any living thing around.

The skull was a fresh one. There were still shreds of boiled flesh clinging to parts of it. The stake had been thrust through the opening where the spinal column had been. Footprints led to and from the grisly thing. It had been put there sometime that morning.

Hrotokar said in a low grating voice: "All-Father curse them. A man's skull they would have kept to drink from."

Then I saw the crooked left upper lateral incisor.

I know, now, what the word *berserker* means. A red haze of absolute hatred came over me. If there had been anyone to vent that hatred against, I damn well would have done it. I don't know how long that red haze lasted. It seemed eternal from inside, but the others were still standing in the same positions when I came out of it, so it couldn't have been too long.

I had not lost the hatred; it had merely become cold and calculating instead of hot and wild. "Hrotokar," I said calmly, "what do we do next?"

"We must tell the Wolfslayer," he said. From the sound of his voice, I could tell that the same cold hatred had come over him.

"And what will he do?"

"All the fighting men will follow these tracks until we find the Eaters-of-Men, and then we will slay them." He turned to one of the men. "Fleet-of-Foot, go and—"

"Hold, Hrotokar Squad-Leader," I said carefully. "This is a trap." Don't ask me how I knew; I just knew. "If Father Wolfslayer sends all the fighting men, that will leave the settlement unguarded. That is what *They* want us to do. Then, while we are following the trail, *They* will go to the settlement and butcher the women, the children, and the old ones."

He frowned. "That very well may be, Tay'or. What, then, should we do?"

"How many of the Eaters-of-Men are there?" I asked.

"Half again as many as we have in the settlement. Maybe more. Perhaps we cannot win." He shrugged. "We must try."

"We can win. Do you trust me, Hrotokar?"

He looked at me for a long moment. "I trust you, Giant Fire-Hair."

"Good. Now, here's what you do: Send Fleet-of-Foot to warn Father Wolfslayer. But Father Wolfslayer is not to send more than another squad to us. The rest should stay at the settlement to hold off the Demons. Meanwhile, we and the new squad will loop around and come upon the Demons from behind. Do you understand?"

A wolfish grin came over his face, and he nodded. "I see. It shall be done."

It took an hour for the second squad to arrive. Then we started following the tracks. But not too far. Only one of the Demons had been needed to place that skull where it would be found, and it was his job to lead us off. As soon as the tracks in the snow began leading off in the wrong direction,

Hrotokar and I led the men around in an arc, back toward the settlement.

Sure enough, the place was under siege.

The besiegers had the place surrounded. Hrotokar had been underestimating when he said that there were half again as many of the invaders as there were of Father Wolfslayer's people. There were over fifty males of the Demons surrounding the log cabins. That meant that their total numbers probably exceeded a hundred.

The Demons were human, of course. There was nothing supernatural about them. They came from the far east of Asia, I think. They were big, about six feet tall, and their faces were definitely Oriental. Mongols? Huns? I don't know. You name it, and you can have it. You wouldn't want it.

They weren't Eskimos; I knew that. But they wore "frost." Polar bear skins. White, you see. And they came from the North.

That makes sense, too. Look at a map of northern Europe. In order to get down into southern Sweden, they'd *have* to come from the North. From the East, they'd have had to come up through Finland and down south again.

Whoever they were, I did not like them.

They were closing in on the settlement when I and the fourteen men with me came up behind them.

"Do we attack now, Fire-Hair?" Hrotokar asked softly. I don't know why, but he had evidently decided to give the leadership to me. He didn't sound very confident—after all, fifteen men against fifty?—but for some reason he trusted me.

"Friend," I asked gently, "how many of those could you kill in a charge?"

His eyes narrowed as he looked at me. "We come from behind. At least fifteen. Perhaps thirty."

"Good. Kill me fifteen, and the rest I shall take care of."

I only had fifty rounds of ammo, and in a firefight you can't be sure every shot will count.

His eyes widened. "Do you swear?"

"I swear by the All-Father and by my life," I said. "Go, Friend Hrotokar. Kill the cannibal sons-of-bitches!" And I added: "When you go, scream like furies! I will be with you every hand of the way."

And I was.

When the two squads charged in, screaming war cries, I was with them. The Demons heard us and turned.

They came at us, spears at the ready. When there was twenty yards between the two opposing ranks, I tossed away my spear and shield, dropped to one knee, and drew my pistol.

The thunder of that weapon echoed across the snowfield as I placed each shot. I think my own men hesitated when they heard that noise, but they charged on when they saw it was me doing the damage.

They didn't know what to make of it, but they saw the Demons, the Eaters-of-Men, fall one after another, and they knew I was doing my part, as I had promised.

Forty-five caliber hardball slugs from service ammo does more damage to living flesh than any other handgun ammo in existence. A man hit solidly with one of those bullets goes down and stays down.

I fired as if I were firing at pop-up targets, except that there was no "friend-or-foe." If it was wearing a polar-bear suit, it was a foe.

The cold hatred for these horrors burned in my brain. They were targets, nothing more. They were things to be shot down and obliterated. When one magazine was empty, I put in another without even thinking about it.

I still had half a magazine left when the fighting was over.

Forty-four of the no-good sons-of-bitches had fallen to me. Hrotokar and his squads had taken care of the rest.

I sat there on the ground, exhausted. Killing is not fun; it is horrible. It is something you must do to preserve your own life, or that of your loved ones.

I don't know how long I sat there, with my pistol in my hand, but the next thing I knew, there was someone towering above me.

"Giant Tay'or Fire-Hair," he began. Then he stopped.

I looked up. It was Father Wolfslayer. He looked rather frightened. He cleared his throat.

I stood up to face him. I still couldn't talk.

All of them backed away from me—not in fear, but in reverence. I didn't like that.

"We know you now for what you are," the Wolfslayer continued. "We will—"

And then something cut him off. The world spun again.

* * *

Ulglossen, having finished the experiments necessary, prepared to return to—

But wait! In the twenty-first decimal, there was an aberration. Some life-form had been dragged from its proper space-time. Poor thing. On the way back, Ulglossen would return the life-form to its proper era. More or less. After all, one should be kind, but one need not be overly solicitous toward life-forms of the past. Still, Ulglossen was a kindly being.

There was no snow on the ground. I was alone in the forest.

Before me was the dead pine that Sten Örnfeld had drawn a target on.

I turned. There was Sten's lodge, fifty yards away.

I went toward it. It didn't fade or go away. It was solid, as it should be. Somehow, some way, I was back in my own time.

I walked to the door. I think it took me at least two minutes to decide to open it.

"Sten?" I said.

"Yah? What do you want? I thought you were going out to shoot."

"Changed my mind," I said. "I'm short of ammo."

"Dumbbell," he said kindly. "Sit down and relax. We'll have a drink together when I'm finished."

"Sure, Sten; sure," I said. I sat down on the couch.

I think I know what happened. I remember hearing Hrotokar in the background saying: "His hammer smashed them! Killed them! And then came back to his hand!"

I can see how that illusion could come about. I hold the hammer in my hand and there is a thunderbolt and the foe falls dead—his head smashed in. And then the hammer is back in my hand. Sure.

Those folk had already shortened my name from "Teydor" to "Tey'or"; why not one syllable further?

My weapon has a name now, as Sten suggested. I looked up a man who knows Norse runes, and I had another man engrave those runes on my pistol, on the right, just above the trigger.

The engraving says: *Mjolnir*.

Yah.

The original.

A NATIVE of Pennsylvania, H. Beam Piper (1904–1964) was a reasonably popular and productive science fiction writer before his tragic suicide. The tragedy was either eased or compounded, depending on your point of view, by his rediscovery and popularity in the mid to late 1970s, a popularity and resulting financial windfall that well might have eliminated the cause of his death. The most famous of his books are probably the "Terran Federation" series, consisting of *Little Fuzzy* (1962), *Space Viking* (1963), and *The Other Human Race* (1964), as well as subsequent works by other writers.

However, our selection is from the equally enjoyable "Paratime" series (*Lord Kalvan of Otherwhen*, 1965, and *Paratime,* 1981) which involves the policing of alternate worlds.

GUNPOWDER GOD

H. Beam Piper

Tortha Karf, Chief of Paratime Police, told himself to stop fretting. Only two hundred odd days till Year-End Day, and then, precisely at midnight, he would rise from this chair and Verkan Vall would sit down in it, and after that he would be free to raise grapes and lemons and wage guerrilla war against the rabbits on the island of Sicily, which he owned on one uninhabited Fifth Level time-line. He wondered how long it would take Vall to become as tired of the chief's seat as he was now.

Vall was tired of it already, in anticipation. He'd never wanted to be chief; prestige and authority meant little to him, and freedom much. It was a job somebody had to do, though, and it was the job for which he had been trained, so Vall would take it, and do it, he suspected, better than he himself had done. The job, policing a near-infinity of different worlds, each one of which was this same planet, Earth, would be safe in the hands of Verkan Vall.

Twelve thousand years ago, facing extinction on an exhausted planet, the First Level race had discovered the existence of a second, lateral dimension of time, and a means of physical transposition to and from the worlds of alternate probability parallel to their own. So the conveyers had gone out by stealth, to bring back wealth in abundance to First Level Home Time-Line, a little from here, a little from there, never enough to be missed.

It all had to be policed. Some Paratimers were unscrupulous in dealing with outtime peoples—he'd have retired five years ago, but for the discovery of a huge paratemporal slave trade, only recently smashed. More often, by somebody's bad luck or indiscretion, the Paratime Secret would be endangered, and that had to be preserved at any cost. Not merely the technique of paratemporal transposition, that went without comment, but the very existence of a race possessing it. If for no other reason, and there were many others, it would be utterly immoral to make any outtime people live with the knowledge that there were among them aliens indistinguishable from themselves, watching and exploiting. So there was the Paratime Police.

Second Level; it had been civilized almost as long as the First, but there had been long Dark-Age interludes. Except for paratemporal transposition, it almost equaled First. Third Level civilization was more recent, but still of respectable antiquity. Fourth Level had started late and advanced slowly; some Fourth Level genius was inventing agriculture when the coal-burning steam engine was obsolescent on the Third. And Fifth Level—on a few time-lines, subhuman brutes, fireless and speechless, were using stones to crack nuts and each other's head; on most of it nothing even humanoid had evolved.

Fourth Level was the big one. The others had devolved from low-probability genetic accidents; Fourth had been the maximum probability. It was divided into many sectors and subsectors, on most of which civilization had first appeared in the Nile and Tigris-Euphrates valleys, and, later, on the Indus and the Yangtze. Europo-American Sector; they might have to pull out of that entirely, that would be Chief Verkan's decision. Too many thermonuclear weapons and too many competing national sovereignties, always a disaster-fraught combination. That had happened all over Third Level within Home Time-Line experience. Alexandrian-Roman, off to a fine start with the pooling of Greek theory and Roman engineering ability, and then, a thousand years ago, two half-forgotten religions had been rummaged out of the dustbin and their respective proselytes had begun massacring each other. They were still at it, with pikes and matchlocks, having lost the ability to make anything better. Europo-American would come to that, if its competing politico-economic sectarians kept on. Sino-Hindic, that wasn't a civilization, was a bad case of cultural paralysis. Indo-Turanian, about where Europo-American had been a thousand years ago.

And Aryan-Oriental; the Aryan migration of three thousand years ago, instead of moving west and south as on most sectors, had rolled east into China.

And Aryan-Transpacific, there was one to watch. An offshoot of Aryan-Oriental; the conquerors of Japan had sailed north and east along the Kuriles and Aleutians, and then spread south and east over North America, bringing with them horses and cattle and iron-working skills, exterminating the Amerinds, splitting into diverse peoples and cultures. There was a civilization along the Pacific coast, and nomads on the plains herding bison and cross-breeding them with Asian cattle, another civilization in the Mississippi Valley, and one around the Great Lakes. And a new one, only four centuries old, on the Atlantic seaboard and back in the Appalachians.

The technological level was about that of Europe in the Middle Ages, a few subsectors slightly higher. But they were going forward. Things, he thought, were about ripe to happen on Aryan-Transpacific.

Well, let Chief Verkan watch that.

She tried to close her mind to the voices around her, and stared at the map between the two candlesticks on the table. There was Tarr-Hostigos overlooking the gap, just a tiny fleck of gold on the parchment, but she could see it all in her mind, the walls, the outer bailey, the citadel and the keep, the watchtower pointing a blunt finger skyward. Below, the little Darro glinted, flowing north to join the Listra and, with it, the broad Athan to the north and east. The town of Hostigos, white walls and slate roofs and busy streets; the checkerboard of fields and forests.

A voice, louder and harsher than the others, brought her back to reality.

"He'll do nothing? What in Dralm's name is a Great King for but to keep the peace?"

She looked along the table, from one to another of them.

The speaker for the peasants, at the foot, uncomfortable in his feast-day clothes and ill at ease seated among his betters, the speakers for the artisans and the merchants and the townsfolk, the lesser family members, the sworn landholders. Chartiphon, the captain-in-chief, his blond beard streaked with gray like the gray lead-splashes on his gilded breastplate, his long sword on the table in front of him. Old Xentos, the cowl of his priestly robe thrown back from his snowy head, his blue eyes troubled. And her father, Prince Ptosphes of Hostigos, beside whom she sat at the table-head, his mouth tight between pointed mustache and pointed beard. How long it had been since she had seen a smile on her father's lips!

Xentos passed a hand negatively in front of his face.

"The Great King, Kaiphranos, said that it was every prince's duty to guard his own realm; that it was for Prince Ptosphes to keep raiders out of Hostigos."

"Well, great Dralm, didn't you tell him it wasn't just bandits?" the other voice bullyragged. "They're Nostori soldiers; it's war! Gormoth of Nostor means to take all Hostigos, as his grandfather took Sevenhills Valley after the traitor we don't name sold him Tarr-Dombra!"

That was a part of the map her eyes had shunned, the bowl valley to the east, where Dombra Gap split the mountains. It was from thence the Nostori raiders came.

"And what hope have we from Styphon's House?" her father asked. He knew the answer; he wanted them all to hear it at first hand.

"Chartiphon spoke with them," Xentos said. "The priests of Styphon hold no speech with priests of other gods."

"The archpriest wouldn't talk to me," Chartiphon said. "Only one of the upper priests. He took our offerings and said that he would pray to Styphon for us. When I asked for fireseed, he would give us none."

"None at all?" somebody cried. "Then we are under the ban!"

Her father rapped with the pommel of his poignard.

"You've heard the worst, now," he said. "What's in your minds to do? You first, Phosg."

The peasant leader rose awkwardly, cleared his throat.

"Lord, my cottage is as dear to me as this fine castle is to you," he said. "I'll fight for mine as you would for yours."

There was a quick mutter of approval along the table. The

others spoke in their turns, a few tried to make speeches. Chartiphon said only: "Fight. What else?"

"Submission to evil is the worst of all sins," Xentos said. "I am a priest of Dralm, and Dralm is a god of peace, but I say, fight with Dralm's blessing."

"Rylla?" her father asked.

"Better die in armor than live in chains," she said. "When the time comes, I will be in armor with the rest of you."

Her father nodded. "I expect no less from any of you." He rose, and all with him. "I thank you all. At sunset, we dine together; until then, servants will attend you. Now, if you please, leave me with my daughter. Xentos, you and Chartiphon stay."

There was a scrape of chairs, a shuffle of feet going out, a murmur of voices in the hall before the door closed. Chartiphon had begun to fill his stubby pipe.

"Sarrask of Sask won't aid us, of course," her father said.

"Sarrask of Sask's a fool," Chartiphon said shortly. "He should know that when Gormoth's conquered Hostigos, his turn will come next."

"He knows it," Xentos said calmly. "He'll try to strike before Gormoth does. But even if he wanted to, he'd not aid us. Not even King Kaiphranos dares aid those whom the priests of Styphon would destroy."

"They want that land in Wolf Valley, for a temple farm," she said slowly. "I know that would be bad, but—"

"Too late," Xentos told her. "Styphon's House is determined upon our destruction, as a warning to others." He turned to her father. "And it was on my advice, Lord, that you refused them."

"I'd have refused against your advice. I swore long ago that Styphon's House should never come into Hostigos while I lived, and by Dralm neither shall they! They come into a princedom, they build a temple, they make a temple farm, and make slaves of the peasants on it. They tax the prince, and force him to tax the people till nobody has anything left. Look at that temple farm in Sevenhills Valley."

"Yes, you'd hardly believe it," Chartiphon said. "They make the peasants on the farms around cart in their manure, till they have none left for their own fields. Dralm only knows what they do with it." He puffed at his pipe. "I wonder why they want Wolf Valley."

"There's something there that makes the water of those springs taste and smell badly," she considered.

"Sulfur," Xentos said. "But why do they want sulfur?"

Corporal Calvin Morrison, Pennsylvania State Police, crouched in the brush at the edge of the old field and looked across the brook at the farmhouse two hundred yards away, scabrous with peeling yellow paint and festooned by a sagging porchroof. A few white chickens pecked disinterestedly in the littered barnyard; there was no other sign of life, but he knew that there was a man inside. A man with a rifle, who would use it; he had murdered once, broken jail, would murder again.

He looked at his watch; the minute hand was squarely on the nine. Jack French and Steve Kovac would be starting down from the road above where they had left the car. He rose, unsnapping the retaining-strap of his holster.

"I'm starting. Watch that middle upstairs window."

"I'm watching," a voice behind assured him. A rifle action clattered softly as a cartridge went into the chamber. "Luck."

He started forward across the weed-grown field. He was scared, as scared as he'd been the first time, back in '52 in Korea, but there was nothing to do about that. He just told his legs to keep moving, knowing that in a few moments he wouldn't have time to be scared. He was almost to the little brook, his hand close to the butt of his Colt, when it happened.

There was a blinding flash, followed by a moment's darkness. He thought he'd been shot; by pure reflex, the .38-special was in his hand. Then, all around him, a flickering iridescence of many colors glowed, in a perfect hemisphere thirty feet across and fifteen high, and in front of him was an oval desk or cabinet, with an instrument panel over it, and a swivel chair from which a man was turning and rising. Young, well-built; wore loose green trousers and black ankle boots and a pale green shirt; a shoulder holster under his left arm, a weapon in his hand.

He was sure it was a weapon, though it looked more like an electric soldering iron, with two slender metal rods instead of a barrel, joined at the front in a blue ceramic knob. It was probably something that made his own Official Police look like a kid's cap pistol, and it was coming up fast to line on him.

He fired, holding the trigger back to keep the hammer down on the fired chamber, and threw himself down, hearing something fall with a crash, landing on his left hand and his left hip and rolling, until the nacreous dome was gone from around him and he bumped hard against something. For a moment, he lay still, then rose to his feet, letting out the trigger of the Colt.

What he'd bumped into was a tree. That wasn't right, there'd been no trees around, nothing but brush. And this tree, and the others, were huge, great columns rising to support a green roof through which only stray gleams of sunlight leaked. Hemlocks, must have been growing here while Columbus was conning Isabella into hocking her jewelry. Come to think of it, there was a stand of trees like this in Alan Seeger Forest. Maybe that was where he was.

He wondered how he was going to explain this.

"While approaching the house," he began aloud and in a formal tone, "I was intercepted by a flying saucer, the operator of which threatened me with a ray pistol. I defended myself with my revolver, firing one round—"

No. That wouldn't do, at all.

He swung out the cylinder of his Colt, ejecting the fired round and replacing it. Then he looked around, and started in the direction of where the farmhouse ought to be, coming to the little brook and jumping across.

Verkan Vall watched the landscape flicker outside the almost invisible shimmer of the transportation field. The mountains stayed the same, but from one time-line to another there was a good deal of randomness about which tree grew where. Occasionally there were glimpses of open country and buildings and installations, the Fifth Level bases his people had established. The red light overhead winked off and on, and each time it went off, a buzzer sounded. The dome of the conveyer became a solid iridescence, and then a cold, inert metal mesh. The red light came on and stayed on. He was picking up the sigma-ray needler from the desk in front of him and holstering it when the door slid open and a lieutenant of Paratime Police looked in.

"Hello, Chief's Assistant. Any trouble?"

In theory, the Ghaldron-Hesthor transposition field was impenetrable from the outside, but in practice, especially when two conveyers going in opposite paratemporal directions interpenetrated, it would go weak, and outside objects, sometimes alive and hostile, would intrude. That was why Paratimers kept weapons at hand, and why conveyers were checked immediately on emergence; it was also why some Paratimers didn't make it home.

"Not this trip. My rocket ready?"

"Yes, sir. Be a little delay about an aircar for the rocketport." The lieutenant stepped inside, followed by a patrolman, who began taking the transportation record tape and the photo-film record out of the cabinet. "They'll call you when it's in."

He and the lieutenant strolled outside into the noise and color of the conveyer-head rotunda. He got out his cigarette case and offered it; the lieutenant flicked his lighter. They had only taken a few first puffs when another conveyer quietly materialized in a vacant space nearby. A couple of Paracops strolled over as the door opened, drawing their needlers. One peeped inside, then holstered his weapon and snatched a radio phone from his belt; the other entered cautiously. Throwing away his cigarette, he strode toward the newly arrived conveyer, the lieutenant following.

The chair was overturned; a Paracop, his tunic off and his collar open, lay on the floor, a needler a few inches from his outstretched hand. His shirt, pale green, was dark with blood. The lieutenant, without touching him, looked at him.

"Still alive," he said. "Bullet, or sword-thrust?"

"Bullet; I can smell nitro powder." Then he saw the hat lying on the floor, and stepped around the fallen man. Two men were coming in with an antigrav stretcher; they and the patrolmen got the wounded man onto it. "Look at this, lieutenant."

The lieutenant glanced at the hat. It was gray felt, wide-brimmed, the crown peaked with four indentations.

"Fourth Level," he said. "Europo-American."

He picked it up, glancing inside. The sweatband was lettered in gold, JOHN B. STETSON COMPANY. PHILADELPHIA, PA., and, hand-inked, *Cpl. Calvin Morrison. Penna. State Police*, and a number.

"I know that outfit," the lieutenant said. "Good men, every bit as good as ours."

"One was a split second better than one of ours." He got out his cigarette case. "Lieutenant, this is going to be a real baddie. This pickup's going to be missed, and the people who'll miss him will be one of the ten best constabulary organizations in the world on their time-line. They won't be put off with the sort of lame-brained explanations that usually get by on Europo-American. They'll want factual proof and physical evidence. And we'll have to find where he came out. A man who can beat a Paracop to the draw won't sink into obscurity on any time-line. He's going to kick up a fuss that'll have to be smoothed over."

"I hope he doesn't come out on a next-door time-line and turn up at a duplicate of his own police post, where a duplicate of himself is on duty. With identical fingerprints," the lieutenant said. "That would kick up a small fuss."

"Wouldn't it?" He went to the cabinet and took out the synchronized transposition record and photo film. "Have that rocket held; I'll want it after a while. But I'm going over these myself. I'm going to make this operation my own personal baby."

Calvin Morrison dangled black-booted legs over the edge of the low cliff and wished, again, that he hadn't lost his hat. He knew exactly where he was, he was on the little cliff, not more than a big outcrop, above the road where they'd left the car, but there was no road under it now, nor ever had been. And there was a hemlock four feet at the butt growing right where the farmhouse ought to be, and no trace of the stone foundations of it or the barn. But the really permanent features, the Bald Eagles to the north and Nittany Mountain to the south, were exactly as they should be.

That flash and momentary darkness could have been subjective; put that in the unproven column. He was sure the strangely beautiful dome of shimmering light had been real, and so had the oval desk and the instrument panel and the man with the odd weapon. And there was certainly nothing subjective about all this virgin forest where farmlands ought to be.

He didn't for an instant consider questioning either his senses or his sanity; neither did he indulge in dirty language like "incredible," or "impossible." Extraordinary; now there was a good word. He was quite sure that something extraordinary had happened to him. It seemed to break into two parts: (One), the dome of pearly light and what had happened inside it, and, (Two), emerging into this same-but-different place.

What was wrong with both was anachronism, and the anachronisms were mutually contradictory. None of (One) belonged in 1964 or, he suspected, for many centuries to come. None of (Two) belonged in 1964, either, or at any time within two centuries in the past. His pipe had gone out; for a while he forgot to relight it, while tossing those two facts back and forth. Then he got out his lighter and thumbed it, and then buttoned it back in his pocket.

In spite—no, because—of his clergyman father's insistence that he study for and enter the Presbyterian ministry, he was an agnostic. Agnosticism, to him, was refusal either to accept or reject without factual proof. A good philosophy for a cop, by the way. Well, he wasn't going to reject the possibility of time machines; not after having been shanghaied out of his own time in one. Whenever he was, it wasn't the Twentieth Century, and he was never going to get back to it. He made up his mind on that once and for all.

Climbing down from the low cliff, he went to the little brook, and followed it to where it joined a larger stream, just as he knew it would. A bluejay made a fuss at his approach. Two deer ran in front of him. A small black bear regarded him with suspicion and hastened away. Now, if he could find some Indians who wouldn't throw tomahawks first and ask questions afterward . . .

A road dipped to cross the stream. For a moment, he accepted that, then caught his breath. A real, wheel-rutted road! And brown horse-droppings in it; they were the most beautiful things he had seen since he came into this here-and-now. They meant that he hadn't beaten Columbus here, after all. He'd have trouble giving a plausible account of himself, but at least he could do it in English. Maybe he was even in time to get into the Civil War. He waded through the ford and started west along the road, toward where Bellefonte ought to be.

The sun went down in front of him. By now, the big hemlocks were gone, lumbered off, and there was a respectable second growth, mostly hardwoods. Finally, in the dusk, he smelled turned earth beside the road. It was full dark before he saw a light ahead.

The house was only a dim shape, the light came from narrow horizontal windows near the roof. Behind, he thought he could make out stables and, by his nose, pigpens. Two dogs ran into the road and began whauff-whauffing in front of him. "Hello, in there!" he called. Through the open windows he heard voices, a man's, a woman's, another man's. He called again. A bar scraped, and the door swung in. A woman, heavy-bodied, in a dark dress, stood aside for him to enter.

It was all one big room, lighted by one candle on a table and one on the mantel and by the fire on the hearth. Double-deck bunks along one wall, table spread with a meal. There were three men and another woman beside the one who had admitted him, and from the corner of his eye he could see children peering around a door that seemed to open into a shed annex. One of the men, big and blond-bearded, stood with his back to the fire, with something that looked like a short gun in his hands. No it wasn't, either; it was a crossbow, bent and quarrel in place.

The other men were younger, the crossbowman's sons for a guess; they were bearded, too, though one's beard was only a fuzz. They all wore short-sleeved jerkins of leather and cross-gartered hose. One of the younger men had a halberd and the other an axe. The older woman spoke in a whisper to the younger; she went through the door, pushing the children ahead of her.

He lifted his hands pacifically as he entered. "I'm a friend," he said. "I'm going to Bellefonte; how far is it?"

The man with the crossbow said something. The man with the halberd said something. The woman replied. The youth with the axe said something, and they all laughed.

"My name's Calvin Morrison. Corporal, Pennsylvania State Police." Hell, they wouldn't know the State Police from the Swiss Marines. "Am I on the road to Bellefonte?"

More back-and-forth. They weren't talking Pennsylvania Dutch, he was sure of that. Maybe Polish; no, he'd heard enough of that to recognize, if he couldn't understand, it. He looked around, while they argued, and saw, in the far corner left of the fireplace, three images on a shelf. He meant to get a closer look at them. Roman Catholics used images, so did Greek Catholics, and he could tell the difference.

The man with the crossbow laid his weapon down, but kept it bent and loaded, and spoke slowly and distinctly. It was no language he had ever heard before. He replied just as distinctly in English. They all looked at one another, passing their hands in front of their faces in bafflement. Finally, by signs, they invited him to sit down and eat, and the children, six of them, trooped in.

The meal was roast ham, potatoes and succotash. The eating tools were knives and a few horn spoons; the men used their sheath knives. He took out his jackknife, a big switch-blade he'd taken off an arrest he'd made. It caused a sensation, and he had to demonstrate it several times. There was also elderberry wine, strong but not particularly good. Then they left the table for the women to clear, and the men filled pipes from a tobacco jar on the mantel, offering it to him. He filled his pipe and lighted it, as they did theirs, with a twig at the fire. Stepping back, he got a look at the images.

The central figure was an elderly man in a white robe, with a blue eight-pointed star on the breast. He was flanked, on one side, by a seated female figure, exaggeratedly pregnant, crowned with a grain, and holding a cornstalk, and, on the other, by a masculine figure in a male shirt, with a spiked mace. The only really unusual thing about him was that he had the head of a wolf. Father-god, fertility-goddess, war-god; no, this gang weren't Catholics, Greek, Roman or any other kind. He bowed to the central figure, touching his forehead, and repeated the gesture to the other two. There was a gratified murmur behind him; anybody could see he wasn't any heathen. Then he sat down on a chest against the wall.

They hadn't re-barred the door. The children had been chased back into the shed after the meal. Nobody was talking, everybody was listening. Now that he remembered, there had been a vacant place at the table. They'd sent one of the youngsters off with a message. As soon as he finished his pipe, he pocketed it, and unobtrusively unsnapped the strap of his holster. It might have been half an hour before he heard galloping hoofs down the road. He affected not to hear; so did everybody else. The older man moved over to where he had put down his crossbow; his elder son got the halberd and a rag as though to polish the blade. The horses clattered to a stop outside, accoutrements jingled. The dogs set up a frantic barking. He slipped the .38 out and cocked it.

The youngest man went to the door. Before he could touch it, it flew open in his face, knocking him backward, and a man—bearded face under a high-combed helmet, steel breastplate, black and orange scarf—burst in, swinging a long sword. Everybody in the room shouted in alarm; this wasn't what they'd been expecting, at all. There was another helmeted head behind the first man, and the muzzle of a short musket. Outside, a shot boomed and one of the dogs howled.

He rose from the chest and shot the man with the sword. Half-cocking with the double action and thumbing the hammer the rest of the way, he shot the man with the musket. The musket went off into the ceiling. A man behind caught a crossbow quarrel through the forehead and pitched forward on top of the other two, dropping a long pistol unfired.

Shifting the Colt to his left hand, he caught up the sword the first man had dropped. It was lighter than it looked, and beautifully balanced. He tramped over the bodies in the doorway, to be confronted by another swordsman outside. For a few moments they cut and parried, and then he drove his point into his opponent's unarmored face and tugged his blade free. The man in front of him went down. The boy who had been knocked down had gotten hold of the dropped pistol and fired it, hitting a man who was holding a clump of horses in the road. The older son dashed out with his halberd, chopping a man down. The father had gotten hold of the musket and ammunition, and was ramming a charge into it.

Driving the point of the sword into the ground, he holstered the .38-special; as one of the loose horses dashed past, he caught the reins and stopped it, vaulting into the saddle. Then, stooping, he retrieved his sword, thankful that even in a motorized age the State Police insisted on teaching their men to ride. The fight was over, at least here. Six attackers were down, presumably dead. The other two were galloping away. Five loose horses milled about, and the two young men were trying to catch them. The older man, priming the pan of the gun, came outside, looking around.

This had only been a sideshow fight, though. The main event was half a mile down the road, where he could hear shots, yells, and screams, and where a sudden orange glare mounted into the night. He was wondering just what he'd cut himself into when the fugitives began streaming up the road. He had no trouble identifying them as such; he'd seen enough of that in Korea. Another fire was blazing up beside the first one.

Some of them had weapons, spears and axes, a few bows, and he saw one big musket. His bearded host shouted at them, and they stopped.

"What's going on, down there?" he demanded loudly.

Babble answered him. One or two tried to push past; he hit at them with his flat, cursing them luridly. The words meant nothing, but the tone did. That had worked for him in Korea, too. They all stopped, in a clump; a few cheered. Many were women and children, and not all the men were armed. Call it twenty effectives. The bodies in the road were quickly stripped of weapons; out of the corner of his eye he saw the two women of the house passing things out the door. Four of the riderless horses had been caught and mounted. More fugitives came up, saw what was going on, and joined.

"All right!" he bawled. "You guys want to live forever?" He swung his sword to include all of them, then stabbed down the road with it. "Let's go!"

A cheer went up, and as he started his horse the whole mob poured after him, shouting. They met more fugitives, who stopped, saw that a counterattack had been organized, if that were the word for it, and joined. The firelight was brighter, half a dozen houses must be burning now, but the shooting had stopped. Nobody left to shoot at, he supposed.

Then, when they were halfway to the burning village, there was a blast of forty or fifty shots in less than ten seconds, and more yelling, much of it in alarm. More shots, and then mounted men began streaming up the road; this was a rout. Everybody with guns or bows let fly at them. A horse went down, and another had its saddle emptied. Considering how many shots it had taken for one casualty in Korea, that wasn't bad. He stood up in his stirrups, which were an inch or so too short for him as it was, and yelled, *"Chaaarge!"*—like Teddy, in "Arsenic and Old Lace."

A man coming in the opposite direction aimed a cut at his bare head. He parried and thrust, his point glanced from a breastplate, and before he could recover the other's horse had carried him past and among the spears and pitchforks behind. Then he was trading thrusts for cuts with another rider, wondering if none of these imbeciles ever heard that a sword had a point. By this time, the road for a hundred yards ahead, and the open field on the left, was a swirl of horsemen, chopping and firing at each other.

He got his point in under his opponent's armpit, almost had the sword wrenched from his hand, and then saw another rider coming at him, unarmored and wearing a wide hat and a cloak, aiming a pistol almost as long as the arm that held it. He urged his horse forward, swinging back for a cut at the weapon, and knew that he wouldn't make it. *O.K., Cal; your luck's run out.* There was an upflash from the pan of the pistol, a belch of flame from the muzzle, and something sledged him in the chest.

He hung onto consciousness long enough to kick his feet free of the stirrups. In that last moment, he was aware that the rider who had shot him had been a young girl.

Vekan Vall put the lighter down on the desk and took the cigarette from his mouth. Tortha Karf leaned back in the chair in which he, himself, would be sitting all too soon.

"We had one piece of luck, right at the start. The time-line is one we've already penetrated. One of our people, in a newspaper office in Philadelphia, that's the nearest large city, reported the disappearance. The press associations have it already, there's nothing we can do about that."

"Well, just what did happen, on the pickup time-line?"

"This Corporal Morrison and three other State Policemen were closing in on a house in which a wanted criminal was hiding. Morrison and another man were in front; the other two were coming in from behind. Morrison started forward, his companion covering for him with a rifle. This other man is the nearest to a witness there is, and he was watching the front of the house and was only marginally aware of Morrison. He heard the other two officers pounding on the back door and demanding admittance, and then the man they were after burst out the front door with a rifle in his hands. Morrison's companion shouted at him to halt; the criminal raised his rifle, and the State Police officer shot him, killing him instantly.

"Then, he says, he realized that Morrison was nowhere in sight. He called to him, without answer. The man they were after was dead, he wouldn't run off, so all three of them hunted for Morrison for almost half an hour. Then they took the body in to the county seat and had to go through a lot of formalities, and it was evening before they were back at their substation. A local reporter happened to be there at the time. He got the story, including the disappearance of Morrison, phoned it to his paper, and the press associations got it from there. Now the State Police refuse to discuss, and are even trying to deny, the disappearance."

"They believe their man lost his nerve, bolted, and is now ashamed to come back," Tortha Karf said. "Naturally they wouldn't want anything like that getting out. Are you going to use that line?"

He nodded. "The hat he lost in the conveyer. It will be planted about a mile from the scene, along a stream. Then one of our people will catch a local, preferably a boy of twelve or so, give him a hypno-injection, and instruct him to find the hat and take it to the State Police. The reporter responsible for the original news break will be notified by anonymous phone call. Later, there will be the usual spate of rumors of Morrison having been seen in all sorts of unlikely places."

"How about his family?"

"We're in luck there, too. Unmarried, parents both dead, only a few relatives with whom he didn't maintain contact."

"That's good. How about the exit?"

"We have that approximated; Aryan-Transpacific. We're not quite sure even of the sector, because the transposition field was weak for several thousand parayears and we can't determine the instant he broke out of the conveyer. It'll be thirty or forty days before we have it pinpointed. We have one positive indication to look for at the scene."

The chief nodded. "The empty cartridge?"

"Yes. He used a revolver, they don't eject automatically. As soon as he was out and no longer immediately threatened, he would open his revolver, remove the empty, and replace it. I'm as sure of that as though I saw him do it. We may not be able to find it, but if we do, it'll be positive proof."

He woke, in bed under soft covers, and for a moment lay with his eyes closed. There was a clicking sound near him, and from a distance an anvil rang, and there was shouting.

Then he opened his eyes. He was in a fairly large room, paneled walls and a painted ceiling; two windows on one side, both open, and nothing but blue sky visible through them. A woman, stout and gray-haired, sat under one, knitting. His boots stood beside a chest across the room, and on its top were piled his clothes and his belt and revolver. A long unsheathed sword with a swept handguard and a copper pommel leaned against the wall by the boots. His body was stiff and sore, and his upper torso was swathed in bandages.

The woman looked up quickly as he stirred, then put down her knitting and rose, going to a table and pouring water for him. Pitcher and cup were silver, elaborately chased. He took the cup, drank, and handed it back, thanking her. She replaced it on the table and went out.

He wasn't a prisoner, the presence of the sword and revolver proved that. This was the crowd that had surprised the raiders at the village. That whole business had been a piece of luck for him. He ran a hand over his chin and estimated about three days' growth of stubble. His fingernails had grown enough since last trimmed to confirm that. He'd have a nasty hole in his chest, and possibly a broken rib.

The woman returned, accompanied by a man in a cowled blue robe with an eight-pointed white star on his breast. Reversed colors from the image at the peasant's farm; a priest, doubling as doctor. The man laid a hand on his brow, felt his pulse, and spoke in a cheerfully optimistic tone; the bedside manner seemed to be a universal constant. With the woman's help, he changed the bandages and smeared the wound with ointment. The woman took out the old bandages and returned with a steaming bowl. It was turkey broth, with finely minced meat in it. While he was finishing it, two more visitors entered.

One was robed like the doctor, his cowl thrown back. He had white hair, and a good face, gentle and pleasant. His companion was a girl with blond hair cut in what would be a page-boy bob in the Twentieth Century; she had blue eyes and red lips and an impudent tilty little nose dusted with golden freckles. She wore a jerkin of something like brown suede, stitched with gold thread, a yellow under-tunic with long sleeves and a high neck, knit hose and thigh-length boots. There was a gold chain around her neck, and a gold-hilted dagger on her belt. He began to laugh when he saw her; they'd met before.

"You shot me!" he accused, then aimed an imaginary pistol, said, "Bang!" and pointed to his chest.

She said something to the older priest, he replied, and she said something to him, pantomiming shame and sorrow, covering her face with one hand and winking at him over it. When he laughed, she laughed with him. Perfectly natural mistake, she hadn't known which side he was on. The two priests held a lengthy colloquy, and the younger brought him about four ounces of something in a tumbler. It tasted alcoholic and medicinally bitter. They told him, by signs, to go to sleep, and went out, all but the gray-haired woman, who went back to her chair and her knitting. He dozed off.

Late in the afternoon he woke briefly. Outside, somebody was drilling troops. Tramping feet, a voice counting cadence, long-drawn preparatory commands, sharp commands, of execution, clattering equipment. That was another universal constant. He smiled; he wasn't going to have much trouble finding a job, here-and-now, whenever now was.

It wasn't the past. Penn's Colony had never been like this. It was more like Sixteenth Century Europe, but no Sixteenth Century cavalryman, who was as incompetent a swordsman as that gang he'd been fighting, would have lived to wear out his first pair of issue boots. And two years in college and a lot of independent reading had given him at least a nodding acquaintance with most of the gods of his own history, and none, back to Egypt and Sumeria, had been like that trio on the peasant's shrine shelf.

So it was the future. A far future, maybe a thousand years later than 1964, AD; a world devastated by atomic wars, blasted back to the Stone Age, and then bootstrap-lifted to something like the end of the Middle Ages. That wasn't important, though. Now was when he was, and now was when he was stuck.

Make the best of it, Cal. You're a soldier; you just got re-assigned, that's all.

He went back to sleep.

The next morning, after breakfast, he sign-talked the woman watching over him to bring him his tunic, and got out his pipe and tobacco and lighter from the pockets. She brought him a stool to set beside the bed to put things on. The badge on the tunic breast was twisted and lead-splotched; that was why he was still alive.

The old priest and the girl were in, an hour later. This time, she was wearing a red and gray knit frock that could have gone into Bergdorf Goodman's window with a $200 price-tag any day, but the dagger she wore with it wasn't exactly Fifth Avenue. They greeted him, then pulled chairs up beside the bed and got to business.

First they taught him words for "You," and "Me," and "He," and "She," and names. The girl was Rylla. The old priest was Xentos. The younger priest, who came in to see his patient, was Mytron. Calvin Morrison puzzled them; evidently they didn't have surnames here-and-now. They settled for calling him Kalvan. They had several shingle-sized boards of white pine, and sticks of charcoal, to draw pictures. Rylla smoked a pipe, with a small stone bowl and a cane stem, which she carried on her belt along with her dagger. His lighter intrigued her, and she showed him her own. It was a tinderbox, the flint held down by a spring against a semicircular striker which was pushed by hand and returned for another push by a spring. With a spring to drive the striker instead of returning it, it would have done for a gunlock. By noon, they were able to tell him that he was their friend, and he was able to tell Rylla he didn't blame her for shooting him in the skirmish on the road.

They were back in the afternoon, accompanied by a gentleman with a gray mustache and imperial, wearing a garment like a fur-collared bathrobe, with a sword-belt over it. He had a large gold chain around his neck. His name was Ptosphes, and after much pantomime and picture-writing it emerged that he was Rylla's father, that he was Prince of this place, and that this place was Hostigos. Rylla's mother was dead. The raiders with whom he had fought had come from a place called Nostor, to the north and east, ruled by a Prince Gormoth. Gormoth was not well thought of in Hostigos.

The next day, he was up in a chair, and they began giving him solid food, and wine. The wine was excellent; so was the tobacco they gave him. He decided he was going to like it, here-and-now. Rylla was in at least twice a day, sometimes alone, sometimes with Xentos, and sometimes with a big man with a graying beard, Chartiphon, who seemed to be Ptosphes' top soldier. He always wore a sword, and often an ornate but battered steel back-and-breast. Sometimes he visited alone, and occasionally accompanied by a younger officer, a cavalryman named Harmakros. Harmakros had been in the skirmish at the raided village, but Rylla had been in command.

"The gods," he explained, "did not give Prince Ptosphes a son. A Prince should have a son, to rule after him, so the Princess Rylla must be a son to him."

The gods, he thought, ought to be persuaded to furnish Ptosphes with a son-in-law, named Calvin Morrison, no, Kalvan. He made up his mind to give the gods a hand on that.

Chartiphon showed him a map, elaborately illuminated on parchment. Hostigos appeared to be all of Centre and Union counties, a snip of Clinton south and west of where Lock Haven ought to be, and southeastern Lycoming, east of the West Branch, which was the Athan, and south of the Bald Eagles, the Mountains of Hostigos. Nostor was the West Branch Valley from above Lock Haven to the forks of the river, and it obtruded south into Hostigos through Ante's Gap, Dombra Gap, to take in Nippenose, Sevenhills Valley. To the west, all of Blair County, and parts of Huntington and Bedford, was the Princedom of Sask, ruled by Prince Sarrask. Sarrask was no friend; Gormoth was an open enemy.

On a bigger map, he saw that all Pennsylvania and Maryland, Delaware and the southern half of New Jersey, was the Great Kingdom of Hos-Harphax, ruled from Harphax City at the mouth of the Susquehanna by King Kaiphranos. Ptosphes, Gormoth, Sarrask and a dozen other princes were his nominal subjects. Judging from what he had seen on the night of his advent here-and-now, Kaiphranos' authority would be maintained for about one day's infantry march around his capital and ignored elsewhere.

He had a suspicion that Hostigos was in a bad squeeze, between Nostor and Sask. Something was bugging these people. Too often, while laughing with him—she was teaching him to read and write, now, and that was fun—Rylla would remember something she wanted to forget, and then her laughter would be strained. Chartiphon was always preoccupied; occasionally he'd forget, for a moment, what he was talking about. And he never saw Ptosphes smile.

Xentos showed him a map of the world. The world, it

seemed, was not round, but flat like a pancake. Hudson's Bay was in the exact center, North America was shaped rather like India, Florida ran almost due east and Cuba north and south. The West Indies were a few random spots to show that the mapmaker had heard about them from somebody. Asia was attached to North America, but it was still blank. An illimitable ocean stretched around the perimeter. Europe, Africa and South America simply weren't. Xentos wanted him to show the country from which he had come. He put his finger down on central Pennsylvania's approximate location. Xentos thought he misunderstood.

"No, Kalvan. This is your home now, and we want you to stay with us, but where is the country you came from?"

"Here," he insisted. "But at another time, a thousand years from now. I had an enemy, an evil sorcerer. Another sorcerer, who was my friend, put a protection on me that I might not be slain by sorcery, so my enemy twisted time around me and hurled me far into the past, before my first known ancestor had been born, and now here I am and here I must stay."

Xentos' hand made a quick circle around the white star on his breast, and he muttered rapidly. Another universal constant.

"What a terrible fate!"

"Yes. I do not like to speak of it, but it was right that you should know. You may tell Prince Ptosphes and Princess Rylla and Chartiphon, but beg them not to speak of it to me. I must forget my old life and make a new one in this time. You may tell the others merely that I come from a far country. From here." He indicated the approximate location of Korea. "I was there, once, fighting in a great war."

"Ah; I knew you had been a warrior." Xentos hesitated, then asked: "Do you know sorcery?"

"No. My father was a priest, as you are, and wished me to become a priest also, and our priest hated sorcery. But I knew that I would never be a good priest, so when this war came, I left my studies and went to fight. Afterward, I was a warrior in my own country, to keep the peace."

Xentos nodded. "If one cannot be a good priest, one should not be a priest at all, and to be a good warrior is almost as good. Tell me, what gods did your people worship?"

"Oh, we had many gods. There was Conformity, and Authority, and Opinion. And there was Status, whose symbols were many and who rode in the great chariot Cadillac, which was almost a god itself. And there was Atombomb, the dread Destroyer, who would someday end the world. For myself, I worshiped none of them. Tell me about your gods, Xentos."

Then he filled his pipe and lit it with the tinderbox he had learned to use in place of his now fuelless Zippo. He didn't need to talk any more; Xentos was telling him about his own god, Dralm, and about Yirtta the All-Mother, and wolf-headed Galzar the god of battle, and Tranth the lame craftsman—funny how often craftsman-gods were lame—and about all the others.

"And Styphon," he added grudgingly. "Styphon is an evil god, and evil men serve him, and are given great wealth and power."

After that, he noticed a subtle change in manner toward him. He caught Rylla looking at him in wondering pity. Chartiphon merely clasped his hand and said, "You'll like it here with us, Kalvan." Prince Ptosphes hemmed and hawed, and said: "Xentos tells me there are things you don't want to talk about, Kalvan. Nobody will mention them to you, ever. We're all happy to have you with us. Stay, and make this your home."

The others treated him with profound respect. They'd been told that he was a prince from a distant land, driven from his throne by treason. They gave him clothes, more than he had ever owned before, and weapons. Rylla gave him a pair of her own pistols, one of which had wounded him in the skirmish. They were two feet long, but lighter than his .38 Colt, the barrels almost paper-thin at the muzzles. They had locks operating on the same principle as the tinderboxes, and Rylla's name was inlaid in gold on the butts. They gave him another, larger room, and a body servant.

As soon as he was able to walk unaided, he went outside to watch the troops being drilled. They had no uniforms except scarves or sashes of Ptosphes' colors, red and blue. The infantry wore leather or canvas jacks sewn with metal plates, and helmets not unlike the one he'd worn in Korea. Some had pikes, some halberds, and some hunting spears, and many had scythe blades with the tangs straightened out, on eight-foot shafts. Foot movements were simple and uncomplicated; the squad was unknown, and they maneuvered by platoons of forty or fifty.

A few of the firearms were huge fifteen-pound muskets, aimed and fired from rests. Most were lighter, arquebuses, calivers, and a miscellany of hunting guns. There would be two or three musketeers and a dozen calivermen or arquebusiers to each spear-and-scythe platoon. There were also archers and crossbowmen. The cavalry were good; they wore cuirasses and high-combed helmets, and were armed with swords and pistols and either lances or short musketoons. The artillery was laughable; wrought-iron six- to twelve-pounders, hand-welded tubes strengthened with shrunk-on bands, without trunnions. They were mounted on four-wheel carts. He made up his mind to do something about that.

He also noticed that while the archers and crossbowmen practiced constantly, not a single practice shot was fired with any firearm.

He took his broadsword to the castle bladesmith and wanted it ground down into a rapier. The bladesmith thought he was crazy. He called in a cavalry lieutenant and demonstrated with a pair of wooden practice swords. Immediately, the lieutenant wanted a rapier, too. The bladesmith promised to make both of them real rapiers. By the next evening, his own was finished.

"You have enemies on both sides, Nostor and Sask, and that's not good," he said one evening as he and Ptosphes and Rylla and Xentos and Chartiphon sat over a flagon of wine in the Prince's study. "You've made me one of you. Now tell me what I can do to help."

"Well, Kalvan," Ptosphes said, "you could better tell us that. You know many things we don't. The thrusting sword"—he glanced down admiringly at his own new rapier—"and what you told Chartiphon about mounting cannon. What else can you give us to help fight our enemies?"

"Well, I can't teach you to make weapons like that six-shooter of mine, or ammunition for it." He tried, as simply as possible, to explain about machine industry and mass production; they only stared in uncomprehending wonder. "I can show you things you don't know but can do with the tools you have. For instance, we cut spiral grooves in the bores of our guns to make the bullets spin. Grooved guns will shoot harder, farther and straighter than smoothbores. I can show your gunsmiths how to do that with guns you already have. And there's another thing." He mentioned never having seen any practice firing. "You have very little powder, fireseed, you call it. Is that it?"

"We haven't enough in Hostigos to fire all the cannon of this castle once," Chartiphon said. "And we can't get any. The priests of Styphon will give us none, and they send cart after cart of it to Nostor."

"You mean, you get fireseed from the priests of Styphon? Can't you get it from anybody else, or make your own?"

They all looked at him, amazed that he didn't know any better.

"Only Styphon's House can make fireseed, and that by Styphon's aid," Xentos said. "That was what I meant when I said that Styphon gives his servants great wealth, and power even over the Great Kings."

He gave Styphon's House the grudging respect any good cop gives a really smart crook. Styphon's House had a real racket. No wonder this country was a snakepit of warring princes and barons. Styphon's House wanted it that way; it kept them in the powder business. He set down his goblet and laughed.

"You think nobody can make fireseed but Styphon's House?" he demanded. "Why, in my time, even the children could do that." Well, children who got as far as high school chemistry; he'd almost gotten expelled, once. "I can make fireseed, right here on this table!"

Ptosphes threw back his head and laughed. Just a trifle hysterically, but it was the first time he'd ever heard the Prince laugh. Chartiphon banged a fist on the table and shouted, "Ha, Gormoth! Now see how soon your head goes up over your own gate!" And no War Crimes foolishness about it, either. Rylla flung her arms around him. "Kalvan! You really and truly can?"

"But it is only by the power of Styphon . . ." Xentos began.

"Styphon's a big fake; his priests are a pack of impudent swindlers. You want to see me make fireseed? Get Mytron in here; he has everything I need in his dispensary. I want sulfur, he has that, and saltpeter, he has that." Mytron gives sulfur mixed with honey for colds; saltpeter was supposed to cool the blood. "And charcoal, and a couple of brass mortars and pestles, and a flour-screen, and balance-scales."

"Go on, man; hurry!" Ptosphes cried. "Bring him anything he wants."

Xentos went out. He asked for a pistol, and Ptosphes brought one from a closet behind him. He opened the pan and dumped out the priming on a sheet of parchment, touching it off with a lighted splinter. It scorched the parchment, which it shouldn't have, and left too much black residue. Styphon wasn't a very honest powdermaker; he cheapened his product with too much charcoal and not enough saltpeter. Xentos returned, accompanied by Mytron; the two priests carried jars, and a bucket of charcoal, and the other things. Xentos seemed dazed; Mytron was scared and trying not to show it.

He put Mytron to work grinding charcoal in one mortar and Xentos to grinding saltpeter in the other. The sulfur was already pulverized. Screening each, he mixed them in a dry goblet, saltpeter .75, charcoal .15, sulfur .10; he had to think a little to remember that.

"But it's just dust," Chartiphon objected.

"Yes. The mixture has to be moistened, worked into a dough, pressed into cakes and dried, and then ground and sieved. We can't do all that now, but this will flash. Look."

He primed the pistol with a pinch of it, aimed at a half burned log in the fireplace, and squeezed. The pistol roared and kicked. Ptosphes didn't believe in reduced charges, that was for sure. Outside, somebody shouted, feet pounded, and the door flew open. A guard with a halberd looked in.

"The Lord Kalvan is showing us something with a pistol," Ptosphes said. "There may be more shots; nobody is to worry."

"All right," he said, when the guard closed the door. "Now we see how it fires." He poured in about forty grains, wadded it with a bit of rag, and primed it, handing it to Rylla. "You fire. This is a great moment in the history of Hostigos. I hope."

She pushed down the striker, aimed into the fireplace and squeezed. The report wasn't quite as loud, but it did fire. They tried it with a bullet, which went into the log half an inch. He laid the pistol on the table. The room was full of smoke, and they were all coughing, but nobody cared.

Chartiphon went to the door and bawled into the hall for more wine.

"But you said no prayers," Mytron faltered. "You just made fireseed. Just like cooking soup."

"That's right. And soon everybody will make fireseed."

And when that day comes, the priests of Styphon will be out on the sidewalk beating a drum for pennies. Chartiphon wanted to know how soon they would be able to march on Nostor.

"It will take more fireseed than Kalvan can make here on this table," Ptosphes told him. "We will need saltpeter, and charcoal, and sulfur. We will have to teach people how to get these things, and grind and mix them. We will need things we don't have, and tools to make them. And nobody knows all this but Kalvan, and there is only one of him."

Well, glory be, Ptosphes had gotten something from the lecture on production, if nobody else had.

"Mytron knows a few things, I think. Where did you get the sulfur and the saltpeter?" he asked the doctor-priest.

Mytron had downed his first goblet of wine at one gulp. He had taken three to the second; now he was working his way down the third and coming out of shock nicely. It was about as he thought. The saltpeter was found in crude lumps under manure piles and refined; the sulfur was gotten by evaporating water from the sulfur springs in Sugar Valley, Wolf Valley here-and-now. For some reason, mention of this threw both Ptosphes and Chartiphon into a fury. He knew how to extract both, on a quart-jar scale. He was a trifle bewildered when told how much would be needed for military purposes.

"But this'll take time," Chartiphon objected. "And as soon as Gormoth hears about it, he'll attack, before we can get any made."

"Don't let him hear about it. Clamp down the security." He had to explain that. "Cavalry patrols, on all the roads and trails out of Hostigos; let anybody in, but don't let anybody out. And here's another thing. I'll have to give orders, and people won't like them. Will I be obeyed?"

"By anybody who wants to keep his head on his shoulders," Ptosphes said. "You speak with my voice."

"And with mine, Lord Kalvan!" Chartiphon was on his feet, extending his sword for him to touch the hilt. "I am at your orders; you command here."

* * *

They gave him a room inside the main gateway of the citadel, across from the guardroom, a big flagstone-floored place with the indefinable but unmistakable flavor of a police court. The walls were white plaster, he could write and draw diagrams on them with charcoal. Paper was unknown, here-and-now. He decided to do something about that, after the war. It was a wonder these people had gotten as far as they had without it. Rylla attached herself to him as adjutant. He gathered in Mytron and the chief priest of Tranth, all the master-artisans in Tarr-Hostigos and some from Hostigo Town, a couple of Chartiphon's officers, and some soldiers to carry messages.

Charcoal was going to be easy, there was plenty of that. For sulfur evaporation he'd need big pans, and sheet iron, larger than a breastplate or a cooking pan—all unavailable. There were bog-iron mines over in Bald Eagle, Listra Valley, and ironworks, but no rolling mill. They'd have to beat sheet iron out by hand in two-foot squares and weld them together like a patch quilt. Saltpeter could be accumulated from all over. Manure piles, at least one to a farm, were the best source, and stables, cellars, underground drains. He set up a saltpeter commission, headed by one of Chartiphon's officers, with authority to go anywhere and enter anything, to hang any subordinate who abused that authority out of hand, and to deal just as summarily with anybody who tried to obstruct.

Mobile units, oxcarts loaded with caldrons, tubs, tools and the like, to go from farm to farm. Peasant women to be collected and taught to leach nitrated soil and purify nitrates.

Grinding mills; there was plenty of water power, and the water wheel was known, here-and-now. Gristmills could be converted. Special grinding equipment, designing of. Sifting screens, cloth. Mixing machines, big casks with counter-rotating paddle wheels inside. Presses to squeeze dough into cakes. Mills to grind caked powder; he spent considerable thought on a set of regulations to prevent anything from striking a spark around them, with bloodthirsty enforcement threats.

During the morning, he ground up the cake he'd made the night before, running it through a couple of sieves to FFFg fineness. A hundred-grain charge in one of the big eight-bore muskets drove the two-ounce ball an inch deeper into a log than an equal charge of Styphon's Best, and fouled the bore much less.

By noon, he was almost sure that most of his War Production Board understood most of what he'd told them. In the afternoon, there was a meeting in the outer bailey of as many of the people who would be working on the Fireseed Project as could be collected. There was an invocation of Dralm by Xentos. Ptosphes spoke, bearing down heavily on the fact that the Lord Kalvan had full authority and would be backed to the limit, by the headsman if necessary. Chartiphon made a speech, picturing the howling wilderness they were going to make of Nostor. He made a speech, himself, emphasizing that there was nothing whatever of a supernatural nature about fireseed. The meeting then broke up into small groups, everybody having his own job explained to him. He was kept running back and forth from one to another to explain to the explainers.

In the evening, they had a feast. By that time, he and Rylla had gotten a rough table of organization charcoaled onto the wall in his headquarters.

Of the next four days, he spent eighteen hours of each in that room, talking to five or six hundred people. The artisans, who had a guild organization, objected to peasants invading their crafts. The masters complained that the apprentices and young journeymen were becoming intractable, which meant that they had started thinking for themselves. The peasants objected to having their dunghills forked down and the ground under them dug up, and to being put to unaccustomed work. The landlords objected to having the peasants taken from the fields, and predicted that the year's crop would be lost.

"Don't worry about that," he told them. "If we win, we'll eat Gormoth's crops. If we lose, we'll all be too dead to eat."

And the Iron Curtain went down. Itinerant packtraders and wagoners began to collect in Hostigos Town, trapped for the duration. Sooner or later, Gormoth and Sarrask would start wondering why nobody was leaving Hostigos, and send spies in through the woods to find out. Organize some counterespionage; get a few spies of his own into both princedoms.

By the fifth day, the sulfur-evaporation plant was operating, and saltpeter production had started, only a few pounds of each, but that would increase rapidly. He put Mytron in charge of the office, and went out to supervise mill construction. It was at this time that he began wearing armor, at least six and often eight hours a day—helmet over a padded coif, with a band of fine-linked mail around his throat and under his chin, steel back-and-breast over a quilted arming-doublet with mail sleeves, mail under the arms, and a mail skirt to below his hips, and double leather hose with mail between. The whole panoply weighed close to forty pounds, and his life was going to depend on accustoming himself to it.

Verkan Vall watched Tortha Karf spin the empty cartridge on the top of his desk. It was a very valuable empty cartridge; it had cost over ten thousand man-hours of crawling on hands and knees and pawing among dead hemlock needles, not counting transposition time.

"A marvel you found it, Vall. Aryan-Transpacific?"

"Oh, yes. We were sure of that from the first. Styphon's House subsector." He gave the numerical designation of the exact time-line.

"Styphon's House. That's that gunpowder theocracy, isn't it?"

That was it. At one time, Styphon had been a minor god of healing. Still was, on most of Aryan-Transpacific. But, three hundred years ago, on one time-line, a priest of Styphon, trying to concoct a new remedy for something, had mixed a batch of saltpeter, charcoal and sulfur—fortunately for him, a small batch—and put it on the fire. For fifty years, the mixture had been a temple miracle, and then its propellant properties were discovered, and Styphon had gone out of medical practice and into the munitions business. The powder had been improved by priestly researchers; weapons to use it were designed. Now no king or prince without gunpowder stood a chance against one with it. No matter who sat on any throne, Styphon's House was his master, because Styphon's House could throw him off it at will.

"I wonder if this Morrison knows how to make gunpowder," Tortha Karf said.

"I'll find that out. I'm going out there myself."

"You don't have to, you know. You have hundreds of men who could do that."

He shook his head obstinately. "After Year-End Day, I'm going to be chained to that chair of yours. But until then, I'm going to work outtime as much as I can." He leaned over to the map-screen and twiddled the selector until he had the Great Kingdom of Hos-Harphax. "I'm going in about here," he said. "I'll be a pack trader, they go anywhere without question. I'll have a saddle horse and three pack horses, with loads of appropriate merchandise. That's in the adjoining princedom of Sask. I'll travel slowly, to let word travel ahead of me. I may even hear something about this Morrison before I enter Hostigos."

"What'll you do when you find him?"

He shrugged. "That will depend on what he's doing, and particularly how he's accounting for himself. I don't want to, the man's a police officer like ourselves, but I'm afraid I'm going to have to kill him. He knows too much."

"What does he know, Vall?"

"First, he's seen the inside of a conveyer. He knows that it was something completely alien to his own culture and technology. Then, he knows that he was shifted in time, because he wasn't shifted to another place, and he will recognize that the conveyer was the means affecting that shift. From that, he will deduce a race of time-travelers.

"Now, he knows enough of the history of his own time-line to know that he wasn't shifted into the past. And he will also know he wasn't shifted into the future. That's all limestone country, where he was picked up and dropped, and on his own time-line it's been quarried extensively for the past fifty or more years. Traces of those operations would remain for tens of thousands of years, and he will find none of them. So what does that leave?"

"A lateral shift, and people who travel laterally in time," the chief said. "Why, that's the Paratime Secret itself."

There would be a feast at Tarr-Hostigos that evening. All morning cattle and pigs, lowing and squealing, had been driven in and slaughtered. Woodcutters' axes thudded for the roasting pits, casks of wine came up from the cellars. He wished the fireseed mills were as busy as the castle kitchens and bakeries. A whole day's production shot to hell. He said as much to Rylla.

"But, Kalvan, they're all so happy." She was pretty excited about it, herself. "And they've worked so hard."

He had to grant that, and maybe the morale gain would offset a day's work lost. And they had a full hundredweight of fireseed, fifty percent better than Styphon's Best, and half of it made in the last two days.

"It's been so long since anybody had anything to be happy about. When we had feasts, everybody would get drunk as soon as they could, to keep from thinking about what was coming. And now, maybe it won't come at all."

And now, they were all drunk on a hundred pounds of black powder. Five thousand arquebus rounds at the most. They'd have to do better than twenty-five pounds a day; have to get it up to a hundred. Mixing, caking and grinding was the bottleneck, that meant still more mill machinery, and there weren't enough men able to build it. It would mean stopping work on the rifling machinery, and on the carriages and limbers for the light four-pounders the ironworks were turning out.

It would take a year to build the sort of army he wanted, and Gormoth or Nostor would attack in two months at most.

He brought that up, that afternoon, at General Staff meeting. Like rifling and trunnions on cannon and teaching swordsmen to use the point, that was new for here-and-now. You just hauled a lot of peasants together and armed them, that was Organization. You picked a march-route, that was Strategy. You lined up your men somehow and shot or hit anybody in front of you, that was Tactics. And Intelligence was something mounted scouts, if any, brought in at the last moment from a mile ahead. It cheered him to recall that that would be Gormoth's idea of the Art of War. Why, with ten thousand men Gustavus Adolphus or the Duke of Parma or Gonzalo de Córdoba could have gone through all five of these Great Kingdoms like a dose of croton oil.

Ptosphes and Rylla were present *ex officio* as Prince and Heiress-Apparent. The Lord Kalvan was Commander-in-Chief. Chartiphon was Field Marshal and Chief of Operations. Harmakros was G-2, an elderly infantry captain was drillmaster, paymaster, quartermaster, inspector-general and head of the draft board. A civilian merchant, who wasn't losing any money on it, was in charge of supply and procurement. Xentos, who was Ptosphes' chancellor as well as chief ecclesiastic, attended to political matters, and also fifth-column activities, another of Lord Kalvan's marvelous new ideas, mainly because he was in touch with the priests of Dralm in Nostor and Sask, all of whom hated Styphon's House beyond expression.

* * *

The first blaze of optimism had died down, he was glad to observe. Chartiphon was grumbling:

"We have three thousand at most; Gormoth has ten thousand, six thousand mercenaries and four thousand of his own people. Making our own fireseed gives us a chance, which we didn't have before, but that's all."

"Two thousand of his own people," somebody said. "He won't take the peasants out of the fields."

"Then he'll attack earlier," Ptosphes said. "While our peasants are getting the harvest in."

He looked at the map painted on one of the walls. Gormoth could invade up the Listra Valley, but that would only give him half of Hostigos—less than that. The whole line of the Mountains of Hostigos was held at every gap except one. Dombra Gap, guarded by Tarr-Dombra, lost by treachery three quarters of a century ago, and Sevenhills Valley behind it.

"We'll have to take Tarr-Dombra and clean Sevenhills Valley out," he said.

Everybody stared at him. It was Chartiphon who first found his voice.

"Man! You never saw Tarr-Dombra, or you wouldn't talk like that. It's smaller than Tarr-Hostigos, but it's even stronger."

"That's right," the retread captain who was G-1 and part of G-4 supported him.

"Do the Nostori think it can't be taken, too?" he asked. "Then it can be. Prince, have you plans of the castle?"

"Oh, yes. On a big scroll, in one of my coffers. It was my grandfather's, and we always hoped . . ."

"I'll want to see them. Later will do. Do you know of any changes made on it since?"

Not on the outside, at least. He asked about the garrison; five hundred, Harmakros thought. A hundred regular infantry of Gormoth's, and four hundred cavalry for patrolling around the perimeter of Sevenhills Valley. They were mercenaries, and they were the ones who had been raiding into Hostigos.

"Then stop killing raiders who can be taken alive. Prisoners can be made to talk." The Geneva Convention was something else unknown here-and-now. He turned to Xentos. "Is there a priest of Dralm in Sevenhills Valley? Can you get in touch with him, and will he help us? Explain that this is a war against Styphon's House."

"He knows that, and he will help, as he can. But he can't get into Tarr-Dombra. There is a priest of Galzar there for the mercenaries, and a priest of Styphon for the lord of the castle. Among the Nostori, Dralm is but a god for the peasants."

That rankled. Yes, the priests of Dralm would help.

"All right. But he can talk to people who can get in, can't he? And he can send messages, and organize an espionage apparatus among his peasants. I want to know everything that can be found out, no matter how trivial. Particularly, I want to know the guard-routine at the castle, and how it's supplied. And I want it observed all the time; Harmakros, you find men to do that. I take it we can't storm the place, or you'd have done that long ago. Then we'll have to surprise it."

Verkan the pack trader went up the road, his horse plodding unhurriedly and the pack horses on the lead-line trailing behind. He was hot and sticky under his steel back-and-breast, and sweat ran down his cheeks from under his helmet into his new beard, but nobody ever saw an unarmed pack trader, so he had to endure it. They were local-made, from an adjoining near-identical time-line, and so were his clothes, his sword, the carbine in the saddle sheath, his horse gear, and the loads of merchandise, all except a metal coffer on top of one pack load.

Reaching the brow of the hill, he started down the other side, and as he did he saw a stir in front of a thatched and whitewashed farm cottage. Men mounting horses; glints of armor, and red-and-blue Hostigi colors. Another cavalry post, the third he'd passed since crossing the border from Sask. The other two had ignored him, but this crowd meant to stop him. Two had lances, the third a musketoon, and the fourth, who seemed to be in command, had his holsters open and his right hand on his horse's neck.

He reined in his horse; the pack horses came to a well-trained stop.

"Good cheer, soldiers," he greeted.

"Good cheer, trader," the man with his hand close to his pistol-butt replied. "From Sask?"

"Sask last. From Ulthor, this trip; Grefftscharr by birth."

Ulthor was the lake port to the northwest; Grefftscharr was the kingdom around the Great Lakes. "I'm for Agrys City."

One of the troopers laughed. The sergeant asked: "Have you any fireseed?"

"About twenty charges." He touched the flask on his belt. "I tried to get some in Sask, but when the priests of Styphon heard that I was coming through Hostigos they'd give me none."

"I know; we're under the ban, here." It did not seem to distress him greatly. "But I'm afraid you'll not see Agrys soon. We're on the edge of war with Nostor, and the Lord Kalvan wants no tales carried, so he's ordered that no one may leave Hostigos."

He cursed; that was expected of him.

"I'd feel ill-used, too, in your place," the sergeant sympathized, "but when princes and lords order, commonfolk obey. It won't be so bad, though. You can get good prices in Hostigos Town or at Tarr-Hostigos, and then, if you know a skilled trade, you can find work at good wages. Or you might take the colors. You're well armed and horsed; the Lord Kalvan welcomes all such."

"The Lord Kalvan? I thought Ptosphes was Prince of Hostigos."

"Why, so he is, Dralm guard him, but the Lord Kalvan, Dralm guard him, too, is the war leader. It's said he's a prince himself, from a far land. It's also said that he's a sorcerer, but that I doubt."

Ah, yes; the stranger prince from afar. And among these people, Corporal Calvin Morrison—he willed himself no longer to think of the man as anything but the Lord Kalvan—would be suspected of sorcery. He chatted pleasantly with the sergeant and the troopers, asking about inns, about prices being paid for things, all the questions a wandering trader would ask, then bade them good luck and rode on. He passed other farms along the road. At most of them, work was going on; men were forking down dunghills and digging under them, fires burned, and caldrons steamed over them. He added that to the cheerfulness with which the sergeant and his men had accepted the ban of Styphon's House.

Styphon, it seemed, had acquired a competitor.

Hostigos Town spread around a low hill and a great spring as large as a small lake, facing the mountains which, on the

Europo-American Sector, had been quarried into sheer cliffs. The Lord Kalvan wouldn't fail to notice that. Above the gap stood a strong castle; that would be Tarr-Hostigos, *tarr* meant castle, or stronghold. The streets were crowded with carts and wagons; the artisans' quarter was noisy with the work of smiths and joiners. He found the Sign of the Red Halberd, the inn the sergeant had commended to him. He put up his horses and safe-stowed the packs, all but his personal luggage, his carbine, and the metal coffer. A servant carried the former; he took the coffer over one shoulder and followed to the room he had been given.

When he was alone, he set the coffer down. It was an almost featureless block of bronze, without visible lock or hinges, only two bright steel ovals on the top. Pressing his thumbs to these, he heard a slight click as the photoelectric lock inside responded to his thumbprint patterns. The lid opened. Inside were four globes of gleaming coppery mesh, a few small instruments with dials and knobs, and a little sigma-ray needler, a ladies' model, small enough to be covered by his hand, but as deadly as the big one he usually carried. It was silent, and it killed without trace that any autopsy would reveal.

There was also an antigrav unit, attached to the bottom of the coffer; it was on, the tiny pilot light glowed red. When he switched it off, the floor boards under the coffer creaked. Lined with collapsed metal, it now weighed over half a ton. He pushed down the lid, which only his thumbprints could open, and heard the lock click.

The common room downstairs was crowded and noisy. He found a vacant place at one of the long tables and sat down. Across from him, a man with a bald head and a small straggling beard grinned at him.

"New fish in the net?" he asked. "Welcome. Where from?"

"Ulthor, with three horse loads. My name's Verkan."

"Mine's Skranga." The bald man was from Agrys City.

"They took them all, fifty of them. Paid me less than I asked, but more than I thought they would, so I guess I got a fair price. I had four Trygathi herders, they're all in the cavalry, now. I'm working in the fireseed mill."

"The what?" He was incredulous. "You mean these people make their own fireseed? But nobody but the priests of Styphon can do that."

Skranga laughed. "That's what I thought, when I came here, but anybody can do it. No more trick than boiling soap. See, they get saltpeter from under dunghills, and . . ."

He detailed the process, step by step. The man facing him joined the conversation; he even understood, dimly, the theory. The charcoal was what burned, the sulfur was the kindling, and the saltpeter made the air to blow up the fire and blow the bullet out of the gun. And there was no secrecy about it, at least inside Hostigos. Except for keeping the news out of Nostor until he had enough fireseed for a war, the Lord Kalvan simply didn't care.

"I bless Dralm for bringing me into this," the horse trader said. "When people can leave here, I'm going some place and start making fireseed myself. Why, I'll be rich in a few years, and so can you."

He finished his meal, said he had to return to work, and left. A cavalry officer who had been sitting a few places down the table picked up his cup and flagon and took the vacant seat.

"You just came in?" he asked. "From Nostor?"

"No, from Sask." The answer seemed to disappoint the cavalryman; he went into the Ulthor-Grefftscharr story again. "How long will I be kept from going on?"

"Till we fight the Nostori and beat them. What do the Saski think we're doing here?"

"Waiting to have your throats cut. They don't know anything about your making fireseed."

The officer laughed. "Ha! Some of them'll get theirs cut, if Prince Sarrask doesn't mind his step. You say you have three horseloads of Grefftscharr wares; any weapons?"

"Some sword blades. Some daggers, a dozen gunlocks, three good shirts of rivet-link mail, bullet molds. And brassware, and jewelry, of course."

"Well, take your loads up to Tarr-Hostigos. They have a little fair each evening in the outer bailey, you can sell anything you have. Go early. Use my name"—he gave it—"and speak to Captain Harmakros. He'll be glad of any news you have."

He re-packed his horses, when he had eaten, and led them up the road to the castle above the gap. Along the wall of the outer bailey, inside the gate, were workshops, all busy. One thing he noticed was a gun carriage for a light fieldpiece being put together, not a little cart, but two big wheels and a trail, to be hauled with a limber. The gun for it was the sort of wrought-iron four-pounder normal for this sector, but it had trunnions, which was not. The Lord Kalvan, again.

Like all the local gentry, Captain Harmakros wore a small neat beard. His armor was rich but well battered, but the long rapier on his belt was new. He asked a few questions, then listened to a detailed account of what Verkan the trader had seen and heard in Sask; the mercenary companies Sarrask had hired, the names of the captains, their strength and equipment.

"You've kept your eyes open and your wits about you," he commented. "I wish you'd come through Nostor instead. Were you ever a soldier?"

"All traders are soldiers, in their own service."

"Yes, well when you've sold your loads, you'll be welcome in ours. Not as a common trooper, as a scout. You want to sell your pack horses, too? We'll give you your own price for them."

"If I sell my loads, yes."

"You'll have no trouble doing that. Stay about, have your meals with the officers here. We'll find something for you."

He had some tools, for both wood and metal work. He peddled them among the artisans, for a good price in silver and a better one in information. Beside cannon with trunnions on regular field-carriages, Kalvan had introduced rifling in small arms. Nobody knew whence Kalvan had come, but they knew it had been a great distance.

The officers with whom he ate listened avidly to what he had to tell about his observations in Sask. Nostor first, and then Sask, seemed to be the schedule. When they talked about the Lord Kalvan, the coldest expressions were of deep respect, and shaded up to hero-worship. But they knew nothing about him before the night he had appeared at a peasant's cottage and rallied a rabble fleeing from a raided village.

He sold the mail and sword blades and gunlocks as a lot to one of the officers; the rest of the stuff he spread to offer to the inmates of the castle. He saw the Lord Kalvan strolling through the crowd, in full armor and wearing a rapier and a Colt .38 Special on his belt. He had grown a small beard since the photograph the Paratime Police had secured on Europo-American had been taken. Clinging to his arm was a beautiful blond girl in male riding dress; Prince Ptosphes' daughter Rylla, he was told. He had already heard the story of how she had shot him by mistake in a skirmish and brought him to Tarr-Hostigos to be cared for. The happy possessiveness with which she held his arm, and the tenderness with which he looked at her, made him smile. Then the smile froze on his lips and died in his eyes as he wondered what Kalvan had told her privately.

Returning to the Red Halberd, he spent some time and money in the taproom. Everybody, as far as he could learn, seemed satisfied that Kalvan had come, with or without divine guidance, to Hostigos in a perfectly normal manner. Finally he went to his room.

Pressing his thumbs to the sensitized ovals, he opened the coffer and lifted out one of the gleaming copper-mesh balls. It opened at pressure on a small stud; he drew out a wire with a mouthpiece attached, and spoke for a long time into it.

"So far," he concluded, "there seems to be no question of anything paranormal about the man in anybody's mind. I have not yet made any contacts with anybody who would confide in me to the contrary. I have been offered an opportunity to take service under him as a scout; I intend doing this. Some assistance can be given me in carrying out this work. I will find a location for a conveyer-head; this will have to be somewhere in the woods near Hostigos Town. I will send a ball through when I do. Verkan Vall, ending communication."

Then he set the timer of the transposition field generator and switched on the antigrav unit. Carrying the ball to the open window, he released it. It rose quickly into the night, and then, high above, among the many visible stars, there was an instant's flash. It could have been a meteor.

Kalvan sat on a rock under a tree, wishing that he could smoke, and knowing that he was beginning to be scared. He cursed mentally. It didn't mean anything, as soon as things got started he'd forget to be scared, but it always happened before, and he hated it. It was quiet on the mountain top, even though there were two hundred men sitting or squatting or lying around him, and another five hundred, under Chartiphon and Prince Ptosphes, five hundred yards behind.

There were fifty more a hundred yards ahead, a skirmish-line of riflemen. Now there was a new word in the here-and-now military lexicon. They were the first riflemen on any battlefield in the history of here-and-now. A few of the rifles were big fifteen- to twenty-pound muskets, eight- to six-bore; mostly they were calivers, sixteen- and twenty-bore, the size and weight of a Civil War musket. They were commanded by the Grefftscharr trader, Verkan. There had been objection to giving an outland stranger so important a command; he had informed the objectors, stiffly, that he had been an outland stranger himself only recently.

Out in front of Verkan's line, in what the defenders of Tarr-Dombra thought was cleared ground, were fifteen sharpshooters. They all had big-bore muskets, rifled and fitted with peep-sights, zeroed in for just that range. The condition of that supposedly cleared approach was the most promising thing about the whole operation. The trees had been felled and the stumps rooted out, but the Nostori thought Tarr-Dombra couldn't be taken and that nobody would try to take it, so they'd gone slack. There were bushes all over it up to a man's waist, and many of them were high enough to hide behind standing up.

His men were hard enough to see even in the open. The helmets have been carefully rusted, so had the body-armor and every gun-barrel or spearhead. Nobody wore anything but green or brown, most of them had bits of greenery fastened to their helmets and clothes. The whole operation, with over twelve hundred men, had been rehearsed a dozen times, each time some being eliminated until they were down to eight hundred of the best.

There was a noise, about what a feeding wild-turkey would make, in front of him, and then a voice said, "Lord Kalvan!" It was Verkan, the Grefftscharrer. He had a rifle in his hand, and wore a dirty green-gray hooded smock; his sword and belt were covered with green and brown rags.

"I never saw you till you spoke," he commented.

"The wagons are coming. They're around the top switchback, now."

He nodded. "We start, then." His mouth was dry. What was that thing in "For Whom the Bell Tolls" about spitting to show you weren't afraid? He couldn't do that, now. He nodded to the boy squatting beside him; he picked up his arquebus and started back toward where Ptosphes and Chartiphon had the main force.

And Rylla! He cursed vilely, in English; there was no satisfaction in taking the name of Dralm in vain, or blaspheming Styphon. She'd announced that she was coming along. He'd told her she was doing nothing of the sort. So had her father, and so had Chartiphon. She'd thrown a tantrum; thrown other things, too. In the end, she had come along. He was going to have his hands full with that girl, when he married her.

"All right," he said softly. "Let's go earn our pay."

The men on either side of him rose, two spears or scythe-blade things to every arquebus, though some of the spearmen had pistols in their belts. He and Verkan went ahead, stopping at the edge of the woods, where the riflemen crouched behind trees, and looked across the open four hundred yards at Tarr-Dombra, the castle that couldn't be taken, its limestone walls rising beyond the chasm that had been quarried straight across the mountain top. The drawbridge was down and the portcullis was up, a few soldiers in black and orange scarves—his old college colors, he oughtn't to shoot them—loitering in the gateway. A few more kept perfunctory watch from the battlements.

Chartiphon and Ptosphes brought their men, one pike to every three calivers and arquebuses, up with a dreadful crashing and clattering that almost stood his hair on end under his helmet and padded coif, but nobody at the castle seemed to have heard it. Chartiphon wore a long sack, with neck and arm holes, over his cuirass, and what looked like a well-used dishrag wrapped around his helmet. Ptosphes was in brown, with browned armor, so was Rylla. They all looked to the left, where the road came up the side and onto the top of the mountain.

Four cavalrymen, black-and-orange scarves and lance-pennons, came into view. They were only fake Princeton men; he hoped they'd remember to tear that stuff off before some other Hostigi shot them. A long ox-wagon followed, piled high with hay and eight Hostigi infantrymen under it, then two more cavalrymen in false Nostori colors, another wagon, and six more cavalry. Two more wagons followed.

The first four cavalrymen clattered onto the drawbridge and

spoke to the guards at the gate, then rode through. Two of the wagons followed. The third rumbled onto the drawbridge and stopped directly under the portcullis. That was the one with the log framework on top and the log slung underneath. The driver must have cut the strap that held that up, jamming the wagon. The fourth wagon, the one loaded to the top of the bed with rocks, stopped on the outer end of the drawbridge, weighting it down. A pistol banged inside the gate, and another; there were shouts of "Hostigos! Hostigos!" The hay seemed to explode off the two wagons in sight as men piled out of them.

He blew his Pennsylvania State Police whistle, and half a dozen big elephant-size muskets bellowed, from places he'd have sworn there had been nobody at all. Verkan's rifle platoon began firing, sharp whip-crack reports like none of the smoothbores. He hoped they were remembering to patch their bullets; that was something new to them. Then he blew his whistle twice and started running forward.

The men who had been showing themselves on the walls were all gone; a musket-shot or so showed that the snipers hadn't gotten all of them. He ran past a man with a piece of fishnet over his helmet, stuck full of oak twigs, who was ramming a musket. Gray powder-smoke hung in the gateway, and everybody who had been outside had gotten in. Yells of "Hostigo!" and "Nostor!" and shots and blade-clashing from within. He broke step and looked back; his two hundred were pouring after him, keeping properly spaced out, the arquebusiers not firing. All the shooting was coming from where Chartiphon—and Rylla, he hoped—had formed a line two hundred yards from the walls and were plastering the battlements, firing as rapidly as they could reload. A cannon went off above when he was almost at the end of the drawbridge, and then, belatedly, the portcullis came down to stop seven feet from the ground on the top of the log framework hidden under the hay on the third wagon.

All six of the oxen on the last wagon were dead; the drivers had been furnished short-handle axes for that purpose. The oxen on the portcullis-stopper had also been killed. The gate towers on both sides had already been taken. There were black-and-orange scarves lying where they had been ripped off, and more on corpses. But shots were beginning to come from the citadel, across the outer bailey, and a mob of

Nostori were pouring out from its gate. This, he thought, was the time to expend some .38's.

Feet apart, left hand on hip, he aimed and emptied the Colt, killing six men with six shots, timed-fire rate. He'd done just as well at that range on silhouette targets many a time; that was all this was. They were the front six; the men behind them stopped momentarily, and then the men behind swept around him, arquebuses banging and pikemen and halberdiers running forward. He holstered the empty Colt, he only had eight rounds left, now, and drew his rapier and poignard. Another cannon on the outside wall thundered; he hoped Rylla and Chartiphon hadn't been in front of it. Then he was fighting his way through the citadel gate.

Behind, in the outer bailey, something beside "Nostor!" and "Hostigos!" was being shouted. It was:

"Mercy, comrade! Mercy; I yield!"

He heard more of that as the morning passed. Before noon, the Nostori garrison had either been given mercy or hadn't needed it. There had only been those two cannon-shots, though between them they had killed and wounded fifty men. Nobody was crazy enough to attack Tarr-Dombra, so they'd left the cannon empty, and had only been given time to load and fire two. He doubted if they'd catch Gormoth with his panzer down again.

The hardest fighting was inside the citadel. He ran into Rylla there, with Chartiphon trying to keep up with her. There was a bright scar on her browned helmet and blood on her sword; she was laughing happily. He expected that taking the keep would be even bloodier work, but as soon as they had the citadel it surrendered. By that time he had used up all his rounds for the Colt.

They hauled down Gormoth's black flag with the orange lily and ran up Ptosphes' halberd-head, blue on red. They found four huge bombards, throwing hundred-pound stone cannon balls, and handspiked them around to bear on the little town of Dyssa, at the mouth of Pine Creek, Gorge River here-and-now, and fired one round from each to announce that Tarr-Dombra was under new management. They set the castle cooks to work cutting up and roasting the oxen from the two rear wagons. Then they turned their attention to the prisoners herded in the inner bailey.

First, there were the mercenaries. They would enter the service of Ptosphes, though they could not be used against Nostor until their captain's terms of contract with Gormoth had run out. They would be sent to the Sask border. Then, there were Gormoth's own troops. They couldn't be used at all, but they could be put to work, as long as they were given soldiers' pay and soldierly treatment. Then, there was the governor of the castle, a Count Pheblon, cousin to Prince Gormoth, and his officers. They would be released, on oath to send their ransoms in silver to Hostigos. The priest of Galzar elected to go to Hostigos with his parishioners.

As for the priest of Styphon, Chartiphon wanted him questioned under torture, and Ptosphes thought he ought merely to be beheaded on the spot.

"Send him to Nostor with Pheblon," Kalvan said. "With a letter for his high priest—no, for the Supreme Priest, Styphon's Voice. Tell Styphon's Voice that we make our own fireseed, that we will teach everybody to make it, and that we will not rest until Styphon's House is utterly destroyed."

Everybody, including those who had been making suggestions for novel and interesting ways of putting the priest to death, shouted in delight.

"And send Gormoth a copy of the letter, and a letter offering him peace and friendship. Tell him we'll teach his soldiers how to make fireseed, and they can make it in Nostor when they're sent home."

"Kalvan!" Ptosphes almost howled. "What god has addled your wits? Gormoth's our enemy!"

"Anybody who can make fireseed will be our enemy, because Styphon's House will be his. If Gormoth doesn't realize that now, he will soon enough."

Verkan the Grefftscharr trader commanded the party that galloped back to Hostigos with the good news—Tarr-Dombra taken, with over two hundred prisoners, a hundred and fifty horses, four tons of fireseed, twenty cannon. And Sevenhills Valley was part of Hostigos again. Harmakros had destroyed a company of mercenary cavalry, killing twenty and capturing the rest, and he had taken Styphon's temple farm, a richly productive nitriary, freeing the slaves and butchering the priests and the guards. And the once persecuted priest of

Dralm had gathered all the peasants for a thanksgiving, telling them that the Hostigi came not as conquerors but as liberators.

He seemed to recall having heard that before, on a number of paratemporal areas, including Calvin Morrison's own.

He also brought copies of the letters Prince Ptosphes had written, or, more likely, which Kalvan had written and Ptosphes had signed, to the Supreme Priest of Styphon and to Prince Gormoth. Dropping a couple of troopers in the town to spread the good news, he rode up to the castle and reported to Xentos. It took a long time to tell the old priest-chancellor the whole story, counting interruptions while Xentos told Dralm about it. When he got away, he was immediately dragged into the officers' hall, where a wine barrel had been tapped. By the time he got back to the Red Halberd in Hostigo Town, it was after dark, and everybody was roaring drunk, and somebody had a little two-pounder in the street and was wasting fireseed that could have been better used to kill Gormoth's soldiers. The bell at the town hall, which had begun ringing while he was riding in through the castle gate, was still ringing.

Going up to his room, he opened the coffer and got out another of the copper balls, putting it under his cloak. He rode a mile out of town, tied his horse in the brush, and made his way to where a single huge tree rose above the scrub oak. Speaking into the ball, he activated and released it. Then he got out his cigarettes and sat down under the tree to wait for the half hour it would take the message-ball to reach Fifth Level Police Terminal Time-Line, and the half hour it would take a mobile antigrav conveyer to come in.

The servant brought him the things, one by one, and Lord Kalvan laid them on the white sheet spread on the table top. The whipcord breeches; he left the billfold in the hip pocket. He couldn't spend United States currency here, and his identity cards belonged to another man, who didn't exist here-and-now. The shirt, torn and bloodstained; the tunic with the battered badge that had saved his life. The black boots, one on either side; the boots they made here were softer and more comfortable. The Sam Browne belt, with the holster and the empty-looped cartridge-carrier and the handcuffs in their pouch. Anybody you needed handcuffs on, here-and-now, you just shot or knocked on the head. The Colt Official Police; he didn't want to part with that, even if there were no more cartridges for it, but the rest of this stuff would seem meaningless without it. He slipped it into the holster, and then tossed the blackjack on top of the pile.

The servant wrapped them and carried the bundle out. There goes Calvin Morrison, he thought; long live Lord Kalvan of Hostigos. Tomorrow, at the thanksgiving service before the feast, these things would be deposited as a votive offering in the temple of Dralm. That had been Xentos' idea, and he had agreed at once. Beside being a general and an ordnance engineer and an industrialist, he had to be a politician, and politicians can't slight their constituents' religion. He filled a goblet from a flagon on the smaller table and sat down, stretching his legs. Unchilled white wine was a crime against nature; have to do something about refrigeration—after the war, of course.

That mightn't be too long, either. They'd already unsealed the frontiers, and the transients who had been blockaded in would be leaving after the feast. They all knew that anybody could make fireseed, and most of them knew how. That fellow they'd gotten those Trygath horses from; he'd had a few words with him, and he was going to Nostor. So were half a dozen agents to work with Xentos' fifth column. Gormoth would begin making his own fireseed, and that would bring him under the ban of Styphon's House.

Gormoth wouldn't think of that. All he wanted was to conquer Hostigos, and without the help of Styphon's House, he couldn't. He couldn't anyhow, now that he had lost his best invasion-route. Two days after Tarr-Dombra had fallen, he'd had two thousand men at the mouth of Gorge River and lost at least three hundred by cannon fire trying to cross the Athan before his mercenary captains had balked, and the night after that Harmakros had come out of McElhattan Gap, Vrylos Gap, with two hundred cavalry and raided western Nostor, burning farms and villages and running off horses and cattle, devastating everything to the end of Listra Valley.

Maybe they'd thrown Gormoth off until winter. That would mean, till next spring. They didn't fight wars in the winter, here-and-now; against mercenary union rules. By then, he should have a real army, trained in new tactics he'd dredged from what he remembered of Sixteenth and Seventeenth Century history. Four or five batteries of little four-pounders, pieces and caissons each drawn by four horses, and as mobile as cavalry. And plenty of rifles, and men trained to use them. And get rid of all these bear spears and scythe blade things, and substitute real eighteen-foot Swiss pikes; they'd hold off cavalry.

Styphon's House was the real enemy. Beat Gormoth once, properly, and he'd stay beaten, and Sarrask of Sask was only a Mussolini to Gormoth's Hilter. But Styphon's House was big; it spread over all five Great Kingdoms, from the mouth of the St. Lawrence to the Gulf of Mexico.

Big but vulnerable, and he knew the vulnerable point. Styphon wasn't a popular god as, say, Dralm was; that was why Xentos' fifth column was building strength in Nostor. Styphon's House had ignored the people and even the minor nobility, and ruled by pressure on the Great Kings and their subject princes, and as soon as they could make their own powder, they'd turn on Styphon's House, and their people with them. This wasn't a religious war, likc the ones in the Sixteenth and Seventeenth Centuries in his own former history. It was just a job of racket-busting.

He set down the goblet and rose, throwing off the light robe, and began to dress for dinner. For a moment, he wondered whether the Democrats or the Republicans would win the election this year—he was sure it was the same year, now, in a different dimension of time—and how the Cold War and the Space Race were coming along.

Verkan Vall, his story finished, relaxed in his chair. There was no direct light on this terrace, only a sky-reflection from the city lights below, so dim that the tips of their cigarettes glowed visibly. There were four of them: the Chief of Paratime Police, the Director of the Paratime Commission, the Chairman of the Paratemporal Board of Trade, and Chief's Assistant Verkan Vall, who would be chief in another hundred days.

"You took no action about him?" the director asked.

"None at all. The man's no threat to the Paratime Secret. He knows he isn't in his own past, and from things he ought to find and hasn't he knows he isn't in his own future. So he knows he's in the corresponding present in a second time dimension, and he knows that somebody else is able to travel laterally in time. I grant that. But he's keeping it to himself.

On Aryan-Transpacific, in the idiom of his original time-line, he has it made. He won't take any chances on unmaking it.

"Look what he has that the Europo-American Sector could never give him. He is a great nobleman; they're out of fashion on Europo-American, where the Common Man is the ideal. He's going to marry a beautiful princess, that's even out of fashion for children's fairy tales. He's a sword-swinging soldier of fortune, and they've vanished from his own nuclear-weapons world. He's in command of a good little army, and making a better one out of it, and he has a cause worth fighting for. Any speculations about what space-time continuum he's in he'll keep inside his own skull.

"Look at the story he put out. He told Xentos that he had been thrown into the past from a time in the far future by sorcery. Sorcery, on that time-line, is a perfectly valid scientific explanation of anything. Xentos, with his permission, passed the story on, under oath of secrecy, to Ptosphes, Rylla, and Chartiphon. The story they gave out is that he's an exiled prince from a country outside local geographical knowledge. Regular defense in depth, all wrapped around the real secret, and everybody has an acceptable explanation."

"How'd you get it, then?" the Board Chairman asked.

"From Xentos, at the feast. I got him into a theological discussion, and slipped some hypno truth-drug into his wine. He doesn't remember, now, that he told me."

"Well, nobody else on that time-line'll get it that way," the Commission director agreed. "But didn't you take a chance getting those things of Morrison's out of the temple? Was that necessary?"

"No. We ran a conveyer in the night of the feast, when the temple was empty. The next morning, the priests all cried, 'A miracle! Dralm has accepted the offering!' I was there and saw it. Morrison doesn't believe that, he thinks some of these pack traders who left Hostigos the next morning stole the stuff. I know Harmakros' cavalrymen were stopping people and searching wagons and packs. Publicly, of course, he has to believe in the miracle.

"As to the necessity, yes. This stuff will be found on Morrison's original time-line, first the clothing, with the numbered badge still on the tunic, and, later, in connection with some crime we'll arrange for the purpose, the revolver. They won't explain anything, they'll make more of a mystery, but it will be a mystery in normal terms of what's locally accepted as possible."

"Well, this is all very interesting," the Trade Board chairman said, "but what have I to do with it, officially?"

"Trenth, you disappoint me," the Commission director said. "This Styphon's House racket is perfect for penetration of that subsector, and in a couple of centuries it'll be a very valuable subsector to have penetrated. We'll just move in on Styphon's House, and take it over, the way we did the Yat-Zar temples on the Hulgun Sector, and build that up to general economic and political control."

"You'll have to stay off Morrison's time-line, though," Tortha Karf said.

"You certainly will!" He was vehement about it. "We'll turn that time-line over to the University, here, for study, and quarantine it absolutely to everybody else. And about five adjoining time-lines, for control study. You know what we have here?" He was becoming excited about it. "We have the start of an entirely new subsector, and we have the divarication point absolutely identified, the first time we've been able to do that except from history. Now, here; I've already established myself with those people as Verkan the Grefftscharr trader. I'll get back, now and then, about as frequently as plausible for traveling by horse, and set up a trading depot. A building big enough to put a conveyer head into . . ."

Tortha Karf began laughing. "I knew it," he said. "You'd find some way!"

"All right. We all have hobbies; yours is fruit-growing and rabbit-hunting on Fifth Level Sicily. Well, my hobby farm is going to be the Kalvan Subsector, Fourth Level Aryan-Transpacific. I'm only a hundred and twenty years old, now. In a couple of centuries, when I'm ready to retire . . ."

JOHN D. MACDONALD (1916–   ) is known as the best-selling author of scores of excellent suspense novels and the creator of Travis McGee, one of the twentieth century's great literary inventions. However, before the fame and the movie sales, John D. MacDonald was a first-rate science fiction writer, the author of such outstanding novels as *Wine of the Dreamers* (1951) and *Ballroom of the Skies* (1952) and about fifty short stories, some of the best of which have been collected as *Other Times, Other Worlds*. Perhaps he will one day return to the field, since he still enjoys it. But in the meantime, we are proud to present a previously unreprinted tale.

AMPHISKIOS*

John D. MacDonald

Any diagrammatic presentation of the time concept must perforce be a simplification. Time is neither pulsations nor is it a winding river nor yet coiled upon itself like a spring. To best understand it and to free it of metaphysical confusions we must revert a full five thousand years to the basic Einstein conjectures, many of them since disproven in the mighty laboratory of stellar space. Draw two lines intersecting. An X. Where they cross is the "now."

The upper half is the past, the lower half the future.

Both the understandable past and the foreseeable future are severely limited by the sides which form a crude, angular hour-glass. The sidelines represent the speed of light, the infinite Fitzgerald Contraction, the bitter barrier of existence.

Each soul is a grain of sand in this hour-glass, but suspended forever at the point of "now." Since the origin of this concept twenty-five generations of experimentation have proved that man, pinned in the focal

---

*Greek word meaning capable of throwing a shadow in either direction.

point of existence, can move timewise neither up into the past nor down into the future.

Thus it has been conceded that escape from this trap of time, from the jaws of inevitability, lies in the possibility of a LATERAL *movement, which, of course, assumes a penetration of the barrier of the speed of light.*

Assuming the possibility of lateral movement, this movement could thus be reversed and the person which had existed for a moment OUTSIDE *the time barrier would return at an alien focal point, thus completing the illusion of a "journey" within time.*

All this is, of course, a simplification so extreme as to render the entire exposition almost meaningless.

—"Narración de Viajes en Tiempo"
Agabanzo Historical Collection
Martian Micro-library

CHAPTER I

Four Are Chosen

Howard Loomis glanced down at the dashboard clock and cursed the long-winded customer who had delayed him for over two hours. His sample cases packed the back seat. He had already reported to the sales manager that he would spend the night in Alexandria, seventy miles away.

He yawned, lit a cigarette and ran the window down, hoping the cold air would keep sleep away. He was a thin and nervous young man with a mobile mouth, a receding hairline and driving ambition.

He began to think of the prospects in Alexandria then as sleep welled up over him. His hands relaxed on the wheel. He awakened with a start as his front right wheel went off onto the shoulder. The big car swerved and he fought it back under control.

It was a clear cold night—below freezing. It had rained during the afternoon but the road was dry.

He decided to increase his speed, depending on the added responsibility to keep him awake.

In the white glow of his headlights he saw a bridge ahead—a bridge over railroad tracks.

The tires whined on the concrete, changed tone as they hit the steel tread of the bridge.

The bridge was coated with thin clear ice.

As the back end began to swing Howard Loomis bit down on his lower lip, fighting both panic and sheer disbelief that this could be happening to him.

The back end swung in the other direction and there was a grinding smash as it tore through the side railing.

The big car tipped. Howard Loomis caught a glimpse of the steel tracks far below. Ridiculously the thought that he could not live through the fall was intermingled with the thoughts of the potential customers in Alexandria.

There was the spinning silence of the fall, the sickening lunge through space, and . . .

The third show was coming up and she knew that it would be rough and unpleasant. During the second show a drunk who fancied himself a comic, after chanting, "Take it off!" had come out onto the floor to offer assistance. There would be more drunks for the third show.

Her name was Mary Callahan—Maurine Callaix on the bill—and she was a tall girl with the blue-black hair, milky skin and blue eyes of her race.

She was checking the concealed hooks in her working dress when Sally, the new singer, came into the dressing room and stood watching her.

"How can you do it, Mary?" she asked.

"Do what, kid?"

"I mean, get out there in front of all those people and—"

Mary smiled tightly. "It's just a business. I was the gal who was going to knock them dead in ballet. But I grew too big. It doesn't bother me any more."

Sally looked at her, shook her head and said, "I could never do it."

Mary Callahan stared at the smaller girl for a moment. Mary Callahan thought of the last three years, of the ten months' hospital bill her mother had accumulated while dying, of the money for milk and meat and bread for the twin nephews.

"I hope you don't have to do it. Ever."

"How about Rick?" Sally asked.

Mary Callahan frowned. "The guy worries me. I don't know what gave him the idea that I was his prize package. He's a hophead, dearie. He stopped me at the door tonight and I had to slap him across the teeth to get by him."

"Was that safe?" Sally asked.

"He hasn't got the nerve to try anything. I hope."

She got the call and went on, pausing just off the floor for the blue spot to pick her up, then walking on in a slow half dance to the sultry beat of the tom-tom, wearing the mechanical lascivious smile, reaching gracefully for the first concealed snap of the evening gown.

When Rick came into the glow of the spot the music faltered and stopped.

Mary Callahan watched his hand, watched the gun.

Suddenly she knew that he would shoot. She saw his pinpoint pupils, the twisted mouth, the stained teeth.

She saw the gun come up. She looked down the barrel, saw his finger whiten on the trigger, saw the first orange-red bloom of the flower of death and . . .

Joe Gresham padded across the I beam, his eyes fixed on the upright opposite him. He had learned three years before that when you're on the high iron you never look at your feet. Because then you'd see the cars below, like beetles, the people like small slow bugs, and something would happen to your stomach.

He was a sun-hardened man, with wide shoulders, knotted hands and an impassive though good-humored face.

Above him he heard the rivets clanking into the bucket, the buck of the hammer. The sun was bright.

When he heard the shout, he stopped dead. The red-hot rivet struck him just above the right ear.

For long seconds he fought for balance, gave up, tried to drop in such a way that his hands would clasp the girder on which he had been walking.

But he had waited too long, and his hands merely slapped the girder.

He spun down through the warm morning air and it was as though the earth spun slowly around him. Each time he saw the street it was startlingly closer. And as he fell he thought,

"This isn't happening to me. This can't be the end of Joe Gresham!"

And . . .

Stacey Murdock took three more smooth crawl strokes, rolled over onto her back and looked back at the lake shore, at the vast white house, the wide green lawns.

She grinned as she wondered if the two muscle-men her father had hired were still sitting in the house waiting for her to get up. Nothing could be more ridiculous than Daddy's periodic kidnapping scares. Why, kidnapping was out of fashion! Even when the gal in question would one day inherit more millions than she had fingers and toes.

Stacey was a trim, small girl with pale blond hair, a rather sallow face and a wide, petulant mouth.

The party last night had been a daisy. The cold water of the lake felt good. Best thing in the world for a hangover.

She had climbed down, dressed in a terrycloth robe, from the terrace outside her bedroom window. She could see the robe on the dock, glinting white in the sun.

It was so much more pleasant to swim without a suit.

Her soaked hair plastered her forehead. She pushed it aside, rolled over and began her long, effortless crawl out into the big lake. The waves were a bit higher way out and sometimes when she rolled her face up to breathe, one would slap her in the face.

Suddenly she felt the churn of nausea. The hangover was worse than she thought. But messy to be sick out in the water like this.

She floated for a time as the feeling got worse. When the paroxysms started, she doubled over, unable to catch her breath, unable to straighten out. She coughed under water and it made a strange bubbling by her ears. Then, stupidly, she had to breathe and she strangled on the water she was sucking into her lungs.

She had no idea where the surface was, and she was climbing up an endless green ladder with arms as limp as wet cloth and then there was a softness of music in her ears and it was so much easier and more delicious just to lie back and relax and sleep and . . .

* * *

It was Baedlik who first penetrated the barrier of the speed of light. The feat was not performed, as one might suppose, in the depths of space but in his laboratory in London. By bombarding the atoms of Baedlium with neutrons, he so increased the mass and attraction of the nuclei that the outer rings of electrons, moving at forty thousand miles per hour, were drawn in toward the nuclei, their speed proportionately increasing.

This decreased the dead space within the atom, resulting in an incredibly heavy material. When the speed of the outer rings passed the speed of light, the samples of Baedlium, to all intents and purposes, naturally ceased to exist at Baedlik's focal point.

This, for over seventy years, was called Baedlik's Enigma, until the lateral movement in time was explained by Glish, who also set forward the first set of formulae designed to predict and control this lateral movement.

—Ibid.

CHAPTER II

The Watching Boxes

Howard Loomis did not have, in his background or experience, any comparable sensation. One moment every fiber of his body was tensed in vain effort to withstand the smash which would tear soul from body.

And, without transition, he lay on a gentle slope, still curled in a seated position, and the air that was cold was warm, the night that was dark was suddenly a new day.

He sat up, still dressed in gray conservative suit, snap-brim hat, buttoned topcoat. His trembling hands rested against the grass. Or was it grass? It was not a proper green, having a bluish cast mixed with it.

Seventy feet away a fairytale forest cast a heavy shadow—mammoth trunks, roots like broken fingers, crowns as high as redwoods, reaching up toward a sky that was too blue. It was a purple blue. The disk of the sun was wide and in its yellow-glare was a tinge of blood.

Breathing hard, he scrambled to his feet, turning, looking

around him, seeing nothing but the expanse of grass, a ragged outcropping of rock that glinted silver, the side of a hill that restricted his horizon.

There was no sign of car, bridge or tracks. And, after the first few seconds, he did not look for any. This was alien, this world. The air was thin, as on a high mountain and to have seen in this place his car or any fragment of the world he knew would have been as grotesque an anachronism as his own presence.

He listened and heard the distant sound of birds. The air was sweet with the scent of sun-warmed grasses.

Howard Loomis dropped to his knees.

His hat rolled away, unheeded. He ran thin fingers through his thinning hair and thought about delirium, Valhalla and death.

He took off his topcoat and threw it aside. He fingered the fabric of his familiar suit, hoping to gain from the touch of the smooth weave a surer grasp on reality. He looked at his sleeve, saw the place where the weaver had fixed the cigarette burn in Baltimore.

He spun to his feet as she coughed.

She was a tall girl in a wine evening dress. Her blue eyes were wide with fear and she stood, her hands at her throat. She looked at something in the air in front of her which did not exist.

"*Rick!*" she gasped.

Howard Loomis began to laugh. He couldn't control it. He fell onto his hands and knees and laughed until the tears dripped ridiculously from the end of his sharp nose.

"Too—too much," he gasped. "Now bring on the—the golden harps."

"Who are you calling a harp?" the girl snapped.

The sound of her angry voice snapped him out of it. He stared at her in silence. "Where is this place? Who are you?"

"Those are my lines, mister."

"I can't tell you where we are, but I'm Howard Loomis. I sell Briskies. I skidded off a railroad bridge but I don't remember hitting the bottom. I ended up right here."

"You don't belong here?" she asked.

"Do I look it? In this decorator's nightmare am I part of the decor?"

"No," she said. "You're the Junior Chamber of Commerce type. You and blue trees don't mix. I'm Mary Callahan. I was starting my strip when a hoppie named Rick walked up and shot me right between the eyes. At least that was where he was aiming. I saw him pull the trigger but I didn't feel it hit."

She reached an unsteady hand up and touched her smooth forehead between her eyebrows with her fingertips.

He took out his cigarettes. She came over and sat down beside him. They smoked in silence.

"Oh, great!" Mary Callahan said.

"Meaning that it's tougher on you than on the common people? Let's take a hike around this glamour pasture and see where we are?"

"In these?" she asked, holding out a slim foot encased in a silver sandal with a four-inch heel. "You walk. I'll wait."

He shrugged. When he was forty feet from her, walking toward the hill, she said, "Hey! Howie! Don't look now but there's something floating over you."

He looked up quickly and his mouth sagged open. It was a little metal box about the size of a cigar box. A fat lens protruded from the bottom of it. It had no visible means of support. Howard stepped quickly to one side. So did the box.

In sudden anger he picked up a rock and threw it at the box.

The rock sailed up, passed through the space where the box had been and continued on.

He turned and looked with exasperation at Mary Callahan. He cocked his head on one side, said, "Hmmm. You have one too."

Fear of the unknown drove them together. Mary Callahan, in her high heels, topped him by two inches, yet she clung to his arm as she stared upward. The two boxes were twenty feet over their heads, drifting quietly side by side.

"They—they're watching us!" said Mary Callahan.

And he knew that she was right. The lenses were cool observant eyes.

"This I'm not going to like," she said grimly. "In spite of my profession I'm a girl who rather likes her privacy. I don't want to be watched, even by floating cameras."

She waited while he went down the slope, struggled up the steep hill. Tough brush aided him as did the outcroppings of rock. At last he gained the summit. He looked out over wild country. There were more forests, a wide river in the distance and several semiflat expanses which he judged to be covered by grass at least ten feet high. He saw no sign of human habitation.

He turned and looked back. The wine dress was brilliant against the blue-green grass. He saw her wave up at him. He started down the hill. She met him at the foot of the hill.

"Howie, did you bring any of those Briskies? They sound as if you eat them. Or are they whiskbrooms? About this time of night—or is it day—I yonk on a steak sandwich."

They both turned as a heavy weight crashed into the top of a small tree. The branches writhed and cracked and a powerful young man dressed in working clothes plummeted down, hitting on the slope, rolling almost to their feet.

He sat up, looked straight up in the air, said, "Heavenly Mary Jane! Where's the building?"

"You lose a building?" Mary Callahan asked sweetly. "I lost a night club and Howie, my pal here, he lost a car and a railroad bridge."

Joe Gresham stared at her, got slowly to his feet, testing arms and legs. He looked around at the landscape, glared at Howard Loomis, looked up again, recoiled as he saw the silver box with lens floating over his head.

"Whassat?" he gasped.

"Oh, we all wear them here. De rigueur, you know," Mary answered. "I assume that you fell off a building. You want the pitch?"

"Pitch? You mean you can tell me what happened?" Joe asked.

"Oh, it's very simple," Mary said. "The fall killed you."

Joe Gresham sat down. He tilted his head on one side and peered at Howard. "Where'd you get this crazy dame?"

"Her name is Mary Callahan and I'm Howard Loomis and we both got here almost the same way you did. If she's crazy, so am I. I haven't said it out loud before but we're all dead. Mary was shot through the head. I went off a bridge. What floor did you fall from?"

"About the forty-first. And my name is Joe Gresham."

"Joe, how many people do you know that fell from the forty-first floor and didn't break even a finger."

Joe took out a bandanna and wiped his sunburned brow. He

said softly, "Al Brunert fell off the top of the tool house and busted his arm and a pint of drinking liquor. You win, pal."

"And *what* do I win? Joe, is this any part of earth you ever heard about?"

Joe took another look around. He stood up and said, "They got the wrong colors here. And that sun is too big and I never seen rocks that look like they're all metal. I don't want to sound like a dope, folks, but is this heaven?"

Mary said, "A—I haven't been a very good girl. B—I don't think you get hungry in heaven. C—This isn't exactly a heavenly dress I've got on."

"Then it's hell," Joe said firmly.

"Don't be so dogmatic," Mary said briskly. "Maybe they've got three deals."

As she spoke Joe took hold of her arm so hard that she gasped. He spun her around and pointed with a big calloused hand. And he whistled softly. "Heaven it might be," he said.

The girl was on the grass twenty feet away, gasping and choking. She was a slightly sallow blonde with a honey tan—all over. Her hair was soaked.

"She represents the ultimate in my profession," Mary said.

The girl sat up, hugged herself and glared at them out of streaming eyes. "Well—do something!" she rasped between coughs.

Howard ran and got his discarded topcoat. Keeping his eyes carefully averted, he held it for the blonde. Mary watched her as she slipped into the coat, buttoned it around her. Mary said, appreciatively, "Sister, you ever want to change your line of work, I can give you the address of my agent."

The blonde stamped her foot on the grass. As it was a bare foot and as she managed to stamp it on a pebble, the gesture was ineffectual. She yelped with pain and hopped on one foot, holding the other.

The three stood and watched her.

Stacey Murdock said, "Get in touch with my father immediately. He's T. Winton Murdock. I'm Stacey Murdock. *The* Stacey Murdock. He'll be worried about me."

They still stared.

She raised her foot to stamp it again, thought better of it. "Didn't you cretins hear me? I insist that you get in touch with my father. He'll be worried. He'll pay you thugs whatever you ask."

Mary nodded, said in an aside to Howard, "You ask me, I think she drowned. Swimming raw too."

"This is no time for silly jokes," Stacey said. "I passed out and you pulled me out of the water and brought me here. Daddy has the note you wrote him."

Howard said tiredly, "I gather that you think we've kidnapped you. Look around, Miss Murdock. Take a good look."

Stacey took a long look and swallowed hard. "This is—a funny place," she said weakly.

"Ha, ha!" said Mary Callahan. "Funny."

"I detest oversized women," Stacey said briskly. She smiled at Joe. "Now you look like a good earthy type. Tell me where I can find a phone."

Joe pointed at his tree. "Lady, I just fell outa the topa that tree. I don't know my way around."

Stacey gave him a dazzling smile. "Now I get it," she said. "They rescued me and I'm still delirious from the shock. You are all figments of my shocked imagination."

Mary grinned tightly. "Figments, eh. Then we can't hurt you a bit?"

"Of course not," Stacey said.

Mary straightarmed Stacey in the forehead with the heel of her hand. Stacey sat down. "Just a love pat from an oversized woman, dearie."

Howard and Joe had to combine forces to pry them apart.

When they had calmed Stacey down they pointed out the floating boxes. She made a tiny bubbling sound. Howard caught her as she fell. He carried her over to the shade of a tree. She was wonderfully light in his arms.

Mary said bleakly, "I'm still starving."

"Could eat something myself," Joe admitted.

Howard shaded his eyes and looked at the sun. "If that sun moves as fast as the one we're used to, kids, we've got two hours to find food, water and a place to sleep."

Mary took off her shoes and hurled them off into the brush. "Better sore feet than a busted ankle. Wake up your dreamboat and we'll trudge."

Ten years after the death of Glish it was O'Dey, expanding the group of basic materials subject to the Baedlik

Enigma, who first managed to test the formulae propounded by Glish. His experiments attracted the attention of the original Planet Foundation, which assigned the Third Integrated Research Team to the task.

Forty-one years after the Third Integrated Research Team took over the task, a method was perfected whereby recording apparatus could be sent to any specific segment of the past after the exact position of the planet in question had been computed.

During the period when the histories of the planets were being rewritten the first basic rules of time travel were being determined, largely by trial and error.

The first truth to come to light was that no specific alteration can be made in the past. By alteration is meant any specific action which, by itself, will cause reactions and interactions that, like a pebble dropped in a pool, might cause alterations in the future.

The second truth to be exposed was that, as the future pre-exists in the variabilities of the present, no travel into the future for prognostic purposes can be made.

—Ibid.

CHAPTER III

Harvest of Bones

Mary Callahan sat on the river bank at dawn and smiled beatifically as she held her bruised feet in the cold water.

She half turned, then relaxed as Howard Loomis came up and sat beside her. In four days Howard had changed a great deal. He had grown more nervous and his hands shook uncontrollably.

"We need food," he snapped, "and rather than sitting here, crooning to your feet, you could be fishing. Stacey found more grubs last night."

"You bore me, Howie," she said, yawning. She looked ruefully at the insect bites on her bare arms. She had torn off the wine dress at knee level. She wondered if she could make crude sleeves from the extra portion of fabric.

"You don't seem to care what happens to us," Howie snapped.

"Kid, you're losing your sense of humor. I haven't had a rest like this in four years. I'm enjoying it. Besides, who was it found out those berries were good to eat?"

"They might have killed you."

She looked at him. "Again?" she asked softly.

Howard shuddered, glanced up at the two silver boxes. At least they went away at nightfall. "I don't feel dead," he said.

"Where's Joe?"

"Puttering around with that fire of his. Trying to burn rocks."

"And the princess?"

"She's still sleeping. And since you brought it up, Mary, I think you could be nicer to her." He waved his hand aimlessly at the surroundings. "She's delicate. All of this is a shock to her. She can't stand the environment the way we can."

Mary smiled without warmth. "The way we men can? Don't be a sucker, Howie. She's as tough as nails. She's just lazy. No work, no eat, I always say."

Howard snorted in disbelief and wandered away.

By concerted effort, they had three fish by lunch time. They were cleaned with Joe's pocket knife, spitted on green twigs and cooked over the flames.

And it was at lunch that Joe showed them the arrowheads he had made.

"For vampires," he said.

When they looked puzzled he said, "Those shiny rocks are silver, I think. Anyway I melted these into a stone mold. I'm cutting a slice off my belt for a bowstring. Find me a dead bird's feather and boom—I got something to use so maybe I can kill one of those little antelopes—the ones that hide out in that big grass."

"You're okay, Joe," Mary said.

Stacey sniffed and Howard reached over and patted her shoulder. It was then that he propounded his theory of heading for a low line of hills in the distance. He said he thought he saw sun glint on rock and, if so, there might be some nice dry caves there, out of the rain that came each night to make them miserable. They had found, according to Howard's watch, that it was only seven hours from dawn to dusk, that the night was not quite six hours long. Thus it might take two or maybe three days to get to the hills.

Stacey cast the only negative vote.

It took five days to reach the hills. And two more days to find the caves.

Four footsore and weary people stood at the base of the cliff and looked up. Joe Gresham had the haunch of a deer wrapped in bluish leaves, slung over his shoulder.

He carried a sturdy bow and three notched arrows in his hand.

Stacey, using thorns and a patience that had elicited Mary's first speck of admiration for her, had made a rather neat costume, shorts and a halter, of the hide of the tiny antelope-like beast. Howie had made a crude knapsack from the topcoat and, when Stacey discovered that her new costume was beginning to smell rather high, it was too late.

Mary noticed with amusement that Howard did not stay as close to Stacey as usual.

Joe had begun to develop an almost animal awareness of his surroundings. And thus it was Joe who saw the length of whitened bone protruding from the thorn brush at the base of the cliff.

Stacey refused to look. Mary, Howard and Joe stared down at the skeleton. It had worn a hide garment. An axe with a stone blade lay under the skeletal arm.

Joe bent over, picked it up, hefted it. "This we can use," he said.

"But don't you see?" Mary exclaimed. "There are people in this screwy world. Honest-to-God people!"

"You missed something," Howard said in a flat voice.

She gave him a quick glance. He was pale. She looked back at the body, saw the glint of metal. It was a fifty-cent piece, tarnished. A hole had been bored through it and it was on a greasy thong around what had been a neck.

She shut her teeth hard, bent over and looked closely at it. Then she straightened up, screamed and fell back against Joe. He steadied her.

Howard looked closely and said, "Joe, it's a U.S. coin all right. But it has a head on it I don't recognize. And the date is nineteen hundred seventy-one."

Joe gave him a puzzled smile. "But nineteen hundred seventy-one don't come along, pal, for another—lemme see—twenty-one years."

"What killed him, Joe?" Mary said.

Joe took a long look. Then he turned and looked up at the cliff. He shook his head. "Thought first he fell. But he's too far out. No, something give him a bash over the ear, caved his head in."

They found three more before nightfall. And one wore a shirt of chain mail, badly rusted.

The fire was in the mouth of the big cave. Howard was the spokesman. They sat back inside the cave, on stones that they had found there, arranged in a half circle, as though they had been used before in just that manner.

Howard said, "We've got to get our heads together. We've been here four days now and we've found—how many bodies, Joe?"

"Seventeen. Fourteen old ones and three fresh ones. Fairly fresh ones."

Mary shivered.

Howard continued. "I'm no historian, folks, but I've been looking at the stuff those people had. Clothes, for example. Now they either came fresh out of a costume play or else they landed here right out of their own world. Understand, I'm just thinking out loud. We've seen only a little part of this country. At the rate we found bodies here they must be all over the place.

"We don't know what the score is. We do know that we can feel hunger and cold and pain—and if these bodies are any proof, we can be killed—even if it is for the second time. I want to stay living if only to find out what this is all about. Agreed?"

The other three nodded.

"Now something killed all these people. Joe, you take it."

"Well, I'd say that most of them got their heads bashed but the fresh ones were carved up a little by something sharp. Not teeth or claws—a little sword, maybe, or a big knife."

"Thanks, Joe. That means there's danger here. I don't think all these people killed each other off. It would have been a help if some of them had written down what was after them."

"Or written it down so we could read it," Joe said grumpily.

"What do you mean?" Howard asked sharply.

"Oh, didn't you see that funny lingo scratched on the wall back there? About twenty feet back into the cave?"

Howard cursed softly, lit a torch and hurried back, Mary and Stacey following him. He found the markings. The flickering flame lighted it.

"Modern French," Stacey said. "Here goes—'I am the one who remains. They came at dawn to hunt us. The shining men. The others, my comrades, have fallen. We killed one. They took away the body, but our dead are—are—' " She faltered.

" 'Unburied,' " Mary said briskly. " 'I do not expect to survive the morrow. It is a strange existence in which one must die twice.' And signed by a character named Lerault."

"How do you—?" Stacey said.

"Education isn't restricted to the upper classes, darling," Mary said.

"Stop that eternal bickering!" Howard yelled. They went back to the fire.

When the flames died down, Joe replenished the blaze.

Mary said softly, "Shining men. Goid your lerns, boys. Tomorrow the battle."

"Shut up!" Howard said, a note of hysteria in his voice.

"Don't let her bother you, darling," Stacey said softly. She took Howard by the arm and the two of them went back into the cave into the darkness.

Joe spat onto the fire. "I was reading once," he said, "or maybe it was a movie or maybe TV. I forget. Anyway, they got this place where they stock it with animals and then if you're a very special guy with a big roll, they let you in there to hunt once in a while."

"Very sharp, Joe," Mary said. "We're thinking alike. Me, I'm going to give them a hell of a time. I know a place where nobody can come up with me plumping rocks down on their heads."

Joe, his voice softer, said, "I should a met you a long time ago, Mary. You got guts."

"Listen to the sweet talk."

Joe stirred restlessly, his voice growing husky. "Kid, on account of maybe this is our last night and—"

"Not so sharp, Joe. Don't let the princess give you wrong ideas. On account of this might be our last night, I'll stay up an hour later and we can have a nice talk."

* * *

Universe organization collapsed when Adolph Kane, egomaniac supervisor of the colonies near Sirius and Alpha Centauri, built a war fleet in secret and, after ten years of bitter warfare, wiped out all organized resistance on the part of the Planet Foundation.

Within fifteen more years he controlled all of the civilized universe, having subjugated the colonies in the Regulus, Formalhaut, Pollux, Aldebaran, Altair, Procryon, Arctures and Capella Sectors. He established new colonies near Archermar, the furthest mankind had yet been from Mother Earth.

He called himself Emperor, built on the gray planet, Lobos, a mighty palace and fortress, protected by the impenetrable ring of satellite warships.

In the shining palace be begat the sons who carried his name and his authority. During three hundred years of the reign of the line of Kane, research for the sake of knowledge ceased to exist. All research was channeled toward the single goal of making the Empire immune to attack, both from within and from without—for men yet feared the possibility of intelligent and warlike races in some yet unconquered corner of the universe.

Yet mankind benefited from the single-minded lust for power of the Empire, for it was through the insistence of the Kanes that the mighty space-ships plunged through the barrier of the speed of light with the lateral time movement aberration canceled down to the point where it was so slight as to be recorded only by the most delicate instruments.

And the Empire, searching the far corners of the universe, found that no enemy was in opposition and they yet lusted for war, as no dictatorship can exist without war.

Bannot, the Ninth in the Succession, turned his attention to past eras in search of a worthy foe.

—Ibid.

CHAPTER IV

They Come to Kill

They did not come the following dawn—or the next.

Joe Gresham had gradually taken over authority from Howard Loomis, yet he deferred to the judgment of Mary Callahan when he was in doubt. The headquarters cave was forty feet from the narrow valley floor, reached by a narrow ledge.

Joe summed up their plan. "We'll try to dicker with these jokers, but if they won't listen we better be ready. It's no use running. This is as good a place as we'll find."

During the two full days of preparation, Mary canceled all attempts at surprise weapons. She pointed up at the hovering boxes and said, "Whatever we do we'll be watched."

At the end of the second day there were six heavy bows. Stacey, pale and upset, displayed a remarkable talent for fashioning arrows. For the sake of speed the tips were fire-hardened. Joe had carried up the rocks. Howard Loomis had fashioned the spears, had made a sling, had traveled to the stream bed to gather small stones for the sling.

Water storage was a problem, unhappily solved by using the hides of the small deer-like creatures to fashion waterbags. Improper curing of the hides gave the water an evil smell, a worse taste.

The initial attack came on the third dawn.

Stacey was on watch at the cave mouth near the embers of the dead fire. Her scream jolted the other three out of sleep.

There were four of them. They stood on the brow of the hill opposite the cliff face. They were a good hundred and fifty yards away, the sun silhouetting them.

Mary shaded her eyes and frowned. "A ham act," she said. "A walk-on part. Spear-carriers. Something out of Shakespeare. J. Caesar, maybe."

The four, even at that distance, looked trim and young. They wore the crested helmets of antiquity, carried oval shields, short swords, unscabbarded. The sun glinted off the silver of their shields, the naked blades, the breastplates, the metallic thongs binding their husky legs.

They merely stood and watched.

"Armor, yet," Joe muttered. "What good are wooden arrows going to be?"

Stacey began to moan.

"Shut up, honey," Mary said softly.

The four men advanced down the slope with cautious steps. As they reached the valley floor their tanned faces were upturned toward the face of the cliff. They wore short stout war axes suspended from their belts.

And above each of them floated a small metallic box.

They seemed wary but confident. Joe growled deep in his throat, backed into the shadow, notched one of the best arrows on the bowstring of the heaviest bow, pulled it back until his thumb touched his cheek, just under his right eye. His big arms trembled slightly with the strain.

He released the arrow. It sped down, whizzing toward the biggest of the four. The man raised his shield with startled speed. The arrow penetrated halfway through the shield. The big man staggered back, lowering his shield. A thin line of blood ran down his cheek. He shouted something in a foreign tongue, a wide smile on his face. With a careless flick of his short sword, he lopped off the protruding arrow.

Howard shouted, his voice shrilled. "What do you want?"

The answer was in English, oddly accented. "To kill you!"

"He couldn't have made it clearer," Mary said.

"Come on and try," Joe yelled.

The four, shields high, inched toward the narrow ledge that wound up to the wide place in front of the cave mouth.

"Let 'em get nearly up here," Joe muttered.

They were so close that the shields overlapped, giving the impression of a vast metallic beetle crawling up the rock.

Joe selected a rock that had taken him much effort to lug up to the cave. His big arms corded with the effort as he lifted it, staying back out of sight. Mary peered over the edge.

She signaled to Joe. He held the rock over his head, stumbled as he came rushing forward.

It took him precious seconds to regain his balance.

The hundred-pound stone crashed down among them. A man yelled in pain as he was smashed against the ledge. Two men fell off, tumbling down into the brush.

But the lead man, the one with the punctured cheek, scrambled up the last ten feet, throwing aside his shield.

He stood enormous in front of the cave, his sword flashing, the war axe in his huge left hand. His mouth was open in a wide grin of battle. Joe charged him with one of the spears but the sword lopped off the spear, along with Joe's first finger and thumb.

Joe fell back. Mary flattened against the inside wall of the cave, stooped and picked up a half pound rock. Her tomboy girlhood had left cunning in her muscles. The rock hit the broad forehead. The man dropped sword and axe, dropped to his knees, his eyes glazed.

Joe took two steps forward and kicked the man in the face. He went over backward, dropped out of sight.

Two of the attackers were uninjured. They had recovered their shields, which they used to protect the injured man who had been hit by the stone Joe dropped among them. They disappeared down the valley into the brush.

The dead giant lay at the foot of the cliff.

They rekindled a fire from the embers while Joe held his right wrist clamped with his strong left hand. With the heated sword blade, Mary seared the stumps of finger and thumb. Joe screamed like a woman. Stacey sat with the face of one slowly going mad. She rocked from side to side and smiled foolishly.

Joe went to the dark interior of the cave and immediately fell into a deep sleep. Howard paced restlessly. Mary sat and watched the valley floor.

In mid-afternoon of the short day, the two uninjured ones made a concerted rush, looped a vine over the foot of the one who had died and dragged him off into the brush. As they did so, one of them glanced up at Mary.

He was dark, lean, powerfully built. But she noticed that there was a contradiction in his face. It had a specific sensibility, sensitivity. He had the look of a man who detested what he was doing.

Long after he had disappeared, she thought about him.

When Bannot, the Ninth Emperor Kane, ordered the court scientists to bring worthy foes from past eras, he had not sufficient training to realize that his request violated the first rule of space travel. Were any man to be taken from a past era the fact of his disappearance would make appreciable change in the future. As the future had already been determined, any effort to alter the past by removing a specific living being would be doomed to failure.

But the court scientists knew that to fail meant death. Their researches carried them far afield. Many of them died painfully when the promises they made to Bannot were not fulfilled within the time interval allotted.

Court secrecy was such that posterity will never know which man it was who first brought a living being from a past era to his own time. His method was dependent upon scanning the person at the moment of death, thus assuring that there would be no specific effect on the past. The lateral movement in time of the person thus transported caused an actual physical split, so that the lifeless duplication of the body remained in the past world.

When the method was first disclosed there was an outcry from the philosophers and from the church, though both institutions had been carefully emasculated by the Kanes.

Bannot, in the week before his death, handled the outcry in typical fashion. He not only ordered the assassination of the more outspoken but explained to the peoples of all planets, in tones of sweet reasonableness, that these persons were not living, even though they seemed to be alive, as they had actually died in times long gone.

When Bannot felt death upon him he ordered the same technique to be used on him after his death, to return a few days to the past and bring him into a new life.

But Bannot died of an exceedingly painful disease, the result of past dissipations. His eldest son, who hated him, found that Bannot could be brought back, only to die again, in agony, within hours.

His eldest son extended those hours into a full year before at last tiring of the game and taking over the golden throne.

—*Ibid.*

CHAPTER V

Battle-Axe Berserk

At dawn the next day, four attackers stood as before on the brow of the opposite hill.

Joe, his right arm badly swollen, laughed mirthlessly. "We

kill one and cripple one and there's still four. A nice game they have."

"That's what it is, Joe," Mary said flatly. "A game. People who can make those little boxes that follow you around could do better than swords. This is like the old Roman amphitheater. Those guys are gladiators. It's a big game with the boxes watching. Maybe the boxes flash the battle on screens. Home movies for the public. Hired entertainers."

Stacey had grown worse during the night. She sat with the empty smile on her lips and her eyes were far away.

Howard said, licking his lips, "Mary, do you think they could have . . ."

"For my money, yes. They want fun, so they grab us somehow just as we get knocked off and here we are and they have their fun."

"It—it's horrible!" Howard said.

"It ain't pretty," Mary agreed.

Howard said, "Why don't we just—well—hold our hands up. If we don't give them any sport, maybe they'll—"

"A lot I can do with one hand," Joe said. "Maybe it's worth a try."

Mary stood up, her lips compressed. "No dice, boys. These kids are bloodthirsty. I think they'd like to cut our throats. Why give them the brass ring?"

"What makes you so sure you're right, Callahan?" Howard asked.

"Take a look," she said tersely.

The four were advancing across the valley floor as cautiously as their predecessors. Mary looked closely. No, two of them were the same as the day before—the uninjured two, including the dark one with the look of disgust in his eyes.

There was nothing reassuring about their advance.

Howard said, "I still think it's—"

With a shrill scream Stacey bounded to her feet, shouldering between Mary and Howard. Though she had always been careful on the ledge she ran down at reckless speed. Mary picked herself up off the floor.

"Stacey!" Howard called after her. "Stacey, darling!"

He started to go after her. Joe caught him, held him, said, "Shut up and we'll see if your plan works. You couldn't catch her in time anyway."

They stood and watched the blond girl. This Stacey Murdock was grotesquely changed from the girl who had demanded that they get in touch with Daddy.

Her tan skin was scratched and torn, her hair dirty, her feet scarred by the rocks. She ran toward the four men, her hands outstretched. They heard her panting voice, her incoherent pleading. The lead man dropped sword and shield. Stacey ran to him. Mary saw the dark man make a move toward the lead man as though to object. But it was too late.

As Stacey ran toward the man's arms he sidestepped her. As she ran by him he caught her blond hair, yanked her backward off her feet. She fell with the small of her back across his bent knee. With one arm across her throat, the other across her hips, he snapped her back like a brittle stick.

He stood up and Mary could see the look of revulsion on his face as though he had disliked touching her. Stacey lay grotesquely bent. The man nudged her with his foot and the four of them looked up at the cave mouth.

Howard Loomis gave an incoherent yell, grabbed the battle axe from the floor and was gone before either Mary or Joe could stop him.

Still yelling in rage and the lust to kill, Howard Loomis, ex-salesman of Briskies, charged the four helmeted warriors.

Mary's throat tightened at the sight of his hopeless bravery.

By the pure fury of his attack he drove the two men back into their companions.

The slashing axe bounced off shield, rang off helmet, a bright arc in the morning light.

Three men dropped back. One of them faced Howard, parried his blows, waiting for the inevitable pause when Howard grew armweary.

With the short sword, as Howard's axe sagged, he spitted him carefully through the middle, twisting the wide blade to let air into the wound.

Howard fell onto his face, toppled over onto his side. The swordsman looked triumphantly up at the cave mouth. As he did so, Howard, with one last convulsive effort of the axe he still clutched, hacked at the swordsman's leg as one would hack at a tree. The axe severed muscle and tendon and artery.

"Good boy!" Joe whispered.

They staunched the flow of blood and one of them helped

the injured man down the valley. The remaining two, the dark one and another one, stared up at the cave.

"They'll wait for their pal," Joe said.

"No. This thing seems to be run by rules. I say that if there are two of us left they'll only toss in two of them."

The two warriors moved cautiously toward the ledge, their shields high, their swords held tightly.

In the beginning a vast planet called Thor was earmarked and set aside for the wars between the soldiers of Kane and the soldiers of the past.

In the beginning there was difficulty in selecting the proper period of the past. To go too far back resulted in poor warfare. To go too short a distance into the past was dangerous. At last it was decided that the savages of the twentieth century were the best. They had the beginnings of a technology and they yet retained much animal cunning.

In the beginning of this mock warfare the soldiers of Kane used the most modern of weapons and the opponents were annihilated so rapidly that the technicians were hard pressed to maintain the supply of combatants.

Also, with such vast armies on Thor, when the available weapons were equalized the loss among the soldiery of Kane was too great. In addition the images of the conflict beamed to all planets were vast, dusty, confusing.

The great-grandson of Bannot, bored with this type of conflict, devised new rules. He changed the scene of the conflict from Thor to Lassa. Lassa was a lush Earth-size planet, circling the bright sun Delta Virginis.

He ordered the manufacture of small individual scanners. He ordered brought from the past young healthy persons of both sexes, savages who could be expected to adjust to the wild conditions of Lassa and put up respectable battle.

In addition his propagandists inculcated a horror of the savages in the minds of those selected to oppose them.

In the beginning, because billions sat entranced before the screens watching the combat, there was intense rivalry among the young men to be selected as they hoped thus to gain fame.

But Orn, the great-grandson of Bannot, was shrewd

enough to realize that he could kill two birds with one stone by making combat with the savages a necessary stepping stone to rank and authority within his elite corps of space warriors.

In this manner he assured his forces of constant supply of bold officer material as hand to hand combat, obsolete for two thousand years, was a screen to sieve out the faint of heart.

It was discovered that, by arming his warriors with short broadsword, shield and battle axe, the thrill of the combat was intensified in close quarters.

And Orn was sufficiently wise to know that the periodic spectacles served to keep reasonably content a mass of humans who otherwise might think of the personal liberty which they lacked, of the restrictions of life under dictatorship.

—Ibid.

CHAPTER VI

No Stage

As dusk came, as the last attempt ceased, Joe laid on his back on the sandy floor of the cave, completely exhausted.

Mary Callahan stared down into the valley, watched the shadows slowly mask the two bodies remaining.

During the bitter afternoon, during the silent combat, neither side had been able to gain any decisive edge.

The crucial moment had come when the dark-haired warrior had, for a moment, gained the flat place in front of the cave. A blow from the club held in Joe's right hand had knocked his sword spinning into the valley. The warrior had left his axe behind so as to simplify the ascent.

He had blocked Joe's further blows with the shield, had beat an orderly retreat back down the ledge.

Joe sighed, inched over to the sagging water-bag, drank deeply.

Mary said ruefully, "Paging DeMille. Only his makeup was never this good."

Joe grunted. He said, "Always with the jokes, eh?"

"Either that or start screaming, laddie. Which'll you have?"

He didn't answer. She looked around, said, "Our best gadget was the rocks. And we're down to three good-sized ones. Can you help me or do I go down and see if I can bring up a few lady-sized ones?"

Joe said, his voice oddly high, "Damn you, Johnny! You promised me that five bucks!"

Mary went over to him. She knelt and put the back of her hand against Joe's forehead. It was like fire. She got some of the fetid water, tore a new strip from the hem of her dress and began to bathe his face.

Joe moaned, rolled from side to side and talked incessantly. At last he went to sleep. Mary suddenly realized that the last of the carefully guarded store of matches was gone and in the heat of combat they had let the last embers die.

The stars shone with hard brilliance. She sat in the cave mouth. For a time she sang softly to herself because it was good to hear the lift of a song. In the starlight she felt her way down the ledge, struggled painfully back up with stones. Four trips was all that she could manage.

And then she talked aloud to herself. She told herself that it was a stupid and empty thing she was doing, to resist. The second death might come as quickly as the first. But she felt the hard core of her courage, the will that would not give up. And she knew a sardonic amusement.

She gnawed on the strips of hard smoked meat until her hunger was gone. Joe shivered in his comatose state, his teeth chattering.

She lay down beside him, warming his body with hers, at last drifting off to uneasy sleep.

The shadow in front of the morning sun awakened her. Even as she rolled to her feet, backed slowly to the cave wall, she knew that she had been fighting to remain asleep, squinting her eyes against the sun.

It was the dark-haired one.

He walked lightly toward her on the balls of his feet. At first he was in silhouette and then he turned so that she could see his face where the light struck it, see the lip lifted away from white teeth.

He lifted the sword, his right arm held in front of his body for a backhand slash.

Mary Callahan lifted her chin, smiled at him and said

softly, "A quick one right across this swanlike neck, honeybun. A real quick one."

The web of muscles stood out on his bronzed forearm. Dawn light shone on the crest of the helmet.

She shut her eyes and waited. But the slashing blow did not come. She heard the thud, the grunt of effort, and opened her eyes to see the dark-haired one drop like a log.

Joe stood on his feet, the wildness gone from his eyes. He held the club in his left hand. The swelling had begun to leave his right arm.

He said, "He was a soft one, Mary. He couldn't quite do it. And while he was making up his mind I got him."

Joe dropped the club, picked up the sword, wedged his toe under the fallen one's shoulder, rolled him over and aimed the point of the sword at the unprotected throat for a downward thrust.

"No!" Mary shouted. "Don't do it, Joe."

He gave her an odd look. "Why not?"

"Because—well, maybe we can use him for a hostage."

The fallen man stirred. Joe shrugged, kicked him on the angle of the jaw, while Mary cut two strips from the empty water bag, tied the man's wrists tightly, then his ankles.

As she finished his ankles, the man opened his eyes and stared calmly at her. Joe once again pressed the tip of the sword to the man's throat. He looked as calmly up at Joe. The keen tip punctured the skin and a tiny rivulet of blood flowed down into the hollow of his strong throat.

Joe cursed. "I could have done it before, Mary, but I can't do it with him looking at me."

Mary pushed the blade away with the flat of her hand. "Go watch for the other one," she said.

Joe stalked to the mouth of the cave, muttering. She turned and glanced up at the two silver boxes which floated, motionless, a few inches from the high roof of the cave.

She smiled up at the lenses and said, "How do you like this, fight fans?"

Shawn, son of Orn, carried on the conflicts as devised by his father, ordering the technicians to make minor improvements.

But Shawn was wearied by the difficulties of administration of the greatest Empire the universe had ever seen.

With the passage of the years, as the blood of the Kanes thinned, unrest had spread throughout the four hundred and eleven colonies and throughout Mother Earth. This unrest was based primarily on the accelerating reduction of the birth rate.

Colonies which once had numbered in the hundreds of millions had shrunk to half their original number. Shawn had kept the court scientists hard at work on the problem but they spoke to him of the tiring germ plasm, of the diminishing vitality of the race. They at last convinced him that the race of man had passed the crest of vitality and was doomed to gradual reduction in numbers until at last, when all vitality was gone, the weeds and the rot would take over the works of man.

When Shawn at last believed the word of his court scientists, when he knew that the Empire would eventually fall with the race, he embarked on a course of personal extravagance, of dissipation, that exceeded anything previously known during the reign of the line of Kane.

His subjects became increasingly discontented, the malcontent spreading even to the officers of his elite corps of warriors of space.

The flames smoldered deep underground and various secret societies were formed, each pledged to overthrow the Empire. Such was the efficacy of the espionage system of the house of Kane that these societies were, for the most part, ignorant of the existence of the others and consequently each underestimated the total power of the spirit of rebellion.

In line with the spirit of malcontent, all decent men wearied of the spectacle of combat, feeling in their hearts that the bitter little battles on Lassa were but an evidence of the harshness of their ruler.

When Shawn found that his billions of subjects were not being entertained by the battles on Lassa, he cleverly recreated their interest by using Lassa as punishment for those he suspected of insubordination, of desiring to overthrow his empire.

He was not so foolish as to send only the rebels against the savages—against the savage dead, as they were called—but carefully kept the proportion down to three loyal and ambitious young officers to one rebel.

There was one minor difference. Once an officer was victorious on Lassa, he was free to rejoin the fleet. But a rebel was condemned to remain until he at last was killed by one of the savages.

What Shawn did not realize was that his subjects, more than sated with the sight of death, had begun to be sympathetic toward the savages and had lost most of the superstitious horror and fear which was the result of the propaganda of his infamous ancestor.

Shawn was careful to see that loyal technicians handled the individual scanners so that, should any condemned rebel attempt to shout his defiance to the listening universe, he would be quickly taken off the receivers of the world.

But Shawn made one mistake. He misjudged the loyalty of one scanner operator, or possibly the operator of the scanner was loyal until he saw what happened in the case of the ex-officer, Anthon.

Or it can be argued that the Empire was in so precarious a state that any incident would have been sufficient.

—Ibid.

CHAPTER VII

Final Gesture

The strands of hide cut deeply into his wrists and ankles and Anthon wondered at the strength of the savage woman who had tied him.

He knew that he was close to the end of his life and felt nothing but fury that his life should have ended in such a meaningless fashion. He would have willingly died in striking one more blow against the rule of the infamous Shawn.

These four savages had fought bravely. At least two of them had.

In the beginning, when he had been searched, when they had found on him the sketch of the castle defenses, when he had been condemned to Lassa to fight against savages until he at last was killed, he had thought it best to go into combat with the idea of being sufficiently clumsy so that death would come easily.

He knew that it would pain his friends, his relatives and those who had plotted with him against Shawn to see his death on the screen, but it had seemed worth the candle to spite Shawn's plan for him to provide sport and entertainment.

Thus, during the training period, he had made no special effort to become adept with sword and axe as had the loyal officers, who looked upon Lassa not as punishment but as a field where they could gain fame.

He had nothing but contempt for those officers who put personal gain above the needs of the race, above the spirit of rebellion. But Anthon was human—he was a victim of hope—and he found that he did not wish to die so pointlessly.

Possibly, if he remained alive for a sufficiently long period, the Empire would be overthrown and he would be free to help build a new world for mankind. Anthon was a sensitive and intelligent man. He recognized the basic weakness of his stand, and the forlorn slimness of his hope. And now the last of his hope was gone.

Incomprehensibly the girl had saved him from his own sword, held in the uninjured hand of the huge sunburned savage. Basically it was his own fault. Had he been able to steel himself to cut the throat of the woman with one back-handed slash he could then have disposed of the man.

He wondered ironically if the savage woman had saved him from the sword thrust out of some desire to repay him for not being able to strike the blow that would kill her. Surely, when Kor attacked, either the girl or the man would have one free moment in which to kill their bound captive before they died.

He pitied the two of them. They had been brought from their own world of the past to fight vainly against a force that would eventually quell them. The girl knelt beside him and, with a bit of cloth, wiped away the blood at the base of his throat. Her eyes were as gentle as her touch.

Anthon wondered at the odd feeling of warmth within him. It had first occurred when he had seen her, standing with the smaller one with the yellow hair. He had not liked the death of the smaller one. He had wanted to interpose himself, to save her, but his resolve had come too late.

And the smaller man had died like a warrior, crippled a strong man even as he died.

He looked up into the blue eyes of the woman in the ragged dark red dress and something in her look was like a note of strange music. He smiled as he thought of the absurdity of feeling affection—even love—for one of the savage dead.

Yet, philosophically speaking, *was* she dead? She could feel pain and cold and fear. Her touch was gentle. Yes, this was a far different sort of being than the lean, rather astringent women of his own class. This savage one had a deep, lusty strength about her. And she was incredibly brave. She had smiled and when she had asked for death the meaning was clear.

He had but few words of her archaic tongue. He said, "Why not kill?"

"Why, it speaks busted English," Mary said. "Why not kill you? Look, pretty boy. I want to live. Mary wants to live. Understand? How can I do that?"

"Mary," he said, rolling the name softly on his lips.

"That's right. Mary. Who are you?"

"Anthon. You will die."

"You say the nicest things, Tony. But you didn't say that fiercely now, did you? You said it like you didn't care for the idea very much but it was inevitable."

"No understand," he said and he wanted her to talk some more. He wanted very much to hear the sound of her voice.

"You're the soft one of the group, aren't you? The only one that doesn't seem to get a crazy joy out of killing off the innocent."

With his few words it was hard to tell her what he wanted to say. "If another way. If not die. Mary and Anthon."

Her laugh was husky silver. "Bless him! I get it, Tony. If not die maybe you're right. I like the look of you, lad."

She stood up quickly as Joe shouted hoarsely. The other warrior stood in the mouth of the cave. Anthon saw the dangling end of vine and knew how the man had been outwitted by Kor.

Kor was between the savage man and the mouth of the cave. The man had no chance. The man fought bravely with his club, but Kor parried the blow, slashed the man across the face. The man, his face spurting blood, staggered back.

With another slash of the sword Kor disemboweled him and

the man toppled slowly over, fell out of sight. Anthon heard the crash as the man struck the floor of the valley below the cave mouth.

The girl, holding the crude spear, rushed at Kor, trying to prod him over the edge. Anthon found himself wishing that she would be successful, wishing it so hard that his teeth almost met in his lower lip.

Kor twisted away from the thrust.

Anthon saw the ready blade and he screamed, "No! Don't—"

His scream faded into a sob. The girl with the dark hair lay face down on the cave floor, coughed once and then was still.

Kor came smiling forward and said, "Rebel, you live to try your luck again. Why they kept you alive I'll never know."

With a flick of the sword blade he severed the thongs that bound Anthon. Anthon moved as though in a dream. He waited a moment until feeling came back to his numbed hands. He reached for his own sword, came up off the floor with a roar of rage, with inhuman strength born of fury.

The startled Kor parried the first blow but the second caught him at the angle of neck and shoulder. The blade severed bone. Kor dropped with the blade still in him.

Still blind with anger, Anthon spread his arms wide, looked up at the silver box above him and said, "Would that it was Shawn who received that blow. Shawn and every one of his assassins and his thieves and the criminals who surround him.

"It is time that we are done with Shawn and his brood. It is time that we were free. It is time for every man of courage to stand upright and fight off oppression. We are not as free as these poor savages who die on Lassa."

And then Anthon realized that with his first words the scanner would have been turned off, that he spoke only to the empty cave of death. He walked two heavy paces, sank on his knees beside the body of the girl and began to sob hoarsely.

History records that the technician operating the scanner turned and fought with bare hands against the supervisor who would have turned it off. By the time the technician was killed, the damage was done.

No battle cry was ever broadcast so instantaneously to all parts of a vast empire.

Everyone had misjudged the strength of the forces of rebellion.

Entire space cruisers, almost to a man, revolted against Shawn. Those who remained loyal died suddenly. The rays of destruction crackled and spat and the air of many planets hummed with the blue fury of released power.

It is recorded that seven hundred millions died in that bloodbath. Shawn and his court died when the Palace of the Kanes became a wide pool of rock and molten metal which bubbled for many months like the crater of a somnolent volcano.

Earth, the mother of the race, was made the home of the new democratic government of the universe.

The organization of government, which has persisted to this day, was the Council of Seven. Anthon, as the man who sparked the rebellion, as the hero of billions, was elected to the original council, was immediately voted Chairman by the other six, who, it seemed, had been the leaders of the unintegrated groups seeking to overthrow Shawn.

For many months after he took over the Chairmanship Anthon was lethargic and depressed. He seemed to be a sick man. Many problems needed solution and there was talk for a time that Anthon, though a hero and a legend during his own lifetime, lacked the administrative ability to discharge properly his responsibilities.

We know, from the diary kept by Calitherous, that it was during a Council discussion of the greatest problem facing the race, that of the regression of procreative powers of the race, that Anthon came alive once more.

He whispered something so softly that no man could make out his words. Then, with eyes that flashed fire, he disbanded the meeting.

His manner was such that no man opposed him.

Anthon was closeted with his scientists for many weeks. One of the peculiarities of that period was the way he occupied himself during every free moment with the acquiring of skill in one of the archaic tongues.

—*Ibid.*

CHAPTER VIII

Re-Run

Howard Loomis spun as he heard a woman cough.

She was a tall girl in a wine evening dress. Her blue eyes were wide with fear and she stood, her hands at her throat. She looked at something in the air in front of her which did not exist.

"*Rick!*" she gasped.

Howard Loomis began to laugh. He couldn't control it. He staggered to the side of the vast luxurious room, furnished in a manner so strange as to give it the appearance of a dream, and laughed until the tears dripped ridiculously from the end of his sharp nose.

"Too—too much," he gasped. "Now bring on the golden harps."

"Who are you calling a harp?" the girl snapped.

The sound of her angry voice brought him out of it. He stared at her in silence. "Where is this place? Who are you?"

"Those are my lines, mister."

"Is your name Mary?" Howard asked. "If so, there's a guy here who—"

There was no need to finish the statement. The young man with the air of authority, with the golden toga that left his bronzed left shoulder bare, pushed by Howard Loomis and advanced toward Mary Callahan.

In his odd English, he said, "Mary, you are more beautiful than before."

"Than before what, friend?"

Anthon took her hands in his. His eyes were warm. "There is much to tell you. There is much that you do not understand."

"That, chum, is a perfect understatement."

"All I have time to tell you right now, Mary, is that this is a world thousands of years ahead of yours. You were brought here once before. I met you then. Others will come after you. I promise you a full and rich life at my side. You and those like you are the hope of this world, Mary. Through you we will gain the strength and vigor of times long past."

Mary Callahan tilted her head on one side. "Brother," she said, "I've been propositioned before but this is the first time I ever heard this line."

"Line?" he said. "All you have to do is to believe me and trust me."

She looked up into his eyes. She said, "Never let anybody say that Callahan doesn't land on her feet."

Anthon took her arm. He said, "Come with me. You must meet the Council. There are things I must explain to them. You can listen and I will translate for you and thus you will learn much."

Mary let herself be led toward the vast doorway. As she passed Howard Loomis she winked broadly at him and said in a stage whisper, "I don't know what the deal is, chum, but something tells me I'm going to like it."

Howard Loomis scratched his head, bewildered and frustrated, as he saw the tall girl, her fingertips on the arm of the oddly dignified young man, pass out through the enormous arched doorway into the sunlight.

Ten minutes later he was hastily wrapping his topcoat around a soaking-wet young lady with blond hair who, in spite of her irate tone, seemed badly in need of a competent man to look after her.

Any good salesman is resourceful.

POUL ANDERSON (1926–   ) is a Hugo and Nebula-winning author who has been publishing science fiction since 1947. Some of his more popular works include *Brain Wave* (1954), *The High Crusade* (1960), and *Three Hearts and Three Lions* (1961). A soon-to-be-released science fiction movie is based on the Hoka stories which he co-authored with Gordon Dickson. And this volume, including a selection from *Guardians of Time* (1960), marks the first of a series of sf adventure anthologies (the next is *Space Wars*) he has agreed to compile exclusively for Tor Books.

DELENDA EST

Poul Anderson

The hunting is good in Europe 40,000 years ago, and the winter sports are unexcelled anywhen. So the Time Patrol, always solicitous for its highly trained personnel, maintains a lodge in the Pleistocene Pyrenees.

Agent Unattached Manse Everard (American, mid-Twentieth A.D.) stood on the glassed-in veranda and looked across ice-blue distances, toward the northern slopes where the mountains fell off into woodland, marsh and tundra. He was a big man, fairly young, with heavy homely features that had once encountered a German rifle butt and never quite straightened out again, gray eyes, and a brown crew cut. He wore loose green trousers and tunic of Twenty-Third-Century insulsynth, boots handmade by a Nineteenth-Century French-Canadian, and smoked a foul old briar of indeterminate origin. There was a vague restlessness about him, and he ignored the noise from within, where half a dozen agents were drinking and talking and playing the piano.

A Cro-Magnon guide went by across the snow-covered yard, a tall handsome fellow dressed rather like an Eskimo (why had romance never credited paleolithic man with enough sense to wear jacket, pants, and footgear in a glacial period?), his face painted, one of the steel knives which had hired him at his belt. The Patrol could act quite freely, this far back in time; there was no danger of upsetting the past, for the metal would rust away and the strangers be forgotten in a few centuries. The main nuisance was that female agents from the more libertine periods were always having affairs with the native hunters.

Piet van Sarawak (Dutch-Indonesian-Venusian, early Twenty-Fourth A.D.), a slim dark young man with good looks and a smooth technique that gave the guides some stiff competition, joined Everard, and they stood for a moment in companionable silence. He was also Unattached, on call to help out in any milieu, and had worked with the American before. They had taken their vacation together.

He spoke first, in Temporal, the synthetic language of the Patrol. "I hear they've spotted a few mammoth near Toulouse." The city would not be built for a long time, but habit was powerful.

"I've got one," said Everard impatiently. "I've also been skiing and mountain climbing and watched the native dances."

Van Sarawak nodded, took out a cigarette, and puffed it into lighting. The bones stood out in his lean brown face as he sucked in the smoke. "A pleasant interlude," he agreed, "but after a time the outdoor life begins to pall."

There were still two weeks of their furlough left. In theory, since he could return almost to the moment of departure, an agent could take indefinite vacations; but actually he was supposed to devote a certain percentage of his probable lifetime to the job. (They never told you when you were scheduled to die—it wouldn't have been certain anyhow, time being mutable. One perquisite of an agent's office was the longevity treatment of the Daneelians, ca. one million A.D., the supermen who were the shadowy chiefs of the Patrol.)

"What I would enjoy," continued van Sarawak, "is some bright lights, music, girls who've never heard of time travel—"

"Done!" said Everard.

"Augustan Rome?" asked the other eagerly. "I've never been there. I could get a hypno on language and customs here."

Everard shook his head. "It's overrated. Unless we want to go 'way upstairs, the most glorious decadence available is right in my own milieu, say New York. If you know the right phone numbers, and I do."

Van Sarawak chuckled. "I know a few places in my own sector," he replied, "but by and large, a pioneer society has little use for the finer arts of amusement. Very good, let's be off to New York, in—when?"

"1955. My public *persona* is established there already."

They grinned at each other and went off to pack. Everard had foresightedly brought along some mid-Twentieth garments in his friend's size.

Throwing clothes and razor into a small handbag, the American wondered if he could keep up with van Sarawak. He had never been a high-powered roisterer, and would hardly have known how to buckle a swash anywhere in space-time. A good book, a bull session, a case of beer, that was about his speed. But even the soberest of men must kick over the traces occasionally.

Briefly, he reflected on all he had seen and done. Sometimes it left him with a dreamlike feeling—that it should have happened to *him*, plain Manse Everard, engineer and ex-soldier; that his ostensible few months' work for the Engineering Studies Company should only have been a blind for a total of years' wandering through time.

Travel into the past involves an infinite discontinuity; it was the discovery of such a principle which made the travel possible in 19352 A.D. But that same discontinuity in the conservation-of-energy law permitted altering history. Not very easily; there were too many factors, the plenum tended to "return" to its "original" shape. But it could be done, and the man who changed the past which had produced him, though unaffected himself, wiped out the entire future. It had never even *been*; something else existed, another train of events. To protect themselves, the Daneelians had recruited the Patrol from all ages, a giant secret organization to police the time lanes. It gave assistance to legitimate traders, scientists, and tourists—that was its main function in practice; but always there was the watching for signs which meant that some mad or ambitious or careless traveler was tampering with a key event in space-time.

If it ever happened, if anyone ever got away with it . . . The room was comfortably heated, but Everard shivered. He and all his world would vanish, would not have existed at all. Language and logic broke down in the face of the paradox.

He dismissed the thought and went to join Piet van Sarawak.

* * *

Their little two-place scooter was waiting in the garage. It looked vaguely like a motorcycle mounted on skids, and an antigravity unit made it capable of flight. But the controls could be set for any place on Earth and any moment of time.

> *"Auprès de ma blonde*
> *Qu'il fait bon, fait bon, fait bon,*
> *Auprès de ma blonde*
> *Qu'il fait bon dormir!"*

Van Sarawak sang it aloud, his breath steaming from him in the frosty air, as he hopped onto the rear saddle. Everard laughed. "Down, boy!"

"Oh, come now," warbled the younger man. "It is a beautiful continuum, a gay and gorgeous cosmos. Hurry up this machine."

Everard was not so sure; he had seen enough human misery in all the ages. You got case-hardened after a while, but down underneath, when a peasant stared at you with sick brutalized eyes, or a soldier screamed with a pike through him, or a city went up in radioactive flame, something wept. He could understand the fanatics who had tried to write a new history. It was only that their work was so unlikely to make anything better. . . .

He set the controls for the Engineering Studies warehouse, a good confidential place to emerge. Thereafter they'd go to his apartment, and then the fun could start.

"I trust you've said goodbye to all your lady friends here," he murmured.

"Oh, most gallantly, I assure you," answered van Sarawak. "Come along there. You're as slow as molasses on Pluto. For your information, this vehicle does not have to be rowed home."

Everard shrugged and threw the main switch. The garage blinked out of sight. But the warehouse did not appear around them.

For a moment, pure shock held them unstirring.

The scene registered in bits and pieces. They had materialized a few inches above ground level—only later did Everard think what would have happened if they'd come out in a solid object—and hit the pavement with a teeth-rattling bump. They were in some kind of square, a fountain jetting nearby.

Around it, streets led off between buildings six to ten stories high, concrete, wildly painted and ornamented. There were automobiles, big clumsy-looking things of no recognizable type, and a crowd of people.

"Ye *gods!*" Everard glared at the meters. The scooter had landed them in lower Manhattan, 23 October 1955, at 11:30 A.M. There was a blustery wind carrying dust and grime, the smell of chimneys, and—

Van Sarawak's sonic stunner jumped into his fist. The crowd was milling away from them, shouting in some babble they couldn't understand. It was a mixed lot: tall fair roundheads, with a great deal of red hair; a number of Amerinds; half-breeds in all combinations. The men wore loose colorful blouses, tartan kilts, a sort of Scotch bonnet, shoes and high stockings. Their hair was long and many favored drooping mustaches. The women had full ankle-length skirts and hair coiled under hooded cloaks. Both sexes went in for jewelry, massive bracelets and necklaces.

"What happened?" whispered the Venusian. "Where are we?"

Everard sat rigid. His mind clicked over, whirling through all the eras he had known or read about. Industrial culture—those looked like steam cars, but why the sharp prows and figureheads?—coal-burning—post-nuclear Reconstruction? No, they hadn't worn kilts then, and they still spoke English—

It didn't fit. There was no such milieu recorded!

"We're getting out of here!"

His hands were on the controls when the big man jumped him. They went over on the pavement in a rage of fists and feet. Van Sarawak fired and sent someone else down unconscious; then he was seized from behind. The mob piled on top of them both, and things became hazy.

Everard had a confused impression of men in shining coppery breastplates and helmets, who shoved a billy-swinging way through the riot. He was fished out and supported while handcuffs were snapped on his wrists. Then he and van Sarawak were searched and hustled off to a big vehicle. The Black Maria is much the same in all times.

He didn't come out of it till they were in a damp and chilly cell with an iron-barred door.

* * *

"Name of a flame!" The Venusian slumped on a wooden cot and put his face in his hands.

Everard stood at the door, looking out. All he could see was a narrow concrete hall and the cell across it. The map of Ireland stared cheerfully through those bars and called something unintelligible.

"What's happened?" Van Sarawak's slim body shuddered.

"I don't know," said Everard very slowly. "I just don't know. That machine was supposed to be foolproof, but maybe we're bigger fools than they allowed for."

"There's no such place as this," said van Sarawak desperately. "A dream?" He pinched himself and lifted a rueful smile. His lip was cut and swelling, and he had the start of a gorgeous shiner. "Logically, my friend, a pinch is no test of reality, but it has a certain reassuring effect."

"I wish it didn't," said Everard.

He grabbed the rails, and the chain between his wrists rattled thinly. "Could the controls have been off, in spite of everything? Is there any city, anywhen on Earth—because I'm damned sure this is Earth, at least—any city, however obscure, which was ever like this?"

"Not to my knowledge," whispered van Sarawak.

Everard hung onto his sanity and rallied all the mental training the Patrol had ever given him. That included total recall . . . and he had studied history, even the history of ages he had never seen, with a thoroughness that should have earned him several Ph.D.'s.

"No," he said at last. "Kilted brachycephalic whites, mixed up with Indians and using steam-driven automobiles, haven't happened."

"Coordinator Stantel V," said van Sarawak faintly. "Thirty-eighth century. The Great Experimenter—colonies reproducing past societies—"

"Not any like this," said Everard.

The truth was growing in him like a cancer, and he would have traded his soul to know otherwise. It took all the will and strength he had to keep from screaming and bashing his brains out against the wall.

"We'll have to see," he said in a flat tone.

A policeman—Everard supposed they were in the hands of the law—brought them a meal and tried to talk to them. Van

Sarawak said the language sounded Celtic, but he couldn't make out more than a few words. The meal wasn't bad.

Toward evening, they were led off to a washroom and got cleaned up under official guns. Everard studied the weapons: eight-shot revolvers and long-barreled rifles. The facilities and the firearms, as well as the smell, suggested a technology roughly equivalent to the 19th century. There were gas lights, and Everard noticed that the brackets were cast in an elaborate intertwined pattern of vines and snakes.

On the way back, he spied a couple of signs on the walls. The script was obviously Semitic, but though van Sarawak had some knowledge of Hebrew through dealing with the Jewish colonies on Venus, he couldn't read it.

Locked in again, they saw the other prisoners led off to do their own washing—a surprisingly merry crowd of bums, toughs, and drunks. "Seems we get special treatment," remarked van Sarawak.

"Hardly astonishing," said Everard. "What would you do with total strangers who appeared out of nowhere and used unheard-of weapons?"

Van Sarawak's face turned to him with an unaccustomed grimness. "Are you thinking what I am thinking?" he asked.

"Probably."

The Venusian's mouth twisted, and horror rode his voice: "Another time line. Somebody *has* managed to change history."

Everard nodded. There was nothing else to do.

They spent an unhappy night. It would have been a boon to sleep, but the other cells were too noisy. Discipline seemed to be lax here. Also, there were bedbugs.

After a bleary breakfast, Everard and van Sarawak were allowed to wash again and shave. Then a ten-man guard marched them into an office and planted itself around the walls.

They sat down before a desk and waited. It was some time till the big wheels showed up. There were two: a white-haired, ruddy-cheeked man in cuirass and green tunic, presumably the chief of police; and a lean, hard-faced half-breed, gray-haired but black-mustached, wearing a blue tunic, a tam o'shanter, and insignia of rank—a golden bull's head. He would have had a certain hawklike dignity had it not been for the skinny hairy legs beneath his kilt. He was followed by younger men, armed and uniformed, who took up their places behind him as he sat down.

Everard leaned over and whispered: "The military, I'll bet. We seem to be of interest."

Van Sarawak nodded sickly.

The police chief cleared his throat with conscious importance and said something to the—general? The latter turned impatiently and addressed himself to the prisoners. He barked his words out with a clarity that helped Everard get the phonemes, but with a manner that was not exactly reassuring.

Somewhere along the line, communication would have to be established. Everard pointed to himself. "Manse Everard," he said. Van Sarawak followed the lead and introduced himself similarly.

The general started and went into a huddle with the chief. Turning back, he snapped: "*Yrn Cimberland*?"

"No spikka da Inglees," said Everard.

"*Gothland*? *Svea*? *Nairoin Teutonach*?"

"Those names—if they are names—they sound a little Germanic, don't they?" muttered van Sarawak.

"So do our names, come to think of it," answered Everard tautly. "Maybe they think we're Germans." To the general: "*Sprechen Sie Deutsch*?" Blankness rewarded him. "*Taler ni svensk*? *Niederlands*? *Dönsk tunga*? *Parlez-vous français*? Goddammit, *¿habla usted español*?"

The police chief cleared his throat again and pointed to himself. "Cadwallader Mac Barca," he said. The general hight Cynyth ap Ceorn.

"Celtic, all right," said Everard. Sweat prickled under his arms. "But just to make sure—" He pointed inquiringly at a few other men, being rewarded with monickers like Hamilcar ap Angus, Asshur yr Cathlann, and Finn O'Carthia. "No . . . there's a distinct Semitic element here too. That fits in with their alphabet—"

Van Sarawak's mouth was dry. "Try Classical languages," he urged harshly. "Maybe we can find out where this time went awry."

"*Loquerisne latine*?" That drew a blank. " 'Ελλενιζεις?"

General ap Ceorn started, blew out his mustache, and narrowed his eyes. "*Hellenach*?" he snapped. "*Yrn Parthia*?"

Everard shook his head. "They've at least heard of Greek,"

he said slowly. He tried a few more words, but no one knew the tongue.

Ap Ceorn growled something and spoke to one of his men, who bowed and went out. There was a long silence.

Everard found himself losing personal fear. He was in a bad spot, yes, and might not live very long; but anything that happened to him was ridiculously insignificant compared to what had been done to the entire world.

God in Heaven! To the universe!

He couldn't grasp it. Sharp in his mind rose the land he knew, broad plains and tall mountains and prideful cities. There was the grave image of his father, and yet he remembered being a small child and lifted up skyward while his father laughed beneath him. And his mother—they had a good life together, those two.

There had been a girl he knew in college, the sweetest little wench a man could ever have been privileged to walk in the rain with; and there was Bernie Aaronson, the long nights of beer and smoke and talk; Phil Brackney, who had picked him out of the mud in France when machine guns were raking a ruined field; Charlie and Mary Whitcomb, high tea and a low little fire in Victoria's London; a dog he had once had; the austere cantos of Dante and the ringing thunder of Shakespeare; the glory which was York Minster and the Golden Gate Bridge—Christ, a man's life, and the lives of who knew how many billions of human creatures, toiling and suffering and laughing and going down into dust to leave their sons behind them— *It had never been!*

He shook his head, dazed with grief, and sat devoid of real understanding.

The soldier came back with a map and spread it out on the desk. Ap Ceorn gestured curtly, and Everard and van Sarawak bent over it.

Yes . . . Earth, a Mercator projection, though eidetic memory showed that the mapping was rather crude. The continents and islands were there in bright colors, but the nations were something else.

"Can you read those names, Van?"

"I can make a guess, on the basis of the Hebraic alphabet," said the Venusian. He read out the alien words, filling in the gaps of his knowledge with what sounded logical.

North America down to about Colombia was Ynys yr

Afallon, seemingly one country divided into states. South America was a big realm, Huy Braseal, with some smaller countries whose names looked Indian. Australasia, Indonesia, Borneo, Burma, eastern India, and a good deal of the Pacific belonged to Hinduraj. Afghanistan and the rest of India were Punjab. Han included China, Korea, Japan, and eastern Siberia. Littorn owned the rest of Russia and reached well into Europe. The British Isles were Brittys, France and the Low Countries Gallis, the Iberian peninsula Celtan. Central Europe and the Balkans were divided into many small states, some of which had Hunnish-looking names. Switzerland and Austria made up Helveti; Italy was Cimberland; the Scandinavian peninsula was split down the middle, Svea in the north and Gothland in the south. North Africa looked like a confederacy, reaching from Senegal to Suez and nearly to the equator under the name of Carthagalann; the southern continent was partitioned among small countries, many of which had purely African titles. The Near East held Parthia and Arabia.

Van Sarawak looked up. There were tears in his eyes.

Ap Ceorn snarled a question and waved his finger about. He wanted to know where they were from.

Everard shrugged and pointed skyward. The one thing he could not admit was the truth. He and van Sarawak had agreed to claim they were from some other planet, since this world hardly had space travel.

Ap Ceorn spoke to the chief, who nodded and replied. The prisoners were returned to their cell.

"And now what?" Van Sarawak slumped on his cot and stared at the floor.

"We play along," said Everard grayly. "We do anything to get at our scooter and escape. Once we're free, we can take stock."

"But what happened?"

"I don't know, I tell you! Offhand it looks as if something upset the Roman Empire and the Celts took over, but I couldn't say what it was." Everard prowled the room. There was a bitter determination growing in him.

"Remember your basic theory," he said. "Events are the result of a complex. That's why it's so hard to change history. If I went back to, say, the Middle Ages, and shot one of FDR's Dutch forebears, he'd still be born in the Twentieth

Century—because he and his genes resulted from the entire world of his ancestors, and there'd have been compensation. The first case I ever worked on was an attempt to alter things in the Fifth Century; we spotted evidence of it in the Twentieth, and went back and stopped the scheme.

"But every so often, there must be a really key event. Only with hindsight can we tell what it was, but some one happening was a nexus of so many world lines that its outcome was decisive for the whole future.

"Somehow, for some reason, somebody has ripped up one of those events back in the past."

"No more Hesperus City," whispered van Sarawak. "No more sitting by the canals in the blue twilight, no more Aphrodite vintages, no more—did you know I had a sister on Venus?"

"Shut up!" Everard almost shouted it. "I know. What counts is what to do.

"Look," he went on after a moment, "the Patrol and the Daneelians are wiped out. But such of the Patrol offices and resorts as antedate the switchpoint haven't been affected. There must be a few hundred agents we can rally."

"*If* we can get out of here."

"We can find that key event and stop whatever interference there was with it. We've got to!"

"A pleasant thought," mumbled van Sarawak, "but—"

Feet tramped outside, and a key clicked in the lock. The prisoners backed away. Then, all at once, van Sarawak was bowing and beaming and spilling gallantries. Even Everard had to gape.

The girl who entered in front of three soldiers was a knockout. She was tall, with a sweep of rusty-red hair past her shoulders to the slim waist; her eyes were green and alight, her face came from all the Irish colleens who had ever lived, the long white dress was snug around a figure meant to stand on the walls of Troy. Everard noticed vaguely that this time-line used cosmetics, but she had small need of them. He paid no attention to the gold and amber of her jewelry, or to the guns behind her.

She smiled, a little timidly, and spoke: "Can you understand me? It was thought you might know Greek—"

The language was classical rather than modern. Everard, who had once had a job in Alexandrine times, could follow it through her accent if he paid close heed—which was inevitable anyway.

"Indeed I do," he replied, his words stumbling over each other.

"What are you snakkering?" demanded van Sarawak.

"Ancient Greek," said Everard.

"It would be," mourned van Sarawak. His despair seemed to have vanished, and his eyes bugged.

Everard introduced himself and his companion. The girl said her name was Deirdre Mac Morn. "Oh, no," groaned van Sarawak. "This is too much. Manse, you've got to teach me Greek, and fast."

"Shut up," said Everard. "This is serious business."

"Well, but why should you have all the pleasure—"

Everard ignored him and invited the girl to sit down. He joined her on a cot, while the other Patrolman hovered unhappily close. The guards kept their weapons ready.

"Is Greek still a living language?" asked Everard.

"Only in Parthia, and there it is most corrupt," said Deirdre. "I am a Classical scholar, among other things. Saorann ap Ceorn is my uncle, so he asked me to see if I could talk with you. There are not many in Afallon who know the Attic tongue."

"Well . . ." Everard suppressed a silly grin. "I am most grateful to your uncle."

Her eyes rested gravely on him. "Where are you from? And how does it happen that you speak only Greek, of all known languages?"

"I speak Latin too."

"Latin?" She frowned briefly. "Oh, yes. The Roman speech, was it not? I'm afraid you'll find no one who knows much about it."

"Greek will do," said Everard.

"But you have not told me whence you came," she insisted.

Everard shrugged. "We've not been treated very courteously," he hinted.

"Oh . . . I'm sorry." It seemed genuine. "But our people are so excitable—especially now, with the international situation what it is. And when you two appeared out of thin air—"

Everard nodded grimly. The international situation? That had a familiar ring. "What do you mean?" he inquired.

"Oh, surely . . . of course you know. With Huy Braseal and Hinduraj about to go to war, and all of us wondering what will happen— It is not easy to be a small power."

"A small power? But I saw a map, and Afallon looked big enough to me."

"We wore ourselves out two hundred years ago, in the great war with Littorn. Now none of our confederated states can agree on a single policy." Deirdre looked directly into his eyes. "What is this ignorance of yours?"

Everard swallowed and said: "We're from another world."

"What?"

"Yes. A . . . planet of Sirius."

"But Sirius is a star!"

"Of course."

"How can a star have planets?"

"How— But it does! A star is a sun like—"

Deirdre shrank back and made a sign with her finger. "The Great Baal aid us," she whispered. "Either you are mad, or— The stars are mounted in a crystal sphere."

Oh, no! Everard asked slowly: "What of the planets you can see—Mars and Venus and—"

"I know not those names. If you mean Moloch, Ashtoreth, and the rest, of course they are worlds like ours. One holds the spirits of the dead, one is the home of witches, one—"

All this and steam cars too. Everard smiled shakily. "If you'll not believe me, then what do you think?"

Deirdre regarded him with large eyes. "I think you must be sorcerers," she said.

There was no answer to that. Everard asked a few weak questions, but learned little more than that this city was Catuvellaunan, a trading and manufacturing center; Deirdre estimated its population at two million, and that of all Afallon at fifty million, but it was only a guess—they didn't take censuses in this world.

The prisoners' fate was also indeterminate. Their machine and other possessions had been sequestrated by the military, but nobody dared to monkey with them, and treatment of the owners was being hotly debated. Everard got the impression that all government, including the leadership of the armed forces, was a sloppy process of individualistic wrangling. Afallon itself was the loosest of confederacies, built out of former nations—Brittic colonies and Indians who had adopted white culture—all jealous of their rights. The old Mayan Empire, destroyed in a war with Texas (Tehannach) and annexed, had not forgotten its time of glory, and sent the most rambunctious delegates of all to the Council of Suffetes.

The Mayans wanted an alliance with Huy Braseal, perhaps out of friendship for fellow Indians. The West Coast states, fearful of Hinduraj, were toadies of the Southeast Asian empire. The Middle West—of course—was isolationist, and the Eastern states were torn every which way but inclined to follow the lead of Brittys.

When he gathered that slavery existed here, though not on racial lines, Everard wondered briefly if the guilty time travelers might not have been Dixiecrats.

Enough! He had his own and Van's necks to think about. "We are from Sirius," he declared loftily. "Your ideas about the stars are mistaken. We came as peaceful explorers, and if we are molested there will be others of our kind to take vengeance."

Deirdre looked so unhappy that he felt conscience-stricken. "Will you spare the children?" she whispered. "They had nothing to do with it." Everard could imagine the frightful vision in her head, helpless captives led off in chains to the slave markets of a world of witches.

"There need be no trouble at all if we are released and our property returned," he said.

"I shall speak to my uncle," she promised, "but even if I can sway him, he is only one on the Council. The thought of what your weapons could mean if we had them has driven men mad."

She rose. Everard clasped her hands, they lay warm and soft in his, and smiled crookedly at her. "Buck up, kid," he said in English. She shivered and made the hex sign again.

"Well," said van Sarawak when they were alone, "what did you find out?" After being told, he stroked his chin and murmured thoughtfully: "That was one sweet little collection of sinusoids. There could be worse worlds than this."

"Or better," said Everard bleakly. "They don't have atomic bombs, but neither do they have penicillin. It's not our job to play god."

"No . . . no, I suppose not." The Venusian sighed.

They spent a restless day. Night had fallen when lanterns

glimmered in the corridor and a military guard unlocked the cell. The prisoners' handcuffs were removed, and they were led silently to a rear exit. A car waited, with another for escort, and the whole troop drove wordlessly off.

Catuvellaunan did not have outdoor lighting, and there wasn't much night traffic. Somehow, that made the sprawling city unreal in the dark. Everard leaned back and concentrated on the mechanics of his vehicle. Steam-powered, as he had guessed, burning powdered coal; rubber-tired wheels; a sleek body with a sharp nose and serpent figurehead; the whole simple to operate but not too well designed. Apparently this world had gradually developed a rule-of-thumb mechanics, but no systematic science worth mentioning.

They crossed a clumsy iron bridge to Long Island, here as at home a residential section for the well-to-do. Their speed was high despite the dimness of their oil-lamp headlights, and twice they came near having an accident—no traffic signals, and seemingly no drivers who did not hold caution in contempt.

Government and traffic . . . hm. It all looked French, somehow, and even in Everard's own Twentieth Century France was largely Celtic. He was no respecter of windy theories about inborn racial traits, but there was something to be said for traditional attitudes so ancient that they were unconsciously accepted. A Western world in which the Celts had become dominant, the Germanic peoples reduced to two small outposts . . . Yes, look at the Ireland of home; or recall how tribal politics had queered Vercingetorix's revolt. . . . But what about Littorn? Wait a minute! In *his* early Middle Ages, Lithuania had been a powerful state; it had held off Germans, Poles, and Russians alike for a long time, and hadn't even taken Christianity till the Fifteenth Century. Without German competition, Lithuania might very well have advanced eastward—

In spite of the Celtic political instability, this was a world of large states, fewer separate nations than Everard's. That argued an older society. If his own Western civilization had developed out of the decaying Roman Empire about, say, 600 A.D., the Celts in this world must have taken over earlier than that.

Everard was beginning to realize what had happened to Rome. . . .

* * *

The cars drew up before an ornamental gate set in a long stone wall. There was an interchange with two armed guards wearing the livery of a private estate and the thin steel collars of slaves. The gate was opened, and the cars went along a graveled driveway between trees and lawns and hedgerows. At the far end, almost on the beach, stood a house. Everard and van Sarawak were gestured out and led toward it.

It was a rambling wooden structure. Gas lamps on the porch showed it painted in gaudy stripes; the gables and beam-ends were carved into dragon heads. Behind it murmured the sea, and there was enough starlight for Everard to make out a ship standing in close—presumably a freighter, with a tall smokestack and a figurehead.

Light glowed through the windows. A slave butler admitted the party. The interior was paneled in dark wood, also carved, the floors thickly carpeted. At the end of the hall there was a living room with overstuffed furniture, several paintings in a stiff conventionalized style, and a merry blaze in a great stone fireplace.

Saorann Cynyth ap Ceorn sat in one chair, Deirdre in another. She laid aside a book as they entered and rose, smiling. The officer puffed a cigar and glowered. There were some words swapped, and the guards disappeared. The butler fetched in wine on a tray, and Deirdre invited the Patrolmen to sit down.

Everard sipped from his glass—the wine was an excellent Burgundy type—and asked bluntly: "Why are we here?"

Deirdre smiled, dazzlingly this time, and chuckled. "Surely you find it more pleasant than the jail."

"Oh, yes. But I still want to know. Are we being released?"

"You are . . ." She hunted for a diplomatic answer, but there seemed to be too much frankness in her. "You are welcome here, but may not leave the estate. We had hopes you could be persuaded to help us. There would be rich reward."

"Help? How?"

"By showing our artisans and wizards the spells to make more machines and weapons like your own."

Everard sighed. It was no use trying to explain. They didn't have the tools to make the tools to make what was needed, but how could he get that across to a folk who believed in witchcraft?

"Is this your uncle's home?" he asked.

"No," said Deirdre. "It is my own. I am the only child of my parents, who were wealthy nobles and died last year."

Ap Ceorn snapped something, and Deirdre translated with a worried frown: "The tale of your magical advent is known to all Catuvellaunan by now; and that includes the foreign spies. We hope you can remain hidden from them here."

Everard, remembering the pranks Axis and Allies had played in little neutral nations like Portugal, shivered. Men made desperate by approaching war would not likely be as courteous as the Afallonians.

"What is this conflict going to be about?" he inquired.

"The control of the Icenian Ocean, of course. Particularly, certain rich islands we call Yyns yr Lyonnach—" Deirdre got up in a single flowing movement and pointed out Hawaii on a globe. "You see," she went on earnestly, "as I told you, the western countries like Brittys, Gallis, and ourselves, fighting Littorn, have worn each other out. Our domains have shrunken, and the newer states like Huy Braseal and Hinduraj are now expanding and quarreling. They will draw in the lesser nations, for it is not only a clash of ambitions but of systems—the monarchy of Hinduraj and the sun-worshipping theocracy of Huy Braseal."

"What is your religion?" asked Everard.

Deirdre blinked. The question seemed almost meaningless to her. "The more educated people think that there is a Great Baal who made all the lesser gods," she answered at last, slowly. "But naturally, we pay our respects to the foreign gods too, Littorn's Perkunas and Czernebog, the Sun of the southerners, Wotan Ammon of Cimberland, and so on. They are very powerful."

"I see. . . ."

Ap Ceorn offered cigars and matches. Van Sarawak inhaled and said querulously: "Damn it, this would have to be a time-line where they don't speak any language I know." He brightened. "But I'm pretty quick to learn, even without hypnos. I'll get Deirdre to teach me."

"You and me both," said Everard hastily. "But listen, Van—" He reported what had been said.

"Hm." The younger man rubbed his chin. "Not so good, eh? Of course, if they'd just let us at our scooter, we could take off at once. Why not play along with them?"

"They're not such fools," answered Everard. "They may believe in magic, but not in undiluted altruism."

"Funny . . . that they should be so backward intellectually, and still have combustion engines."

"No. It's quite understandable. That's why I asked about their religion. It's always been purely pagan; even Judaism seems to have disappeared. As Whitehead pointed out, the medieval idea of one almighty God was important to science, by inculcating the notion of lawfulness in nature. And Mumford added that the early monasteries were probably responsible for the mechanical clock—a very basic invention—because of having regular hours for prayer. Clocks seem to have come late in this world." Everard smiled wryly, but there was a twisting sadness in him. "Odd to talk that way. Whitehead and Mumford never lived. If Jesus did, his message has been lost."

"Still—"

"Just a minute." Everard turned to Deirdre. "When was Afallon discovered?"

"By white men? In the year 4827."

"Um . . . when does your reckoning start from?"

Deirdre seemed immune to further startlement. "The creation of the world—at least, the date some philosophers have given. That is 5959 years ago."

"4004 B.C. . . . Yes, definitely a Semitic element in this culture. The Jews had presumably gotten their traditional date from Babylon; but Everard doubted that the Jews were the Semites in question here.

"And when was steam (*pneuma*) first used to drive engines?"

"About a thousand years ago. The great Druid Boroihme O'Fiona—"

"Never mind." Everard smoked his cigar and mulled his thoughts for a while. Then he turned back to van Sarawak.

"I'm beginning to get the picture," he said. "The Gauls were anything but the barbarians most people think. They'd learned a lot from Phoenician traders and Greek colonists, as well as from the Etruscans in Cisalpine Gaul. A very energetic and enterprising race. The Romans, on the other hand, were a stolid lot, with few intellectual interests. There was very little technological progress in our world till the Dark Ages, when the Empire had been swept out of the way.

"In *this* history, the Romans vanished early and the Gauls

got the power. They started exploring, building better ships, discovering America in the 9th century. But they weren't so far ahead of the Indians that those couldn't catch up . . . even be stimulated to build empires of their own, like Huy Braseal today. In the 11th century, the Celts began tinkering with steam engines. They seem to have got gunpowder too, maybe from China, and to have made several other inventions; but it's all been cut-and-dry, with no basis of real science."

Van Sarawak nodded. "I suppose you're right. But what did happen to Rome?"

"I'm not sure . . . yet . . . but our key point is back there somewhere."

Everard returned to Deirdre. "This may surprise you," he said smoothly. "Our people visited this world about 2500 years ago. That's why I speak Greek but don't know what has occurred since. I would like to find out from you—I take it you're quite a scholar."

She flushed and lowered long dark lashes. "I will be glad to help as much as I can." With a sudden appeal that cut at his heart: "But will you help us in return?"

"I don't know," said Everard heavily. "I'd like to, but I don't know if we can."

Because after all, my job is to condemn you and your entire world to death.

When Everard was shown to his room, he discovered that local hospitality was more than generous. He was too tired and depressed to take advantage of it . . . but at least, he thought on the edge of sleep, Van's slave girl wouldn't be disappointed.

They got up early here. From his upstairs window, Everard saw guards pacing the beach, but they didn't detract from the morning's freshness. He came down with van Sarawak to breakfast, where bacon and eggs, toast and coffee added the last incongruous note of dream. Ap Ceorn was gone back to town to confer, said Deirdre; she herself had put wistfulness aside and chattered gaily of trivia. Everard learned that she belonged to a dramatic group which sometimes gave plays in the original Greek—hence her fluency; she liked to ride, hunt, sail, swim—"And shall we?" she asked.

"Huh?"

"Swim, of course!" Deirdre sprang from her chair on the

lawn, where they had been sitting under flame-colored leaves in the wan autumn sunlight, and whirled innocently out of her clothes. Everard thought he heard a dull clunk as van Sarawak's jaw hit the ground.

"Come!" she laughed. "Last one in is a Sassenach!"

She was already tumbling in the cold gray waves when Everard and van Sarawak shuddered their way down to the beach. The Venusian groaned. "I come from a warm planet," he objected. "My ancestors were Indonesians—tropical birds."

"There were some Dutchmen too, weren't there?" grinned Everard.

"They had the sense to go to Indonesia."

"All right, stay ashore."

"Hell! If she can do it, I can!" Van Sarawak put a toe in the water and groaned again.

Everard summoned up all the psychosomatic control he had ever learned and ran in. Deirdre threw water at him. He plunged, got hold of a slender leg, and pulled her under. They tumbled about for several minutes before running back to the house. Van Sarawak followed.

"Speak about Tantalus," he mumbled. "The most beautiful girl in the whole continuum, and I can't talk to her and she's half polar bear."

Everard stood quiet before the living-room fire, while slaves toweled him dry and dressed him in the local garb. "What pattern is this?" he asked, pointing to the tartan of his kilt.

Deirdre lifted her ruddy head. "My own clan's," she answered. "A house guest is always taken as a clan member during his stay, even if there is a blood feud going on." She smiled shyly. "And there is none between us, Manslach."

It cast him back into bleakness. He remembered what his purpose was.

"I'd like to ask you about history," he said. "It is a special interest of mine."

She nodded, adjusted a gold fillet on her hair, and got a book from a crowded shelf. "This is the best world history, I think. I can look up details you might wish to know."

And tell me what I must do to destroy you. Seldom had Everard felt himself so much a skunk.

He sat down with her on a couch. The butler wheeled in lunch, and he ate moodily.

To follow up his notion—"Did Rome and Carthage ever fight a war?"

"Yes. Two, in fact. They were allied at first, against Epirus. Then they fell out. Rome won the first war and tried to restrict Carthaginian enterprise." Her clean profile bent over the pages, like a studious child. "The second war broke out twenty-three years later, and lasted . . . hm . . . eleven years all told, though the last three were only mopping up after Hannibal had taken and burned Rome."

Ah-hah! Somehow, Everard did not feel happy about it.

The Second Punic War, or rather some key incident thereof, was the turning point. But—partly out of curiosity, partly because he feared to tip his hand—Everard did not ask for particulars. He'd first have to get straight in his mind what had actually happened, anyway. (No . . . what had not happened. The reality was here, warm and breathing beside him, and he was the ghost.)

"So what came next?" he inquired tonelessly.

"There was a Carthaginian Empire, including Spain, southern Gaul, and the toe of Italy," she said. "The rest of Italy was impotent and chaotic, after the Roman confederacy had been broken up. But the Carthaginian government was too venal to endure; Hannibal himself was assassinated by men who thought him too honest. Meanwhile, Syria and Parthia fought for the eastern Mediterranean, with Parthia winning.

"About a hundred years after the Punic Wars, some Germanic tribes invaded and conquered Italy." (Yes . . . that would be the Cimbri, with their allies the Teutones and Ambrones, whom Marius had stopped in Everard's world.) "Their destructive path through Gaul set the Celts moving too, into Spain and North Africa as Carthage declined; and from Carthage the Gauls learned much.

"There followed a long period of wars, during which Parthia waned and the Celtic states grew. The Huns broke the Germans in middle Europe, but were in turn scattered by Parthia, so the Gauls moved in and the only Germans left were in Italy and Hyperborea." (That must be the Scandinavian peninsula.) "As ships improved, there was trade around Africa with India and China. The Celtanians discovered Afallon, which they thought was an island—hence the 'Ynys'—but were thrown out by the Mayans. The Brittic colonies further north had better luck, and eventually won their independence.

"Meanwhile Littorn was growing vastly. It swallowed up central Europe and Hyperborea for a while, and those countries only regained their freedom as part of the peace settlement after the Hundred Years' War you know of. The Asian countries have shaken off their European masters and modernized themselves, while the Western nations have declined in their turn." Deirdre looked up. "But this is only the barest outline. Shall I go on?"

Everard shook his head. "No, thanks." After a moment: "You are very honest about the situation of your own country."

Deirdre shrugged. "Most of us won't admit it, but I think it best to look truth in the eyes."

With a surge of eagerness: "But tell me of your own world. This is a marvel past belief."

Everard sighed, turned off his conscience, and began lying.

The raid took place that afternoon.

Van Sarawak had recovered himself and was busily learning the Afallonian language from Deirdre. They walked through the garden hand in hand, stopping to name objects and act out verbs. Everard followed, wondering vaguely if he was a third wheel or not, most of him bent to the problem of how to get at the scooter.

Bright sunlight spilled from a pale cloudless sky. A maple stood like a shout of scarlet, and a drift of yellow leaves scudded across sere grass. An elderly slave was raking the yard in a leisurely fashion, a young-looking guard of Indian race lounged with his rifle slung on one shoulder, a pair of wolfhounds dozed with dignity under a hedge. It was a peaceful scene—hard to believe that men schemed murder beyond these walls.

But man was man, in any history. This culture might not have the ruthless will and sophisticated cruelty of Western civilization; in some ways it looked strangely innocent. Still, that wasn't for lack of trying; and in this world, a genuine science might never emerge, man might endlessly repeat the weary cycle of war, empire, collapse, and war. In Everard's future, the race had finally broken out of it.

For what? He could not honestly say that this new continuum was worse or better than his own. It was different, that was all; and didn't these people have as much right to their existence as—as his own, who were damned to nullity if he failed to act?

He shook his head and felt fists knot at his side. It was too big. No man should have to decide something like this.

In the showdown, he knew, it would be no abstract sense of duty which compelled him, but the little things and the little folk he remembered.

They rounded the house and Deirdre pointed to the sea. "*Awarlann*," she said. Her loose hair was flame in the wind.

"Now does that mean 'ocean' or 'Atlantic' or 'water'?" asked van Sarawak, laughing. "Let's go see." He led her toward the beach.

Everard trailed. A kind of steam launch, long and fast, was skipping over the waves, a mile or so offshore. Gulls flew up in a shrieking snowstorm of wings. He thought that if he'd been in charge, there would have been a Navy ship on picket out there.

Did he even have to decide anything? There were other Patrolmen in the pre-Roman past. They'd return to their respective eras and—

Everard stiffened. A chill ran down his back and into his belly.

They'd return, and see what had happened, and try to correct the trouble. If any of them succeeded, this world would blink out of space-time, and he would go with it.

Deirdre paused. Everard, standing in a cold sweat, hardly noticed what she was staring at, till she cried out and pointed. Then he joined her and squinted across the sea.

The launch was coming in close, its high stack fuming smoke and sparks, the gilt snake figurehead agleam. He could see the dwarfed forms of men aboard, and something white, with wings. It rose from the poopdeck and trailed at the end of a rope, mounting. A glider! Celtic aeronautics had gotten that far, at least—

"Pretty thing," said van Sarawak. "I suppose they have balloons too."

The glider cast its tow and swooped inward. One of the guards on the beach shouted. The rest came running from behind the house, sunlight flashed off their guns. The launch sped for the shore and the glider landed, plowing a furrow in the beach.

An officer yelled, waving the Patrolmen back. Everard had a glimpse of Deirdre's face, white and uncomprehending.

Then a turret on the glider swiveled—a detached part of his mind assumed it was manually operated—and a cannon spoke.

Everard hit the dirt. Van Sarawak followed, dragging the girl with him. Grapeshot plowed hideously through the Afallonian soldiers.

There came a spiteful crack of guns. Men were emerging from the aircraft, dark-faced men in turbans and sarongs. *Hinduraj!* thought Everard. They traded shots with the surviving guards, who rallied about their captain.

That man roared and led a charge. Everard looked up to see him almost at the glider and its crew. Van Sarawak leaped up and ran to join the fight. Everard rolled over, caught his leg, and pulled him down.

"Let me *go!*" The Venusian writhed. There was a sobbing in his throat. The racket of battle seemed to fill the sky.

"No, you bloody fool! It's us they're after, and that wild Irishman did the worst thing he could have—" Everard slapped his friend's face and looked up.

The launch, shallow-draught and screw-propelled, had run up to the beach and was retching armed men. The Afallonians realized too late that they had discharged their weapons and were being attacked from the rear.

"Come on!" Everard yanked Deirdre and van Sarawak to their feet. "We've got to get out of here—get to the neighbors—"

A detachment of the boat crew saw him and veered. He felt rather than heard the flat smack of a bullet into turf. Slaves were screaming around the house. The two wolfhounds charged and were gunned down.

Everard whirled to flee. Crouched, zigzag, that was the way, over the wall and out onto the road! He might have made it, but Deirdre stumbled and fell. Van Sarawak halted and stood over her with a snarl. Everard plunged to a stop, and by that time it was too late. They were covered.

The leader of the dark men snapped something at the girl. She sat up, giving him a defiant answer. He laughed shortly and jerked his thumb at the launch.

"What do they want?" asked Everard in Greek.

"You." She looked at him with horror. "You two—" The officer spoke. "And me to translate— No!"

She twisted in the arms that held her and clawed at a man's face. Everard's fist traveled in a short arc that ended in a lovely squashing of nose. It was too good to last: a clubbed rifle descended on his head, and he was only dimly aware of being carried off to the launch.

The crew left the glider behind, shoved their boat into deeper water, and revved it up. They left all the guardsmen slain, but took their own casualties along.

Everard sat on a bench on the plunging deck and stared with slowly clearing eyes as the shoreline dwindled. Deirdre wept on van Sarawak's shoulder, and the Venusian tried to console her. A chill noisy wind blew across indifferent waves, spindrift stung their faces.

It was when the two white men emerged from a cabin that Everard's mind was jarred back into motion. Not Asians after all—these were Europeans. And the rest of the crew had Caucasian features . . . grease paint!

He regarded his new owners warily. One was a portly, middle-aged man of average height, in a red silk blouse and baggy white trousers and a sort of astrakhan hat; he was clean-shaven and his dark hair was twisted into a queue. The other was somewhat younger, a shaggy blond giant in a tunic sewn with copper links, legginged breeches, a leather cloak, and a horned helmet. Both wore revolvers at their belts and were treated deferentially.

"What the devil—" Everard looked around. They were already out of sight of land and bending north. The engine made the hull quiver, spray sheeted when the bows bit into a wave.

The older man spoke first in Afallonian. Everard shrugged. Then the bearded Nordic tried, first in a completely unrecognizable dialect but afterward: "*Taelan thu Cimbric?*"

Everard, who knew German, Swedish, and Anglo-Saxon, took a chance, while van Sarawak pricked up his Dutch ears. Deirdre huddled back wide-eyed, too bewildered to move.

"*Ja*," said Everard, "*ein wenig*." When Goldilocks looked uncertain, he amended it: "A little."

"*Ah, aen litt. Gode!*" The big man rubbed hairy hands. "*Ik hait Boierik Wulfilasson ok main gefreond heer erran Boleslav Arkonsky.*"

It was not any language Everard had ever heard of—it couldn't even be the original Cimbrian, after all these centuries—but the Patrolman could follow it tolerably well.

The trouble would be in speaking; he couldn't predict how it had evolved.

"What the hell erran thu maching, anyway?" he blustered. "Ik bin aen man auf Sirius—the stern Sirius, mit planeten ok all. Set uns gebach or willen be der Teufel to pay!"

Boierik Wulfilasson looked pained and suggested that the discussion be continued inside, with the young lady for interpreter. He led the way back into the cabin, which turned out to be small but comfortably furnished. The door remained open, with an armed guard looking in and more on call.

Boleslav Arkonsky said something in Afallonian to Deirdre. She nodded, and he gave her a glass of wine. It seemed to steady her, but she spoke to Everard in a thin voice.

"We've been taken, Manslach. Their spies found out where you were kept. Another group is supposed to capture your machine—they know where that is, too."

"So I imagined," replied Everard. "But who in Baal's name are they?"

Boierik guffawed at the question and expounded lengthily on his own cleverness. The idea was to make the Suffetes of Afallon think that Hinduraj was responsible. Actually, the secret alliance of Littorn and Cimberland had built up quite an effective spy service of its own. They were now bound for the Littornian Embassy's summer retreat on Ynys Llangollen (Nantucket), where the wizards would be induced to explain their spells and the great powers get a surprise.

"And if we don't . . . ?"

Deirdre translated Arkonsky's answer word for word: "I regret the consequences to you. We are civilized men, and will pay well in gold and honor for your free cooperation; but the existence of our countries is at stake."

Everard looked at them. Boierik seemed embarrassed and unhappy, the boastful glee evaporated from him. Boleslav Arkonsky drummed on the table, his lips compressed but a certain mute appeal in his eyes. *Don't make us do this. We have to live with ourselves.*

They were probably husbands and fathers, they must enjoy a mug of beer and a friendly game of dice as well as the next man, maybe Boierik bred horses in Italy and Arkonsky was a rose fancier on the Baltic shores. But none of it would do their captives a bit of good, not when the almighty Nation locked horns with its kin.

Everard paused briefly to admire the sheer artistry of this operation and began wondering what to do. The launch was fast, but would need something like twenty hours to reach Nantucket if he remembered the trip. There was that much time at least.

"We are weary," he said in English. "May we not rest a while?"

"*Ja, deedly*," said Boierik with a clumsy graciousness. "*Ok wir skallen gode gefreonds bin, ni*?"

Sunset smoldered redly to the west. Deirdre and van Sarawak stood at the rail, looking across a gray waste of waters. Three crewmen, their brown paint and Asian garments removed, poised alert and weaponed on the poop; a man steered by compass; Boierik and Everard paced the quarterdeck, talking. All wore heavy cloaks against a stiff, stinging wind.

Everard was getting some proficiency in the Cimbrian language; his tongue still limped, but he could make himself understood. Mostly, though, he let Boierik do the talking.

"So you are from the stars? These matters I do not understand. I am a simple man. Had I my way, I would manage my Tuscan estate in peace and let the world rave as it will. But we of the Folk have our obligations." The Teutons seemed to have replaced the Latins altogether in Italy, as the Saxons had done the Britons in Everard's world.

"I know how you feel," said the Patrolman. "It is a strange thing, that so many should fight when so few want to."

"Oh, but it is necessary." Almost a whine there. "You don't understand. Carthagalann stole Egypt, our rightful possession."

"*Italia irredenta*," murmured Everard.

"Huh?"

"Never mind. So you Cimbri are allied with Littorn, and hope to grab off Europe and Africa while the big powers are fighting in the East."

"Not at all!" replied Boierik indignantly. "We are merely asserting our rightful and historic territorial claims. Why, the king himself said—" And so on and so on.

Everard braced himself against the roll of the deck. "It seems to me that you treat us wizards rather hardily," he declared. "Beware lest we get really angered at you."

"All of us are protected against curses and shapings."

"Well—"

"I wish you would help us freely," said Boierik. "I will be happy to demonstrate to you the justice of our cause, if you have a few hours to spare."

Everard shook his head and stopped by Deirdre. Her face was a blur in the thickening dusk, but he caught a forlorn defiance in her voice: "I hope you are telling him what to do with his plans, Manslach."

"No," said Everard heavily. "We are going to help them."

She stood as if struck.

"What are you saying, Manse?" asked van Sarawak.

Everard told him.

"No!" said the Venusian.

"Yes," said Everard.

"By God, no! I'll—"

Everard grabbed his arm and said coldly: "Be still. I know what I'm doing. We can't take sides in this world, we're against everybody and you'd better realize it. The only thing to do is play along with these fellows for a while. And don't tell that to Deirdre."

Van Sarawak bent his head and stood for a moment, thinking. "All right," he said dully.

The Littornian resort was on the southern shore of Nantucket, near a fishing village but walled off from it. The embassy had built in the style of its homeland, long timber houses with roofs arched like a cat's back, a main hall and its outbuildings enclosing a flagged courtyard. Everard finished a night's sleep and a breakfast made miserable by Deirdre's eyes by standing on deck as they came to the private pier. Another, bigger launch was already there, and the grounds swarmed with hard-looking men. Arkonsky's eyes kindled, and he said in Afallonian: "I see the magic engine has been brought. We can go right to work."

When Boierik interpreted, Everard felt his heart slam.

The guests, as the Cimbrian insisted on calling them, were led into a great room where Arkonsky bent the knee to an idol with four faces, that Svantevit which the Danes had chopped up for firewood in the other history. There was a blaze on the hearth against the autumn chill, and guards posted around the walls. Everard had eyes only for the scooter, where it stood gleaming on the floor.

"I hear it was a hard fight in Catuvellaunan," remarked Boierik to him. "Many were killed, but our folk got away without being followed." He touched a handlebar gingerly. "And this wain can truly appear anywhere it wishes, out of thin air?"

"Yes," said Everard.

Deirdre gave him a look of scorn such as he had never known. She stood haughtily away from him and van Sarawak.

Arkonsky spoke to her, something he wanted translated. She spat at his feet. Boierik sighed and gave the word to Everard:

"We wish the engine demonstrated. You and I will go for a ride on it. I warn you, I will have a revolver at your back; you will tell me in advance everything you mean to do, and if aught untoward happens I will shoot. Your friends will remain here as hostages, also to be shot on the first suspicion. But I'm sure we will all be good friends."

Everard nodded. There was a tautness thrumming in him, and his palms felt cold and wet. "First I must say a spell," he answered.

His eyes flicked. One glance memorized the spatial reading of the position meters and the time reading of the clock on the scooter. Another look showed van Sarawak seated on a bench, under Arkonsky's drawn pistol and the rifles of the guards; Deirdre sat down too, stiffly, as far from him as she could get. Everard made a close estimate of the bench's position relative to the scooter's, lifted his arms, and chanted in Temporal:

"Van, I'm going to try to pull you out of here. Stay exactly where you are now; repeat, exactly. I'll pick you up on the fly. If all goes well, that'll happen about one minute after I blink out of here with our shaggy comrade."

The Venusian sat wooden-faced. There was a thin beading of sweat on his forehead.

"Very good," said Everard in his pidgin Cimbrian. "Mount on the rear saddle, Boierik, and we'll put this magic horse through her paces."

The big man nodded and obeyed. As Everard took the front seat, he felt a gun muzzle held shakily against his back. "Tell Arkonsky we'll be back in half an hour," he added; they had approximately the same time units here as in his world, both descended from the Babylonian. When that had been taken care of, Everard said: "The first thing we will do is appear in midair over the ocean and hover."

"F-f-fine," said Boierik. He didn't sound very convinced.

Everard set the space controls for ten miles east and a thousand feet up and threw the main switch.

They sat like witches astride a broom, looking down on a greenish-gray sweep of waters and the distant blur which was land. The wind was high; it caught at them and Everard gripped tight with his knees. He heard Boierik's oath and smiled wanly.

"Well," he asked, "how do you like this?"

"It . . . it is wonderful." As he grew accustomed to the idea, the Cimbrian gathered enthusiasm. "Why, with machines like this, we can soar above enemy cities and pelt them with fire."

Somehow, that made Everard feel better about what he was going to do.

"Now we will fly ahead," he announced, and sent the scooter gliding through the air. Boierik whooped exuberantly. "And now we will make the instantaneous jump to your homeland."

Everard threw the maneuver switch. The scooter looped the loop and dropped at a three-gee acceleration.

Forewarned, the Patrolman could still barely hang on. He never knew whether the curve or the dive had thrown Boierik; he only had a moment's hideous glimpse of the man plunging down through windy spaces to the sea.

For a little while, then, Everard hung above the waves. His first reaction was a cold shudder . . . suppose Boierik had had time to shoot? His second was a gray guilt. Both he dismissed, and concentrated on the problem of rescuing van Sarawak.

He set the space verniers for one foot in front of the prisoners' bench, the time unit for one minute after he had departed. His right hand he kept by the controls—he'd have to work fast—and his left free.

Hang on to your seats, fellahs. Here we go again.

The machine flashed into existence almost in front of van Sarawak. Everard clutched the Venusian's tunic and hauled him close, inside the spatiotemporal field, even as his right hand spun the time dial back and snapped over the main switch.

A bullet caromed off metal. Everard had a moment's glimpse of Arkonsky shouting. And then it was all gone and they were on a grassy hill sloping down to the beach. It was 2,000 years ago.

He collapsed shivering over the handlebars.

A cry brought him back to awareness. He twisted around, looking at van Sarawak where the Venusian sprawled on the hillside. One arm was still around Deirdre's waist.

The wind lulled, and the sea rolled into a broad white strand, and clouds walked high in heaven.

"I can't say I blame you, Van." Everard paced before the scooter and looked at the ground. "But it does complicate matters greatly."

"What was I supposed to do?" There was a raw note in the other's voice. "Leave her there for those bastards to kill—or to be snuffed out with her entire universe?"

"In case you've forgotten, we're conditioned against revealing the Patrol's existence to unauthorized people," said Everard. "We couldn't tell her the truth even if we wanted to . . . and I, for one, don't want to."

He looked at the girl. She stood breathing heavily, with a dawn in her eyes. The wind caressed her hair and the long thin dress.

She shook her head, as if clearing a mist of nightmare, and ran over to clasp their hands. "Forgive me, Manslach," she whispered. "I should have known you'd not betray us."

She kissed him and van Sarawak. The Venusian responded eagerly, but Everard couldn't bring himself to. He would have remembered Judas.

"Where are we?" she chattered. "It looks almost like Llangollen, but no men— Have you taken us to the Happy Isles?" She spun on one foot and danced among summer flowers. "Can we rest here a while before returning home?"

Everard drew a long breath. "I've bad news for you, Deirdre," he said.

She grew silent, and he saw her gather herself.

"We can't go back."

She waited mutely.

"The—the spells I had to use, to save our lives . . . I had no choice, but those spells debar us from returning home."

"There is no hope?" He could barely hear her.

Everard's eyes stung. "No," he said.

She turned and walked away. Van Sarawak moved to follow her, but thought better of it and sat down beside Everard. "What'd you tell her?" he asked.

Everard repeated his words. "It seemed the best compromise," he finished. "I can't send her back to—what's waiting for this world."

"No." Van Sarawak sat quiet for a while, staring across the sea. Then: "What year is this? About the time of Christ? Then we're still upstairs of the turning point."

"Yeah. And we still have to find out what it was."

"Let's go back to the farther past. Lots of Patrol offices. We can recruit help there."

"Maybe." Everard lay back in the grass and regarded the sky. Reaction overwhelmed him. "I think I can locate the key event right here, though, with Deirdre's help. Wake me up when she comes back."

She returned dry-eyed, a desolate calm over her. When Everard asked if she would assist in his own mission, she nodded. "Of course. My life is yours who saved it."

After getting you into that mess in the first place. Everard said carefully: "All I want from you is some information. Do you know about . . . about putting people to sleep, a sleep in which they may believe anything they're told?"

"Y-yes," she said doubtfully. "I've seen medical Druids do that."

"It won't harm you. I only wish to make you sleep so you can remember everything you know, things you believe forgotten. It won't take long."

Her trustfulness was hard to endure. Using Patrol techniques, Everard put her in a hypnotic state of total recall and dredged out all she had ever read or heard about the Second Punic War. That added up to enough for his purposes.

Roman interference with Carthaginian enterprise south of the Ebro, in direct violation of treaty, had been the last roweling. In 219 B.C. Hannibal Barca, governor of Carthaginian Spain, laid siege to Saguntum. After eight months he took it, and thus provoked his long-planned war with Rome. At the beginning of May, 218, he crossed the Pyrenees with 90,000 infantry, 12,000 cavalry, and 37 elephants, marched through Gaul, and went over the Alps. His losses en route were gruesome: only 20,000 foot and 6,000 horse reached Italy late in the year. Nevertheless, near the Ticinus River he met and broke a superior Roman force. In the course of the following year, he fought several bloodily victorious battles and advanced into Apulia and Campania.

The Apulians, Lucaninas, Bruttians, and Samnites went over to his side. Quintus Fabius Maximus fought a grim guerrilla war, which laid Italy waste and decided nothing. But meanwhile Hasdrubal Barca was organizing Spain, and in 211 he arrived with reinforcements. In 210 Hannibal took and burned Rome, and in 207 the last cities of the confederacy surrendered to him.

"That's it," said Everard. He stroked the coppery hair of the girl lying beside him. "Go to sleep now. Sleep well and wake up glad of heart."

"What'd she tell you?" asked van Sarawak.

"A lot of detail," said Everard—the whole story had required more than an hour. "The important thing is this: her knowledge of history is good, but never mentions the Scipios."

"The who's?"

"Publius Cornelius Scipio commanded the Roman army at Ticinus, and was beaten there. But later he had the intelligence to turn westward and gnaw away the Carthaginian base in Spain. It ended with Hannibal being effectively cut off in Italy, and the Iberian help which could be sent was annihilated. Scipio's son of the same name also held a high command, and was the man who finally whipped Hannibal at Zama; that's Scipio Africanus the Elder.

"Father and son were by far the best leaders Rome had—but Deirdre never heard of them."

"So—" Van Sarawak stared eastward across the sea, where Gauls and Cimbri and Parthians were ramping through the shattered Classical world. "What happened to them in this time-line?"

"My own total recall tells me that both the Scipios were at Ticinus, and very nearly killed; the son saved his father's life during the retreat, which I imagine was more like a stampede. One gets you ten that in *this* history the Scipios died there."

"Somebody must have knocked them off," said van Sarawak on a rising note. "Some time traveler . . . it could only have been that."

"Well, it seems probable, anyhow. We'll see." Everard looked away from Deirdre's slumbrous face. "We'll see."

At the Pleistocene resort—half an hour after having left it—the Patrolmen put the girl in charge of a sympathetic Greek-speaking matron and summoned their colleagues. Then the message capsules began jumping through space-time.

All offices prior to 218 B.C.—the closest was Alexandria, 250–230—were "still" there, two hundred or so agents altogether. Written contact with the future was confirmed to be impossible, and a few short jaunts upstairs clinched the proof. A worried conference met at the Academy, back in the Oligocene Period. Unattached agents ranked those with steady assignments but not each other; on the basis of his own experience, Everard found himself the chairman of a committee of top-bracket officers.

It was a frustrating job. These men and women had leaped centuries and wielded the weapons of gods; but they were still human, with all the ingrained orneriness of their race.

Everyone agreed that the damage would have to be repaired. But there was fear for those agents who had gone ahead into time before being warned; if they weren't back when history was re-altered, they would never be seen again. Everard deputized parties to attempt rescue, but doubted there'd be much success; he warned them sternly to return in a day or face the consequences.

A man from the Scientific Renaissance had another point to make. Granted, it was the survivors' plain duty to restore the original time track. But they had a duty to knowledge as well. Here was a unique chance to study a whole new phase of humankind; there should be several years' anthropological work done before—Everard slapped him down with difficulty. There weren't so many Patrolmen left that they could take the risk.

Study groups had to determine the exact moment and circumstances of the change. The wrangling over methods went on interminably. Everard glared out the window, into the prehuman night, and wondered if the sabertooths weren't doing a better job after all than their simian successors.

When he had finally gotten his bands dispatched, he broke out a bottle and got drunk with van Sarawak.

Reconvening the next day, the steering committee heard

from its deputies, who had run up a total of years in the future. A dozen Patrolmen had been rescued from more or less ignominious situations; another score would simply have to be written off. The spy group's report was more interesting. It seemed that there had been two Helvetian mercenaries who joined Hannibal in the Alps and won his confidence. After the war, they had risen to high positions in Carthage; under the names of Phrontes and Himilco, they had practically run the government, engineered Hannibal's murder, and set new records for luxurious living. One of the Patrolmen had seen their homes and the men themelves. "A lot of improvements that hadn't been thought of in Classical times. The fellows looked to me like Neldorians, 205th millennium."

Everard nodded. That was an age of bandits who had "already" given the Patrol a lot of work. "I think we've settled the matter," he said. "It makes no difference whether they were with Hannibal before Ticinus or not. We'd have hell's own time arresting them in the Alps without tipping our hand and changing the future ourselves. What counts is that they seem to have rubbed out the Scipios, and that's the point we'll have to strike at."

A Nineteenth-Century Britisher, competent but with elements of Colonel Blimp, unrolled a map and discoursed on his aerial observations of the battle. He'd used an infra-red telescope to look through low clouds. "And here the Romans stood—"

"I know," said Everard. "A thin red line. The moment when they took flight is the crucial one, but the confusion then also gives us our chance. Okay, we'll want to surround the battlefield unobtrusively, but I don't think we can get away with more than two agents actually on the scene. The Alexandria office can supply Van and me with costumes."

"I say," exclaimed the Englishman. "I thought I'd have the privilege."

"No. Sorry." Everard smiled with one corner of his mouth. "It's no privilege, anyway. Risk your neck, and all to wipe out a world of people like yourself."

"But dash it all—"

Everard rose. "I've got to go," he said flatly. "I don't know why, but I've got to."

Van Sarawak nodded.

* * *

They left their scooter in a clump of trees and started across the field.

Around the horizon and up in the sky waited a hundred armed Patrolmen, but that was small consolation here among spears and arrows. Lowering clouds hurried before a cold whistling wind, there was a spatter of rain, sunny Italy was enjoying its late fall.

The cuirass was heavy on Everard's shoulders as he trotted across blood-slippery mud. He had helmet, greaves, a Roman shield on his left arm and a sword at his waist; but his right hand gripped a stunner. Van Sarawak loped behind, similarly equipped, eyes shifting under the wind-ruffled officer's plume.

Trumpets howled and drums stuttered. It was all but lost among the yells of men and tramp of feet, screaming horses and whining arrows. The legion of Carthage was pressing in, hammering edged metal against the buckling Roman lines. Here and there the fight was already breaking up into small knots, where men cursed and cut at strangers.

The combat had passed over this area and swayed beyond. Death lay around him. Everard hurried behind the Roman force, toward the distant gleam of the eagles. Across helmets and corpses, he made out a banner that fluttered triumphant, vivid red and purple against the unrestful sky. And there, looming gray and monstrous, lifting their trunks and bellowing, came a squad of elephants.

He had seen war before. It was always the same—not a neat affair of lines across maps, nor a hallooing gallantry, but men who gasped and sweated and bled in bewilderment.

A slight, dark-faced youth squirmed nearby, trying feebly to pull out the javelin which had pierced his stomach. He was a cavalryman from Carthage, but the burly Italian peasant who sat next to him, staring without belief at the stump of an arm, paid no attention.

A flight of crows hovered overhead, riding the wind and waiting.

"This way," muttered Everard. "Hurry up, for God's sake! That line's going to break any minute."

The breath was raw in his throat as he panted toward the standards of the Republic. It came to him that he'd always rather wished Hannibal had won. There was something repellent about the cold, unimaginative greed of Rome. And here he was, trying to save the city. Well-a-day, life was often an odd business.

It was some consolation that Scipio Africanus was one of the few decent men left after the war.

Screaming and clangor lifted, and the Italians reeled back. Everard saw something like a wave smashed against a rock. But it was the rock which advanced, crying out and stabbing, stabbing.

He began to run. A legionary went past, howling his panic. A grizzled Roman veteran spat on the ground, braced his feet, and stood where he was till they cut him down. Hannibal's elephants squealed and lifted curving tusks. The ranks of Carthage held firm, advancing to the inhuman pulse of their drums. Cavalry skirmished on the wings in a toothpick flash of lances.

Up ahead, now! Everard saw men on horseback, Roman officers. They held the eagles aloft and shouted, but nobody could hear them above the din.

A small group of legionaries came past and halted. Their leader hailed the Patrolmen: "Over here! We'll give them a fight, by the belly of Venus!"

Everard shook his head and tried to go past. The Roman snarled and sprang at him. "Come here, you cowardly—" A stun beam cut off his words and he crashed into the muck. His men shuddered, someone screamed, and the party broke into flight.

The Carthaginians were very near, shield to shield and swords running red. Everard could see a scar livid on the cheek of one man, and the great hook nose of another. A hurled spear clanged off his helmet, he lowered his head and ran.

A combat loomed before him. He tried to go around, and tripped on a gashed corpse. A Roman stumbled over him in turn. Van Sarawak cursed and dragged him away. A sword furrowed the Venusian's arm.

Beyond, Scipio's men were surrounded and battling without hope. Everard halted, sucking air into starved lungs, and looked into the thin rain. Armor gleamed wetly, Roman horsemen galloping in with mud up to their mounts' noses—that must be the son, Scipio Africanus to be, hastening to his father. The hoofbeats were like thunder in the earth.

"Over there!"

Van Sarawak cried it out and pointed. Everard crouched where he was, rain dripping off his helmet and down his face. A small troop of Carthaginians was riding toward the battle around the eagles, and at their head were two men with the height and craggy features of Neldor. They were clad in the usual G.I. armor, but each of them held a slim-barreled gun.

"This way!" Everard spun on his heel and dashed toward them. The leather in his cuirass creaked as he ran.

They were close to the newcomers before they were seen. A Carthaginian face swung to them and called the warning. Everard saw how he grinned in his beard. One of the Neldorians scowled and aimed his blast-rifle.

Everard went on his stomach, and the vicious blue-white beam sizzled where he had been. He snapped a shot and one of the African horses went over in a roar of metal. Van Sarawak stood his ground and fired steadily. Two, three, four—and there went a Neldorian, down in the mud!

Men hewed at each other around the Scipios. The Neldorians' escort yelled with terror. They must have had the blasters demonstrated, but these invisible blows were something else. They bolted. The second of the bandits got his horse under control and turned to follow.

"Take care of the one you potted," gasped Everard. "Haul him off the battlefield—we'll want to question—" He himself scrambled to his feet and made for a riderless horse. He was in the saddle and after the remaining Neldorian before he was fully aware of it.

They fled through chaos. Everard urged speed from his mount, but was content to pursue. Once they'd got out of sight, a scooter could swoop down and make short work of his quarry.

The same thought must have occurred to the time rover. He reined in and took aim. Everard saw the blinding flash and felt his cheek sting with a near miss. He set his pistol to wide beam and rode in shooting.

Another fire-bolt took his horse full in the breast. The animal toppled and Everard went out of the saddle. Trained reflexes softened the fall, he bounced dizzily to his feet and staggered toward his enemy. His stunner was gone, no time to look for it. Never mind, it could be salvaged later, if he lived. The widened beam had found its mark; it wasn't strong enough to knock a man out, but the Neldorian had dropped his rifle and the horse stood swaying with closed eyes.

Rain beat in Everard's face. He slogged up to the mount. The Neldorian jumped to earth and drew a sword. Everard's own blade rasped forth.

"As you will," he said in Latin. "One of us will not leave this field."

The moon rose over mountains and turned the snow to a sudden wan glitter. Far in the north, a glacier threw back the light in broken shards, and a wolf howled. The Cro-Magnons chanted in their cave, it drifted faintly through to the veranda.

Deirdre stood in darkness, looking out. Moonlight dappled her face and caught a gleam of tears. She started as Everard and van Sarawak came up behind her.

"Are you back so soon?" she asked. "You only came here and left me this morning."

"It didn't take long," said van Sarawak. He had gotten a hypno in Attic Greek.

"I hope . . ." She tried to smile. "I hope you have finished your task and can rest from your labors."

"Yes," said Everard. "Yes, we finished it."

They stood side by side for a while, looking out on a world of winter.

"Is it true what you said, that I can never go home?" asked Deirdre.

"I'm afraid so. The spells—" Everard shrugged and swapped a glance with van Sarawak.

They had official permission to tell the girl as much as they wished and take her wherever they thought she could live best. Van Sarawak maintained that that would be Venus in his century, and Everard was too tired to argue.

Deirdre drew a long breath. "So be it," she said. "I'll not waste a life weeping for it . . . but the Baal grant that they have it well, my people at home."

"I'm sure they will," said Everard.

Suddenly he could do no more. He only wanted to sleep. Let van Sarawak say what had to be said, and reap whatever rewards there might be.

He nodded at his companion. "I'm turning in," he declared. "Carry on, Van."

The Venusian took the girl's arm. Everard went slowly back to his room.

ANNE McCAFFREY (1926–   ) is a phenomenally successful writer whose recent novel, *Moreta: DragonLady of Pern,* has soared to eighth place on *The New York Times Book Review* bestseller list as these words are typed. Her "Dragonrider" series, which the following story is part of, has millions of readers, somewhat obscuring her other non-series novels like *Dinosaur Planet* (1977), *Restoree* (1967), and *Decision at Doona* (1969). A talented singer, her voice was well known to science fiction convention goers before she moved to Ireland, where she farms and raises thoroughbred horses for stud. She is one of the very few writers to have won the Nebula, the Hugo, and the Gandalf Award.

DRAGONRIDER

Anne McCaffrey

The Finger Points
At an Eye blood red.
Alert the Weyrs
To sear the Thread.

"You still doubt, R'gul?" F'lar asked, appearing slightly amused by the older bronze rider's perversity.

R'gul, his handsome features stubbornly set, made no reply to the Weyrleader's taunt. He ground his teeth together as if he could grind away F'lar's authority over him.

"There have been no Threads in Pern's skies for over four hundred Turns. There are no more!"

"There is always that possibility," F'lar conceded amiably. There was not, however, the slightest trace of tolerance in his amber eyes. Nor the slightest hint of compromise in his manner.

He was more like F'lon, his sire, R'gul decided, than a son had any right to be. Always so sure of himself, always slightly contemptuous of what others did and thought. Arrogant, that's what F'lar was. Impertinent, too, and underhanded in the matter of that young Weyrwoman. Why, R'gul had trained her up to be one of the finest Weyrwomen in many Turns. Before he'd finished her instruction, she knew all the teaching ballads and sagas letter perfect. And then the silly child had turned to F'lar. Didn't have sense enough to appreciate the merits of an older, more experienced man. Undoubtedly she felt a first obligation to F'lar, he having discovered her at Ruath Hold during Search.

"You do, however," F'lar was saying, "admit that when the sun hits the Finger Rock at the moment of dawn, winter solstice has been reached?"

"Any fool knows that's what Finger Rock is for," R'gul grunted.

"Then why don't you, you old fool, admit that the Eye Rock was placed on Star Stone to bracket the Red Star when it's about to make a Pass?" burst out K'net, the youngest of the dragonriders.

R'gul flushed, half-starting out of his chair, ready to take the young sprout to task for such insolence.

"K'net," F'lar's voice cracked authoritatively, "do you really like flying the Igen Patrol so much you want another few weeks at it?"

K'net hurriedly seated himself, flushing at the reprimand and the threat.

"There is, you know, R'gul, incontrovertible evidence to support my conclusions," F'lar went on with deceptive mildness. " 'The Finger points/At an Eye blood red . . .' "

"Don't quote me verses I taught you as a weyrling," R'gul exclaimed, heatedly.

"Then have faith in what you taught," F'lar snapped back, his amber eyes flashing dangerously.

R'gul, stunned by the unexpected forcefulness, sank back into his chair.

"You cannot deny, R'gul," F'lar continued quietly, "that no less than half an hour ago, the sun balanced on the Finger's tip at dawn and the Red Star was squarely framed by the Eye Rock."

The other dragonriders, bronze as well as brown, murmured and nodded their agreement to that phenomenon. There was also an undercurrent of resentment for R'gul's continual contest of F'lar's policies as the new Weyrleader. Even old S'lel, once R'gul's avowed supporter, was following the majority.

"There have been no Threads in four hundred years. There are no Threads," R'gul muttered.

"Then, my fellow dragonman," F'lar said cheerfully, "all you have taught is falsehood. The dragons are, as the Lords of the Holds wish to believe, parasites on the economy of Pern, anachronisms. And so are we.

"Therefore, far be it from me to hold you here against the dictates of your conscience. You have my permission to leave the Weyr and take up residence where you will."

R'gul was too stunned by F'lar's ultimatum to take offense at the ridicule. Leave the Weyr? Was the man mad? Where would he go? The Weyr had been his life. He had been bred up to it for generations. All his male ancestors had been dragonriders. Not all bronze, true, but a decent percentage. His own dam's sire had been a Weyrleader just as he, R'gul, had been until F'lar's Mnementh had flown the new queen and that young upstart had taken over as traditional Weyrleader.

But dragonmen never left the Weyr. Well, they did if they were negligent enough to lose their dragons, like that Lytol fellow who was now Warden at Ruath Hold. And how could he leave the Weyr *with* a dragon?

What did F'lar want of him? Was it not enough that the young one was Weyrleader now in R'gul's stead? Wasn't F'lar's pride sufficiently swollen by having bluffed the lords of Pern into disbanding their army when they were all set to coerce the Weyr and dragonmen? Must F'lar dominate *every* dragonman, body and will, too? He stared a long moment, incredulous.

"I do not believe we are parasites," F'lar said, breaking the silence with his soft, persuasive voice. "Nor anachronistic. There have been long Intervals before. The Red Star does not always pass close enough to drop Threads on Pern. Which is why our ingenious ancestors thought to position the Eye Rock and the Finger Rock as they did . . . to confirm *when* a Pass will be made. And another thing," his face turned grave, "there have been other times when dragonkind has all but died out . . . and Pern with it because of skeptics like you." F'lar smiled and relaxed indolently in his chair. "I prefer not to be recorded as a skeptic. How shall we record you, R'gul?"

The Council Chamber was tense. R'gul was aware of someone breathing harshly and realized it was himself. He looked at the adamant face of the young Weyrleader and knew that the threat was not empty. He would either concede to F'lar's authority, completely, though concession rankled deeply, or leave the Weyr.

And where could he go, unless to one of the other Weyrs, deserted for hundreds of Turns? And, R'gul's thoughts were savage, wasn't that indication enough of the cessation of the Threads? Five empty Weyrs? No, by the Egg of Faranth, he would practice some of F'lar's own brand of deceit and bide his time. When all Pern turned on the arrogant fool, he, R'gul, would be there to salvage something from the ruins.

"A dragonman stays in his Weyr," R'gul said with what dignity he could muster from the remains of his pride.

"And accepts the policies of the current Weyrleader?" The tone of F'lar's voice made it less of a question and more of an order.

Relieved he would not have to perjure himself, R'gul gave a curt nod of his head. F'lar continued to stare at him until R'gul wondered if the man could read his thoughts as his dragon might. He managed to return the gaze calmly. His turn would come. He'd wait.

Apparently accepting the capitulation, F'lar stood up and crisply delegated patrol assignments for the day.

"T'bor, you're weather-watch. Keep an eye on those tithe trains as you do. What's the morning's report?"

"Weather is fair at dawning . . . all across Telgar and Keroon . . . if all too cold," T'bor said with a wry grin. "Tithing trains have good hard roads, though, so they ought to be here soon." His eyes twinkled with anticipation of the feasting that would follow the supplies' arrival; a mood shared by all, to judge by the expressions around the table.

F'lar nodded. "S'lan and D'nol, you are to continue an adroit Search for likely boys. They should be striplings, if possible, but do not pass over anyone suspected of talent. It's all well and good to present, for Impression, boys reared up in the Weyr traditions." F'lar gave a one-sided smile.

"But there are not enough in the lower caverns. We, too, have been behind in begetting. Anyway, dragons reach full growth faster than their riders. We must have more young *men* to Impress when Ramoth hatches. Take the southern holds, Ista, Nerat, Fort, and south Boll, where maturity comes earlier. You can use the guise of inspecting holds for greenery to talk to the boys. And, take along firestone. Run a few flaming passes on those heights that haven't been scoured in oh . . . dragon's years. A flaming beast impresses the young and rouses envy."

F'lar deliberately looked at R'gul to see the ex-Weyrleader's reaction to the order. R'gul had been dead set against going outside the Weyr for more candidates. In the first place, R'gul had argued that there were eighteen youngsters in the Lower Caverns, some quite young, to be sure, but R'gul would not admit that Ramoth would lay more than the dozen Nemorth had always dropped. In the second place, R'gul persisted in wanting to avoid any action that might antagonize the Lords.

R'gul made no overt protest and F'lar went on.

"K'net, back to the mines. I want the dispositions of each firestone dump checked and quantities available. R'gul, continue drilling recognition points with the weyrlings. They must be positive about their references. They may be sent out quickly and with no time to ask questions, if they're used as messengers and suppliers.

"F'nor, T'sum," and F'lar turned to his own brown riders, "you're clean-up squad today." He allowed himself a grin at their dismay. "Try Ista Weyr. Clear the Hatching Cavern and enough weyrs for a double wing. And, F'nor, don't leave a single record behind. They're worth preserving.

"That will be all, dragonmen. Good flying." And with that, F'lar rose and strode from the Council Room up to the queen's weyr.

Ramoth still slept, her hide gleaming with health, its color deepening to a shade of gold closer to bronze, indicating her pregnancy. As he passed her, the tip of her long tail twitched slightly.

All the dragons were restless these days, F'lar reflected. Yet when he asked Mnementh, the bronze dragon could give no reason. He woke, he went back to sleep. That was all. F'lar couldn't ask a leading question for that would defeat his purpose. He had to remain discontented with the vague fact that the restlessness was some kind of instinctive reaction.

Lessa was not in the sleeping room nor was she still bathing. F'lar snorted. That girl was going to scrub her hide off with this constant bathing. She'd had to live grimy to protect herself in Ruath Hold but bathing twice a day? He was beginning to wonder if this might be a subtle, Lessa-variety insult to him personally. F'lar sighed. That girl. Would she never turn to him of her own accord? Would he ever touch that elusive inner core of Lessa? She had more warmth for his half brother, F'nor, and K'net, the youngest of the bronze riders, than she had for F'lar who shared her bed.

He pulled the curtain back into place, irritated. Where had she got to today when, for the first time in weeks, he had been able to get all the wings out of the Weyr just so he could teach her to fly *between?*

Ramoth would soon be too egg-heavy for such activity. He had promised the Weyrwoman and he meant to keep that promise. She had taken to wearing the wher-hide riding gear as a flagrant reminder of his unfulfilled pledge. From certain remarks she had dropped, he knew she would not wait much longer for his aid. That she should try it on her own didn't suit him at all.

He crossed the queen's weyr again and peered down the passage that led to the Records Room. She was often to be found there, poring over the musty skins. And that was one more matter that needed urgent consideration. Those records were deteriorating past legibility. Curiously enough, earlier ones were still in good condition and readable. Another technique forgotten.

That girl! He brushed his thick forelock of hair back from his brow in a gesture habitual to him when he was annoyed or worried. The passage was dark which meant she could not be below in the Records Room.

Mnementh, he called silently to his bronze dragon, sunning on the ledge outside the queen's weyr. *What is that girl doing?*

Lessa, the dragon replied, stressing the Weyrwoman's name with pointed courtesy, *is talking to Manora. She's dressed for riding,* he added after a slight pause.

F'lar thanked the bronze sarcastically and strode down the passage to the entrance. As he turned the last bend, he all but ran Lessa down.

You hadn't asked me where *she was,* Mnementh answered plaintively to F'lar's blistering reprimand.

* * *

Lessa rocked back on her heels from the force of their encounter. She glared up at him, her lips thin with displeasure, her eyes flashing.

"Why didn't I have the opportunity of seeing the Red Star through the Eye Rock?" she demanded in a hard, angry voice.

F'lar pulled at his hair. Lessa at her most difficult would complete the list of this morning's trials.

"Too many to accommodate as it was on the Peak," he muttered, determined not to let her irritate him today. "And you already believe."

"I'd've liked to see it," she snapped and pushed past him towards the weyr. "If only in my capacity of Weyrwoman and Recorder."

He caught her arm and felt her body tense. He set his teeth, wishing as he had a hundred times since Ramoth rose in her first mating flight that Lessa had not been virgin, too. He had not thought to control his dragon-incited emotions and Lessa's first sexual experience had been violent. It had surprised him to be first, considering her adolescent years had been spent drudging for lascivious warders and soldier-types. Evidently no one had bothered to penetrate the curtain of rags and the coat of filth she had carefully maintained as a disguise. He had been a considerate and gentle bedmate ever since but, unless Ramoth and Mnementh were involved, he might as well call it rape.

Yet he knew someday, somehow, he would coax her into responding wholeheartedly to his love-making. He had a certain pride in his skill and he was in a position to persevere.

Now he took a deep breath and released her arm slowly.

"How fortunate you're wearing riding gear. As soon as the wings have cleared out and Ramoth wakes, I shall teach you to fly *between*."

The gleam of excitement in her eyes was evident even in the dimly lit passageway. He heard her inhale sharply.

"Can't put it off too much longer or Ramoth'll be in no shape to fly at all," he continued amiably.

"You do mean it?" Her voice was low and breathless, its usual acid edge missing. "You will teach us today?" He wished he could see her face clearly.

Once or twice, he had caught an unguarded expression on

her face, loving and tender. He would give much to have that look turned on him. However, he admitted wryly to himself, he ought to be glad that melting regard was directed only at Ramoth and not at another human.

"Yes, my dear Weyrwoman, I mean it. I will teach you to fly *between* today. If only to keep you from trying it yourself."

Her low chuckle informed him his taunt was well-aimed.

"Right now, however," he said, indicating for her to lead the way back to the weyr, "I could do with some food. We were up before the kitchen."

They had entered the well-lighted weyr so he did not miss the trenchant look she shot him over her shoulder. She would not so easily forgive being left out of the group at the Star Stone this morning; certainly not with the bribe of flying *between*.

How different this inner room was now Lessa was Weyrwoman, F'lar mused as Lessa called down the service shaft for food. During Jora's incompetent tenure as Weyrwoman, the sleeping quarters had been crowded with junk, unwashed apparel, uncleared dishes. The state of the Weyr and the reduced number of dragons were as much Jora's fault as R'gul's for she had indirectly encouraged sloth, negligence and gluttony.

Had he, F'lar, been just a few years older when F'lon, his father, had died . . . Jora had been disgusting but when dragons rose in mating flight, the condition of your partner counted for nothing.

Lessa took a tray of bread and cheese, and mugs of the stimulating *klah* from the platform. She served him deftly.

"You've not eaten either?" he asked.

She shook her head vigorously, the braid into which she had plaited her thick, fine dark hair bobbing across her shoulders. The hairdressing was too severe for her narrow face but it did not, if that were her intention, disguise her femininity nor the curious beauty of her delicate features. Again F'lar wondered that such a slight body contained so much shrewd intelligence and resourceful . . . cunning, yes, that was the word, cunning. F'lar did not make the mistake, as others had, of underestimating her abilities.

"Manora called me to witness the birth of Kylara's child."

F'lar maintained an expression of polite interest. He knew perfectly well that Lessa suspected the child was his and it could have been, he admitted privately, but he doubted it. Kylara had been one of the ten candidates from the same Search three years ago which had discovered Lessa. Like others who survived Impression, Kylara had found certain aspects of Weyr life exactly suited to her temperament. She had gone from one rider's weyr to another's. She had even seduced F'lar, not at all against his will, to be sure. Now that he was Weyrleader, he found it wiser to ignore her efforts to continue the relationship. T'bor had taken her in hand and had his hands full until he retired her to the Lower Caverns, well-advanced in pregnancy.

Aside from having the amorous tendencies of a green dragon, Kylara was quick and ambitious. She would make a strong Weyrwoman so F'lar had charged Manora and Lessa with the job of planting the notion in Kylara's mind. In the capacity of Weyrwoman . . . of another Weyr . . . her intense drives would be used to Pern's advantage. She had not learned the severe lessons of restraint and patience that Lessa had and she didn't have Lessa's devious mind. Fortunately she was in considerable awe of Lessa and, F'lar suspected, that Lessa was subtly influencing this attitude. In Kylara's case, F'lar preferred not to object to Lessa's meddling.

"A fine son," Lessa was saying.

F'lar sipped his *klah*. She was not going to get him to admit any responsibility.

After a long pause, Lessa added, "She has named him T'kil."

F'lar suppressed a grin at Lessa's failure to get a rise from him.

"Discreet of her."

"Oh?"

"Yes," F'lar replied blandly. "T'lar might be confusing if she took the second half of her name as is customary. 'T'kil,' however, still indicates sire as well as dam."

"While I was waiting for Council to end," Lessa said, after clearing her throat, "Manora and I checked the supply caverns. The tithing trains, which the Holds have been so gracious as to send us," her voice was sharp, "are due within the week. There shortly will be bread fit to eat," she added, wrinkling her nose at the crumbling gray pastry she was attempting to spread with cheese.

"A nice change," F'lar agreed.

She paused.

"The Red Star performed its scheduled antic?"

He nodded.

"And R'gul's doubts have been wiped away in the enlightening red glow?"

"Not at all," F'lar grinned back at her, ignoring her sarcasm. "Not at all, but he will not be so vocal in his criticism."

She swallowed quickly so she could speak. "You'd do well to cut out his criticism," she said ruthlessly, gesturing with her knife as if plunging it into a man's heart. "He is never going to accept your authority with good grace."

"We need every bronze rider . . . there are only seven, you know," he reminded her pointedly. "R'gul's a good wingleader. He'll settle down when the Threads fall. He needs proof to lay his doubts aside."

"And the Red Star in the Eye Rock is not proof?" Lessa's expressive eyes were wide.

F'lar was privately of Lessa's opinion, that it might be wiser to remove R'gul's stubborn contentiousness. But he could not sacrifice a wingleader, needing every dragon and rider as badly as he did.

"I don't trust him," she added, darkly. She sipped at her hot drink, her gray eyes dark over the rim of her mug. As if, F'lar mused, she didn't trust him either.

And she didn't, past a certain point. She had made that plain and, in honesty, he couldn't blame her. She did recognize that every action F'lar took was towards one end . . . the safety and preservation of dragonkind and weyrfolk, and, consequently, the safety and preservation of Pern. To effect that end, he needed her full cooperation. When weyr business or dragonlore were discussed, she suspended the antipathy he knew she felt for him. In conferences, she supported him wholeheartedly and persuasively but always he suspected the double edge to her comments and saw a speculative, suspicious look in her eyes. He needed not only her tolerance but her empathy.

"Tell me," she said after a long silence, "did the sun touch the Finger Rock before the Red Star was bracketed in the Eye Rock or after?"

"Matter of fact, I'm not sure as I did not see it myself . . .

the concurrence lasts only a few moments . . . but the two are supposed to be simultaneous."

She frowned at him sourly. "Whom did you waste it on? R'gul?" She was provoked; her angry eyes looked everywhere but at him.

"I am Weyrleader," he informed her curtly. She was unreasonable.

She awarded him one long, hard look before she bent to finish her meal. She ate very little, quickly and neatly. Compared to Jora, she didn't eat enough in the course of an entire day to nourish a sick child. But then, there was no point in ever comparing Lessa to Jora.

He finished his own breakfast, absently piling the mugs together on the empty tray. She rose silently and removed the dishes.

"As soon as the Weyr is free, we'll go," he told her.

"So you said," and she nodded towards the sleeping queen, visible through the open arch. "We still must wait upon Ramoth."

"Isn't she rousing? Her tail's been twitching an hour."

"She always does that about this time of day."

F'lar leaned across the table, his brows drawn together thoughtfully as he watched the golden forked tip of the queen's tail jerk spasmodically from side to side.

"Mnementh, too. And always at dawn and early morning. As if somehow they associate that time of day with trouble . . ."

". . . Or the Red Star's rising?"

Some subtle difference in her tone caused F'lar to glance quickly at her. It wasn't anger, now, for missing the morning's phenomenon. Her eyes were fixed on nothing; her face, smooth at first, was soon wrinkled with a vaguely anxious frown as tiny lines formed between her arching, well-defined brows.

"Dawn . . . that's when all warnings come," she murmured.

"What kind of warnings?" he asked with quiet encouragement.

"There was that morning . . . a few days before . . . before you and Fax descended on Ruath Hold. Something woke me . . . a feeling, like a very heavy pressure . . . the sensation of some terrible danger threatening." She was silent. "The Red Star was just rising." The fingers of her left hand opened and closed. She gave a convulsive shudder. Her eyes refocused on him.

"You and Fax did come out of the northeast from Crom," she said sharply, ignoring the fact, F'lar noticed, that the Red Star also rises north of true east.

"Indeed we did," he grinned at her, remembering that morning vividly. He remembered, too, how certain he had been as Fax's procession wound down the long valley to Ruath Hold that he and Fax would find some excuse for a mortal duel. And that he had somehow convinced himself that Ruatha Valley held a woman who had the unusual talents it would take to become the Weyrwoman Pern needed to impress the unhatched queen. "Indeed we did," he chuckled. "Although," he added, gesturing around the great cavern to emphasize, "I prefer to believe I served you well that day. You remember it with displeasure?"

The look she gave him was coldly inscrutable.

"Danger comes in many guises."

"I agree," he replied amiably, determined not to rise to her bait. "Had any other rude awakenings?" he inquired conversationally.

The absolute stillness in the room brought his attention back to her. Her face had drained of all color.

"The day Fax invaded Ruath Hold." Her voice was a barely articulated whisper. Her eyes were wide and staring. Her hands clenched the edge of the table. She said nothing for such a long interval F'lar became concerned. This was an unexpectedly violent reaction to a casual question.

"Tell me," he suggested softly.

She spoke in unemotional, impersonal tones, as if she were reciting a Traditional Ballad or something that had happened to an entirely different person.

"I was a child—just eleven. I woke at dawn . . ." her voice trailed off. Her eyes remained focused on nothing, staring at a scene that had happened long ago.

F'lar was stirred by an irresistible desire to comfort her. It struck him forcibly, even as he was stirred by this unusual compassion, that he had never thought that Lessa, of all people, would be troubled by so old a terror.

Mnementh sharply informed his rider that Lessa was obviously bothered a good deal. Enough so that her mental anguish was rousing Ramoth from sleep. In less accusing tones, Mnementh informed F'lar that R'gul had finally taken off with his weyrling pupils. His dragon, Hath, however, was in a fine state of disorientation due to R'gul's state of mind. Must F'lar unsettle everyone in the Weyr . . .

"Oh, be quiet," F'lar retorted under his breath.

"Why?" Lessa demanded in her normal voice.

"I didn't mean you, my dear Weyrwoman," he assured her, smiling pleasantly, as if the entranced interlude had never occurred. "Mnementh is full of advice these days."

"Like rider, like dragon," she replied tartly.

Ramoth yawned mightily. Lessa was instantly on her feet, running to her dragon's side, her slight figure dwarfed by the six-foot dragon head.

A tender, adoring expression flooded her face as she gazed into Ramoth's gleaming opalescent eyes. F'lar clenched his teeth, envious, by the Egg, of a rider's affection for her dragon.

In his mind, he heard Mnementh's dragon equivalent of laughter.

"She's hungry," Lessa informed F'lar, an echo of her love for Ramoth lingering in the soft line of her mouth, in the kindness in her gray eyes.

"She's always hungry," he observed and followed them out of the weyr.

Mnementh hovered courteously just beyond the ledge until Lessa and Ramoth had taken off. They glided down the Weyr Bowl, over the misty bathing lake, towards the feeding ground at the opposite end of the long oval that comprised the floor of Benden Weyr. The striated, precipitous walls were pierced with the black mouths of single weyr entrances, deserted at this time of day by the few dragons who might otherwise doze on their ledges in the wintry sun. Benden Weyr, that could house five hundred beasts, accommodated a scant two hundred these days.

As F'lar vaulted to Mnementh's smooth bronze neck, he hoped that Ramoth's clutch would be spectacular, erasing the ignominy of the paltry dozen Nemorth had laid in each of her last few clutches.

He had no serious doubts of the improvement after Ramoth's remarkable mating flight with his Mnementh. The bronze dragon smugly echoed his rider's certainty and both looked on the queen possessively as she curved her wings to land. She was twice Nemorth's size, for one thing; her wings half-a-wing again longer than Mnementh's who was the biggest of the seven male bronzes. F'lar looked to Ramoth to repopulate the five empty Weyrs, even as he looked to himself, and Lessa, to rejuvenate the pride and faith of dragonriders and of Pern itself. He only hoped time enough remained to him to do what was necessary. The Red Star had been bracketed by the Eye Rock. the Threads would soon be falling. Somewhere, in one of the other Weyrs' records, must be the information he needed to ascertain *when*, exactly, Threads would fall.

Mnementh landed. F'lar jumped down from the curving neck to stand beside Lessa. The three watched as Ramoth, a buck grasped in each of her forefeet, rose to a feeding ledge.

"Will her appetite never taper off?" Lessa asked with affectionate dismay.

As a dragonet, Ramoth had been eating to grow. Her full stature attained, she was, of course, now eating for her young and she applied herself conscientiously.

F'lar chuckled and squatted, hunter fashion. He picked up shale flakes, skating them across the flat dry ground, counting the dust puffs boyishly.

"The time will come when she won't eat everything in sight," he assured Lessa. "But she's still young . . ."

". . . And needs her strength," Lessa interrupted, her voice a fair imitation of R'gul's pedantic tones.

F'lar looked up at her, squinting against the wintry sun that slanted down at them.

"She's a finely grown beast, especially compared to Nemorth." He gave a contemptuous snort. "In fact, there *is* no comparison. However, look here," he ordered peremptorily.

He tapped the smoothed sand in front of him and she saw that his apparently idle gestures had been to a purpose. With a sliver of stone, he drew a design in quick strokes.

"In order to fly a dragon *between*, he has to know where to go. And so do you." He grinned at the astonished and infuriated look of comprehension on her face. "Ah, but there are certain consequences to an ill-considered jump. Badly visualized reference points often result in staying *between*." His voice dropped ominously. Her face cleared of its resentment. "So, there are certain reference, or recognition points, arbitrarily taught all weyrlings. That," he pointed first to his facsimile and then to the actual Star Stone with its Finger and Eye Rock companions, on Benden Peak, "that is the first recognition point a weyrling learns. When I take you aloft, you will reach an altitude just above the Star Stone, near enough for you to be able to see the hole in the Eye Rock clearly. Fix that picture sharply in your mind's eye, relay it to Ramoth. That will always get you home."

"Understood. But how do I learn recognition points of places I've never seen?"

He grinned up at her. "You're drilled in them. First by your instructor," and he pointed the sliver at his chest, "and then by going there, having directed your dragon to get the visualization from her instructor," and he indicated Mnementh. The bronze dragon lowered his wedge-shaped head until one eye was focused on his rider and his mate's rider. He made a pleased noise deep in his chest.

Lessa laughed up at the gleaming eye and, with unexpected affection, patted the soft nose.

F'lar cleared his throat in surprise. He was aware that Mnementh showed an unusual affection for the Weyrwoman but he had had no idea Lessa was fond of the bronze. Perversely, he was irritated.

"However," he said, and his voice sounded unnatural to himself, "we take the young riders constantly to and from the main reference points all across Pern, to all the Holds so that they have eyewitness impressions on which to rely. As a rider becomes adept in picking out landmarks, he gets additional references from other riders. Therefore, to go *between,* there is actually only one requirement: a clear picture of where you want to go. *And* a dragon!" He grinned at her. "Also, you should always plan to arrive above your reference point in clear air."

Lessa frowned.

"It is better to arrive in open air," F'lar waved a hand above his head, "rather than underground," and he slapped his open hand into the dirt. A puff of dust rose warningly.

"But the wings took off within the Bowl itself the day the Lords of the Hold arrived," Lessa reminded him.

F'lar chuckled at her uptake. "True, but only the most seasoned riders. Once we came across a dragon and a rider entombed together in solid rock. They . . . were . . . very young.'' His eyes were bleak.

''I take the point,'' she assured him gravely. ''That's her fifth,'' she added, pointing towards Ramoth who was carrying her latest kill up to the bloody ledge.

''She'll work them off today, I assure you,'' F'lar remarked. He rose, brushing off his knees with sharp slaps of his riding gloves. ''Test her temper.''

Lessa did so with a silent, *Had enough?* She grimaced at Ramoth's indignant rejection of the thought.

The queen went swooping down for a huge fowl, rising in a flurry of gray, brown and white feathers.

''She's not as hungry as she's making you think, the deceitful creature,'' F'lar chuckled and saw that Lessa had reached the same conclusion. Her eyes were snapping with vexation.

''When you've finished the bird, Ramoth, do let us learn how to fly *between*,'' Lessa said aloud for F'lar's benefit, ''before our good Weyrleader changes his mind.''

Ramoth looked up from her gorging, turned her head towards the two riders at the edge of the feeding ground. Her eyes gleamed. She bent her head again to her kill but Lessa could sense the dragon would obey.

It was cold aloft. Lessa was glad of the fur lining in her riding gear, and the warmth of the great golden neck which she bestrode. She decided not to think of the absolute cold of *between* which she had experienced only once, coming from Ruath Hold to Benden Weyr three Turns before. She glanced below on her right where bronze Mnementh hovered and caught his amused thought.

F'lar tells me to tell Ramoth to tell you to fix the alignment of the Star Stone firmly in your mind as a homing. Then, Mnementh went on amiably, *we shall fly down to the lake. You will return from* between *to this exact point. Do you understand?*

Lessa found herself grinning foolishly with anticipation and nodded vigorously. How much time was saved because she could speak directly to the dragons! Ramoth made a disgruntled noise deep in her throat. Lessa patted her reassuringly.

''Have you got the picture in your mind, dear one?'' she

asked and Ramoth again rumbled, less annoyed because she was catching Lessa's excitement.

Mnementh stroked the cold air with his wings, greenish brown in the sunlight, and curved down gracefully towards the lake on the plateau below Benden Weyr. His flight line took him very low over the rim of the Weyr. From Lessa's angle, it looked like a collision course. Ramoth followed closely in his wake. Lessa caught her breath at the sight of the jagged boulders just below Ramoth's wing tips.

It was exhilarating, Lessa crowed to herself, doubly stimulated by the elation that flowed back to her from Ramoth.

Mnementh halted above the farthest shore of the lake and there, too, Ramoth came to hover.

Mnementh flashed the thought to Lessa that she was to place the picture of where she wished to go firmly in her mind and direct Ramoth to get there.

Lessa complied. The next instant the awesome, bone-penetrating cold of black *between* enveloped them. Before either she or Ramoth was aware of more than that invidious touch of cold and impregnable darkness, they were above the Star Stone.

Lessa let out a cry of triumph.

It is extremely simple. Ramoth seemed disappointed.

Mnementh reappeared beside and slightly below them.

You are to return by the same route to the Lake, he ordered and before the thought had finished, Ramoth took off.

Mnementh was beside them above the lake, fuming with his own and F'lar's anger. *You did not visualize before transferring. Don't think a first successful trip makes you perfect. You have no conception of the dangers inherent in* between. Never *fail to picture your arrival point again.*

Lessa glanced down at F'lar. Even two wingspans apart, she could see the vivid anger on his face, almost feel the fury flashing from his eyes. And laced through the wrath, a terrible sinking fearfulness for her safety that was a more effective reprimand than his wrath. Lessa's safety, she wondered bitterly, or Ramoth's?

You are to follow us, Mnementh was saying in a calmer tone, *rehearsing in your mind the two reference points you have already learned. We shall jump to and from them this morning, gradually learning other points around Benden.*

They did. Flying as far away as Benden Hold itself, nestled

against the foothills above Benden Valley, the Weyr Peak a far point against the noonday sky, Lessa did not neglect to visualize a clearly detailed impression, each time.

This was as marvelously exciting as she had hoped it would be, Lessa confided to Ramoth. Ramoth replied: *Yes, it was certainly preferable to the time-consuming methods others had to use but she didn't think it was exciting, at all, to jump* between *from Benden Weyr to Benden Hold and back to Benden Weyr again. It was dull.*

They had met with Mnementh above the Star Stone again. The bronze dragon sent Lessa the message that this was a very satisfactory initial session. They would practice some distant jumping tomorrow.

Tomorrow, thought Lessa glumly, some emergency will occur or our hardworking Weyrleader willl decide today's session constitutes keeping his promise and that will be that.

There was one jump she could make *between,* from anywhere on Pern, and not miss her mark.

She visualized Ruatha for Ramoth, as seen from the heights above the Hold . . . to satisfy that requirement. To be scrupulously clear, Lessa projected the pattern of the firepits. Before Fax invaded and she had had to manipulate its decline, Ruatha had been such a lovely prosperous valley. She told Ramoth to jump *between.*

The cold was intense and seemed to last for many heartbeats. Just as Lessa began to fear she had somehow lost them *between*, they exploded into the air above the Hold. Elation filled her. That for F'lar and his excessive caution. With Ramoth she could jump anywhere! For there was the distinctive pattern of Ruatha's fire-guttered heights. It was just before dawn, the Breast Pass between Crom and Ruatha, black cones against the lightening gray sky. Fleetingly she noticed the absence of the Red Star that now blazed in the dawn sky. And fleetingly she noticed a difference in the air. Chill, yes, but not wintry . . . the air held that moist coolness of early spring.

Startled she glanced downward, wondering if she could have, for all her assurance, erred in some fashion. But no, this was Ruath Hold. The Tower, the inner Court, the aspect of the broad avenue leading down to the crafthold were just as they should be. Wisps of smoke from distant chimneys indicated people were making ready for the day.

Ramoth caught the tenor of her insecurity and began to press for an explanation.

This is Ruatha, Lessa replied stoutly. *It can be no other. Circle the heights. See, there are the fire-pit lines I gave you . . .*

Lessa gasped, the coldness in her stomach freezing her muscles.

Below her in the slowly lifting pre-dawn gloom, she saw the figures of many men toiling over the breast of the cliff from the hills beyond Ruatha: men moving with quiet stealth like criminals.

She ordered Ramoth to keep as still as possible in the air so as not to direct their attention upward. The dragon was curious but obedient.

Who would be attacking Ruatha? It seemed incredible. The present Warder, Lytol, was a former dragonman and had savagely repelled one attack already. Was there thought of aggression among the Holds now that F'lar was Weyrleader? What Hold Lord would be mounting a territorial war in the winter?

No, not winter. The air here was spring-like.

The men crept on, over the fire-pits to the edge of the heights. Suddenly Lessa realized they were lowering rope ladders over the face of the cliff, down towards the open shutters of the Inner Hold.

Wildly she clutched at Ramoth's neck, certain of what she saw.

This was the invader Fax, now dead nearly three Turns—Fax and his men as they began their attack on Ruatha nearly thirteen Turns ago.

Yes, there was the Tower guard, his face a white blot turned towards the cliff itself, watching. He had been paid his bribe to stand silent this morning.

But the watch-wher, trained to give alarm for any intrusion, why was it not trumpeting its warning? Why was it silent?

Because, Ramoth informed her rider with calm logic, *it senses your presence as well as mine so how could the Hold possibly be in danger?*

No. No! Lessa moaned. *What can I do now? How can I*

wake them? Where is the girl I was? I was asleep and then I woke. I remember. I dashed from my room. I was so scared. I went down the steps and nearly fell. I knew I had to get to the watch-wher's kennel . . . I knew . . .

Lessa clutched at Ramoth's neck for support as past acts and mysteries became devastatingly clear.

She herself had warned herself, just as it was her presence on the queen dragon that had kept the watch-wher from giving alarm. For as she watched, stunned and speechless, she saw the small, gray-robed figure that could only be herself as a youngster, burst from the Hold hall door, race down the cold stone steps into the Court and disappear into the watch-wher's stinking den. Faintly she heard it lurring in piteous confusion.

Just as Lessa-the-girl reached that doubtful sanctuary, Fax's invaders swooped into the open window embrasures and began the slaughter of her sleeping family.

Back—back to the Star Stone! Lessa cried. In her wide and staring eyes she held the image of the guiding rocks like a rudder for her sanity as well as Ramoth's direction.

The intense cold acted as a restorative. And then they were above the quiet, peaceful wintry Weyr as if they had never paradoxically visited Ruatha.

F'lar and Mnementh were nowhere to be seen.

Ramoth, however, was unshaken by the experience. She had only gone where she had been told and had not quite understood that going *when* she had been told had shocked Lessa. She suggested to her rider that Mnementh had probably followed them to Ruatha so if Lessa would give her the *proper* references, she'd take her there. Ramoth's sensible attitude was comforting.

Lessa carefully drew for Ramoth, not the child's memory of a long-vanished, idyllic Ruatha, but her more recent recollection of the Hold, gray, sullen, at dawning, with a Red Star pulsing on the horizon.

And there they were again, hovering over the Valley, the Hold below them on the right. The grasses grew untended on the heights, clogging firepit and brickwork; the scene showed all the deterioration she had encouraged in her effort to thwart Fax of any profit from conquering Ruath Hold.

But, as she watched, vaguely disturbed, she saw a figure emerge from the kitchen, saw the watch-wher creep from its lair and follow the raggedly dressed figure as far across the Court as the chain permitted. She saw the figure ascend the Tower, gaze first eastward, then northeastward. This was still not Ruatha of today and now! Lessa's mind reeled, disoriented. This time she had come back to visit herself of three Turns ago, to see the filthy drudge plotting revenge on Fax.

She felt the absolute cold of *between* as Ramoth snatched them back, emerging once more above the Star Stone. Lessa was shuddering, her eyes frantically raking the reassuring sight of the Weyr Bowl, hoping she had not somehow shifted backwards in time yet again. Mnementh suddenly erupted into the air a few lengths below and beyond Ramoth. Lessa greeted him with a cry of intense relief.

Back to your weyr! There was no disguising the white fury in Mnementh's tone. Lessa was too unnerved to respond in any way other than instant compliance. Ramoth glided swiftly to their ledge, quickly clearing the perch for Mnementh to land.

The rage on F'lar's face as he leaped from Mnementh and advanced on Lessa brought her wits back abruptly. She made no move to evade him as he grabbed her shoulders and shook her violently.

"How dare you risk yourself and Ramoth? Why must you defy me at every opportunity? Do you realize what would happen to all Pern if we lost Ramoth? Where did you go?" He was spitting with anger, punctuating each question that tumbled from his lips by shaking her.

"Ruatha," she managed to say, trying to keep herself erect. She reached out to catch at his arms but he shook her again.

"Ruatha? We were there. You weren't. Where did you go?"

"Ruatha!" Lessa cried louder, clutching at him distractedly because he kept jerking her off balance. She couldn't organize her thoughts with him jolting her.

She was *at Ruatha,* Mnementh said firmly.

We were there twice, Ramoth added.

As the dragons' calmer words penetrated F'lar's fury, he stopped shaking Lessa. She hung limply in his grasp, her hands weakly plucking at his arms, her eyes closed, her face gray. He picked her up and strode rapidly into the queen's weyr, the dragons following. He placed her upon the couch, wrapping her tightly in the fur cover. He called down the service shaft for the duty cook to send up hot *klah*.

"All right, what happened?" he demanded.

She didn't look at him but he got a glimpse of her haunted eyes. She blinked constantly as if she longed to erase something she had recently seen.

Finally she got herself somewhat under control and said in a low tired voice, "I did go to Ruatha. Only . . . I went *back* to Ruatha."

"Back to Ruatha?" F'lar repeated the words stupidly. The significance momentarily eluded him.

Certainly, Mnementh agreed, and flashed to F'lar the two scenes he had picked out of Ramoth's mind.

Staggered by the import of the visualization, F'lar found himself slowly sinking to the edge of the bed.

"You . . . you went *between* times?"

Lessa nodded slowly. The terror was beginning to leave her eyes.

"*Between* times," F'lar murmured. "I wonder . . ."

His mind raced through the possibilities. It might well tip the scales of survival in the Weyr's favor. He couldn't think exactly how to use this extraordinary ability but there *must* be an advantage in it for dragonfolk.

The service shaft rumbled. He took the pitcher from the platform and poured two cups.

Lessa's hands were shaking so much she couldn't get hers to her lips. He steadied it for her, wondering if going *between* times would cause this kind of shock regularly. If so, it wouldn't be any advantage at all. He wondered if she'd had enough of a scare this day so she might not be so contemptuous of his orders the next time.

Outside in the weyr, Mnementh snorted his opinion on that. F'lar ignored him.

Lessa was trembling violently now. He put an arm around her, pressing the fur against her slender body. He held the mug to her lips, forcing her to drink. He could feel the tremors ease off. She finally held the cup and took long, slow, deep breaths between swallows, equally determined to get herself under control. The moment he felt her stiffen under his arm, he released her. He wondered if Lessa had ever had someone to turn to. Certainly not after Fax invaded her family Hold. She had been only eleven; a child. Had hate and revenge been the only emotions the growing girl had practiced?

She lowered the cup, cradling it in her hands carefully as if it had assumed some undefinable importance to her.

"Now. Tell me," he ordered.

After a long deep breath she began to speak, her hands tightening around the mug. Her inner turmoil had not lessened; it was merely under control now.

"Ramoth and I were bored with the weyrling exercises," she admitted candidly.

Grimly F'lar recognized that, while the adventure might have taught her to be more circumspect, it had not scared her into obedience. He doubted that anything would.

"I gave her the picture of Ruatha so we could go *between* there." She did not look at him but her profile was outlined against the dark fur of the rug. "The Ruatha I knew so well: I accidentally sent myself backward in time to the day Fax invaded."

Her shock was now comprehensible to him.

"And . . ." he prompted her, his voice carefully neutral.

"And I saw myself . . ." her voice broke off. With an effort she continued. "I had visualized for Ramoth the designs of the firepits and the angle of the Hold if one looked down from the pits into the Inner Court. That was where we emerged. It was just dawn"—she lifted her chin with a nervous jerk—"and there was no Red Star in the sky." She gave him a quick defensive look as if she expected him to contest this detail. "And I saw men creeping over the firepits, lowering rope ladders to the top windows of the Hold. I saw the Tower guard watching. Just watching." She clenched her teeth at such treachery and her eyes gleamed malevolently. "And I saw myself run from the Hall into the watch-wher's lair. And do you know why," her voice lowered to a bitter whisper, "the watch-wher did not alarm the Hold?"

"Why?"

"Because there was a dragon in the sky and *I*, Lessa of Ruatha, was on her." She flung the mug from her as if she wished she could reject the knowledge, too. "Because *I* was there, the watch-wher did not alarm the Hold, thinking the intrusion legitimate, with one of the Blood on a dragon in the sky. So I," her body grew rigid, her hands clasped so tightly the knuckles were white, "*I* was the cause of my family's massacre. Not Fax! If I had not acted the captious fool today, I would not have been there with Ramoth and the watch-wher would . . ."

Her voice had risen to an hysterical pitch of recrimination. He slapped her sharply across the cheeks, grabbing her, robe and all, to shake her.

The stunned look in her eyes and the tragedy in her face alarmed him. His indignation over her willfulness disappeared. Her unruly independence of mind and spirit attracted him as much as her curious dark beauty. Infuriating as her fractious ways might be, they were too vital a part of her integrity to be exorcised. Her indomitable will had taken a grievous shock today and her self-confidence had better be restored quickly.

"On the contrary, Lessa," he said sternly, "Fax would still have murdered your family. He had planned it very carefully, even to scheduling his attack on the morning when the Tower guard was one who could be bribed. Remember, too, it was dawn and the watch-wher, being a nocturnal beast, blind by daylight, is relieved of responsibility at dawn and knows it. Your presence, damnable as it may appear to you, was not the deciding factor by any means. It did, and I draw your attention to this very important fact, it did cause you to save yourself, by warning Lessa-the-child. Don't you see that?"

"I could have called out," she murmured but the frantic look had left her eyes and there was a faint hint of normal color in her lips.

"If you wish to flail around in guilt, go right ahead," he said with deliberate callousness.

Ramoth interjected a thought that, since they, too, had been there that previous time as Fax's men had prepared to invade, it had already happened, so how could it be changed? The act was inevitable both that day and today. For how else could Lessa have lived to come to the Weyr and impress Ramoth at the hatching?

Mnementh relayed Ramoth's message scrupulously, even to imitating Ramoth's egocentric nuances. F'lar looked sharply at Lessa to see the effect of Ramoth's astringent observation.

"Just like Ramoth to have the final word," she said with a hint of her former droll humor.

F'lar felt the muscles along his neck and shoulders begin to relax. She'd be all right, he decided, but it might be wiser to make her talk it all out now, to put the whole experience into proper perspective.

"You said you were there twice?" He leaned back on the couch, watching her closely. "When was the second time?"

"Can't you guess?" she asked sarcastically.

"No," he lied.

"When else but the dawn I wakened, feeling the Red Star was a menace to me. Three days before you and Fax came out of the northeast."

"It would seem," he remarked drily, "that you were your own premonition both times."

She nodded.

"Have you had any more of these presentiments . . . or should I say, reinforced warnings?"

She shuddered but answered him with more of her old spirit.

"No, but if I should, *you* go. I don't want to."

F'lar grinned maliciously.

"I would, however," she added, "like to know why and how it could happen."

"I've never run across a mention of it anywhere," he told her candidly. "Of course, if you have done it, and you undeniably have," he assured her hastily at her indignant protest, "it obviously can be done. You say you thought of Ruatha, but you thought of it as it was on that particular day. Certainly a day to be remembered. You thought of spring, before dawn, no Red Star . . . yes I remember you mentioning that . . . so one would have to remember references peculiar to a significant day to return *between* times to the past."

She nodded slowly, thoughtfully.

"You used the same method the second time, to get to the Ruatha of three Turns ago. Again, of course, it was spring."

He rubbed his palms together, then brought his hands down on his knees with an emphatic slap and rose to his feet.

"I'll be back," he said and strode from the room, ignoring her half-articulated cry of warning.

Ramoth was curling up in the weyr as he passed her. He noticed that her color remained good in spite of the drain of her energies by the morning's exercises. She glanced at him, her many-faceted eye already covered by the inner, protective lid.

Mnementh awaited his rider on the ledge, and the moment F'lar leaped to his neck, took off. He circled upward, hovering above the Star Stone.

You wish to try Lessa's trick, Mnementh said, unperturbed by the prospective experiment.

F'lar stroked the great curved neck affectionately. *You understand how it worked for Ramoth and Lessa?*

As well as anyone can, Mnementh replied with the approximation of a shrug. *When did you have in mind?*

At that moment, F'lar had had no idea. Now, unerringly, his thoughts drew him backwards to the summer day R'gul's bronze Hath had flown to mate the grotesque Nemorth, and R'gul had become Weyrleader in place of his dead father, F'lon.

Only the cold of *between* gave them any indication they had transferred; they were still hovering above the Star Stone. F'lar wondered if they had missed some essential part of the transfer. Then he realized that the sun was in another quarter of the sky, and the air was warm and sweet with summer. The Weyr below was empty, there were no dragons sunning themselves on the ledges, no women busy at tasks in the Bowl. Noises impinged on his senses; raucous laughter, yells, shrieks, and a soft crooning noise that dominated the bedlam.

Then, from the direction of the weyrling barracks in the lower Caverns, two figures emerged; a stripling and a young bronze dragon. The boy's arm lay limply along the beast's neck. The impression that reached the hovering observers was one of utter dejection. The two halted by the lake, the boy peering into the unruffled blue waters, then glancing upward towards the queen's weyr.

F'lar knew the boy for himself, and compassion for that younger self filled him. If only he could reassure that boy, so torn by grief, so filled with resentment, that he would one day become Weyrleader . . .

Abruptly, startled by his own thoughts, he ordered Mnementh to transfer back. The utter cold of *between* was like a slap in his face, replaced almost instantly as they broke out of *between* into the cold of normal winter.

Slowly, Mnementh flew back down to the queen's weyr, as sobered as F'lar by what they had seen.

Rise high in glory,
Bronze and gold.
Dive entwined,
Enhance the Hold.

Count three months and more,
And five heated weeks,
A day of glory and
In a month, who seeks?

A strand of silver
In the sky . . .
With heat, all quickens
And all times fly.

"I don't know why you insisted F'nor unearth these ridiculous things from Ista Weyr," Lessa exclaimed in a tone of exasperation. "They consist of nothing but trivial notes on how many measures of grain were used to bake daily bread."

F'lar glanced up at her from the records he was studying. He sighed, leaned back in his chair in a bone-popping stretch.

"And I used to think," Lessa said with a rueful expression on her vivid, narrow face, "that those venerable Records would hold the total sum of all dragonlore and human wisdom. Or so I was led to believe," she added pointedly.

F'lar chuckled. "They do, but you have to disinter it."

Lessa wrinkled her nose. "*Phew.* They smell as if we had . . . and the only decent thing to do would be to rebury them."

"Which is another item I'm hoping to find . . . the old preservative technique that kept the skins from hardening and smelling."

"It's stupid, anyhow, to use skins for recording. There ought to be something better. We have become, dear Weyrleader, entirely too hidebound."

While F'lar roared with appreciation of her pun, she regarded him impatiently. Suddenly she jumped up, fired by another of her mercurial moods.

"Well, you won't find it. You won't find the facts you're

looking for. Because I know what you're really after and it isn't recorded!''

''Explain yourself.''

''It's time we stopped hiding a rather brutal truth from ourselves.''

''Which is?''

''Our mutual feeling that the Red Star is a menace and that the Threads *will* come! *We* decided that out of pure conceit and then went back *between* times to particularly crucial points in our lives and strengthened that notion, in our earlier selves. And for you, it was when you decided you were destined,'' her voice mocked the word, ''to become Weyrleader one day.

''Could it be,'' she went on scornfully, ''that our ultraconservative R'gul has the right of it? That there have been no Threads for four hundred Turns because there are no more? And that the reason we have so few dragons is because the dragons sense they are no longer essential to Pern? That we *are* anachronisms as well as parasites?''

F'lar did not know how long he sat looking at her bitter face, nor how long it took him to find answers for her probing questions.

''Anything is possible, Weyrwoman,'' he heard his voice replying calmly. ''Including the unlikely fact that an eleven-year-old child, scared stiff, could plot revenge on her family's murderer and—against all odds—succeed.''

She took an involuntary step forward, struck by his unexpected rebuttal. She listened intently.

''I prefer to believe,'' he went on inexorably, ''that there is more to life than raising dragons and playing spring games. That is not enough for me. And I have made others look further, beyond self-interest and comfort. I have given them a purpose, a discipline. Everyone, dragonfolk and Holder alike, profits.

''I am not looking in these Records for reassurance. I'm looking for solid facts.

''I can prove, Weyrwoman, that there have been Threads. I can prove that there have been Intervals during which the Weyrs have declined. I can prove that if you sight the Red Star directly bracketed by the Eye Rock at the moment of winter solstice, the Red Star will pass close enough to Pern to throw off Threads. Since I can prove those facts, I believe Pern is in danger. *I* believe . . . not the youngster of fifteen Turns ago. F'lar, the bronze rider, the Weyrleader, believes it!"

He saw her eyes reflecting shadowy doubts but he sensed his arguments were beginning to reassure her.

"You felt constrained to believe in me once before," he went on in a milder voice, "when I suggested that you could be Weyrwoman. You believed me and . . ." he made a gesture around the weyr as substantiation.

She gave him a weak, humorless smile.

"That was because I had never planned what to do with my life once I did have Fax lying dead at my feet. Of course, being Ramoth's weyrmate is wonderful but"—and she frowned slightly—"it isn't enough anymore either. That's why I wanted so to learn to fly and then . . ."

". . . that's how this argument started in the first place," F'lar finished for her with a sardonic smile.

He leaned across the table, urgently.

"Believe with me, Lessa, until you have cause not to. I respect your doubts. There's nothing wrong in doubting. It sometimes leads to greater faith. But believe in me until spring. If the Threads have not fallen by then . . ." He shrugged fatalistically.

She looked at him for a long moment and then inclined her head slowly, in agreement.

He tried to suppress the relief he felt at her decision. Lessa, as Fax had discovered, was a ruthless adversary and a canny advocate. Besides these, she was Weyrwoman: essential to his plans.

"Now, let's get back to the contemplation of trivia. They do tell me, you know: time, place and duration of Thread incursions," he grinned up at her reassuringly. "And those are facts I must have to make up my timetable."

"Timetable? But you said you didn't know the time."

"Not the day to the second when the Threads may spin down. For one thing, while the weather holds so unusually cold for this time of year, the Threads simply turn brittle and blow away like dust. They're harmless. However, when the air is warm, they are viable and . . . deadly." He made fists of both hands, placing one above and to one side of the other.

"The Red Star is my right hand, my left is Pern. The Red Star turns very fast and in the opposite direction to us. It also wobbles erratically."

"How do you know that?"

"Diagram on the walls of the Fort Weyr Hatching Ground. *That was the very first Weyr*. So, when the Star makes a pass, the Threads spin off, down towards us, in attacks that last six hours and occur about fourteen hours apart."

"Attacks last six hours?"

He nodded gravely. "When the Red Star is closest to us. Right now, it is just beginning its Pass."

She frowned.

He rummaged among the skin sheets on the table and an object dropped to the stone floor with a metallic clatter.

Curious, Lessa bent to pick it up, turning the thin sheet over in her hands. "What's this?" She ran an exploratory finger lightly across the irregular design on one side.

"I don't know. F'nor brought it back from Fort Weyr. It was nailed to one of the chests in which Records had been stored. He brought it along, thinking it might be important. Said there was a plate like it just under the Red Star diagram on the wall of the Hatching Ground.

"This first part is plain enough: 'Mother's father's father, who departed for all time *between*, said this was the key to the mystery, and it came to him while doodling. He said that he said: ARRHENIUS? EUREKA! MYCORRHIZA . . .' Of course that part doesn't make any sense at all. It isn't even Pernese; just babbling, the last three words.

"I have studied it, Lessa. The only way to depart for all time *between* is to die, right? People can't just fly away on their own, obviously. So it is a death vision, dutifully recorded by a grandchild, who couldn't spell very well. 'Doodling' as the present tense of dying!" He smiled indulgently. "And as for the rest of it, after the nonsense; like most death-visions, it 'explains' what everyone has always known. The second part says simply: '. . . flame-throwing fire-lizards to wipe out the spores. Q. E. D.' No, this is no help in our researches, just a primitive rejoicing that he is a dragonman, who didn't even know the right word for Threads."

Lessa wet one fingertip to see if the patterns were inked on. The metal was shiny enough to be a good mirror. However, the patterns remained smooth and precise. "Primitive or no, they had a more permanent way of recording their visions than well-preserved skins."

"Well-preserved babblings," said F'lar, turning back to the skins he was checking for understandable data.

"A badly-scored ballad, perhaps," said Lessa, dismissing it. "The design isn't even pretty."

F'lar pulled forward a chart that showed overlapping horizontal bands imposed on the projection of Pern's continental mass.

"Here," he said, "this represents waves of attack and this one," he pulled forward the second map with vertical bands, "shows time bands. So you can see, that with a fourteen-hour break, only certain parts of Pern are affected in each attack. One reason for the spacing of the weyrs."

"Six full weyrs," she murmured, "close to three thousand dragons."

"I'm aware of the statistics," he replied in a voice devoid of expression. "It meant no one weyr was overburdened during the height of the attacks, not that three thousand beasts must be available. However, with these timetables, we can manage until Ramoth's first clutches have matured."

She turned a cynical look on him. "You've a lot of faith in one queen's capacity."

He waved that remark aside impatiently. "I've more faith, no matter what your opinion is, in the startling repetitions of events in these Records."

"Ha!"

"I don't mean how many measures for daily bread, Lessa," he retorted, his voice rising. "I mean such things as the time such and such a wing was sent out on patrol, how long the patrol lasted, how many riders were hurt. The brooding capacities of queens, during the fifty years a Pass lasts and the Intervals between such Passes. Yes, it tells that. By all I've studied here," and he pounded emphatically on the nearest stack of dusty, smelly skins, "Nemorth should have been mating twice a Turn for the last ten. Had she even kept to her paltry twelve a clutch, we'd have two hundred and forty more beasts . . . Don't interrupt. But we had Jora as Weyrwoman and R'gul as Weyrleader and we had fallen into planet-wide disfavor during a four hundred Turn interval. Well, Ramoth will brood over no measly dozen and she'll lay a queen egg, mark my words. She will rise often to mate and lay generously. By the time the Red Star is passing closest to us and the attacks become frequent, we'll be ready."

She stared at him, her eyes wide with incredulity. "Out of Ramoth?"

"Out of Ramoth and out of the queens she'll lay. Remember, there are Records of Faranth laying sixty eggs at a time, including several queen eggs."

Lessa could only shake her head slowly in wonder.

" 'A Strand of silver
In the sky.
With heat, all quickens,
All times fly!' " F'lar quoted to her.

"She's got weeks more to go before laying and then the eggs must hatch . . ."

"Been on the Hatching Ground recently? Wear your boots. You'll be burned through sandals."

She dismissed that with a guttural noise. He sat back, outwardly amused by her disbelief.

". . . And then you have to make Impression and wait till the riders . . ." she went on.

". . . Why do you think I've insisted on older boys? The dragons are mature long before their riders."

"Then the system is faulty."

He narrowed his eyes slightly, shaking the stylus at her.

"Dragon tradition started out as a guide . . . but there comes a time when man becomes too traditional . . . too—what was it you said the other day—too hidebound. Yes, it's traditional to use the weyrbred, because it's been convenient. And because this sensitivity to dragons strengthens when both sire and dam are weyrbred. That doesn't mean weyrbred is best. You, for example . . ."

"There's Weyrblood in the Ruathan Line," she said proudly.

"Granted. Take young Naton; he's craftbred from Nabol, yet F'nor tells me he can make Canth understand him."

"Oh, that's not hard to do," she interjected.

"What do you mean?" F'lar jumped on her statement.

They were both interrupted by a high-pitched, penetrating whine. F'lar listened intently for a moment and then shrugged, grinning.

"Some green's getting herself chased again."

"And that's another item these so-called all-knowing records of yours never mention. Why is it only the gold dragons can reproduce?"

F'lar did not suppress a lascivious chuckle.

"Well, for one thing, firestone inhibits reproduction. If they never chewed stone, a green could lay but, at best, they produce small beasts and we need big ones. And, for another thing," his chuckle rolled out as he went on deliberately, grinning mischievously, "if the greens could reproduce, considering their amorousness, and the numbers we have of them, we'd be up to our ears in dragons in next to no time."

The first whine was joined by another and then a low hum throbbed as if carried by the stones of the Weyr itself.

F'lar, his face changing rapidly from surprise to triumphant astonishment, dashed up the passage before Lessa could open her mouth.

"What's the matter?" she demanded, picking up her skirts to run after him. "What does that mean?"

The hum, resonating everywhere, was deafening in the echo-chamber of the queen's weyr. Lessa registered the fact that Ramoth was gone. She heard F'lar's boots pounding down the passage to the ledge, a sharp *ta-ta-tat* over the kettledrum booming hum. The whine was so high-pitched now it was inaudible, but nerve-wracking. Disturbed, frightened, Lessa followed F'lar out.

By the time she reached the ledge, the Bowl was a-whir with dragons on the wing, making for the high entrance to the Hatching Ground. Weyrfolk, riders, women, children, all screaming with excitement, were pouring across the Bowl to the lower entrance to the Ground.

She caught sight of F'lar charging across to the tunnel entrance and she shrieked at him to wait. He couldn't have heard her across the bedlam.

Fuming because she had the long stairs to descend, then must double back as the stairs faced the feeding grounds at the opposite end of the Bowl from the Hatching Ground, Lessa realized that she, the Weyrwoman, would be the last one there.

Why had Ramoth decided to be secretive about laying? Wasn't she close enough to her own weyrmate to want her with her?

A dragon knows what to do, Ramoth calmly informed Lessa.

"You could have told me," Lessa wailed, feeling much abused.

Why, at the time F'lar had been going on largely about huge clutches and three thousand beasts, that infuriating dragon-child had been doing it!

It didn't improve Lessa's temper to have to recall another remark of F'lar's—on the state of the Hatching Grounds. The moment she stepped into the mountain-high cavern, she felt the heat through the soles of her sandals. Everyone was crowded in a loose circle around the far end of the cavern. And everyone was swaying from foot to foot. As Lessa was short to begin with, this only decreased the likelihood of her ever seeing what Ramoth had done.

"Let me through!" she demanded imperiously, pounding on the wide backs of two tall riders.

An aisle was reluctantly opened for her and she went through, looking neither to her right nor left at the excited weyrfolk. She was furious, confused, hurt and knew she looked ridiculous because the hot sand made her walk a curious, quick-step mince.

She halted, stunned and wide-eyed at the mass of eggs, and forgot such trivial things as hot feet.

Ramoth was curled around the clutch, looking enormously pleased with herself. She, too, kept shifting, closing and opening a protective wing over her eggs so it was difficult to count them.

"No one will steal them, silly, so stop fluttering," Lessa exclaimed as she tried to make a tally.

Obediently, Ramoth folded her wings. To relieve her maternal anxiety, however, she snaked her head out across the circle of mottled, glowing eggs, looking all around the cavern, flicking her forked tongue in and out.

An immense sigh, like a gust of wind, swept through the cavern. For there, now Ramoth's wings were furled, gleamed an egg of glowing gold among the tan, the green and the blue ones. A queen egg!

"A queen egg!" The cry went up simultaneously from half a hundred throats. The Hatching Ground rang with cheers, yells, screams and howls of exultation.

Someone seized Lessa and swung her around in an excess of feeling. A kiss landed in the vicinity of her mouth. No sooner did she recover her footing than she was hugged by someone else, she thought it was Manora, and then pounded and buffeted around in congratulation until she was reeling in a kind of dance between avoiding the celebrants and easing the growing discomfort of her feet.

She broke from the milling revelers and ran across the Ground to Ramoth. She came to a sudden stop before the eggs. They seemed to be pulsing. The shells looked flaccid. She could have sworn they were hard the day she Impressed Ramoth. She wanted to touch one, just to make sure, and dared not.

You may, Ramoth assured her condescendingly. She touched Lessa's shoulder gently with her tongue.

The egg was soft to touch and Lessa drew her hand back quickly, afraid of doing injury.

The heat will harden it, Ramoth said.

"Ramoth, I'm so proud of you," Lessa sighed, looking adoringly up at the great eyes which shone in rainbows of pride. "You are the most marvelous queen ever. I do believe you will redragon all the Weyrs. I do believe you will."

Ramoth inclined her head regally, then began to sway it from side to side over the eggs, protectingly. She began to hiss suddenly, raising up from her crouch, beating the air with her wings, before settling back into the sands to lay yet another egg.

The weyrfolk, uncomfortable on the hot sands, were beginning to leave the Hatching Ground, now they had paid tribute to the arrival of the golden egg. A queen took several days to complete her clutch so there was no point to waiting. Seven eggs already lay beside the important golden one and if there were seven already, this augured well for the eventual total. Wagers were being made and taken even as Ramoth produced her ninth mottled egg.

"A queen egg, by the mother of us all," F'lar's voice said in Lessa's ear. "And I'll wager there'll be ten bronzes at least."

She looked up at him, completely in harmony with the Weyrleader at this moment. She was conscious, now, of Mnementh, crouching proudly on a ledge, gazing fondly at his mate. Impulsively, Lessa laid her hand on F'lar's arm.

"F'lar, I do believe you."

"Only now?" F'lar teased her, but his smile was wide and his eyes proud.

> Weyrman, watch; Weyrman, learn
> Something new in every Turn.
> Oldest may be coldest, too.
> Sense the right; find the true!

If F'lar's orders over the next months caused no end of discussion and muttering among the weyrfolk, they seemed, to Lessa, to be only the logical outcomes of their discussion after Ramoth had finished laying her gratifying total of forty-one eggs.

F'lar discarded tradition right and left, treading on more than R'gul's conservative toes.

Out of perverse distaste for outworn doctrines against which she herself had chafed during R'gul's leadership, and out of respect for F'lar's intelligence, Lessa backed him completely. She might not have respected her earlier promise to him that she would believe in his ways until spring if she had not seen his predictions come true one after another. These were based, however, not on the premonitions she no longer trusted after her experience *between* times, but on recorded facts.

As soon as the eggshells hardened and Ramoth had rolled her special queen egg to one side of the mottled clutch for attentive brooding, F'lar brought the prospective riders into the Hatching Ground. Traditionally the candidates saw the eggs for the first time on the day of Impression. To this precedent, F'lar added others: Very few of the sixty-odd were weyrbred and most of them were in their late teens. The candidates were to get used to the eggs, touch them, caress them, be comfortable with the notion that out of these eggs, young dragons would hatch, eager and waiting to be Impressed. F'lar felt that such a practice might cut down on casualties during Impression when the boys were simply too scared to move out of the way of the awkward dragonets.

F'lar also had Lessa persuade Ramoth to let Kylara near her precious golden egg. Kylara readily enough weaned her son and spent hours, with Lessa acting as her tutor, beside the golden egg. Despite Kylara's loose attachment to T'bor, she showed an open preference for F'lar's company. Therefore,

Lessa took great pains to foster F'lar's plan for Kylara since it meant her removal, with the new-hatched queen, to Fort Weyr.

F'lar's use of the Hold-born as riders served an additional purpose. Shortly before the actual Hatching and Impression, Lytol, the Warder appointed at Ruath Hold, sent another message.

"The man positively delights in sending bad news," Lessa remarked as F'lar passed the message skin to her.

"He's gloomy," F'nor agreed. He had brought the message. "I feel sorry for that youngster cooped up with such a pessimist."

Lessa frowned at the brown rider. She still found distasteful any mention of Gemma's son, now Lord of her ancestral Hold. Yet . . . she had inadvertently caused his mother's death. As she could not be Weyrwoman and Lady Holder at the same time, it was fitting that Gemma's Gaxom be Lord at Ruatha.

"I, however," F'lar said, "am grateful to his warnings. I suspected Meron would cause trouble again."

"He's got shifty eyes, like Fax," Lessa remarked.

"Shifty-eyed or not, he's dangerous," F'lar answered. "And I cannot have him spreading rumors that we are deliberately choosing men of the Blood to weaken Family Lines."

"There are more craftsmen's sons than Holders' boys in any case," F'nor snorted.

"I don't like him questioning that the Threads have not appeared," Lessa said gloomily.

F'lar shrugged. "They'll appear in due time. Be thankful the weather has continued cold. When the weather warms up and still no Threads, then I will worry." He grinned at Lessa in an intimate reminder of her promise.

F'nor cleared his throat hastily and looked away.

"However," the Weyrleader went on briskly, "I can do something about the other accusation."

So, when it was apparent the eggs were about to hatch, he broke another long-standing tradition and sent riders to fetch the fathers of the young candidates from craft and Hold.

The great Hatching cavern gave the appearance of being almost full as Holder and Weyrfolk watched from the tiers above the heated Ground. This time, Lessa observed, there was no aura of fear. The youthful candidates were tense, yes, but not frightened out of their wits by the rocking, shattering eggs. When the ill-coordinated dragonets awkwardly stumbled—it seemed to Lessa they deliberately looked around at the eager faces as though pre-Impressed—the youths either stepped to one side, or eagerly advanced as a crooning dragonet made his choice. The Impressions were made quickly and with no accidents. All too soon, Lessa thought, the triumphant procession of stumbling dragons and proud new riders moved erratically out of the Hatching Ground to the barracks.

The young queen burst from her shell and moved unerringly for Kylara, standing confidently on the hot sands. The watching beasts hummed their approval.

''It was over too soon,'' Lessa said in a disappointed voice that evening to F'lar.

He laughed indulgently, allowing himself a rare evening of relaxation now that another step had gone as planned. The Holder folk had been ridden home, stunned, dazed and themselves impressed by the Weyr and the Weyrleader.

''That's because you were watching this time,'' he remarked, brushing a lock of her hair back. It obscured his view of her profile. He chuckled again. ''You'll notice Naton . . .''

''. . . N'ton . . .'' she corrected him.

''. . . All right, N'ton . . . Impressed a bronze.''

''Just as you predicted,'' she said with some asperity.

''And Kylara is Weyrwoman for Pridith.''

Lessa did not comment on that and she did her best to ignore his laughter.

''I wonder which bronze will fly her,'' he murmured softly.

''It had better be T'bor's Orth,'' Lessa said, bridling.

He answered her the only way a wise man could.

Crack dust, blackdust,
Turn in freezing air,
Waste dust, spacedust,
From Red Star bare.

Lessa woke abruptly, her head aching, her eyes blurred, her mouth dry. She had the immediate memory of a terrible nightmare which, just as quickly, escaped recall. She brushed her hair out of her face and was surprised to find she had been sweating heavily.

"F'lar?" she called in an uncertain voice. He had evidently risen early. "F'lar," she called again, louder.

He's coming, Mnementh informed her. Lessa sensed that the dragon was just landing on the ledge. She touched Ramoth and found that the queen, too, had been bothered by formless, frightening dreams. The dragon roused briefly and then fell back into deeper sleep.

Disturbed by her vague fears, Lessa rose and dressed, foregoing a bath for the first time since she had arrived at the Weyr.

She called down the shaft for breakfast, plaiting her hair with deft fingers as she waited.

The tray appeared on the shaft platform just as F'lar entered. He kept looking back over his shoulder at Ramoth.

"What's got into her?"

"Echoing my nightmare. I woke in a cold sweat."

"You were sleeping quietly enough when I left to assign patrols. You know, at the rate those dragonets are growing, they're already capable of limited flight. All they do is eat and sleep and that is . . ."

". . . What makes a dragon grow . . ." Lessa finished for him and sipped thoughtfully at her steaming hot *klah*. "You are going to be extra careful about their drill procedures, aren't you?"

"You mean to prevent an inadvertent flight *between* times? I certainly am," he assured her. "I don't want bored dragonriders irresponsibly popping in and out." He gave her a long, stern look.

"Well, it wasn't my fault no one taught me to fly early enough," she replied in the sweet tone she used when she was being especially malicious. "If I'd been drilled from the day of Impression to the day of my first flight, I'd never have discovered that trick."

"True enough," he said solemnly.

"You know, F'lar, if I discovered it, someone else must have and someone else may. If they haven't already."

F'lar drank, making a face as the *klah* scalded his tongue. "I don't know how to find out discreetly. We would be foolish to think we were the first. It is, after all, an inherent ability in dragons or you would never have been able to do it."

She frowned, took a quick breath and then let it go, shrugging.

"Go on," he encouraged her.

"Well, isn't it possible that our conviction about the imminence of the Threads could stem from one of us coming back when the Threads are actually falling . . . I mean . . ."

"My dear girl, we have both analyzed every stray thought and action—even your dream this morning upset you although it was no doubt due to all the wine you drank last night—until we wouldn't know an honest presentiment if it walked up and slapped us in the face."

"I can't dismiss the thought that this *between* times ability is of crucial value," she said emphatically.

"That, my dear Weyrwoman, *is* an honest presentiment."

"But why?"

"Not 'why,' " he corrected her cryptically, "*when*." An idea stirred vaguely in the back of his mind. He tried to nudge it out where he could mull it over. Mnementh announced that F'nor was entering the weyr.

"What's the matter with you?" F'lar demanded of his half brother for F'nor was choking and sputtering, his face red with the paroxysm.

"Dust . . ." he coughed, slapping at his sleeves and chest with his riding gloves. "Plenty of dust, but no Threads," he said, describing a wide arc with one arm as he fluttered his fingers suggestively. He brushed his tight, wher-hide pants, scowling as a fine black dust drifted off.

F'lar felt every muscle in his body tense as he watched the dust float to the floor.

"Where did you get so dusty?" he demanded.

F'nor regarded him with mild surprise. "Weather patrol in Tillek. Entire north has been plagued with dust storms lately. But what I came in for . . ." He broke off, alarmed by F'lar's taut immobility. "What's the matter with dust?" he asked in a baffled voice.

F'lar pivoted on his heel and raced for the stairs to the Record Room. Lessa was right behind him, F'nor belatedly trailing after.

"Tillek, you said?" F'lar barked at his wingsecond. He was clearing the table of stacks for the four charts he then laid out. "How long have these storms been going on? Why didn't you report them?"

"Report dust storms? You wanted to know about warm air masses."

"How long have these storms been going on?" F'lar's voice crackled.

"Close to a week."

"*How close?*"

"Six days ago, the first storm was noticed in upper Tillek. They have been reported in Bitra, upper Telgar, Crom and the High Reaches," F'nor reported tersely.

He glanced hopefully at Lessa but saw she, too, was staring at the four unusual charts. He tried to see why the horizontal and vertical strips had been superimposed on Pern's land mass, but the reason was beyond him.

F'lar was making hurried notations, pushing first one map and then another away from him.

"Too involved to think straight, to see clearly, to understand," the Weyrleader snarled to himself, throwing down the stylus angrily.

"You did say only warm air masses," F'nor heard himself saying humbly, aware that he had somehow failed his Weyrleader.

F'lar shook his head impatiently.

"Not your fault, F'nor. Mine. I should have asked. I knew it was good luck that the weather held so cold." He put both hands on F'nor's shoulders, looking directly in his eyes. "The Threads have been falling," he announced gravely. "Falling into cold air, freezing into bits to drift on the wind," and F'lar imitated F'nor's finger-fluttering, "as specks of black dust."

" 'Crack dust, blackdust,' " Lessa quoted. "In the Ballad of Moreta's Ride, the chorus is all about black dust."

"I don't need to be reminded of Moreta right now," F'lar growled, bending to the maps. "She could talk to any dragon in the Weyrs."

"But I can do that!" Lessa protested.

Slowly, as if he didn't quite credit his ears, F'lar turned back to Lessa. "What did you just say?"

"I said, I can talk to any dragon in the Weyr."

* * *

Still staring at her, blinking in utter astonishment, F'lar sank down to the table top.

"How long," he managed to say, "have you had *this* particular skill?"

Something in his tone, in his manner, caused Lessa to flush and stammer like an erring weyrling.

"I . . . I always could. Beginning with the watch-wher at Ruatha . . ." and she gestured indecisively in Ruatha's westerly direction, "and I talked to Mnementh at Ruatha. And . . . when I got here, I could—" her voice faltered at the accusing look in F'lar's cold, hard eyes. Accusing and worse, contemptuous.

"I thought you had agreed to help me, to believe in me."

"I'm truly sorry, F'lar. It never occurred to me it was any use to anyone but—"

F'lar exploded onto both feet, his eyes blazing with aggravation.

"The one thing I could not figure out was how to direct the wings and keep in contact with the Weyr during an attack. How was I going to get reinforcements and firestone in time. And you . . . you have been sitting there, spitefully hiding the—"

"I am NOT spiteful," she screamed at him. "I said I was sorry. I am. But you've a nasty smug habit of keeping your own council. How was I to know you didn't have the same trick? You're F'lar, the Weyrleader. You can do *any*thing. Only you're just as bad as R'gul because you never *tell* me half the things I ought to know."

F'lar reached out and shook her until her angry voice was stopped.

"Enough. We can't waste time arguing like children." Then his eyes widened, his jaw dropped. "Waste time? That's it."

"Go *between* times?" Lessa gasped.

"*Between* times!"

F'nor was totally confused. "What are you two talking about?"

"The Threads started falling at dawn in Nerat," F'lar said, his eyes bright, his manner decisive.

F'nor could feel his guts congealing with apprehension. At dawn in Nerat? Why, the rainforests would be demolished.

He could feel a surge of adrenalin charging through his body at the thought of danger.

"So we're going *back* there, *between* times, and be there when the Threads started falling, two hours ago. F'nor, the dragons can go not only where we direct them, but *when*."

"Where? When?" F'nor repeated, bewildered. "That could be dangerous."

"Yes, but today it will save Nerat. Now, Lessa," and F'lar gave her another shake, compounded of pride and affection, "order out all the dragons, young, old—any that can fly. Tell them to load themselves down with firestone sacks. I don't know if you can talk across time . . ."

"My dream this morning . . ."

"Perhaps. But right now, rouse the Weyr." He pivoted to F'nor. "If Threads are falling . . . were falling . . . at Nerat at dawn, they'll be falling on Keroon and Ista right now, because they are in that time pattern. Take two wings to Keroon. Arouse the plains. Get them to start the firepits blazing. Take some weyrlings with you and send them on to Igen and Ista. Those Holds are not in as immediate danger as Keroon. I'll reinforce you as soon as I can. And . . . keep Canth in touch with Lessa."

F'lar clapped his brother on the shoulder and sent him off, the brown rider too used to taking orders to argue.

"Mnementh says R'gul is duty officer and R'gul wants to know . . " Lessa began.

"C'mon, girl," F'lar said, his eyes brilliant with excitement. He grabbed up his maps and propelled her up the stairs.

They arrived in the weyr just as R'gul entered with T'sum. R'gul was muttering about this unusual summons.

"Hath told me to report," he complained. "Fine thing when your own dragon . . ."

"R'gul, T'sum, mount your wings. Arm them with all the firestone they can carry and assemble above Star Stone. I'll join you in a few minutes. We go to Nerat at dawn."

"Nerat? I'm watch officer, not patrol . . ."

"This is no patrol," F'lar cut him off.

"But sir," T'sum interrupted, his eyes wide, "Nerat's dawn was two hours ago, same as ours."

"And that is *when* we are going to, brown rider. The dragons, we have discovered, can go *between* places temporally as well as geographically. At dawn, Threads fell at Nerat. We're going back, *between* times, to sear them from the sky."

F'lar paid no attention to R'gul's stammered demand for explanation. T'sum, however, grabbed up firestone sacks and raced back to the ledge and his waiting Munth.

"Go on, you old fool," Lessa told R'gul irascibly. "The Threads are here. You were wrong. Now be a dragonman! Or go *between* and stay there!"

Ramoth, awakened by the alarms, poked at R'gul with her man-sized head and the ex-Weyrleader came out of his momentary shock. Without a word, he followed T'sum down the passageway.

F'lar had thrown on his heavy wher-hide tunic and shoved on his riding boots.

"Lessa, be sure to send messages to all the Holds. Now, this attack will stop about four hours from now. So the farthest west it can reach will be Ista. But I want every Hold and craft warned."

She nodded, her eyes intent on his face lest she miss a word.

"Fortunately the Star is just beginning its Pass so we won't have to worry about another attack for a few days. I'll figure out the next one when I get back.

"Now, get Manora to organize her women. We'll need pails of ointment. The dragons are going to be laced and that hurts. Most important, if something goes wrong, you'll have to wait till a bronze is at least a year old to fly Ramoth . . ." Suddenly F'lar crushed her against him, his mouth bruising hers as if all her sweetness and strength must come with him. He released her so abruptly she staggered back against Ramoth's lowered head. She clung for a moment to her dragon, as much for support as for reassurance.

Wheel and turn
Or bleed and burn.
Fly between,
Blue and green.

Soar, dive down,
Bronze and brown
Dragonmen must fly
When Threads are in the sky.

As F'lar raced down the passageway to the ledge, firesacks bumping against his thighs, he was suddenly grateful for the tedious sweeping patrols over every Hold and hollow of Pern. He could see Nerat clearly in his mind's eye. He could see the many petaled vineflowers which were the distinguishing feature of the rainforests at this time of year. Their ivory blossoms would be glowing in the first beams of sunlight like dragon-eyes among the tall, wide-leaved plants.

Mnementh, his eyes flashing with excitement, hovered skittishly at the ledge. F'lar vaulted to the bronze neck.

The Weyr was seething with wings of all colors, noisy with shouts and countercommands. The atmosphere was electric but F'lar could sense no panic in that ordered confusion. Dragon and human bodies oozed out of openings around the Bowl walls. Women scurried across the floor from one lower cavern to another. The children playing by the lake were sent to gather wood for a fire. The weyrlings, supervised by old C'gan, were forming outside their barracks. F'lar looked up to the Peak and approved the tight formation of the wings assembled there in close flying order. Another wing formed up as he watched. He recognized brown Canth, F'nor on his neck, just as the entire wing vanished.

He ordered Mnementh aloft. The wind was cold and carried a hint of moisture. A late snow? This was the time for it, if ever.

R'gul's wing and T'bor's fanned out on his left, T'sum and D'nol on his right. He noted each dragon was well-laden with sacks. Then he gave Mnementh the visualization of the early spring rainforest in Nerat, just before dawn, the vineflowers gleaming, the sea breaking against the rocks of the High Shoal . . .

He felt the searing cold of *between*. And he felt a stab of doubt. Was he injudicious, sending them all, possibly to their deaths *between* times, in this effort to out-time the Threads at Nerat?

Then, they were all there, in the crepuscular light that promises day. The lush, fruity smells of the rainforest drifting up to them. Warm, too, and that was frightening. He looked up and slightly to the north. Pulsing with menace, the Red Star shown down.

The men had realized what had happened, their voices

raised in astonishment. Mnementh told F'lar that the dragons were mildly surprised at their riders' fuss.

"Listen to me, dragonriders," F'lar called, his voice harsh and distorted in an effort to be heard by all. He waited till the men had moved as close as possible. He told Mnementh to pass the information on to each dragon. Then he explained what they had done and why. No one spoke but there were many nervous looks exchanged across bright wings.

Crisply he ordered the wings to fan out in a staggered formation, keeping a distance of five-wings' spread up or down between them.

The sun came up.

Slanting across the sea, like an ever-thickening mist, Threads were falling; silent, beautiful, treacherous. Silvery gray were those space-traversing spores, spinning from hard frozen ovals into coarse filaments as they penetrated the warm atmospheric envelope of Pern. Less than mindless, they had been ejected from their barren planet towards Pern, a hideous rain that sought organic matter to nourish it into growth. The southern continent of Pern had already been sucked dry. One Thread sinking into fertile soil would burrow deep, propagating thousands in the warm earth, rendering it into a black-dusted wasteland.

A stifled roar from the throats of eighty men and dragons broke the dawn air above Nerat's green heights—as if the Threads might hear this challenge, F'lar mused.

As one, dragons swiveled their wedge-shaped heads to their riders for firestone. Great jaws macerated the hunks. The fragments were swallowed and more firestone was demanded. Inside the beasts, acids churned and the poisonous phosphenes were readied. When the dragons belched forth the gas, it would ignite in the air, into ravening flame to sear the Threads from the sky. And burn them from the soil.

Dragon instinct took over the moment the Threads began to fall above Nerat's shores.

As much admiration as F'lar had always held for his bronze companion, it achieved newer heights in the next hours. Beating the air in great strokes, Mnementh soared with flaming breath to meet the down-rushing menace. The fumes, swept back by the wind, choked F'lar until he thought to crouch low on the lea side of the bronze neck. The dragon squealed as Threads flicked the tip of one wing. Instantly F'lar and he ducked into *between*, cold, calm, black. In the flicker of an eye, they were back to face the reality of Threads.

Around him, F'lar saw dragons winking in and out of *between*, flaming as they returned, diving, soaring. As the attack continued, and they drifted across Nerat, F'lar began to recognize the pattern in the dragons' instinctive evasion-attack movements—and in the Threads. For, contrary to what he had gathered from his study of the Records, the Threads fell in patches. Not as rain will, in steady unbroken sheets, but like flurries of snow; here, above, there, whipped to one side suddenly. Never fluidly, despite the continuity their name implied.

You could see a patch above you. Flaming, your dragon would rise. You'd have the intense joy of seeing the clump shrivel from bottom to top. Sometimes, a patch would fall between riders. One dragon would signal he would follow and, spouting flame, would dive and sear.

Gradually the dragonriders worked their way over the rainforests, so densely, so invitingly green. F'lar refused to dwell on what just one live Thread burrow would do to that lush land. He would send back a low-flying patrol to quarter every foot. One Thread! Just one Thread could put out the ivory eyes of every luminous vineflower.

A dragon screamed somewhere to his left. Before he could identify the beast, it had ducked *between*. F'lar heard other cries of pain, from men as well as dragons. He shut his ears and concentrated, as dragons did, on the here-and-now. Would Mnementh remember those piercing cries later? F'lar wished he could forget them now.

He, F'lar, the bronze rider, felt suddenly superfluous. It was the dragons who were fighting this engagement. You encouraged your beast, comforted him when the Threads burned, but you depended on his instinct and speed.

Hot fire dripped across F'lar's cheek, burrowing like acid into his shoulder . . . a cry of surprised agony burst from F'lar's lips. Mnementh took them to merciful *between*. The dragonman batted with frantic hands at the Threads, felt them crumble in the intense cold of *between* and break off. Revolted, he slapped at injuries still afire. Back in Nerat's humid air, the sting seemed to ease. Mnementh crooned comfortingly and then dove at a patch, breathing fire.

Shocked at self-consideration, F'lar hurriedly examined his mount's shoulder for telltale score marks.

I duck very quickly, Mnementh told him and veered away from a dangerously close clump of Threads. A brown dragon followed them down and burned them to ash.

It might have been moments, it might have been a hundred hours later when F'lar looked down in surprise at the sunlit sea. Threads now dropped harmlessly into the salty waters. Nerat was to the east of him on his right, the rocky tip curling westward.

F'lar felt weariness in every muscle. In the excitement of frenzied battle, he had forgotten the bloody scores on cheek and shoulder. Now, as he and Mnementh glided slowly, the injuries ached and stung.

He flew Mnementh high and when they had achieved sufficient altitude, they hovered. He could see no Threads falling landward. Below him, the dragons ranged, high and low, searching for any sign of a burrow, alert for any suddenly toppling trees or disturbed vegetation.

"Back to the Weyr," he ordered Mnementh in a heavy sigh. He heard the bronze relay the command even as he himself was taken *between*. He was so tired he did not even visualize where—much less, when—relying on Mnementh's instinct to bring him safely home through time and space.

Honor those the dragons heed,
In thought and favor, word and deed.
Worlds are lost or worlds are saved
From those dangers dragon-braved.

Craning her neck towards the Star Stone at Benden Peak, Lessa watched from the ledge until she saw the four wings disappear from view.

Sighing deeply to quiet her inner fears, Lessa raced down the stairs to the floor of Benden Weyr. She noticed someone was building a fire by the lake and that Manora was already ordering her women around, her voice clear but calm.

Old C'gan had the weyrlings lined up. She caught the envious eyes of the newest dragonriders at the barracks' windows. They'd have time enough to fly a flaming dragon. From what F'lar had intimated, they'd have years.

She shuddered as she stepped up to the weyrlings but managed to smile at them. She gave them their orders and sent them off, checking quickly with each dragon to be sure the riders had given clear references. The Holds would shortly be stirred up to a froth.

Canth told her that there were Threads at Keroon, falling on the Keroon side of Nerat Bay. He told her that F'nor did not think two wings were enough to protect the meadowlands.

Lessa stopped in her tracks, trying to think how many wings were already out.

K'net's wing is still here, Ramoth informed her. *On the Peak.*

Lessa glanced up and saw bronze Piyanth spread his wings in answer. She told him to get *between* to Keroon, close to Nerat Bay. Obediently the entire wing rose and then disappeared.

She turned with a sigh to say something to Manora when a rush of wind and a vile stench almost overpowered her. The air above the Weyr was full of dragons. She was about to demand of Piyanth why he hadn't gone to Keroon when she realized there were far more beasts a-wing than K'net's twenty.

But you just left, she cried as she recognized the unmistakable bulk of bronze Mnementh.

That was two hours ago for us, Mnementh said with such weariness in his tone, Lessa closed her eyes in sympathy.

Some dragons were gliding in, fast. From their awkwardness it was evident they were hurt.

As one, the weyrwomen grabbed salve pots and clean rags, and beckoned the injured down. The numbing ointment was smeared on score marks where wings resembled black and red etched lace.

No matter how badly injured they might be, every rider tended his beast first.

Lessa kept one eye on Mnementh, sure that F'lar would not keep the huge bronze hovering like that if he'd been hurt. She was helping T'sum with Munth's cruelly pierced right wing when she realized the sky above the Star Stone was empty.

She forced herself to finish with Munth before she went to find the bronze and his rider. When she did locate them, she also saw Kylara smearing salve on F'lar's cheek and shoulder. She was advancing purposefully across the sands towards the pair when Canth's urgent plea reached her. She saw Mnementh's head swing upwards as he, too, caught the brown's thought.

"F'lar, Canth says they need help," Lessa cried. She didn't even notice, then, that Kylara slipped away into the busy crowd.

F'lar wasn't badly hurt. She reassured herself about that. Kylara had treated the wicked burns which looked to be shallow. Someone had found him another fur to replace the tatters of the threadbare one. He frowned, and winced because the frown creased his burned cheek. He gulped hurriedly at his *klah*.

"Mnementh, what's the tally of able-bodied? Oh, never mind, just get 'em aloft with a full load of firestone."

"You're all right?" Lessa asked, a detaining hand on his arm. He couldn't just go off like this, could he?

He smiled tiredly down at her, pressed his empty mug into her hands, giving them a quick squeeze. Then he vaulted to Mnementh's neck. Someone handed him a heavy load of sacks.

Blue, green, brown and bronze dragons lifted from the Weyr Bowl in quick order. A trifle more than sixty dragons hovered briefly above the Weyr where eighty had lingered so few minutes before.

So few dragons. So few riders. How long could they take such toll?

Canth said F'nor needed more firestone.

She looked about anxiously. None of the weyrlings were back yet from their messenger rounds. A dragon was crooning plaintively and she wheeled, but it was only young Pridith, stumbling across the Weyr to the feeding grounds, butting playfuly at Kylara as they walked. The only other dragons were injured or . . . her eyes fell on C'gan, emerging from the weyrling barracks.

"C'gan, can you and Tagath get more firestone to F'nor at Keroon?"

"Of course," the old blue rider assured her, his chest lifting with pride, his eyes flashing. She hadn't thought to send him anywhere yet he had lived his life in training for this emergency. He shouldn't be deprived of a chance at it.

She smiled her approval at his eagerness as they piled heavy sacks on Tagath's neck. The old blue dragon snorted and danced as if he were young and strong again. She gave them the references Canth had visualized to her.

She watched as the two blinked out above the Star Stone.

It isn't fair. They have all the fun, said Ramoth peevishly. Lessa saw her sunning herself on the weyr ledge, preening her enormous wings.

"You chew firestone and you're reduced to a silly green," Lessa told her weyrmate sharply. She was inwardly amused by the queen's disgruntled complaint.

She passed among the injured then. B'fol's dainty green beauty moaned and tossed her head, unable to bend one wing which had been threaded to bare cartilage. She'd be out for weeks but she had the worst injury among the dragons. Lessa looked quickly away from the misery in B'fol's worried eyes.

As she did the rounds, she realized more men were injured than beasts. Two in R'gul's wing had serious head damages. One man might lose an eye completely. Manora had dosed him unconscious with numb-weed. Another man's arm had been burned clear to the bone. Minor though most of the wounds were, the tally dismayed Lessa. How many more would be disabled at Keroon?

Out of one hundred and seventy-two dragons, fifteen already were out of action; some only for a day or two, to be sure.

A thought struck Lessa. If N'ton had actually ridden Canth, maybe he could ride out on the next dragonade on an injured man's beast, since there were more injured riders than dragons. F'lar broke traditions as he chose. Here was another one to set aside—if the dragon was agreeable.

Presuming N'ton was not the only new rider able to transfer to another beast, what good would such flexibility do in the long run? F'lar had definitely said the incursions would not be so frequent at first, when the Red Star was just beginning its fifty-turn-long circling pass of Pern. How frequent was frequent? He would know but he wasn't here.

Well, he *had* been right this morning about the appearance of Threads at Nerat so his exhaustive study of those old Records had been worthwhile.

No, that wasn't quite accurate. He had forgotten to have the men alert for signs of black dust as well as warming weather. As he had put the matter right by going *between* times, she would graciously allow him that minor error. But he did have an infuriating habit of guessing correctly. Lessa corrected herself again. He didn't guess. He studied. He planned. He thought and then he used common good sense. Like figuring out where and when Threads would strike according to entries in those smelly Records. Lessa began to feel better about their future.

Now, if he would just make the riders learn to trust their dragons' sure instinct in battle, they would keep casualties down, too.

A shriek pierced air and ear as a blue dragon emerged above the Star Stone.

"*Ramoth!*" Lessa screamed in an instinctive reaction, hardly knowing why. The queen was a-wing before the echo of her command had died. For the careening blue was obviously in grave trouble. He was trying to brake his forward speed, yet one wing would not function. His rider had slipped forward over the great shoulder, precariously clinging to his dragon's neck with one hand.

Lessa, her hands clapped over her mouth, watched fearfully. There wasn't a sound in the Bowl but the flapping of Ramoth's immense wings. The queen rose swiftly to position herself against the desperate blue, lending him wing support on the crippled side.

The watchers gasped as the rider slipped, lost his hold and fell—landing on Ramoth's shoulders.

The blue dropped like a stone. Ramoth came to a gentle stop near him, crouching low to allow the weyrfolk to remove her passenger.

It was old C'gan.

Lessa felt her stomach heave as she saw the ruin the Threads had made of the old harper's face. She dropped beside him, pillowing his head in her lap. The weyrfolk gathered in a respectful, silent circle.

Manora, her face as always serene, had tears in her eyes. She knelt and placed her hand on the old rider's heart. Concern flickered in her eyes as she looked up at Lessa. Slowly she shook her head. Then, setting her lips in a thin line, she began to apply the numbing salve.

"Too toothless old to flame and too slow to get *between*,"

C'gan mumbled, rolling his head from side to side. "Too old. 'But dragonmen must fly/When Threads are in the sky . . .' " His voice trailed off into a sigh. His eyes closed.

Lessa and Manora looked at each other in anguish. A terrible, ear-shattering note cut the silence. Tagath sprang aloft in a tremendous leap. C'gan's eyes rolled slowly open, sightless. Lessa, breath suspended, watched the blue dragon, trying to deny the inevitable as Tagath disappeared in midair.

A low moan sprang up around the weyr, like the torn, lonely cry of a keening wind. The dragons were uttering tribute.

"Is he . . . gone?" Lessa asked, although she knew.

Manora nodded slowly, tears streaming down her cheeks as she reached over to close C'gan's dead eyes.

Lessa rose slowly to her feet, motioning to some of the women to remove the old rider's body. Absently she rubbed her bloody hands dry on her skirts, trying to concentrate on what might be needed next.

Yet her mind turned back to what had just happened. A dragonrider had died. His dragon, too. The Threads had claimed one pair already. How many more would die this cruel Turn? How long could this one Weyr survive? Even after Ramoth's forty had matured, and the ones she soon would conceive, and her queen-daughters, too?

Lessa walked apart to quiet her uncertainties and ease her grief. She saw Ramoth wheel and glide aloft, to land on the Peak. One day soon, would Lessa see those golden wings laced red and black from Thread marks? Would Ramoth . . . disappear?

No, Ramoth would not. Not while Lessa lived.

F'lar had told her long ago that she must learn to look beyond the narrow confines of Hold Ruatha and mere revenge. He was, as usual, right. As Weyrwoman under his tutelage, she had further learned that living *was* more than raising dragons and spring games. Living was struggling to do something impossible—to succeed, or die, knowing you had tried!

Lessa realized that she had, at last, fully accepted her role: as Weyrwoman and mate, to help F'lar shape men and events for many Turns to come—to secure Pern against the Threads.

Lessa threw her shoulders back and lifted her chin high.

Old C'gan had had the right of it.

Dragonmen *must* fly

When Threads are in the sky!
And yet—how long would there be dragonmen?

Worlds are lost or worlds are saved
By those dangers dragon-braved.

As F'lar had predicted, the attack ended by high noon, and weary dragons and riders were welcomed by Ramoth's high-pitched trumpeting from the Peak.

Once Lessa assured herself that F'lar had no serious injury, that F'nor's were superficial and that Manora was keeping Kylara busy in the kitchens, she applied herself to organizing the care of the injured and the comfort of the worried.

As dusk fell, an uneasy peace settled on the Weyr: the quiet of minds and bodies too tired, or too hurtful, to talk. Lessa's own words mocked her as she made out the list of wounded men and beasts. Twenty-eight men or dragons were out of the air for the next Thread battle. C'gan was the only fatality but there had been four more seriously injured dragons at Keroon and seven badly scored men, out of action entirely for months to come.

Lessa crossed the Bowl to her weyr, reluctant but resigned to giving F'lar this unsettling news.

She expected to find him in the sleeping room but it was vacant. Ramoth was asleep already as Lessa passed her on the way to the Council Room, also empty. Puzzled and a little alarmed, Lessa half-ran down the steps to the Records Room, to find F'lar, haggard of face, poring over musty skins.

"What are you doing here?" she demanded, angrily. "You ought to be asleep."

"So should you," he drawled, amused.

"I was helping Manora settle the wounded—"

"Each to his own craft," F'lar drawled. But he did lean back from the table, rubbing his neck and rotating the uninjured shoulder to ease stiffened muscles.

"I couldn't sleep," he admitted. "So I thought I'd see what answers I might turn up in the Records."

"More answers? To what?" Lessa cried, exasperated with him. As if the Records ever answered anything. Obviously the tremendous responsibilities of Pern's defense against the Threads were beginning to tell on the Weyrleader. After all, there had been the stress of the first battle; not to mention the drain of the traveling *between* times itself to get to Nerat to forestall the Threads.

F'lar grinned and beckoned Lessa to sit beside him on the wall bench.

"I need the answer to the very pressing question of how one understrength Weyr can do the fighting of six."

Lessa fought the panic that rose.

"Oh, your time schedules will take care of that," she replied gallantly. "You'll be able to conserve the dragon power until the new forty can join the ranks."

F'lar raised a mocking eyebrow.

"Let us be honest between ourselves, Lessa."

"But there have been Long Intervals before," she argued, "and since Pern survived them, Pern can again."

"Before there were always six Weyrs. And twenty or so Turns before the Red Star was due to begin its Pass, the queens would start to produce enormous clutches. All the queens, not just one faithful golden Ramoth. Oh, how I curse Jora!" He slammed to his feet and started pacing, irritably brushing the lock of black hair that fell across his eyes.

Lessa was torn with the desire to comfort him and the sinking, choking fear that made it difficult to think at all.

"You were not so doubtful . . ."

He whirled back to her, ". . . Not until I had actually had an encounter with the Threads and reckoned up the numbers of injuries. That sets the odds against us. Even supposing we can mount other riders to uninjured dragons, we will be hard put to keep a continuously effective force in the air, and still maintain a ground guard." He caught her puzzled frown. "There's Nerat to be gone over on foot tomorrow. I'd be a fool indeed if I thought we'd caught and seared every Thread midair."

"Get the Holders to do that. They can't just immure themselves safely in their inner Holds and let us do all. If they hadn't been so miserly and stupid . . ."

He cut off her complaint with an abrupt gesture. "They'll do their part all right," he assured her. "I'm sending for a full Council tomorrow, all Hold Lords and all Craftmasters. But there's more to it than just marking where Threads fall. How do you destroy a burrow that's gone deep under the surface? A dragon's breath is fine for the air and surface work but no good three feet down."

"Oh, I hadn't thought of that aspect. But the fire pits . . ."

". . . Are only on the heights and around human habitations, not on the meadowlands of Keroon or on Nerat's so green rainforests."

This consideration was daunting indeed. She gave a rueful little laugh.

"Shortsighted of me to suppose our dragons are all poor Pern needs to dispatch the Threads. Yet . . ." she shrugged expressively.

"There are other methods," F'lar said, "or there were. There must have been. I have run across frequent mention of the Holds organizing ground groups and that they were armed with fire. What kind is never mentioned because it was so well known." He threw up his hands in disgust and sagged back down on the bench. "Not even five hundred dragons could have seared all the Threads that fell today. Yet *they* managed to keep Pern Thread-free."

"Pern, yes, but wasn't the southern continent lost? Or did they just have their hands too full with Pern itself?"

"No one's bothered with the southern continent in a hundred thousand Turns," F'lar snorted.

"It's on the maps," Lessa reminded him.

He scowled, disgustedly, at the Records, piled in uncommunicative stacks on the long table.

"The answer must be there. Somewhere."

There was an edge of desperation in his voice, the hint that he held himself to blame for not having discovered those elusive facts.

"Half those things couldn't be read by the man who wrote them," Lessa said tartly. "Besides that, it's been your *own* ideas that have helped us the most so far. You compiled the timemaps and look how valuable they are already."

"I'm getting too hidebound again, huh?" he asked, a half-smile tugging at one corner of his mouth.

"Undoubtedly," she assured him with more confidence than she felt. "We both know the Records are guilty of the most ridiculous omissions."

"Well said, Lessa. So, let us forget these misguiding and antiquated precepts and think up our own guides. First, we need more dragons. Second, we need them now. Third, we need something as effective as a flaming dragon to destroy Threads which have burrowed."

"Fourth, we need sleep, or we won't be able to think of anything," she added with a touch of her usual asperity.

F'lar laughed outright, hugging her.

"You've got your mind on one thing, haven't you?" he teased.

She pushed ineffectually at him, trying to escape. For a wounded, tired man, he was remarkably amorous. One with that Kylara. Imagine that woman's presumption, dressing his wounds.

"My responsibility as Weyrwoman includes care of you, the Weyrleader."

"But you spend hours with blue dragonriders and leave me to Kylara's tender ministrations."

"You didn't look as if you objected."

F'lar threw back his head and roared. "Should I open Fort Weyr and send Kylara on?" he taunted her.

"I'd as soon Kylara were Turns as well as miles away from here," Lessa snapped, thoroughly irritated.

F'lar's jaw dropped, his eyes widened. He leaped to his feet with an astonished cry.

"You've said it!"

"Said what?"

"Turns away! That's it. We'll send Kylara back, *between* times, with her queen and the new dragonets." F'lar excitedly paced the room while Lessa tried to follow his reasoning. "No, I'd better send at least one of the older bronzes. F'nor, too . . . I'd rather have F'nor in charge . . . Discreetly, of course."

"Send Kylara back . . . where to? When to?" Lessa interrupted him.

"Good point," and F'lar dragged out the ubiquitous charts. "Very good point. Where can we send them around here without causing anomalies by being present at one of the other Weyrs? The High Reaches are remote. No, we've found remains of fires there, you know, still warm, and no inkling as to who built them or why. And if we had already sent them back, they'd've been ready for today and they weren't. So they can't have been in two places already . . ." He shook his head, dazed by the paradoxes.

Lessa's eyes were drawn to the blank outline of the neglected southern continent.

"Send them there," she suggested sweetly, pointing.

"There's nothing there."

"They bring in what they need. There must be water for Threads can't devour that. We fly in whatever else is needed, fodder for the herdbeasts, grain . . ."

F'lar drew his brows together in concentration, his eyes sparkling with thought, the depression and defeat of a few moments ago forgotten.

"Threads wouldn't be there ten Turns ago. And haven't been there for close to four hundred. Ten Turns would give Pridith time to mature and have several clutches. Maybe more queens."

Then he frowned and shook his head. "No, there's no Weyr there. No Hatching Ground, no . . ."

"How do we know that?" Lessa caught him up sharply, too delighted with many aspects of this project to give it up easily. "The Records don't mention the southern continent, true, but they omit a great deal. How do we know it isn't green again in the four hundred Turns since the Threads last spun? We do know that Threads can't last long unless there is something organic on which to feed and that once they've devoured all, they dry up and blow away."

F'lar looked at her admiringly. "Now, why hasn't someone wondered about that before?"

"Too hidebound," Lessa wagged her finger at him, dedicated completely to this venture. "And there's been no need to bother with it."

"Necessity . . . or is it jealousy . . . hatches many a tough shell." There was a smile of pure malice on his face and Lessa whirled away as he reached for her.

"The good of the Weyr," she retorted.

"Furthermore, I'll send you along with F'nor tomorrow to look. Only fair, since it is your idea."

Lessa stood still. "You're not going?"

"I feel confident I can leave this project in your very capable, interested hands," he laughed and caught her against his uninjured side, smiling down at her, his eyes glowing. "I must play ruthless Weyrleader and keep the Hold Lords from slamming shut their Inner Doors. And I'm hoping," he raised his head, frowning slightly, "one of the Craftmasters may know the solution to the third problem . . . getting rid of Thread burrows."

"But . . ."

"The trip will give Ramoth something to stop her fuming." He pressed the girl's slender body more closely to him, his full attention at last on her odd, delicate face. "Lessa, you are my fourth problem." He bent to kiss her.

At the sound of hurried steps in the passageway, F'lar scowled irritably, releasing her.

"At this hour?" he muttered, ready to reprove the intruder scathingly. "Who goes there?"

"F'lar?" It was F'nor's voice, anxious, hoarse.

The look on F'lar's face told Lessa that not even his half brother would be spared a reprimand and it pleased her irrationally. But the moment F'nor burst into the room, both Weyrleader and Weyrwoman were stunned silent. There was something subtly wrong with the brown rider. And, as the man blurted out his incoherent message, the difference suddenly registered in Lessa's mind. He was tanned! He wore no bandages and hadn't the slightest trace of the Thread mark along his cheek that she had tended this evening!

"F'lar, it's not working out! You can't be alive in two times at once!" F'nor was exclaiming distractedly. He staggered against the wall, grabbing the sheer rock to hold himself upright. There were deep circles under his eyes, visible despite the tan. "I don't know how much longer we can last like this. We're all affected. Some days not as badly as others."

"I don't understand."

"Your dragons are all right," F'nor assured the Weyrleader with a bitter laugh. "It doesn't bother them. They keep all their wits about them. But their riders . . . all the weyrfolk. We're shadows, half-alive, like dragonless men, part of us gone forever. Except Kylara." His face contorted with intense dislike. "All she wants to do is go back and watch herself. The woman's egomania will destroy us all, I'm afraid."

His eyes suddenly lost focus and he swayed wildly. His eyes widened and his mouth fell open. "I can't stay. I'm here already. Too close. Makes it twice as bad. But I had to warn you. I promise, F'lar, we'll stay as long as we can but it won't be much longer . . . so it won't be long enough, but we tried. We tried!"

Before F'lar could move, the brown rider whirled and ran, half-crouched, from the room.

"But he hasn't gone yet!" Lessa gasped. "He hasn't even gone yet!"

F'lar stared after his half brother, his brows contracting with the keen anxiety he felt.

"What can have happened?" Lessa demanded of the Weyrleader. "We haven't even told F'nor. We ourselves just finished considering the idea of exploring the southern continent; to see if we could send dragons back and give Pridith a chance to lay a few clutches. And he looked so tanned and healthy." Her hand flew to her own cheek. "And the Threadmark—I dressed it myself tonight—it's gone. Gone. So he's been gone a long while." She sank down to the bench.

"However, he has come back. So he did go," F'lar remarked slowly in a reflective tone of voice. "Yet we now know the venture is not entirely successful even before it begins. And knowing this we have sent him back ten Turns for whatever good it is doing." F'lar paused thoughtfully. "Consequently we have no alternative but to continue with the experiment."

"But what could be going wrong?"

"I think I know and there is no remedy." He sat down beside her, his eyes intent on hers. "Lessa, you were very upset when you got back from going *between* to Ruatha that first time. But I think now it was more than just the shock of seeing Fax's men invading your own Hold or in thinking your return might have been responsible for that disaster. I think it has to do with being in two times at once." He hesitated again, trying to understand this immense new concept even as he voiced it.

Lessa regarded him with such awe that he found himself laughing with embarrassment.

"It's unnerving under any conditions," he went on, "to think of returning and seeing a younger self."

"That must be what he meant about Kylara," Lessa gasped, "about her wanting to go back and watch herself . . . as a child. Oh, that wretched girl!" Lessa was filled with anger for Kylara's self-absorption. "Wretched selfish creature. She'll ruin everything."

"Not yet," F'lar reminded her. "Look, although F'nor warned us that the situation in his time is getting desperate, he didn't tell us how much he was able to accomplish. But you noticed that his scar had healed to invisibility, consequently some Turns must have elapsed. Even if Pridith lays only one good-sized clutch, even if just the forty of Ramoth's are mature enough to fight in three days' time, we have accomplished something. Therefore, Weyrwoman," and he noticed how she straightened up at the sound of her title, "we must disregard F'nor's return. When you fly to the southern continent tomorrow, make no allusion to it. Do you understand?"

Lessa nodded gravely and then gave a little sigh. "I don't know if I'm happy or disappointed to realize, even before we get there tomorrow, that the southern continent obviously will support a Weyr," she said with dismay. "It was kind of exciting to wonder."

"Either way," F'lar told her with a sardonic smile, "we have found only part of the answers to problems one and two."

"Well, you'd better answer number four right now!" Lessa suggested. "Decisively!"

Weaver, Miner, Harper, Smith,
Tanner, Farmer, Herdsman, Lord,
Gather wingspeed, listen well
To the Weyrman's urgent word.

They both managed to guard against any reference to his premature return when they spoke to F'nor the next morning. F'lar asked brown Canth to send his rider to the queen's weyr as soon as he awoke and was pleased to see F'nor almost immediately. If the brown rider noticed the curiously intent stare Lessa gave his bandaged face, he gave no sign of it. As a matter of fact, the moment F'lar outlined the bold venture of scouting the southern continent with the possibility of starting a weyr ten Turns back in time, F'nor forgot all about his wounds.

"I'll go willingly only if you send T'bor along with Kylara. I'm not waiting till N'ton and his bronze are big enough to take her on. T'bor and she are as . . ." F'nor broke off with a grimace in Lessa's direction, ". . . well, they're as near a pair as can be. I don't object to being . . . importuned, but there are limits to what a man is willing to do out of loyalty to dragonkind.''

F'lar barely managed to restrain the amusement he felt over F'nor's reluctance. Kylara tried her wiles on every rider and, because F'nor had not been amenable, she was determined to succeed with him.

''I hope two bronzes are enough. Pridith may have a mind of her own, come mating time.''

''You can't turn a brown into a bronze!'' F'nor exclaimed with such dismay F'lar could no longer restrain himself.

''Oh, stop it!'' And that touched off Lessa's laughter. ''You're as bad a pair,'' he snapped, getting to his feet. ''If we're going south, Weyrwoman, we'd better get started. Particularly if we're going to give this laughing maniac a chance to compose himself before the solemn Lords descend. I'll get provisions from Manora. Well, Lessa? *Are* you coming with me?''

Muffling her laughter, Lessa grabbed up her furred flying cloak and followed him. At least, the adventure was starting off well.

F'lar grabbed the pitcher of *klah* and his cup and adjourned to the Council Room, debating whether to tell the Lords and Craftmasters of this southern venture or not. The dragon's ability to fly *between* times as well as places was not yet well known. The Lords might not yet realize it had been used the previous day to forestall the Threads. If he could be sure that project was going to be successful, well, it would add an optimistic note to the meeting.

Let the charts, with the waves and times of the Thread attacks clearly visible, reassure the Lords.

The visitors were not long in assembling. Nor were they all successful in hiding their apprehension and the shock they had received now that Threads had again spun down from the Red Star to menace all life on Pern. This was going to be a difficult session, F'lar decided grimly. He had a fleeting wish, which he quickly suppressed, that he had gone with F'nor and Lessa to the southern continent. Instead, he bent with apparent industry to the charts before him.

Soon there were but two more to come, Meron of Nabol (whom he would have liked not to include for the man was a troublemaker) and Lytol of Ruatha. He had sent for Lytol last because he did not wish Lessa to encounter the man. She was still overly and, to his mind, foolishly, sensitive over resigning her claim to Ruatha Hold for Lady Gemma's posthumous son. Lytol as Warder of Ruatha had a place in this conference. The man was also an ex-dragonman, and his return to the Weyr was painful enough without Lessa compounding it with her resentment. Lytol had turned to the Weaver's craft after his dragon's death and his compulsory exile from the Weyr. He was, with the exception of young Larad of Telgar, the Weyr's most valuable ally.

S'lel came in with Meron a step behind him. The Holder was furious at this summons; it showed in his walk, in his eyes, in his haughty bearing. But he was also as inquisitive as he was devious. He nodded only to Larad among the Lords and took the seat left vacant for him by Larad's side. Meron's manner made it obvious that that place was too close to F'lar by half a room.

The Weyrleader acknowledged S'lel's salute and indicated the bronze rider should be seated. F'lar had given thought to the seating arrangements in the Council Room, carefully interspersing brown and bronze dragonriders with Holders and Craftsmen. There was now barely room to move in the generously proportioned cavern, but there was also no room in which to draw daggers if tempers got hot.

A hush fell on the gathering and F'lar looked up to see that the stocky, glowering ex-dragonman from Ruatha had stopped at the threshold of the Council. He slowly brought his hand up in a respectful salute to the Weyrleader. As F'lar returned the salute, he noticed that the tic in Lytol's left cheek jumped almost continuously.

Lytol's eyes, dark with pain and inner unquiet, ranged the room. He nodded to the members of his former wing, to Larad and Zurg, head of his own Weaver's Craft. Stiff-legged he walked to the remaining seat, murmuring a greeting to T'sum on his left.

F'lar rose.

"I appreciate your coming, good Lords and Craftmasters. The Threads spin once again. The first attack has been met and seared from the sky. Lord Vincet," and the worried Holder of Nerat looked up in alarm, "we have dispatched a patrol to the rainforest to do a low-flight sweep to make certain there are no burrows."

Vincet swallowed nervously, his face paling at the thought of what Threads could do to his fertile, lush holdings.

"We shall need your best junglemen to help . . ."

"Help . . . but you said . . . the Threads were seared in the sky?"

"There is no point in taking the slightest chance," F'lar replied, implying the patrol was only a precaution instead of the necessity he knew it would be.

Vincet gulped, glancing anxiously around the room for sympathy—and found none. Everyone would soon be in his position.

"There is a patrol due at Keroon and at Igen," and F'lar looked first at Lord Corman, then Lord Banger who gravely nodded. "Let me say, by way of reassurance, that there will be no further attacks for three days and four hours." F'lar tapped the appropriate chart. "The Threads will begin approximately here on Telgar, drift westward through the southernmost portion of Crom, which is mountainous, and on, through Ruatha and the southern end of Nabol."

"How can you be so certain of that?"

F'lar recognized the contemptuous voice of Meron of Nabol.

"The Threads do not fall like a child's tumble-sticks, Lord Meron," F'lar replied. "They fall in a definitely predictable pattern; the attacks last exactly six hours. The intervals between attacks will gradually shorten over the next few Turns as the Red Star draws closer. Then, for about forty full Turns, as the Red Star swings past and around us, the attacks occur every fourteen hours, marching across our world in a timetable fashion."

"So *you* say," Meron sneered and there was a low mumble of support.

"So the Teaching Ballads say," Larad put in firmly.

Meron glared at Telgar's Lord and went on, "I recall another of your predictions about how the Threads were supposed to begin falling right after Solstice."

"Which they did," F'lar interrupted him. "As black dust in the Northern Holds. For the reprieve we've had, we can thank our lucky stars that we have had an unusually hard and long Cold Turn."

"Dust?" demanded Nessel of Crom. "That dust was

Threads?'' The man was one of Fax's blood connections and under Meron's influence: an older man who had learned lessons from his conquering relative's bloody ways and had not the wit to improve on or alter the original. ''My Hold is still blowing with them. They're dangerous?''

F'lar shook his head emphatically. ''How long has the black dust been blowing in your Hold? Weeks? Done any harm yet?''

Nessel frowned.

''I'm interested in your charts, Weyrleader,'' Larad of Telgar said smoothly. ''Will they give us an accurate idea of how often we may expect Threads to fall in our own Holds?''

''Yes. You may also anticipate that the dragonmen will arrive shortly before the invasion is due,'' F'lar went on. ''However, additional measures of your own are necessary and it is for this that I called the Council.''

''Wait a minute,'' Corman of Keroon growled. ''I want a copy of those fancy charts of yours for my own. I want to know what those bands and wavy lines really mean. I want . . .''

''Naturally you'll have a time-table of your own. I mean to impose on Masterharper Robinton,'' and F'lar nodded respectfully towards that Craftmaster, ''to oversee the copying and make sure everyone understands the timing involved.''

Robinton, a tall, gaunt man with a lined, saturnine face, bowed deeply. A slight smile curved his wide lips at the now hopeful glances favored him by the Hold Lords. His craft, like that of the dragonmen, had been much mocked and this new respect amused him. He was a man with a keen eye for the ridiculous, and an active imagination. The circumstances in which doubting Pern found itself were too ironic not to appeal to his innate sense of justice. He now contented himself with a deep bow and a mild phrase.

''Truly all shall pay heed to the master.'' His voice was deep, his words enunciated with no provincial slurring.

F'lar, about to speak, looked sharply at Robinton as he caught the double barb of that single line. Larad, too, looked around at the Masterharper, clearing his throat hastily.

''We shall have our charts,'' Larad said, forestalling Meron who had opened his mouth to speak, ''we shall have the Dragonmen when the Threads spin. What are these additional measures? And why are they necessary?''

* * *

All eyes were on F'lar again.

"We have one Weyr where six once flew."

"But word is that Ramoth has hatched forty more," someone in the back of the room declared. "And why did you Search out still more of our young men?"

"Forty as yet unmatured dragons," F'lar said aloud, privately hoping that this southern venture would still work out. There was real fear in that man's voice. "They grow well and quickly. Just at present, while the Threads do not strike with great frequency as the Red Star begins its Pass, our Weyr is sufficient . . . if we have your cooperation on the ground. Tradition is that," and he nodded tactfully toward Robinton, the dispenser of Traditional usage, "you Holders are responsible for only your dwellings which, of course, are adequately protected by firepits and raw stone. However, it is spring and our heights have been allowed to grow wild with vegetation. Arable land is blossoming with crops. This presents a vast acreage vulnerable to the Threads which one Weyr, at this time, is not able to patrol without severely draining the vitality of our dragons and riders."

At this candid admission, a frightened and angry mutter spread rapidly throughout the room.

"Ramoth rises to mate again soon," F'lar continued, in a matter-of-fact way. "Of course in other times, the queens started producing heavy clutches many Turns before the critical solstice, and more queens. Unfortunately, Jora was ill and old, and Nemorth intractable. The matter . . ." He was interrupted.

"You dragonmen with your high and mighty airs will bring destruction on us all!"

"You've yourselves to blame," Robinton's voice stabbed across the ensuing shouts. "Admit it one and all! You've paid less honor to the Weyr than you would your watch-wher's kennel—and that not much! But now the thieves are on the heights and you are screaming because the poor reptile is nigh to death from neglect. Beat him, will you, when you exiled him to his kennel because he tried to warn you, tried to get you to prepare against the invaders? It's on *your* conscience, not the Weyrleader's nor the dragonriders', who had honestly done their duty these hundreds of Turns in keeping dragonkind alive . . . against all your protests. How many of you," and his tone was scathing, "have been generous in thought and favor towards dragonkind? Even since I became Master of my craft, how often have my Harpers told me of being beaten for singing the old songs as is their duty? You earn only the right, good Lords and Craftsmen, to squirm inside your stony Holds and writhe as your crops die aborning." He rose.

" 'No Threads will fall. It's a Harper's winter tale,' " he whined, in faultless imitation of Nessel. " 'These dragonmen leech us of heir and harvest,' " and his voice took on the constricted, insinuating tenor that could only be Meron's. "And now the truth is as bitter as a brave man's fear and as difficult as mock-weed to swallow. For all the honor you've done them, the dragonmen should leave you to be spun on the Threads' distaff."

"Bitra, Lemos and I," spoke up Raid, the wiry Lord of Benden, his blunt chin lifted belligerently, "have always done our duty to the Weyr."

Robinton swung round to him, his eyes flashing as he gave that speaker a long, slow look.

"Aye, and you have. Of all the Great Holds, you three have been loyal. But you others," and his voice rose indignantly, "as spokesmen for my Craft, I know, to the last full stop in the score, your opinion of dragonkind. I heard the first whisper of your attempt to ride out against the Weyr." He laughed harshly and pointed a long finger at Vincet. "Where would you be today, good Lord Vincet, if the Weyr had *not* sent you packing back, hoping your ladies would be returned you? All of you," and his accusing finger marked each of the Lords of that abortive effort, "actually rode against the Weyr because . . . 'there . . . were . . . no . . . more . . . Threads!' "

He planted his fists on either hip and glared at the assembly. F'lar wanted to cheer. It was easy to see why the man was Masterharper and he thanked circumstances that such a man was the Weyr's partisan.

"And now, at this critical moment, you actually have the incredible presumption to protest against any measure the Weyr suggests?" Robinton's supple voice oozed derision and amazement. "Attend what the Weyrleader says and spare him your petty carpings!" He snapped those words out as a father might enjoin an erring child. "You were," and he switched to the mildest of polite conversational tones as he addressed

F'lar, "I believe asking our cooperation, good F'lar? In what capacities?"

F'lar hastily cleared his throat.

"I shall require that the Holds police their own fields and woods, during the attacks if possible, definitely once the Threads have passed. All burrows which might land must be found, marked and destroyed. The sooner they are located, the easier it is to be rid of them."

"There's no time to dig firepits through all the lands . . . we'll lose half our growing space . . ." Nessel exclaimed.

"There were other ways, used in olden times, which I believe our Mastersmith might know," and F'lar gestured politely toward Fandarel, the archetype of his profession if ever such existed.

The Smith Craftmaster was by several inches the tallest man in the Council Room, his massive shoulders and heavily muscled arms pressed against his nearest neighbors, although he had made an effort not to crowd against anyone. He rose, a giant tree-stump of a man, hooking thumbs like beast-horns in the thick belt that spanned his waistless midsection. His voice, by no means sweet after Turns of bellowing above roaring hearths and hammers, was, by comparison to Robinton's superb delivery, a diluted, unsupported light baritone.

"There were machines, that much is true," he allowed in deliberate, thoughtful tones. "My father told me of them as a curiosity of the Craft. There may be sketches in the Hall. There may not. Such things do not keep on skins for long," and he cast an oblique look under beetled brows at the Tanner Craftmaster.

"It is our own hides we must worry about preserving," F'lar remarked to forestall any inter-craft disputes.

Fandarel grumbled in his throat in such a way that F'lar was not certain whether the sound was the man's laughter or a guttural agreement.

"I shall consider the matter. So shall all my fellow craftsmen," Fandarel assured the Weyrleader. "To sear Threads from the ground without damaging the soil may not be so easy. There are, it is true, fluids which burn and sear. We use an acid to etch design on dagger and ornamental metals. We of the Craft call it agenothree. There is also the black heavy-water that lies on the surface of pools in Igen and Boll. It burns hot and long. And, if as you say, the Cold Turn made the Threads break into dust, perhaps ice from the coldest northlands might freeze and break grounded Threads. However, the problem is to bring such to the Threads where they fall since they will not oblige us by falling where we want them . . ." he screwed up his face in a grimace.

F'lar stared at him, surprised. Did the man realize how humorous he was? No, he was speaking with sincere concern. Now the Mastersmith scratched his head, his tough fingers making audible grating sounds along his coarse hair and heat-toughened scalp.

"A nice problem. A nice problem," he mused, undaunted. "I shall give it every attention." He sat down, the heavy bench creaking under his weight.

The Masterfarmer raised his hand tentatively.

"When I became Craftmaster, I recall coming across a reference to the sandworms of Igen. They were once cultivated as a protective . . ."

"Never heard Igen produced anything useful except heat and sand . . ." quipped someone.

"We need every suggestion," F'lar said sharply, trying to identify that heckler. "Please find that reference, Craftmaster. Lord Banger of Igen, find me some of those sandworms!"

Banger, equally surprised that his arid Hold had a hidden asset, nodded vigorously.

"Until we have more efficient ways of killing Threads, all Holders must be organized on the ground during attacks, to spot and mark burrows, to set firestone to burn in them. I do not wish any man to be scored but we know how quickly Threads burrow deep and no burrow can be left to multiply. You stand to lose more," and he gestured emphatically at the Holder Lords, "than any others. Guard not just yourselves, for a burrow on one man's border may grow across to his neighbor's. Mobilize every man, woman and child, farm and crafthold. Do it now."

The Council Room was fraught with tension and stunned reflection until Zurg, the Masterweaver, rose to speak.

"My Craft, too, has something to offer . . . which is only fair since we deal with thread each day of our lives . . . in regard to the ancient methods." Zurg's voice was light and dry and his eyes, in their creases of spare, lined flesh, were busy, darting from one face in his audience to another. "In Ruath Hold I once saw upon the wall . . . where the tapestry now resides, who knows? . . ." and he slyly glanced at Meron of Nabol and then Bargen of the High Reaches who had succeeded to Fax's title there. "The work was as old as dragonkind and showed, among other things, a man on foot, carrying upon his back a curious contraption. He held within his hand a rounded, sword-long object from which tongues of flame . . . magnificently woven in the orange-red dyes now lost to us . . . spouted towards the ground. Above, of course, were dragons in close formation, bronzes predominating . . . again we've lost that true dragon-bronze shade. Consequently I remember the work as much for what we now lack as for its subject matter."

"A flamethrower?" the Smith rumbled. "A flamethrower," he repeated with a falling inflection. "A flamethrower," he murmured thoughtfully, his heavy brows drawn into a titanic scowl. "A thrower of what sort of flame? It requires thought." He lowered his head and didn't speak, so engrossed in the required thought that he lost interest in the rest of the discussions.

"Yes, good Zurg, there have been many tricks of every trade lost in recent Turns," F'lar commented sardonically. "If we wish to continue living, such knowledge must be revived . . . fast. I would particularly like to recover the tapestry of which Master Zurg speaks."

F'lar looked significantly at those Hold Lords who had quarreled over Fax's seven Holds after that usurper's death in Ruath Great Hall.

"It may save all of you much loss. I suggest that it appear at Ruatha, at Zurg's or Fandarel's Crafthall. Whichever is most convenient."

There was some shuffling of feet but no admission of ownership.

"It might then be returned to Fay's son who is now Ruatha's Lord," F'lar added, wryly amused at such magnanimous justice.

Lytol, Ruatha's Warder, snorted softly and glowered round the room. F'lar supposed Lytol to be amused and experienced a fleeting regret for the orphaned Gaxom, reared by such a cheerless, if scrupulously honest, guardian.

"If I may, Lord Weyrleader," Robinton broke in, "we

might all benefit, as your maps prove to us, from research in our own records.'' He smiled suddenly, an unexpectedly embarrassed smile. ''I own I find myself in some disgrace for we Harpers have let slip unpopular ballads and skimped on some of the longer Teaching Sagas . . . for lack of listeners and, occasionally, in the interest of preserving our skins.''

F'lar stifled a laugh. Robinton was a genius.

''I must see the Ruathan tapestry,'' Fandarel suddenly boomed out.

''I'm sure it will be in your hands very soon,'' F'lar assured him with more confidence than he dared feel. ''My Lords, there is much to be done. Now that you understand what we all face, I leave it in your hands as leaders in your separate Holds and crafts how best to organize your own people. Craftsmen, turn your best minds to our special problems: review all records which might turn up something to our purpose. Lords Telgar, Crom, Ruatha and Nabol, I shall be with you in three days. Nerat, Keroon and Igen, I am at your disposal to help destroy any burrow on your lands. While we have the Masterminer here, tell him your needs. How stands your craft?''

''Happy to be so busy at our trade, Weyrleader,'' piped up the Masterminer.

Just then F'lar caught sight of F'nor, hovering about in the shadows of the hallway, trying to catch his eye. The brown rider wore an exultant grin and it was obvious he was bursting with news.

F'lar wondered how they could have returned so swiftly from the southern continent and then he realized that F'nor—again—was tanned. He gave a jerk of his head, indicating that F'nor take himself off to the sleeping quarters and wait.

''Lords and Craftmasters, a dragonet will be at the disposal of each of you for messages and transportation. Now, good morning.''

He strode out of the Council Room, up the passageway into the queen's weyr, and parted the still swinging curtains into the sleeping room just as F'nor was pouring himself a cup of wine.

''Success!'' F'nor cried as the Weyrleader entered. ''Though how you knew to send just thirty-two candidates I'll never understand. I thought you were insulting our noble Pridith.

But thirty-two eggs she laid in four days. It was all I could do to keep from riding out when the first appeared.''

F'lar responded with hearty congratulations, relieved that there would be at least that much benefit from this apparently ill-fated venture. Now, all he had to figure out was how much longer F'nor had stayed south until his frantic visit the night before. For there were no worry lines or strain in F'nor's grinning, well-tanned face.

''No queen egg?'' asked F'lar hopefully. With thirty-two in the one experiment, perhaps they could send a second queen back and try again.

F'nor's face lengthened. ''No, and I was sure there would be. But there are fourteen bronzes, which outmatches Ramoth there,'' he added proudly.

''Indeed it does. How goes the Weyr otherwise?''

F'nor frowned, shaking his head against an inner bewilderment. ''Kylara's . . . well, she's a problem. Stirs up trouble constantly. T'bor leads a sad time with her and he's so touchy everyone keeps a distance from him.'' F'nor brightened a little. ''Young N'ton is shaping up into a fine wingleader and his bronze may outfly T'bor's Orth when Pridith flies to mate the next time. Not that I'd wish Kylara on N'ton . . . or anyone.''

''No trouble then with supplies?''

F'nor laughed outright. ''If you hadn't made it so plain we must not communicate with you here, we could supply you with fruits and fresh greens that are superior to anything in the north. We eat the way dragonmen should! Really, F'lar, we must consider a supply Weyr down there. Then we shall never have to worry about tithing trains and . . .''

''In good time. Get back now. You know you must keep these visits short.''

F'nor grimaced. ''Oh, it's not so bad. I'm not here in this time anyway.''

''True,'' F'lar agreed, ''but don't mistake the time and come while you're still here.''

''Hm-m-m? Oh, yes, that's right. I forget time is creeping for us and speeding for you. Well, I shan't be back again till Pridith lays the second clutch.''

With a cheerful good-bye, F'nor strode out of the weyr. F'lar watched him thoughtfully as he slowly retraced his steps to the Council Room. Thirty-two new dragons, fourteen of them bronzes, was no small gain and seemed worth the hazard. Or would the hazard wax greater?

Someone cleared his throat deliberately. F'lar looked up to see Robinton standing in the archway that led to the Council Room.

"Before I can copy and instruct others about those maps, Weyrleader, I must myself understand them completely. I took the liberty of remaining behind."

"You make a good champion, Masterharper."

"You have a noble cause, Weyrleader," and then Robinton's eyes glinted maliciously. "I've been begging the Egg for an opportunity to speak out to so noble an audience."

"A cup of wine first?"

"Benden grapes are the envy of Pern."

"If one has the palate for such a delicate bouquet."

"It is carefully cultivated by the knowledgeable."

F'lar wondered when the man would stop playing with words. He had more on his mind than studying the time charts.

"I have in mind a ballad which, for lack of explanation, I had set aside when I became the Master of my Crafthall," he said judiciously after an appreciative savoring of his wine. "It is an uneasy song, both the tune and the words. One develops, as a Harper must, a certain sensitivity for what will be received and what will be rejected . . . forcefully," and he winced in retrospect. "I found that this ballad unsettled singer as well as audience and retired it from use. Now, like that tapestry, I think it bears rediscovery."

After his death, C'gan's instrument had been hung on the Council Room wall till a new Weyrsinger could be chosen. The guitar was very old, its wood thin. Old C'gan had kept it well-tuned and covered. The Masterharper handled it now with reverence, lightly stroking the strings to hear the tone, raising his eyebrows at the fine voice of the instrument.

He plucked a chord, a dissonance. F'lar wondered if the instrument were out of tune or if the Harper had, by some chance, struck the wrong string. But Robinton repeated the odd dischord, then modulated into a weird minor that was somehow more disturbing than the first notes.

"I told you it was an uneasy song. And I wonder if you

know the answers to the questions it asks. For I've turned the puzzle over in my mind many times of late."

Then abruptly he shifted from the spoken to the sung tone.

"Gone away, gone ahead,
Echoes roll unanswered.
Empty, open, dusty, dead,
Why have all the weyrfolk fled?

Where have dragons gone together?
Leaving weyrs to wind and weather?
Setting herdbeasts free of tether?
Gone, our safeguards, gone, but whither?

Have they flown to some new weyr
Where cruel Threads some others fear?
Are they worlds away from here?
Why, oh why, the empty Weyr?"

The last plaintive chord reverberated.

"Of course, you realize that that song was first recorded in the Craft-annals some four hundred Turns ago," Robinton said lightly, cradling the guitar in both arms. "The Red Star had just passed beyond attack-proximity. The people had ample reason to be stunned and worried over the sudden loss of the populations of five Weyrs. Oh, I imagine at the time they had any one of a number of explanations but none . . . not one explanation . . . is recorded." Robinton paused significantly.

"I have found none recorded either," F'lar replied. "As a matter of fact, I had all the Records brought here from the other Weyrs—in order to compile accurate attack time-tables. And those other Weyr Records simply end," F'lar made a chopping gesture with one hand. "In Benden's records, there is no mention of sickness, death, fire, disaster; not one word of explanation for the sudden lapse of the usual intercourse between the Weyrs. Benden's records continue blithely, but only for Benden. There is one entry that pertains to the mass disappearance . . . the initiation of a Pern-wide patrol routing, not just Benden's immediate responsibility. And that is all."

"Strange," Robinton mused. "Once the danger from the Red Star was past, the dragons and riders may have gone *between* to ease the drain on the Holds. But I simply cannot believe that. Our Craft-records do mention that harvests were bad and that there had been several natural catastrophes . . . other than the Threads. Men may be gallant and your breed the most gallant of all, but mass suicide? I simply do not accept that explanation . . . not for dragonmen."

"My thanks," F'lar said with mild irony.

"Don't mention it," Robinton replied graciously.

F'lar chuckled appreciatively. "I see we have been too weyrbound as well as too hidebound."

Robinton drained his cup, and looked at it mournfully until F'lar refilled it.

"Well, your isolation served some purpose, you know, and you handled that uprising of the Lords magnificently. I nearly choked to death laughing," Robinton remarked, grinning broadly. "Stealing their women in the flash of a dragon's breath!" He chuckled again and suddenly sobered, looking F'lar straight in the eye. "Accustomed as I am to hearing what a man does *not* say aloud, I suspect there is much you glossed over in that Council Meeting. You may be sure of my discretion . . . and . . . you may be sure of my wholehearted support and that of my not ineffectual Craft. To be blunt, how may my Harpers aid you?" and he strummed a vigorous marching air. "Stir men's pulses with ballads of past glories and success?" The tune, under his flashing fingers, changed abruptly to a stern but determined rhythm. "Strengthen their mental and physical sinews for hardship?"

"If all your harpers could stir men as you yourself do, I should have no worries that five hundred or so additional dragons would not immediately end."

"Oho, then despite your brave words and marked charts, the situation is"—a dissonant twang on the guitar accented his final words—"more desperate than you carefully did not say."

"It may be."

"The flamethrowers old Zurg remembered and Fandarel must reconstruct? Will they tip the scales?"

F'lar regarded this clever man thoughtfully, and made a quick decision.

"Even Igen's sandworms will help but as the world turns and the Red Star nears, the interval between daily attacks shortens and we have only seventy-two new dragons to add to those we had yesterday. One is now dead and several will not fly for several weeks."

"Seventy-two?" Robinton caught him up sharply. "Ramoth hatched but forty and they are still too young to eat firestone."

F'lar outlined F'nor and Lessa's expedition, taking place at that moment. He went on to F'nor's reappearance and warning, as well as the fact that the experiment had been successful in part with the hatching of thirty-two new dragons for Pridith's first clutch.

Robinton caught him up. "How can F'nor already have returned when you haven't heard from Lessa and him that there is a breeding place on the southern continent?"

"Dragons can go *between* times as well as places. They go easily from a when to a *where*."

Robinton's eyes widened as he digested this astonishing news.

"That is how we forestalled the attack on Nerat yesterday morning. We jumped back two hours *between* times to meet the Threads as they fell."

"You can actually jump backwards? How far back?"

"I don't know. Lessa, when I was teaching her to fly Ramoth, inadvertently returned to Ruath Hold, to the dawn twelve Turns ago when Fax's men invaded from the heights. When she returned to the present, I attempted a *between* times jump of some ten Turns. To the dragons it is a simple matter to go *between* times or spaces, but there appears to be a terrific drain on the rider. Yesterday, by the time we returned from Nerat and had to go on to Keroon, I felt as though I had been pounded flat and left to dry for a summer on Igen plain." F'lar shook his head. "We have obviously succeeded in sending Kylara, Pridith and the others ten Turns *between*, because F'nor has already reported to me that he has been there several Turns. The drain on humans, however, is becoming more and more marked. However, even seventy-two more mature dragons will be a help."

"Send a rider ahead in time and see if it is sufficient," Robinton suggested helpfully. "Save you a few days worrying."

"I don't know how to get some-*when* which has not yet happened. You must give your dragon reference points, you know. How can you refer him to times which have not yet occurred?"

"You've got an imagination. Project it."

"And perhaps lose a dragon when I have none to spare? No, I must continue . . . because obviously I have, judging by F'nor's returns . . . as I decided to start. Which reminds me, I must give orders to start packing. Then I shall go over the time charts with you."

It was just after the noonmeal, which Robinton took with the Weyrleader, before the Masterharper was confident he understood the charts and left to begin their copying.

Across a waste of lonely tossing sea,
Where no dragonwings had lately spread,
Flew a gold and a sturdy brown in spring,
Searching if a land be dead.

As Ramoth and Canth bore Lessa and F'nor up to the Star Stone, they saw the first of the Hold Lords and Craftmasters arriving for the Council.

In order to get back to the southern continent of ten Turns ago, Lessa and F'nor had decided it was easiest to transfer first *between* times to the Weyr of ten Turns back which F'nor remembered. Then they would go *between* places to a seapoint just off the coast of the neglected southern continent which was as close to it as the Records gave any references.

F'nor put Canth in mind of a particular day he remembered ten Turns back and Ramoth picked up the references from the brown's mind. The awesome cold of *between* times took Lessa's breath away and it was with intense relief she caught a glimpse of the normal weyr activity before the dragons took them *between* places to hover over the turgid sea.

Beyond them, smudged purple on this overcast and gloomy day, lurked the southern continent. Lessa felt a new anxiety replace the uncertainty of the temporal displacement. Ramoth beat forward with great sweeps of her wings, making for the distant coast. Canth gallantly tried to maintain a matching speed.

"He's only a brown," Lessa scolded her golden queen.

If he is flying with me, Ramoth replied coolly, *he must stretch his wings a little.*

Lessa grinned, thinking very privately that Ramoth was still piqued that she had not been able to fight with her weyrmates. All the males would have a hard time with her for a while.

They saw the flock of wherries first and realized that there would have to be some vegetation on the continent. Wherries needed greens to live although they could subsist on a few grubs if necessary.

Lessa had Canth relay questions to his rider. "If the southern continent were rendered barren by the Threads, how did new growth start? Where did the wherries come from?"

"Ever notice the seed pods split open and the flakes carried away by the winds? Ever notice that wherries fly south after the autumn solstice?"

"Yes, but . . ."

"Yes, but!"

"But the land was thread-bared!"

"In less than four hundred Turns even the scorched hill tops of our continent begin to sprout in the springtime," F'nor replied by way of Canth, "so it is easy to assume the southern continent could revive, too."

Lessa was dubious and berated herself sternly, forcing her mind from F'nor's cryptic warning.

Even at the pace Ramoth set, it took time to reach the jagged shoreline with its forbidding cliffs, stark stone in the sullen light. Lessa groaned inwardly but urged Ramoth higher to see over the masking highlands. All seemed gray and desolate from that altitude.

Suddenly the sun broke through the cloud cover and the gray dissolved into dense greens and browns, living colors, the live greens of lush tropical growth, the browns of vigorous trees and vines. Lessa's cry of triumph was echoed by F'nor's hurrah and the brass voices of the dragons. Wherries, startled by the unusual sound, rose up in alarm from their perches.

Beyond the headland, the land sloped away to jungle and grassy plateau, similar to mid-Boll. Though they searched all morning, they found no hospitable cliffs wherein to found a new Weyr. Was that a contributing factor in the southern venture's failure, Lessa wondered?

Discouraged, they landed on a high plateau by a small lake. The weather was warm but not oppressive and while F'nor and Lessa ate their noonday meal, the two dragons wallowed in the water, refreshing themselves.

Lessa felt uneasy and had little appetite for the meat and bread. She noticed F'nor was restless, too, shooting surreptitious glances around the lake and the jungle verge.

"What under the sun are we expecting? Wherries don't charge and wild whers would come nowhere near a dragon. We're ten Turns before the Red Star so there can't be any Threads."

F'nor shrugged, grimacing sheepishly as he tossed his unfinished bread back into the food pouch.

"Place just feels so empty, I guess," he tendered, glancing around. He spotted ripe fruit hanging from a moonflower vine. "Now that looks familiar and good enough to eat, without tasting like dust in the mouth."

He climbed nimbly and snagged the orange-red fruit down.

"Smells right, feels ripe, looks ripe," he announced and deftly sliced the fruit open. Grinning, he handed Lessa the first slice, carving another for himself. He lifted it challengingly. "Let us eat and die together!"

She couldn't help but laugh and saluted him back. They bit into the succulent flesh simultaneously. Sweet juices dribbled from the corners of her mouth and Lessa hurriedly licked her lips to capture the least drop of the delicious liquid.

"Die happy, I will," F'nor cried, cutting more fruit.

Both were subtly reassured by the experiment and were able to discuss their discomposure.

"I think," F'nor suggested, "it is the lack of cliff and cavern and the still, still quality of the place; the knowing that there are no other men or beasts about but us."

Lessa nodded her head in agreement. "Ramoth, Canth, would having no weyr upset you?"

We didn't always live in caves, Ramoth replied, somewhat haughtily as she rolled over in the lake. Sizable waves rushed up the shore almost to where Lessa and F'nor were seated on a fallen tree trunk. *The sun here is warm and pleasant, the water cooling. I could enjoy it here but I am not to come.*

"She is out of sorts," Lessa whispered to F'nor. "Let Pridith have it, dear one," she called soothingly to the golden queen, "you've the Weyr and all!"

Ramoth ducked under the water, blowing up a froth in disgruntled reply.

Canth admitted that he had no reservations at all about

living weyrless. The dry earth would be warmer than stone to sleep in, once a suitably comfortable hollow had been achieved. No, he couldn't object to the lack of the cave as long as there was enough to eat.

"We'll have to bring herdbeasts in," F'nor mused. "Enough to start a good-sized herd. Of course, the wherries here are huge. Come to think of it, I believe this plateau has no exits. We wouldn't need to pasture it off. I'd better check. Otherwise, this plateau with the lake and enough clear space for Holds seems ideal. Walk out and pick breakfast from the tree."

"It might be wise to choose those who were not Hold-reared," Lessa added. "They would not feel so uneasy away from protecting heights and stone-security." She gave a short laugh. "I'm more a creature of habit than I suspected. All these open spaces, untenanted and quiet, seem . . . indecent." She gave a delicate shudder, scanning the broad and open plain beyond the lake.

"Fruitful and lovely," F'nor amended, leaping up to secure more of the orange-red succulents. "This tastes uncommon good to me. Can't remember anything this sweet and juicy from Nerat and yet it's the same variety."

"Undeniably superior to what the Weyr gets. I suspect Nerat serves home first, Weyr last."

They both stuffed themselves greedily.

Further investigation proved that the plateau was isolated, and ample to pasture a huge herd of food beasts for the dragons. It ended in a sheer drop of several dragon-lengths into more dense jungle on one side, the seaside escarpment on the other. The timber stands would provide raw material from which dwellings could be made for the weyrfolk. Ramoth and Canth stoutly agreed dragonkind would be comfortable enough under the heavy foliage of the dense jungle. As this part of the continent was similar, weatherwise, to upper Nerat, there would be neither intense heat nor cold to give distress.

However, Lessa was glad enough to leave. F'nor seemed reluctant to start back.

"We can go *between* time and place on the way back," Lessa insisted finally, "and be in the Weyr by late afternoon. The Lords will surely be gone by then."

F'nor concurred and Lessa steeled herself for the trip *between*. She wondered why the *when between* bothered her more than the *where* for it had no effect on the dragons at all. Ramoth, sensing Lessa's depression, crooned encouragingly. The long, long black suspension of the utter cold of *between* where and when ended suddenly in sunlight above the Weyr.

Somewhat startled, Lessa saw bundles and sacks spread out before the Lower Caverns as dragonriders supervised the loading of their beasts.

"What has been happening?" F'nor exclaimed.

"Oh, F'lar's been anticipating success," she assured him glibly.

Mnementh, who was watching the bustle from the ledge of the queen's weyr, sent a greeting to the travelers and the information that F'lar wished them to join him in the weyr as soon as they returned.

They found F'lar, as usual, bent over some of the oldest and least legible Record skins which he had had brought to the Council Room.

"And?" he asked, grinning a broad welcome at them.

"Green, lush and livable," Lessa declared, watching him intently. He knew something else, too. Well, she hoped he'd watch his words. F'nor was no fool and this foreknowledge was dangerous.

"That is what I had so hoped to hear you say," F'lar went on smoothly. "Come, tell me in detail. It'll be good to fill in the blank spaces on the chart."

Lessa let F'nor give most of the account to which F'lar listened with sincere attention, making notes.

"On the chance that it would be practical, I started packing supplies and alerting the riders to go with you," he told F'nor when the account was finished. "Remember, we've but three days in this time in which to start you back ten Turns ago. *We* have no moments to spare. And we must have many more mature dragons ready to fight at Telgar in three days' time. So, though ten Turns will have passed for you, three days only will elapse here. Lessa, your thought that the farm-bred might do better is well-taken. We're lucky that our recent Search for rider candidates for the dragons Pridith will have came mainly from the crafts and farms. No problem there. And most of the thirty-two are in their early teens."

"Thirty-two?" F'nor exclaimed. "We should have fifty.

The dragonets must have some choice even if we get the candidates used to the dragonets before they're hatched.''

F'lar shrugged negligently. ''Send back for more. *You'll* have time, remember,'' and F'lar chuckled as though he had started to add something and decided against it.

F'nor had no time to debate with the Weyrleader for F'lar immediately launched on other rapid instructions.

F'nor was to take his own wingriders to help train the weyrlings. They would also take the forty young dragons of Ramoth's first clutch: Kylara with her queen Pridith, T'bor and his bronze Orth. N'ton's young bronze might also be ready to fly and mate by the time Pridith was, so that gave the young queen two bronzes at least.

''Supposing we'd found the continent barren?'' F'nor asked, still puzzled by F'lar's assurance. ''What then?''

''Oh, we'd've sent them back to say the High Reaches,'' F'lar replied far too glibly but quickly went on. ''I should send on other bronzes but I'll need everyone else here to ride burrow-search on Keroon and Nerat. They've already unearthed several at Nerat. Vincet, I'm told, is close to a heart attack from fright.''

Lessa made a short comment on that Hold Lord.

''What of the meeting this morning?'' F'nor asked, remembering.

''Never mind that now. You've got to start shifting *between* by evening, F'nor.''

Lessa gave the Weyrleader a long hard look and decided she'd have to find out what had happened in detail very soon.

''Sketch me some references, will you, Lessa?'' F'lar asked.

There was a definite plea in his eyes as he drew clean hide and a stylus to her. He wanted no questions from her now that would alarm F'nor. She sighed and picked up the drawing tool.

She sketched quickly, with one or two details added by F'nor until she had rendered a reasonable map of the plateau they had chosen. Then abruptly, she had trouble focusing her eyes. She felt lightheaded.

''Lessa?'' F'lar bent to her.

''Everything's . . . moving . . . circling . . .'' and she collapsed backward into his arms.

As F'lar raised her slight body into his arms, he exchanged an alarmed look with his half brother.

"I'll call for Manora," F'nor suggested.

"How do you feel?" the Weyrleader called after his brother.

"Tired but no more than that," F'nor assured him as he shouted down the service shaft to the kitchens for Manora to come and for hot *klah*. He needed that and no doubt of it.

F'lar laid the Weyrwoman on the sleeping couch, covering her gently.

"I don't like this," he muttered, rapidly recalling what F'nor had said of Kylara's decline which F'nor could not know was yet to come in his future. Why should it start so swiftly with Lessa?

"Time-jumping makes one feel slightly . . ." F'nor paused, groping for the exact wording, "not entirely . . . whole. You fought *between* times at Nerat yesterday yourself . . ."

"I fought," F'lar reminded him, "but neither you nor Lessa battled anything today. There may be some inner . . . mental . . . stress simply to going *between* times. Look, F'nor, I'd rather only you came back once you reach the southern weyr. I'll make it an order and get Ramoth to inhibit the dragons. That way no rider can take it into his head to come back even if he wants to. There is some factor which may be more serious than we can guess. Let's take no unnecessary risks."

"Agreed."

"One other detail, F'nor. Be very careful which times you pick to come back to see me. I wouldn't jump *between* too close to any time you were actually here. I can't imagine what would happen if you walked into your own self in the passageway and I can't lose you."

With a rare demonstration of affection, F'lar gripped his half brother's shoulder tightly.

"Remember, F'nor. I was here all morning and you did not arrive back from the first trip till mid-afternoon. And remember, too, *we* have only three days. You have ten Turns."

F'nor left, passing Manora in the hall.

The woman could find nothing obviously the matter with Lessa and they finally decided it might be simple fatigue; yesterday's strain when Lessa had to relay messages between dragons and fighters followed by the disjointing *between* times trip today.

When F'lar went to wish the southern venturers a good trip, Lessa was in a normal sleep, her face pale but her breathing easy.

F'lar had Mnementh relay to Ramoth the prohibition he wished the queen to instill in all dragonkind assigned to the venture. Ramoth obliged, but added in an aside to bronze Mnementh, which he passed on to F'lar, that everyone else had adventures while she, the Weyr Queen, was forced to stay behind.

No sooner had the laden dragons, one by one, winked out of the sky above the Star Stone, than the young weyrling assigned to Nerat Hold as messenger came gliding down, his face white with fear.

"Weyrleader, many more burrows have been found and they cannot be burned out with fire alone. Lord Vincet wants you."

F'lar could well imagine Vincet did.

"Get yourself some dinner, boy, before you start back. I'll go shortly."

As he passed through to the sleeping quarters, he heard Ramoth rumbling in her throat. She had settled herself down for the night.

Lessa still slept, one hand curled under her cheek, her dark hair trailing over the edge of the bed. She looked fragile, childlike and very precious to him. F'lar smiled to himself. So she was jealous of Kylara's attentions yesterday. He was pleased and flattered. Never would Lessa learn from him that Kylara, for all her bold beauty and sensuous nature, did not have one tenth the attraction for him that the unpredictable, dark and delicate Lessa held. Even her stubborn intractableness, her keen and malicious humor, added zest to their relationship. With a tenderness he would never show her awake, F'lar bent and kissed her lips. She stirred and smiled, sighing lightly in her sleep.

Reluctantly returning to what must be done, F'lar left her so. As he paused by the queen, Ramoth raised her great, wedge-shaped head; her many-faceted eyes gleamed with bright luminescence as she regarded the Weyrleader.

"Mnementh, please ask Ramoth to get in touch with the dragonet at Fandarel's Crafthall. I'd like the Mastersmith to come with me to Nerat. I want to see what his agenothree does to Threads."

Ramoth nodded her head as the bronze dragon relayed the message to her.

"She has done so and the green dragon will come as soon as he can," Mnementh reported to his rider. "It is easier to do, this talking about, when Lessa is awake," he grumbled.

F'lar agreed, heartily thankful that Lessa could talk to any dragon in the Weyr. It had been quite an advantage yesterday in the Battle and would be more and more of an asset.

Maybe it would be better if she tried to speak, across time, to F'nor . . . but no, F'nor had come back.

F'lar strode into the Council Room, still hopeful that somewhere within the illegible portions of the old Records was the one clue he so desperately needed. There must be a way out of this impasse. If not the southern venture, then something else. Something!

Fandarel showed himself a man of iron will as well as sinew; he looked calmly at the exposed tangle of perceptibly growing Threads that writhed and intertwined obscenely.

"Hundreds and thousands in this one burrow," Lord Vincet of Nerat was exclaiming in a frantic tone of voice. He waved his hands distractedly around the plantation of young trees in which the burrow had been discovered. "These stalks are already withering even as you hesitate. Do something! How many more young trees will die in this one field alone? How many more burrows escaped dragon's breath yesterday? Where is a dragon to sear them? Why are you just standing there?"

F'lar and Fandarel paid no attention to the man's raving, both fascinated as well as revolted by their first sight of the burrowing stage of their ancient foe. Despite Vincet's panicky accusations, it was the only burrow on this particular slope. F'lar did not like to contemplate how many more might have slipped through the dragons' efforts to reach Nerat's warm and fertile soil. If they had only had time enough to set out watchmen to track the fall of stray clumps . . . they could, at least, remedy that error in Telgar, Crom and Ruatha in three days. But it was not enough. Not enough.

Fandarel motioned forward the two craftsmen who had accompanied him. They were burdened with an odd contraption: a large cylinder of metal to which was attached a wand with a wide nozzle. At the other end of the cylinder was another short pipe length and then a short cylinder with an inner plunger. One craftsman worked the plunger vigorously, while the second, barely keeping his hands steady, pointed the nozzle end towards the Thread burrow. At a nod from his pumper, the man released a small knob on the nozzle, extending it carefully away from him and over the burrow. A thin spray danced from the nozzle and drifted down into the burrow. No sooner had the spray motes contacted the Thread tangles than steam hissed out of the burrow. Before long, all that remained of the pallid writhing tendrils was a smoking mass of blackened strands. Long after Fandarel had waved the craftsmen back, he stared at the grave. Finally he grunted and found himself a long stick with which he poked and prodded the remains. Not one Thread wriggled.

"Humph," he grunted with evident satisfaction. "However, we can scarcely go around digging up every burrow. I need another."

With Lord Vincet a hand-wringing moaner in their wake, they were escorted by the junglemen to another undisturbed burrow on the seaside of the rainforest. The Threads had entered the earth by the side of a huge tree which was already drooping.

With his prodding stick, Fandarel made a tiny hole at the top of the burrow and then waved his craftsmen forward. The pumper made vigorous motions at his end while the nozzle-holder adjusted his pipe before inserting it in the hole. Fandarel gave the sign to start and counted slowly before he waved a cutoff. Smoke oozed out of the tiny hole.

After a suitable lapse of time, Fandarel ordered the junglemen to dig, reminding them to be careful not to come in contact with the agenothree liquid. When the burrow was uncovered, the acid had done its work, leaving nothing but a thoroughly charred mass of tangles.

Fandarel grimaced but this time scratched his head in dissatisfaction.

"Takes too much time, either way. Best to get them still at the surface," the Mastersmith grumbled.

"Best to get them in the air," Lord Vincet chattered. "And what will that stuff do to my young orchards? What will it do?"

Fandarel swung round, apparently noticing the distressed Holder for the first time.

"Little man, agenothree in diluted form is what you use to fertilize your plants in the spring. True, this field has been burned out for a few years, but it is *not* Thread-full. It *would* be better if we could get the spray up high in the air. Then it would float down and dissipate harmlessly—fertilizing very evenly, too." He paused, scratched his head gratingly. "Young dragons could carry a team aloft . . . Hm-m-m. A possibility but the apparatus is bulky yet." He turned his back on the surprised Hold Lord then and asked F'lar if the tapestry had been returned. "I cannot yet discover how to make a tube throw flame. I got this mechanism from what we make for the orchard farmers."

"I'm still waiting for word," F'lar replied, "but this spray of yours is effective. The Thread burrow is dead."

"The sandworms are effective too, but not really efficient." Fandarel grunted in dissatisfaction. He beckoned abruptly to his assistants and stalked off into the increasing twilight to the dragons.

Robinton awaited their return at the Weyr, his outward calm barely masking his inner excitement. He inquired politely, however, of Fandarel's efforts. The Mastersmith grunted and shrugged.

"I have all my Craft at work."

"The Mastersmith is entirely too modest," F'lar put in. "He has already put together an ingenious device that sprays agenothree into Thread burrows and sears them into a black pulp."

"Not efficient. *I* like the idea of flamethrowers," the Smith said, his eyes gleaming in his expressionless face. "A thrower of flame," he repeated, his eyes unfocusing. He shook his heavy head with a bone-popping crack. "I go," and with a curt nod to the Harper and the Weyrleader, he left.

"I like that man's dedication to an idea," Robinton observed. Despite his amusement with the man's eccentric behavior, there was a strong undercurrent of respect for the Smith. "I must set my apprentices a task for an appropriate Saga on the Mastersmith. I understand," he said turning to F'lar, "that the southern venture has been inaugurated."

F'lar nodded unhappily.

"Your doubts increase?"

"This *between* times travel takes its own toll," he admitted, glancing anxiously towards the sleeping room.

"The Weyrwoman is ill?"

"Sleeping, but today's journey affected her. We need another, less dangerous answer!" and F'lar slammed one fist into the other palm.

"I came with no real answer," Robinton said then, briskly, "but with what I believe to be another part of the puzzle. I have found an entry. Four hundred Turns ago, the then Masterharper was called to Fort Weyr not long after the Red Star retreated away from Pern in the evening sky."

"An entry? What is it?"

"Mind you, the Thread attacks had just lifted and the Masterharper was called one late evening to Fort Weyr. An unusual summons. However," and Robinton emphasized the distinction by pointing a long, callous-tipped finger at F'lar, "no further mention is ever made of that visit. There ought to have been, for all such summonses have a purpose. All such meetings are recorded yet no explanation of this one is given. The record is taken up several weeks later by the Masterharper as though he had not left his Crafthall at all. Some ten months afterwards, the Question Song was added to compulsory Teaching Ballads."

"You believe the two are connected with the abandonment of the five Weyrs?"

"I do, but I could not say why. I only feel that the events, the visit, the disappearances, the Question Song, are connected."

F'lar poured them both cups of wine.

"I have checked back, too, seeking some indications." He shrugged. "All must have been normal right up to the point they disappeared. There are records of tithe trains received, supplies stored, the list of injured dragons and men returning to active patrols. And then the records cease at full Cold, leaving only Benden Weyr occupied."

"And why that one Weyr of the six to choose from?" Robinton demanded. "Nerat, in the tropics, or island Ista would be better choices if only one Weyr was to be left. Benden so far north is not a likely place to pass four hundred Turns."

"Benden is high and isolated. A disease that struck the others and was prevented from reaching Benden?"

"And no explanation of it? They can't all, dragons, riders, weyrfolk, have dropped dead on the same instant and left no carcasses rotting in the sun."

"Then let us ask ourselves, why was the Harper called? Was he told to construct a Teaching Ballad covering this disappearance?"

"Well," Robinton snorted, "it certainly wasn't meant to reassure us, not with that tune—if one cares to call it a tune at all, and I don't—nor does it answer any questions! It poses them."

"For us to answer?" suggested F'lar softly.

"Aye," and Robinton's eyes shone. "For us to answer, indeed, for it is a difficult song to forget. Which means it was meant to be remembered. Those questions are important, F'lar!"

"Which questions are important?" demanded Lessa who had entered quietly.

Both men were on their feet. F'lar, with unusual attentiveness, held a chair for Lessa and poured her wine.

"I'm not going to break apart," she said tartly, almost annoyed at the excess of courtesy. Then she smiled up at F'lar to take the sting out of her words. "I slept and I feel much better. What were you two getting so intense about?"

F'lar quickly outlined what he and the Masterharper had been discussing. When he mentioned the Question Song, Lessa shuddered.

"That's one I can't forget either. Which, I've always been told," and she grimaced, remembering the hateful lessons with R'gul, "means it's important. But why? It only asked questions." Then she blinked, her eyes went wide with amazement.

" 'Gone away, gone . . . *ahead!*' " she cried, on her feet. "That's it! All five Weyrs went . . . *ahead*. But to when?"

F'lar turned to her, speechless.

"They came ahead. To our time, five weyrs full of dragons," she repeated in an awed voice.

"No, that's impossible," F'lar contradicted.

"Why?" Robinton demanded excitedly. "Doesn't that solve the problem we're facing? The need for fighting dragons?

Doesn't it explain why they left so suddenly with no explanation except that Question Song?''

F'lar brushed back the heavy lock of hair that overhung his eyes.

''It would explain their actions in leaving,'' he admitted, ''because they couldn't leave any clues saying where they went or it would cancel the whole thing. Just as I couldn't tell F'nor I knew the southern venture would have problems. But how do they get here—if here is *when* they came. They aren't here now. And how would they have known they were needed—or *when* they were needed? And this is the real problem, how can you conceivably give a dragon references to a *when* that has not yet occurred?''

''Someone here must go back to give them the proper references,'' Lessa replied in a very quiet voice.

''You're mad, Lessa,'' F'lar shouted at her, alarm written on his face. ''You know what happened to you today. How can you consider going back to a *when* you can't remotely imagine? To a *when* four hundred Turns ago? Going back ten Turns left you fainting and half-ill.''

''Wouldn't it be worth it?'' she asked him, her eyes grave. ''Isn't Pern worth it?''

F'lar grabbed her by the shoulders, shaking her, his eyes wild with fear.

''Not even Pern is worth losing you, or Ramoth. Lessa, Lessa, don't you dare disobey me in this.'' His voice dropped to an intense, icy whisper, shaking with anger.

''Ah, there may be a way of effecting that solution, momentarily beyond us, Weyrwoman,'' Robinton put in adroitly. ''Who knows what tomorrow holds? It certainly is not something one does without considering every angle.''

Lessa did not shrug off F'lar's vise-like grip on her shoulders as she gazed at Robinton.

''Wine?'' The Masterharper suggested, pouring a mug for her. His diversionary action broke the tableau of Lessa and F'lar.

''Ramoth is not afraid to try,'' Lessa said, her mouth set in a determined line.

F'lar glared at the golden dragon who was regarding the humans, her neck curled round almost to the shoulder joint of her great wing.

"Ramoth is young," F'lar snapped and then caught Mnementh's wry thought even as Lessa did.

She threw her head back, her peal of laughter echoing in the vaulted chamber.

"I'm badly in need of a good joke myself," Robinton remarked pointedly.

"Mnementh told F'lar that he was neither young nor afraid to try either. It was just a long step," Lessa explained, wiping tears from her eyes.

F'lar glanced dourly at the passageway, at the end of which Mnementh lounged on his customary ledge.

A laden dragon comes, the bronze warned those in the weyr. *It is Lytol beyond young B'rant on brown Fanth.*

"Now he brings his own bad news?" Lessa asked sourly.

"It is hard enough for Lytol to ride another's dragon or come here at all, Lessa of Ruatha. Do not increase his torment one jot with your childishness," F'lar said sternly.

Lessa dropped her eyes, furious with F'lar for speaking so to her in front of Robinton.

Lytol stumped into the queen's weyr, carrying one end of a large rolled rug. Young B'rant, struggling to uphold the other end, was sweating with the effort. Lytol bowed respectfully towards Ramoth and gestured the young brownrider to help him unroll their burden. As the immense tapestry uncoiled, F'lar could understand why Masterweaver Zurg had remembered it. The colors, ancient though they undoubtedly were, remained vibrant and undimmed. The subject matter was even more interesting.

"Mnementh, send for Fandarel. Here's the model he needs for his flamethrower," F'lar said.

"That tapestry is Ruatha's," Lessa cried indignantly. "I remember it from my childhood. It hung in the Great Hall and was the most cherished of my Bloodline's possessions. Where has it been?" Her eyes were flashing.

"Lady, it is being returned where it belongs," Lytol said stolidly, avoiding her gaze. "A masterweaver's work, this," he went on, touching the heavy fabric with reverent fingers. "Such colors, such patterning. It took a man's life to set up the loom: a craft's whole effort to complete, or I am no judge of true craftsmanship."

F'lar walked along the edge of the immense arras, wishing

it could be hung to get the proper perspective of the heroic scene. A flying formation of three wings of dragons dominated the upper portion of half the hanging. They were breathing flame as they dove upon gray, falling clumps of Threads in the brilliant sky. A sky, just that perfect autumnal blue, F'lar decided, that cannot occur in warmer weather. Upon the lower slopes of the hills depicted, foliage was turning yellow from chilly nights. The slaty rocks suggested Ruathan country. Was that why the tapestry had hung in Ruatha Hall? Below, men had left the protecting Hold, cut into the cliff itself. The men were burdened with the curious cylinders of which Zurg had spoken. The tubes in their hands belched brilliant tongues of flame in long streams, aimed at the writhing Threads that attempted to burrow in the ground.

Lessa gave a startled exclamation, walking right onto the tapestry, staring down at the woven outline of the Hold, its massive door ajar, the details of its bronze ornamentation painstakingly rendered in fine yarns.

"I believe that's the design on the Ruatha Hold door," F'lar remarked.

"It is . . . and it isn't," Lessa replied in a puzzled voice.

Lytol glowered at her, and then at the woven door. "True. It isn't and yet it is and I went through that door a scant hour ago." He scowled down at the door before his toes.

"Well, here are the designs Fandarel wants to study," F'lar said with relief, as he peered at the flamethrowers.

Whether the Smith could produce a working model from this woven one in time to help them three days hence, F'lar couldn't guess. But if Fandarel could not, no man could.

The Mastersmith was, for him, jubilant over the presence of the tapestry. He lay upon the rug, his nose tickled by the nap as he studied the details. He grumbled, moaned and muttered as he sat cross-legged to sketch and peer.

"Has been done. Can be done. Must be done," he was heard to rumble.

Lessa called for *klah,* bread and meat when she learned from young B'rant that neither he nor Lytol had eaten yet. She served all the men, her manner gay and teasing. F'lar was relieved for Lytol's sake. Lessa even pressed food and *klah* on Fandarel, a tiny figure beside the mammoth man, insisting that he come away from the tapestry and eat and drink. After taking nourishment he could return to his mumbling and drawing.

Fandarel finally decided he had enough sketches and disappeared, to be flown back to his Crafthold.

"No point in asking him when he'll be back. He's too deep in thought to hear," F'lar remarked, amused.

"If you don't mind, I shall excuse myself as well," Lessa said, smiling graciously to the four remaining around the table. "Good Warder Lytol, young B'rant should soon be excused, too. He's half asleep."

"I most certainly am not, Weyrlady," B'rant assured her hastily, widening his eyes with simulated alertness.

Lessa merely laughed as she retreated into the sleeping chamber. F'lar stared thoughtfully after her.

"I mistrust the Weyrwoman when she uses that particularly docile tone of voice," he said slowly.

"Well, we must all depart . . ." Robinton suggested, rising.

"Ramoth is young but not that foolish," F'lar murmured after the others had left.

Ramoth slept, oblivious of his scrutiny. He reached for the consolation Mnementh could give him, without response. The big bronze was dozing on his ledge.

Black, blacker, blackest
And cold beyond frozen things.
Where is *between* when there is naught
To Life but fragile dragon wings?

"I just want to see that tapestry back on the wall at Ruatha," Lessa insisted to F'lar the next day. "I want it where it belongs."

They had been to check on the injured, and had had one argument already over F'lar's having sent N'ton along with the southern venture. Lessa had wanted him to try riding another's dragon. F'lar had preferred for him to learn to lead a wing of his own in the south, given the years to mature in. He had reminded Lessa, in the hope that it might prove inhibiting to any ideas she had about going four hundred Turns back, about F'nor's return trips and bore down hard on the difficulties she had already experienced.

She had become very thoughtful although she had said nothing.

Therefore, when Fandarel sent word he would like to show F'lar a new mechanism, the Weyrleader felt reasonably safe in allowing Lessa the triumph of returning the purloined tapestry to Ruatha. She went to have the arras rolled and strapped to Ramoth's back.

He watched Ramoth rise with great sweeps of her wide wings, up to the Star Stone before going *between* to Ruatha. R'gul appeared at the ledge, just then, reporting that a huge train of firestone was entering the tunnel. Consequently, busy with such details, it was mid-morning before he could get to see Fandarel's crude and not yet effective flamethrower . . . the fire did not "throw" from the nozzle of the tube with any force at all. It was late afternoon before he reached the Weyr again.

R'gul announced sourly that F'nor had been looking for him, twice, in fact.

"Twice?"

"Twice, as I said. He would not leave a message with me for you," and R'gul was clearly insulted by F'nor's refusal.

By the evening meal, when there was still no sign of Lessa, F'lar sent to Ruatha to learn that she had indeed brought the tapestry. She had badgered and bothered the entire Hold until the thing was properly hung. For upwards of several hours, she had sat and looked at it, pacing its length occasionally.

She and Ramoth had then taken to the sky above the Great Tower and disappeared. Lytol had assumed, as had everyone at Ruatha, that she had returned to Benden Weyr.

"Mnementh?" F'lar bellowed when the messenger had finished, "Mnementh, where are they?"

Mnementh's answer was a long time in coming.

I cannot hear them, he said finally, his mental voice soft and as full of worry as a dragon's could be.

F'lar gripped the table with both hands, staring at the queen's empty weyr. He knew, in the anguished privacy of his mind, where Lessa had tried to go.

> Cold as death, death-bearing,
> Stay and die, unguided.
> Brave and braving, linger.
> This way was twice decided.

Below them was Ruatha's Great Tower. Lessa coaxed

Ramoth slightly to the left, ignoring the dragon's acid comments, knowing that she was excited, too.

"That's right, dear, this is exactly the angle at which the tapestry illustrates the Hold door. Only when that tapestry was designed, no one had carved the lintels or capped the door. And there was no Tower, no inner Court, no gate." She stroked the surprisingly soft skin of the curving neck, laughing to hide her own tense nervousness and apprehension at what she was about to attempt.

She told herself there were good reasons prompting her action in this matter. The ballad's opening phrase, "gone away, gone ahead" was clearly a reference to *between* times. And the tapestry gave the required reference points for the jump *between* whens. Oh, how she thanked the masterweaver who had woven that doorway. She must remember to tell him how well he had wrought. She hoped she'd be able to. Enough of that. Of course, she'd be able to. For hadn't the Weyrs disappeared? Knowing they had gone ahead, knowing how to go back to bring them ahead, it was she, obviously, who must go back and lead them. It was very simple and only she and Ramoth could do it. Because they already had.

She laughed again, nervously, and took several deep, shuddering breaths.

"All right, my golden love," she murmured. "You have the reference. You know when I want to go. Take me *between*, Ramoth, *between* four hundred Turns."

The cold was intense, even more penetrating than she had imagined. Yet it was not a physical cold. It was the awareness of the absence of *everything*. No light. No sound. No touch. As they hovered, longer and longer, in this nothingness, Lessa recognized the fullblown panic of a kind that threatened to overwhelm her reason. She knew she sat on Ramoth's neck yet she could not feel the great beast under her thighs, under her hands. She tried to cry out inadvertently and opened her mouth to . . . nothing . . . no sound in her own ears. She could not even feel the hands that she knew she had raised to her own cheeks.

I am here, she heard Ramoth say in her mind. *We are together*, and this reassurance was all that kept her from losing her grasp on sanity in that terrifying eon of unpassing, timeless nothingness.

* * *

Someone had sense enough to call for Robinton. The Masterharper found F'lar sitting at the table, his face deathly pale, his eyes staring at the empty weyr. The craftmaster's entrance, his calm voice, reached F'lar in his shocked numbness. He sent the others out with a peremptory wave.

"She's gone. She tried to go back four hundred Turns," F'lar said in a tight, hard voice.

The Masterharper sank into the chair opposite the Weyrleader.

"She took the tapestry back to Ruatha," F'lar continued in that same choked voice. "I'd told her about F'nor's returns. I told her how dangerous this was. She didn't argue very much and I know going *between* times had frightened her, if anything could frighten Lessa." He banged the table with an impotent fist. "I should have suspected her. When she thinks she's right, she doesn't stop to analyze, to consider. She just does it!"

"But she's not a foolish woman," Robinton reminded him slowly. "Not even she would jump *between* times without a reference point. Would she?"

" 'Gone away, gone ahead' . . . that's the only clue we have!"

"Now wait a moment," Robinton cautioned him, then snapped his fingers. "Last night, when she walked upon the tapestry, she was uncommonly interested in the Hall door. She discussed it with Lytol."

F'lar was on his feet and halfway down the passageway.

"Come on, man, we've got to get to Ruatha."

Lytol lit every glow in the Hold for F'lar and Robinton to examine the tapestry clearly.

"She spent the afternoon just looking at it," the Warder said, shaking his head. "You're sure she has tried this incredible jump?"

"She must have. Mnementh can't hear either her or Ramoth anywhere. Yet he says he can get an echo from Canth many Turns away and in the southern continent." F'lar stalked past the tapestry. "What is it about the door, Lytol? Think, man!"

"It is much as it is now, save that there are no carved lintels, there is no outer Court, nor Tower . . ."

"That's it. Oh, by the first Egg, it is so simple. Zurg said this tapestry is old. Lessa must have decided it was four hundred Turns and she has used it as the reference point to go back *between* times."

"Why, then, she's there and safe," Robinton cried, sinking with relief in a chair.

"Oh, no, Harper. It is not as easy as that," F'lar murmured.

Robinton caught his stricken look and the despair echoed in Lytol's face. "What's the matter?"

"There is nothing *between*," F'lar said in a dead voice. "To go *between* places takes only as much time as for a man to cough three times. *Between* four hundred Turns . . ." his voice trailed off.

Who wills,
Can.
Who tries,
Does.
Who loves,
Lives.

There were voices that first were roars in her aching ears and then hushed beyond the threshold of sound. She gasped as the whirling, nauseating sensation apparently spun her, and the bed which she felt beneath her, round and round. She clung to the sides of the bed as pain jabbed through her head, from somewhere directly in the middle of her skull. She screamed, as much in protest at the pain as from the terrifying, rolling, whirling, dropping, lack of a solid ground.

Yet some frightening necessity kept her trying to gabble out the message she had come to give. Sometimes she felt Ramoth trying to reach her in that vast swooping darkness that enveloped her. She would try to cling to Ramoth's mind, hoping the golden queen could lead her out of this torturing nowhere. Exhausted she would sink down, down, only to be torn from oblivion by the desperate need to communicate.

She was finally aware of a soft, smooth hand upon her arm, of a liquid, warm and savory, in her mouth. She rolled it around her tongue and it trickled down her sore throat. A fit of coughing left her gasping and weak. Then she experimentally opened her eyes and the images before her did not lurch and spin.

"Who . . . are . . . you?" she managed to croak.

"Oh, my dear Lessa . . ."

"Is that who I am?" she asked, confused.

"So your Ramoth tells us," she was assured. "I am Mardra of Fort Weyr."

"Oh, F'lar will be so angry with me," Lessa moaned as her memory came rushing back. "He will shake me and shake me. He always shakes me when I disobey him. But I was right. I was right. Mardra? . . . Oh, that . . . awful . . . nothingness," and she felt herself drifting off into sleep, unable to resist that overwhelming urge. Comfortingly, her bed no longer rocked beneath her.

The room, dimly lit by wallglows, was both like her own at Benden Weyr and subtly different. Lessa lay still, trying to isolate that difference. Ah, the Weyr walls were very smooth here. The room was larger, too, the ceiling higher and curving. The furnishings, now that her eyes were used to the dim light and she could distinguish details, were more finely crafted. She stirred restlessly.

"Ah, you're awake again, mystery lady," a man said. Light beyond the parted curtain flooded in from the outer weyr. Lessa sensed rather than saw the presence of others in the room beyond.

A woman passed under the man's arm, moving swiftly to the bedside.

"I remember you. You're Mardra," Lessa said with surprise.

"Indeed I am and here is M'ron, Weyrleader at Fort."

M'ron was tossing more glows into the wallbasket, peering over his shoulder at Lessa to see if the light bothered her.

"Ramoth!" Lessa exclaimed, sitting upright, aware for the first time that it was not Ramoth's mind she touched in the outer weyr.

"Oh, that one," Mardra laughed with amused dismay. "She'll eat us out of the Weyr and even my Loranth has had to call the other queens to restrain her."

"She perches on the Star Stones as if she owned them and keens constantly," M'ron added, less charitably. He cocked an ear. "Ha. She's stopped."

"You can come, can't you?" Lessa blurted out.

"Come? Come where, my dear?" Mardra asked, confused. "You've been going on and on about our 'coming,' and Threads approaching, and the Red Star bracketed in the Eye Rock and . . . my dear, don't you realize, the Red Star has been past Pern these two months?"

"No, no, they've started. That's why I came back *between* times . . ."

"Back? *Between* times?" M'ron exclaimed, striding over to the bed, eyeing Lessa intently.

"Could I have some *klah?* I know I'm not making much sense and I'm not really awake yet. But I'm not mad or still sick and this is rather complicated."

"Yes, it is," M'ron remarked with deceptive mildness. But he did call down the service shaft for *klah*. And he did drag a chair over to her bedside, settling himself to listen to her.

"Of course you're not mad," Mardra soothed her, glaring at her weyrmate. "Or she wouldn't ride a queen."

M'ron had to agree to that. Lessa waited for the *klah* to come, sipping gratefully at its stimulating warmth.

Lessa took a deep breath and began, telling them of the Long Interval between the dangerous passes of the Red Star: How the sole Weyr had fallen into disfavor and contempt. How Jora had deteriorated and lost control over her queen, Nemorth, so that, as the Red Star neared, there was no sudden increase in the size of clutches. How she had impressed Ramoth to become Benden's Weyrwoman. How F'lar had outwitted the dissenting Hold Lords the day after Ramoth's first mating flight and taken firm command of Weyr and Pern, preparing for the Threads he knew were coming. She told her by now rapt audience of her own first attempts to fly Ramoth and how she had inadvertently gone back *between* times to the day Fax had invaded Ruath Hold.

"Invade . . . my family's Hold?" Mardra had cried, aghast.

"Ruatha has given the Weyrs many famous Weyrwomen," Lessa said with a sly smile at which M'ron burst out laughing.

"She's Ruathan, no question," he assured Mardra.

She told them of the situation in which dragonmen now found themselves, with an insufficient force to meet the Thread attacks. Of the Question Song and the great tapestry.

"A tapestry?" Mardra cried, her hand going to her cheek in alarm. "Describe it to me!"

And when Lessa did, she saw—at last—belief in both their faces.

"My father has just commissioned a tapestry with such a scene. He told me of it the other day because the last battle with the Threads was held over Ruatha.'' Incredulous, Mardra turned to M'ron who no longer looked amused. ''She must have done what she has said she'd done. How could she possibly know about the tapestry?''

''You might also ask your queen dragon, and mine,'' Lessa suggested.

''My dear, we do not doubt you now,'' Mardra said sincerely, ''but it is a most incredible feat.''

''I don't think,'' Lessa said, ''that I would ever try it again, knowing what I do now.''

''Yes, this shock makes a forward jump *between* times quite a problem if your F'lar must have an effective fighting force,'' M'ron remarked.

''You will come? You will?''

''There is a distinct possibility we will,'' M'ron said gravely and his face broke into a lopsided grin. ''You said we left the Weyrs . . . abandoned them, in fact, and left no explanation. We went somewhere . . . somewhen, that is, for we are still here now . . .''

They were all silent for the same alternative occurred to them simultaneously. The Weyrs had been left vacant, but Lessa had no way of proving that the five Weyrs reappeared in her time.

''There must be a way. There must be a way,'' Lessa cried distractedly. ''And there's no time to waste. No time at all!''

M'ron gave a bark of laughter. ''There's plenty of time at this end of history, my dear.''

They made her rest, then, more concerned than she was that she had been ill some weeks, deliriously screaming that she was falling, and could not see, could not hear, could not touch. Ramoth, too, they told her, had suffered from the appalling nothingness of a protracted stay *between,* emerging above ancient Ruatha a pale yellow wraith of her former robust self.

The Lord of Ruath Hold, Mardra's father, had been surprised out of his wits by the appearance of a staggering rider and a pallid queen on his stone verge. Naturally and luckily he had sent to his daughter at Fort Weyr for help. Lessa and Ramoth had been transported to the Weyr and the Ruathan Lord kept silent on the matter.

When Lessa was strong enough, M'ron called a Council of Weyrleaders. Curiously, there was no opposition to going

. . . provided they could solve the problem of time-shock and find reference points along the way. It did not take Lessa long to comprehend why the dragonriders were so eager to attempt the journey. Most of them had been born during the present Thread incursions. They had now had close to four months of unexciting routine patrols and were bored with monotony. Training Games were pallid substitutes for the real battles they had all fought. The Holds, which once could not do dragonmen favors enough, were beginning to be indifferent. The Weyrleaders could see these incidents increasing as Thread-generated fears receded. It was a morale decay as insidious as a wasting disease in Weyr and Hold. The alternative which Lessa's appeal offered was better than a slow decline in their own time.

Of Benden, only the Weyrleader himself was privy to these meetings. Because Benden was the only Weyr in Lessa's time, it must remain ignorant, and intact, until her time. Nor could any mention be made of Lessa's presence for that, too, was unknown in her Turn.

She insisted that they call in the Masterharper because her Records said he had been called. But, when he asked her to tell him the Question Song, she smiled and demurred.

"You'll write it, or your successor will, when the Weyrs are found to be abandoned," she told him. "But it must be your doing, not my repeating."

"A difficult assignment to know one must write a song that four hundred Turns later gives a valuable clue."

"Only be sure," she cautioned him, "that it is a Teaching tune. It must *not* be forgotten for it poses questions that I have to answer."

As he started to chuckle, she realized she had already given him a pointer.

The discussions—how to go so far safely with no sustained sense deprivations—grew heated. There were more constructive notions, however impractical, on how to find reference points along the way. The five Weyrs had not been ahead in time and Lessa, in her one gigantic backward leap, had not stopped for intermediate time marks.

"You did say that a *between* times jump of ten years caused no hardship?" M'ron asked of Lessa as all the Weyrleaders and the Masterharper met to discuss this impasse.

"None. It takes . . . oh, twice as long as a *between* places jump."

"It is the four hundred Turn leap that left you imbalanced, hm-m-m. Maybe twenty or twenty-five Turn segments would be safe enough."

That suggestion found merit until Ista's cautious leader, D'ram, spoke up.

"I don't mean to be a Hold-hider, but there is one possibility we haven't mentioned. How do we know we made the jump *between* to Lessa's time? Going *between* is a chancy business. Men go missing often. And Lessa barely made it here alive."

"A good point, D'ram," M'ron concurred briskly, "but I feel there is more to prove that we do—did—will—go forward. The clues, for one thing; they were aimed at Lessa. The very emergency which left five Weyrs empty that sent her back to appeal for our help . . ."

"Agreed, agreed," D'ram interrupted earnestly, "but what I mean is can you be sure we reached Lessa's time? It hadn't happened yet. Do we know it can?"

M'ron was not the only one who searched his mind for an answer to that. All of a sudden, he slammed both hands, palms down, on the table.

"By the Egg, it's die slow, doing nothing, or die quick, trying. I've had a surfeit of the quiet life we dragonmen must lead after the Red Star passes, till we go *between* in old age. I confess I'm almost sorry to see the Red Star dwindle further from us in the evening sky. I say, grab the risk with both hands and shake it till it's gone. We're dragonmen, aren't we, bred to fight the Threads? Let's go hunting . . . four hundred Turns ahead!"

Lessa's drawn face relaxed. She had recognized the validity of D'ram's alternate possibility and it had touched off bitter fear in her heart. To risk herself was her own responsibility but to risk these hundreds of men and dragons, the weyrfolk who could accompany their men . . . ?

M'ron's ringing words for once and all dispensed with that consideration.

"And I believe," the Masterharper's exultant voice cut through the answering shouts of agreement, "I believe I have your reference points." A smile of surprised wonder illuminated his face. "Twenty Turns or twenty-hundred, you have a guide! And M'ron said it. 'As the Red Star dwindles in the evening sky . . .' "

Later, as they plotted the orbit of the Red Star, they found how easy that solution actually was, and chuckled that their ancient foe should be their guide.

Atop Fort Weyr, as on all the Weyrs, were great stones. They were so placed that at certain times of the year they marked the approach and retreat of the Red Star, as it orbited in its erratic, two hundred Turn-long course around their sun. By consulting the Records which, among other morsels of information, included the Red Star's wanderings, it was not hard to plan jumps *between* of twenty-five Turns for each Weyr. It had been decided that the complement of each separate Weyr would jump *between* above its own base, for there would unquestionably be accidents if close to eighteen hundred laden beasts tried it at one point.

Each moment now was one too long away from her own time for Lessa. She had been a month away from F'lar and missed him more than she had thought could be possible. Also, she was worried that Ramoth would mate away from Mnementh. There were, to be sure, bronze dragons and bronze riders eager to do that service, but Lessa had no interest in them.

M'ron and Mardra occupied her with the many details in organizing the exodus so that no clues, past the tapestry and the Question Song which would be composed at a later date, remained in the Weyrs.

It was with a relief close to tears that Lessa urged Ramoth upward in the night sky to take her place near M'ron and Mardra above the Fort Weyr Star Stone. At five other Weyrs, great wings were ranged in formation, ready to depart their own times.

As each Weyrleader's dragon reported to Lessa that all were ready—reference points, determined by the Red Star's travels in mind—it was this traveler from the future who gave the command to jump *between*.

> The blackest night must end in
> dawn,
> The sun dispel the dreamer's fear:

When shall my soul's bleak, hopeless pain
Find solace in its darkening weyr?

They had made eleven jumps *between,* the Weyrleaders' bronzes speaking to Lessa as they rested briefly between each jump. Of the eighteen hundred odd travelers, only four failed to come ahead, and they had been older beasts. All five sections agreed to pause for a quick meal and hot *klah,* before the final jump which would be but twelve Turns.

"It is easier," M'ron commented as Mardra served around the *klah,* "to go twenty-five Turns than twelve." He glanced up at the Red Dawn Star, their winking and faithful guide. "It does not alter its position as much. I count on you, Lessa, to give us additional references."

"I want to get us back to Ruatha before F'lar discovers I have gone." She shivered as she looked up at the Red Star and sipped hastily at the hot *klah.* "I've seen the Star just like that, once . . . no, twice . . . before at Ruatha." She stared at M'ron, her throat constricting as she remembered that morning: the time she had decided that the Red Star was a menace to her, three days after which Fax and F'lar had appeared at Ruath Hold. Fax had died on F'lar's dagger and she had gone to Benden Weyr. She felt suddenly dizzy, weak, strangely unsettled. She had not felt this way as they paused between other jumps.

"Are you all right, Lessa?" Mardra asked with concern. "You're so white. You're shaking." She put her arm around Lessa, glancing, concerned, at her weyrmate.

"Twelve Turns ago I was at Ruatha," Lessa murmured, grasping Mardra's hand for support. "I was at Ruatha twice. Let's go on quickly. I'm too many in this morning. I must get back. I must get back to F'lar. He'll be so angry."

The note of hysteria in her voice alarmed both Mardra and M'ron. Hastily the latter gave orders for the fires to be extinguished, for the weyrfolk to mount and prepare for the final jump ahead.

Her mind in chaos, Lessa transmitted the references to the other Weyrleaders' dragons: Ruatha in the evening light, the Great Tower, the inner Court, and the land at springtime . . .

A fleck of red in a cold night sky,
A drop of blood to guide them by,
Turn away, Turn away, Turn, be
gone,
A Red Star beckons the travelers
on.

Between them, Lytol and Robinton forced F'lar to eat, deliberately plying him with wine. At the back of his mind he knew he would have to keep going but the effort was immense, the spirit gone from him. It was no comfort that they still had Pridith and Kylara to continue dragonkind, yet he delayed sending someone back for F'nor, unable to face the reality of that admission: that in sending for Pridith and Kylara, he had acknowledged the fact that Lessa and Ramoth would not return.

Lessa, Lessa, his mind cried endlessly, damning her one moment for her reckless, thoughtless daring; loving her the next for attempting such an incredible feat.

"I said, F'lar, you need sleep now more than wine," Robinton's voice penetrated his preoccupation.

F'lar looked at him, frowning in perplexity. He realized that he was trying to lift the wine jug that Robinton was holding firmly down.

"What did you say?"

"Come. I'll bear you company to Benden. Indeed, nothing could persuade me to leave your side. You have aged years, man, in the course of hours."

"And isn't it understandable . . . ?" F'lar shouted, rising to his feet, the impotent anger boiling out of him at the nearest target in the form of Robinton.

Robinton's eyes were full of compassion as he reached for F'lar's arm, gripping it tightly.

"Man, not even this Masterharper has words enough to express the sympathy and honor he has for you. But you must sleep; you have tomorrow to endure and the tomorrow after that you have to fight. The dragonmen must have a leader . . ." and his voice trailed off. "Tomorrow you must send for F'nor . . . and Pridith."

F'lar pivoted on his heel and strode towards the fateful door of Ruatha's great hall.

Oh, Tongue, give sound to joy
and sing
Of hope and promise on dragon-
wing.

Before them loomed Ruatha's Great Tower, the high walls of the Outer Court clearly visible in the fading light.

The klaxon rang violent summons into the air, barely heard over the ear-splitting thunder as hundreds of dragons appeared, ranging in full fighting array wing upon wing, up and down the valley.

A shaft of light stained the flagstones of the Court as the Hold door opened.

Lessa ordered Ramoth down, close to the Tower, and dismounted, running eagerly forward to greet the men who piled out of the door. She made out the stocky figure of Lytol, a handbasket of glows held high about his head. She was so relieved to see him, she forgot her previous antagonism to the Warder.

"You misjudged the last jump by two days, Lessa," he cried as soon as he was near enough for her to hear him over the noise of settling dragons.

"Misjudged? How could I?" she breathed.

M'ron and Mardra came up beside her.

"It is not to worry," Lyton reassured her, gripping her hands tightly in his, his eyes dancing. He was actually smiling at her. "You overshot the day. Go back *between*, return to Ruatha of two days ago. That's all." His grin widened at her confusion. "It is all right," he repeated, patting her hands. "Take this same hour, the Great Court, everything, but visualize F'lar, Robinton and myself here on the flagstones. Place Mnementh on the Great Tower and a blue dragon on the verge. Now go."

Mnementh? Ramoth queried Lessa, eager to see her weyrmate. She ducked her great head and her huge eyes gleamed with scintillating fire.

"I don't understand," Lessa wailed. Mardra slipped a comforting arm around her shoulders.

"But I do, I do, trust me," Lytol pleaded, patting her shoulder awkwardly and glancing at M'ron for support. "It is as F'nor has said. You cannot be several places in time without experiencing great distress and when you stopped twelve Turns back, it threw Lessa all to pieces."

"You know that?" M'ron cried.

"Of course. Just go back two days. You see, I *know* you have. I shall, of course, be surprised then, but now, tonight, I know you reappeared two days earlier. Oh, go. Don't argue. F'lar was half out of his mind with worry for you."

"He'll shake me," Lessa cried, like a little girl.

"Lessa!" M'ron took her by the hand and led her back to Ramoth who crouched so her rider could mount.

M'ron took complete charge and had his Fidranth pass the order to return to the references Lytol had given, adding by way of Ramoth a description of the humans and Mnementh.

The cold of *between* restored Lessa to herself although her error had badly jarred her confidence. But then, there was Ruatha again. The dragons happily arranged themselves in tremendous display. And there, silhouetted against the light from the Hall, stood Lytol, Robinton's tall figure and . . . F'lar.

Mnementh's voice gave a brassy welcome and Ramoth could not land Lessa quickly enough to go and twine necks with her mate.

Lessa stood where Ramoth had left her, unable to move. She was aware that Mardra and M'ron were beside her. She was conscious only of F'lar, racing across the Court towards her as fast as he could. Yet she could not move.

He swung her up in his arms, hugging her so tightly she could not doubt the joy of his welcome.

"My darling, my love, how could you gamble so? I have been lost in an endless *between,* fearing for you." He kissed her, hugged her, held her and then kissed her with rough urgency again. Then he suddenly set her on her feet and gripped her shoulders. "Lessa, if you ever . . ." he said, punctuating each word with a flexing of his fingers, and stopped, aware of a grinning circle of strangers surrounding them.

"I told you he'd shake me," Lessa was saying, dashing tears from her face. "But, F'lar, I brought them all . . . all but Benden Weyr. And that is why the five Weyrs were abandoned. I brought them."

F'lar looked around him, looked beyond the leaders to the

masses of dragons settling in the Valley, on the heights, everywhere he turned. There were dragons, blue, green, bronze, brown, and a whole wingful of golden queen dragons alone.

"You brought the Weyrs?" he echoed, stunned.

"Yes, this is Mardra and M'ron of Fort Weyr, D'ram and . . ."

He stopped her with a little shake, pulling her to his side so he could see and greet the newcomers.

"I am more grateful than you can know," he said and could not go on with all the many words he wanted to add.

M'ron stepped forward, holding out his hand which F'lar seized and held firmly.

"We bring eighteen hundred dragons, seventeen queens, and all that is necessary to implement our Weyrs."

"And they brought flamethrowers, too," Lessa put in excitedly.

"But, to come . . . to attempt it . . ." F'lar murmured in admiring wonder.

M'ron and D'ram and the others laughed.

"Your Lessa showed the way."

". . . With the Red Star to guide us . . ." she said.

"We are dragonmen," M'ron continued solemnly, "as you are yourself, F'lar of Benden. We were told there are Threads here to fight and that's work for dragonmen to do . . . in any time!"

Drummer, beat, and piper, blow,
Harper, strike, and soldier, go.
Free the flame and sear the grasses
'Til the dawning Red Star passes.

Even as the five Weyrs had been settling around Ruatha valley, F'nor had been compelled to bring forward in time his southern weyrfolk. They had all reached the end of endurance in double-time life, gratefully creeping back to quarters they had vacated two days and ten Turns ago.

R'gul, totally unaware of Lessa's backward plunge, greeted F'lar and his Weyrwoman on their return to the Weyr, with the news of F'nor's appearance with seventy-two new dragons and the further word that he doubted any of the riders would be fit to fight.

"Never seen such exhausted men in my life," R'gul rattled

on, "can't imagine what could have got into them, with sun and plenty of food and all, and no responsibilities."

F'lar and Lessa exchanged glances.

"Well, the southern Weyr ought to be maintained, R'gul. Think it over."

"I'm a fighting dragonman, not a womanizer," the old dragonrider grunted. "It'd take more than a trip *between* times to reduce me like those others."

"Oh, they'll be themselves again in next to no time," Lessa said and, to R'gul's intense disapproval, she giggled.

"They'll have to be if we're to keep the skies Threadfree," R'gul snapped testily.

"No problem about that now," F'lar assured him easily.

"No problem? With only a hundred and forty-four dragons?"

"Two hundred and sixteen," Lessa corrected him firmly.

Ignoring her, R'gul asked, "Has that smithmaster found a flamethrower that'll work?"

"Indeed he has," F'lar said.

The five Weyrs had indeed brought forward their equipment. Fandarel all but snatched examples from their backs and, undoubtedly, every hearth and smithy through the continent would be ready to duplicate the design by morning. M'ron had told F'lar that, in his time, each Hold had ample flamethrowers for every man on the ground. In the course of the Long Interval, however, the throwers must have been either smelted down or lost as incomprehensible devices. D'ram, particularly, was very interested in Fandarel's agenothree sprayer, considering it better than thrown-flame since it would also act as a fertilizer.

"Well," R'gul admitted gloomily, "a flamethrower or two will be some help day after tomorrow."

"We have found something else that will help a lot more," Lessa remarked and then hastily excused herself, dashing into the sleeping quarters.

The sounds which drifted past the curtain were either laughter or sobs and R'gul frowned on both. That girl was just too young to be Weyrwoman at such a time. No stability.

"Has she realized how critical our situation is—even with F'nor's additions—that is, if they can fly?" R'gul demanded testily. "You oughtn't to let her leave the Weyr at all."

F'lar ignored that and began pouring himself a cup of wine.

"You once pointed out to me that the five empty Weyrs of

Pern supported your theory that there would be no more Threads."

R'gul cleared his throat, thinking that apologies—even if they might be due the Weyrleader—were scarcely effective against the Threads.

"Now there was merit in that theory," F'lar went on, filling a cup for R'gul. "Not, however, as you interpreted it. The five Weyrs were empty because they . . . they came here."

R'gul, his cup halfway to his lips, stared at F'lar. This man also was too young to bear his responsibilities. But . . . he seemed actually to believe what he was saying.

"Believe it or not, R'gul—and in a bare day's time you will—the five Weyrs are empty no longer. They're here, in the Weyrs, in this time. And they shall join us, eighteen hundred strong, tomorrow at Telgar, with flamethrowers and with plenty of battle experience to help us overcome our ancient foe."

R'gul regarded the poor man stolidly for a long moment. Carefully he put his cup down and, turning on his heel, left the weyr. He refused to be an object of ridicule. He'd better plan to take over the leadership tomorrow if they were to fight Threads the day after.

The next morning, when he saw the clutch of great bronze dragons bearing the Weyrleaders and their wingleaders to the conference, R'gul got quietly drunk.

Lessa exchanged good mornings with her friends and then, smiling sweetly, left the weyr, saying she must feed Ramoth. F'lar stared after her thoughtfully, then went to greet Robinton and Fandarel who had been asked to attend the meeting, too. Neither Craftmaster said much, but neither missed a word said. Fandarel's great head kept swiveling from speaker to speaker, his deepset eyes blinking occasionally. Robinton sat with a bemused smile on his face, utterly delighted by the circumstance of ancestral visitors.

F'lar was quickly talked out of resigning his titular position as Weyrleader of Benden on the grounds that he was too inexperienced.

"You did well enough at Nerat and Keroon. Well indeed," M'ron said.

"You call twenty-eight men or dragons out of action good leadership?"

"For a first battle, with every dragonman green as a hatchling? No, man, you were on time at Nerat, however you got there," and M'ron grinned maliciously at F'lar, "which is what a dragonman must do. No, that was well flown, I say. Well flown." The four other Weyrleaders muttered complete agreement with that compliment. "Your Weyr is understrength, though, so we'll lend you enough odd-wing riders till you've got the Weyr up to full strength again. Oh, the queens love these times!" And his grin broadened to indicate that bronze riders did, too.

F'lar returned that smile, thinking that Ramoth was about ready for another mating flight and this time, Lessa . . . Oh, that girl was being too deceptively docile. He'd better watch her closely.

"Now," M'ron was saying, "we left with Fandarel's Crafthold all the flamethrowers we brought up so that the groundmen will be armed tomorrow."

"Aye, and my thanks," Fandarel grunted. "We'll turn out new ones in record time and return yours soon."

"Don't forget to adapt that agenothree for air spraying, too," D'ram put in.

"It is agreed," and M'ron glanced quickly around at the other riders, "that all the Weyrs will meet, full strength, three hours after dawn above Telgar, to follow the Threads' attack across to Crom. By the way, F'lar, those charts of yours that Robinton showed me are superb. We never had them."

"How did you know when the attacks would come?"

M'ron shrugged. "They were coming so regularly even when I was a weyrling, you kind of knew when one was due. But this way is much much better."

"More efficient," Fandarel added approvingly.

"After tomorrow, when all the Weyrs show up at Telgar, we can request what supplies we need to stock the empty Weyrs," M'ron grinned. "Like old times, squeezing extra tithes from the Holders," and he rubbed his hands in anticipation.

"There's the southern Weyr," F'nor suggested. "We've been gone from there six Turns in this time, and the herdbeasts were left. They'll have multiplied and there'll be all that fruit and grain."

"It would please me to see that southern venture continued," F'lar remarked, nodding encouragingly at F'nor.

"Yes, and continue Kylara down there, please, too," F'nor added urgently, his eyes sparkling with irritation.

They discussed sending for some immediate supplies to help out the newly occupied Weyrs, and then adjourned the meeting.

"It is a trifle unsettling," M'ron said as he shared wine with Robinton, "to find the Weyr you left the day before in good order has become a dusty hulk." He chuckled. "The women of the lower Caverns were a bit upset."

"We cleaned up those kitchens," F'nor replied indignantly. A good night's rest in a fresh time had removed much of his fatigue.

M'ron cleared his throat. "According to Mardra, no man can *clean* anything."

"Do you think you'll be up to riding tomorrow, F'nor?" F'lar asked solicitously. He was keenly aware of the stress of years showing in his half brother's face despite his improvement overnight. Yet those strenuous Turns had been necessary, nor had they become futile even by hindsight with the arrival of eighteen hundred dragons from past time. When F'lar had ordered F'nor ten Turns backward to breed the desperately needed replacements, they had not yet brought to mind the Question Song or known of the Tapestry.

"I wouldn't miss that fight if I were dragonless," F'nor declared stoutly.

"Which reminds me," F'lar remarked, "we'll need Lessa at Telgar tomorrow. She can speak to any dragon, you know," he explained almost apologetically, to M'ron and D'ram.

"Oh, we know," M'ron assured him. "And Mardra doesn't mind." Seeing F'lar's blank expression, he added, "As senior Weyrwoman, Mardra, of course, leads the queens' wing."

F'lar's face grew blanker. "Queens' wing?"

"Certainly," and M'ron and D'ram exchanged questioning glances at F'lar's surprise. "You don't keep your queens from fighting, do you?"

"Our *queens?* M'ron, we at Benden have had but *one* queen dragon—at a time—for so many generations, that there are those who denounce the legends of queens in battle as black sacrilege!"

M'ron looked rueful. "I had not truly realized how small your numbers were, till this instant." But his enthusiasm overtook him. "Just the same, queens're very useful with flamethrowers. They get clumps other riders might miss. They fly in low, under the main wings. That's one reason D'ram's so interested in the agenothree spray. Doesn't singe the hair off the Holders' heads, so to speak, and is far better over tilled fields."

"Do you mean to say that you allow your queens to fly—against Threads?" F'lar ignored the fact that F'nor was grinning, and M'ron, too.

"Allow?" D'ram bellowed. "You can't stop them. Don't you know your Ballads?"

" 'Moreta's Ride'?"

"Exactly."

F'nor laughed aloud at the expression on F'lar's face as he irritably pulled the hanging forelock from his eyes. Then, sheepishly, he began to grin.

"Thanks. That gives me an idea."

He saw his fellow Weyrleaders to their dragons, waved cheerfully to Robinton and Fandarel, more lighthearted than he would have thought he'd be the morning before the second battle. Then he asked Mnementh where Lessa might be.

Bathing, the bronze dragon replied.

F'lar glanced at the empty queen's weyr.

Oh, Ramoth is on the Peak, as usual. Mnementh sounded agrieved.

F'lar heard the sound of splashing in the bathing room suddenly cease, so he called down for hot *klah*. He was going to enjoy this.

"Oh, did the meeting go well?" Lessa asked sweetly as she emerged from the bathing room, drying-cloth wrapped tightly around her slender figure.

"Extremely. You realize, of course, Lessa, that you'll be needed at Telgar?"

She looked at him intently for a moment before she smiled again.

"I *am* the only Weyrwoman who can speak to any dragon," she replied archly.

"True," F'lar admitted blithely. "And no longer the only queen's rider in Benden . . ."

"I hate you!" Lessa snapped, unable to evade F'lar as he pinned her cloth-swathed body to his.

"Even when I tell you that Fandarel has a flamethrower for you so you can join the queens' wing?"

She stopped squirming in his arms and stared at him, disconcerted that he had outguessed her.

"And that Kylara will be installed as Weyrwoman in the south . . . in this time? As Weyrleader, I need all the peace and quiet I can get between battles . . ."

From the Weyr and from the Bowl
Bronze and brown and blue and
  green,
Rise the dragonmen of Pern,
Aloft, on wing; seen, then unseen.

Ranged above the Peak of Benden Weyr, a scant three hours after dawn, two hundred and sixteen dragons held their formations as F'lar on bronze Mnementh inspected their ranks.

Below in the Bowl were gathered all the weyrfolk and some of those injured in the first battle. All the weyrfolk, that is, except Lessa and Ramoth. They had gone on to Fort Weyr where the queens' wing was assembling. F'lar could not quite suppress a twinge of concern that she and Ramoth would be fighting, too. A holdover, he knew, from the days when Pern had had but the one queen. If Lessa could jump four hundred Turns *between* and lead five Weyrs back, she could take care of herself and her dragon against Threads.

He checked to be sure that every man was well loaded with firestone sacks, that each dragon was in good color, especially those in from the southern Weyr. Of course, the dragons were fit but the faces of the men still showed evidences of the temporal strains they had endured. He was procrastinating and the Threads would be dropping in the skies of Telgar.

He gave the order to go *between*. They reappeared above, and to the south of Telgar Hold itself, and were not the first arrivals. To the west, to the north and yes, to the east now, wings arrived until the horizon was patterned with the great V's of several thousand dragon wings. Faintly he heard the klaxon bell on Telgar Hold Tower as the unexpected dragon strength was acclaimed from the ground.

"Where is she?" F'lar demanded of Mnementh. "We'll need her presently to relay orders . . ."

She's coming, Mnementh interrupted him.

Right above Telgar Hold another wing appeared. Even at this distance, F'lar could see the difference: the golden dragons shone in the bright morning sunlight.

A hum of approval drifted down the dragon ranks and despite his fleeting worry, F'lar grinned with proud indulgence at the glittering sight.

Just then the eastern wings soared straight upward in the sky as the dragons became instinctively aware of the presence of their ancient foe.

Mnementh raised his head, echoing back the brass thunder of the war cry. He turned his head, even as hundreds of other beasts turned to receive firestone from their riders. Hundreds of great jaws masticated the stone, swallowed it, their digestive acids transforming dry stone into flame producing gases, igniting on contact with oxygen.

Threads! F'lar could see them clearly now against the spring sky. His pulses began to quicken, not with apprehension, but with a savage joy. His heart pounded unevenly. Mnementh demanded more stone and began to speed up the strokes of his wings in the air, gathering himself to leap upward when commanded.

The leading Weyr already belched gouts of orange-red flame into the pale-blue sky. Dragons winked in and out, flamed and dove.

The great golden queens sped at cliff-skimming height to cover what might have been missed.

Then F'lar gave the command to gain altitude to meet the Threads halfway in their abortive descent. As Mnementh surged upward, F'lar shook his fist defiantly at the winking Red Eye of the Star.

"One day," he shouted, "we will not sit tamely here, awaiting your fall. We will fall on you, where you spin, and sear you on your own ground."

By the Egg, he told himself, if we can travel four hundred Turns backward, and across seas and lands in the blink of an eye, what is travel from one world to another but a different kind of step?

F'lar grinned to himself. He'd better not mention that audacious notion in Lessa's presence.

Clumps ahead, Mnementh warned him.

As the bronze dragon charged, flaming, F'lar tightened his knees on the massive neck. Mother of us all, he was glad that now, of all times conceivable, he, F'lar, rider of bronze Mnementh, was a Dragonman of Pern!

KEITH LAUMER (1925–   ) is remarkable in several respects—he has been tremendously prolific and very popular, having published dozens of excellent novels and collections featuring at least four series characters or settings plus excellent individual works. His series about the adventures of interstellar diplomat Jamie Retief combines great adventure with wonderful humor, and reflects the author's own experiences as a member of the United States Foreign Service in the 1950s. Also remarkable is his recovery from a serious stroke that temporarily reduced his output. A former captain in the United States Air Force, he writes some of the best action and combat stories extant, including the following story later expanded into *Dinosaur Beach* (1971).

THE TIMESWEEPERS

Keith Laumer

The man slid into the seat across from me, breathing a little hard, and said, "Do you mind?" He was holding a filled glass in his hand; he waved it at the room, which was crowded, but not that crowded. It was a slightly run-down bar in a run-down street in a run-down world. Just the place for meeting strangers.

I looked him over, not too friendly a look. The smile he was wearing slipped a little and wasn't a smile anymore, just a sick smirk. He had a soft, round face, very pale blue eyes, the kind of head that ought to be bald but was covered with a fine blond down, like baby chicken feathers. He was wearing a striped sport shirt with a very wide collar laid back over a bulky plaid jacket with padded shoulders and wide lapels. His neck was smooth-skinned, and too thin for his head. The hand that was holding the glass was small and well-lotioned, with short, immaculately manicured fingers. There was a big, cumbersome-looking ring on one of the fingers. The whole composition looked a little out of tune, like something assembled in a hurry by somebody who was short on material and had to make do with what was at hand. Still, it wasn't a bad job, under the circumstances. It had passed—up until now.

"Please don't misunderstand," he said. His voice was like

the rest of him: not feminine enough for a woman, but not anything you'd associate with a room full of cigar smoke, either.

"It's vital that I speak with you, Mr. Starv," he went on, talking fast, as if he wanted to get it all said before he was thrown out. "It's a matter of great importance to your future."

He must not have liked what went across my face then; he started to get up and I caught his wrist—as soft and smooth as a baby's—and levered him back into his seat.

"You might as well stay and tell me about it," I said. I looked at him over my glass while he got his smile fixed up and back in position. "My future, eh?" I prompted him. "I wasn't sure I had one."

"Oh, yes," he said, and nodded quickly. "Yes indeed. And I might add that your future is a great deal larger than your past, Mr. Starv."

"Have we met somewhere?"

He shook his head. "Please—I know I don't make a great deal of sense; I'm under a considerable strain. But please listen . . ."

"I'm listening, Mr. . . . what was the name?"

"It really doesn't matter, Mr. Starv. I myself don't enter into the matter at all; I was merely assigned to contact you and deliver the information."

"Assigned?"

He looked at me with an expression like a slave bringing ill tidings to a bad-tempered king.

"Mr. Starv—what would you say if I told you I was a member of a secret organization of supermen?"

"What would you expect me to say?"

"That I'm insane," he said promptly. "Naturally, that's why I'd prefer to speak directly to the point. Mr. Starv, your life is in danger."

"Go on."

"In precisely"—he glanced at the watch strapped to the underside of his wrist—"one and one half minutes, a man will enter this establishment. He will be dressed in a costume of black, and will carry a cane—ebony, with a silver head. He will go to the bar, order a straight whiskey, drink it, turn, raise the cane and fire three lethal darts into your chest."

I took another swallow of my drink. It was the real stuff; one of the compensations of the job.

"Uh-huh," I said. "Then what?"

"Then? Then?" my little man said rather wildly. "Then you are dead, Mr. Starv!" He leaned across the table and threw this at me in a hiss, with quite a lot of spit.

"Well, I guess that's that," I said.

"No!" His fat little hand shot out and clutched my arm with more power than I'd given him credit for. "This is what will happen—*unless* you act at once to avert it."

"I take it that's where the big future you mentioned comes in."

"Mr. Starv—you must leave here at once." He fumbled in a pocket of his coat, brought out a card with an address printed on it: *309 Turkon Place*.

"It's an old building, very stable, quite near here. Go to the third floor. You'll have to climb a wooden stairway, but it's quite safe. A door marked with the numeral 9 is at the back. Enter the room and wait."

"Why would I do that?" I asked him.

He wiped at his face with his free hand.

"In order to save your life," he said.

"What's the idea—that the boy in black can't work in rooms marked 9?"

"Please, Mr. Starv—time is short. Won't you simply trust me?"

"Where'd you get my name?"

"Does that matter more than your life?"

"The name's a phony. I made it up about an hour and a half ago, when I registered at the hotel across the street."

His earnest look went all to pieces; he was still trying to reassemble it when the street door of the bar opened and a man in a black overcoat, black velvet collar, black homburg and carrying a black swagger stick walked in.

My new chum's fingers clamped into the same grooves they'd made last time.

"You see? Just as I said. Now, quickly, Mr. Starv—"

I brushed his hand off me and slid out of the booth. The man in black went to the bar without looking my way, took a stool near the end.

I went across and took the stool on his left.

He didn't look at me. He was so busy not looking at me

that he didn't even look around when my elbow dug into his side. If there was a gun in his pocket, I couldn't feel it.

I leaned a little toward him. "Who is he?" I said, about eight inches from his ear. His head jerked. He put his hands on the bar and turned. His face was thin, white around the nostrils from anger or illness, gray everywhere else. His eyes looked like little black stones.

"Are you addressing me?" he said in a tone with a chill like Scott's last camp on the ice cap.

"Your friend with the sticky hands is waiting over in the booth. Why not join the party?"

"You've made an error," Blackie said, and turned away.

From the corner of my eye I saw the other half of the team trying a sneak play around left end. I caught him a few yards past the door.

It was a cold night. Half an inch of snow squeaked under our shoes as he tried to jerk free of the grip I took on his upper arm.

"Tell me about it," I said. "After I bought the mind-reading act, what was to come next?"

"You fool—I'm trying to save your life—have you no sense of gratitude?"

"What made it worth the trouble? My suit wouldn't fit you, and the cash in my pocket wouldn't pay cab fare over to Turkon Place and back."

"Let me go! We must get off the street!" He tried to kick my ankle, and I socked him under the ribs hard enough to fold him against me wheezing like a bagpipe. I took a quick step back and heard the flat *whak!* of a silenced pistol and the whisper that a bullet makes when it passes an inch from your ear: Blackie's cane going into action from the door to the bar.

There was an alleymouth a few feet away. We made it in one jump. My little pal had his feet working again, and tried to use them to wreck my knee. I had to bruise his shins a little.

"Easy," I told him. "That slug changes things. Quiet down and I'll let go of your neck."

He nodded as well as he could with my thumb where it was and I eased him back against the wall. I put my back against it, beside him, with him between me and the alleymouth. I made a little production of levering back the hammer of my Mauser.

Two or three minutes went past like geologic ages.

"We'll take a look. You first." I prodded him forward. Nobody shot at him. I risked a look. Except for a few people not in black overcoats, the sidewalk was empty.

My car was across the street. I walked him across and waited while he got in and slid across under the wheel, then got in after him. There were other parked cars, and plenty of dark windows up above for a sniper to work from, but nobody did.

"309 Turkon Place, you said." I nudged him with the Mauser. "Let's go have a look."

He drove badly, like a middle-aged widow who only learned to drive after her husband died. We clashed gears and ran stoplights across town to the street he had named. It was a badly-lit unpatched brick dead end that rose steeply toward a tangle of telephone poles at the top. The house was tall and narrow, slanted against the sky, showing no lights. I prodded my guide ahead of me along the narrow walk that ran back beside the house, went in via the back door. It resisted a little, but gave without making any more noise than a dropped xylophone.

We stood on some warped linoleum and smelled last week's cabbage and listened to some dense silence.

"Don't be afraid," the little man said. "There's no one here." He led me along a passage a little wider than my elbows, past a tarnished mirror and a stand full of umbrellas, up steep steps with black rubber matting held by tarnished brass rods. The flooring creaked on the landing. Another flight brought us into a low-ceilinged hall with gray-painted doors made visible by the pale light coming through a wire-glass skylight.

He found number 9, put an ear against it, opened up and went in. I followed.

It was a small bedroom, with a double bed, a dresser with a doily on it, a straight chair, a rocker, an oval rag rug, a hanging fixture in the center with a colored glass bowl. My host placed the chairs into a cozy *tête-à-tête* arrangement, offered me the rocker, and perched on the edge of the other.

"Now," he said, and put his fingertips together comfortably, like a pawnbroker about to beat you down on the value of the family jewels, "I suppose you want to hear all about the man in black, how I knew just when he'd appear, and so on."

"It was neat routine," I said. "Up to a point. After you fingered me, if I didn't buy the act, Blackie would plug me—with a dope dart. If I did—I'd be so grateful, I'd come here."

"As indeed you have." My little man looked different now, more relaxed, less eager to please. "I suppose I need not add that the end result will be the same." He made a nice hip draw and showed me a strange-looking little gun, all shiny rods and levers.

"You will now tell me about yourself, Mr. Starv—or whatever you may choose to call yourself."

"Wrong again—Karge," I said.

For an instant it didn't register. Then his fingers twitched and the gun made a spitting sound and needles showered off my chest. I let him fire the full magazine. Then I shot him under the left eye with the pistol I had palmed while he was settling himself on his chair.

He settled further; his head was bent over his left shoulder as if he were trying to admire the water spots on the ceiling. His little pudgy hands opened and closed a couple of times. He leaned sideways quite slowly and hit the floor like a hundred and fifty pounds of heavy machinery.

Which he was, of course.

The shots hadn't made much noise—no more than the one fired at me by the Enforcer had. I listened, heard nothing in the way of a response. I laid the Karge out on his back—or on its back—and cut the seal on his reel compartment, lifted out the tape he'd been operating on. It was almost spent, indicating that his mission had been almost completed. I checked his pockets but turned up nothing, not even a ball of lint.

It took me twenty minutes to go over the room. I found a brain-reader focused on the rocker from the stained-glass ceiling light. He'd gone to a lot of effort to make sure he cleaned me before disposing of the remains.

I took time to record my scan to four-point detail, then went back down to the street. A big square car went past, making a lot of noise in the silent street, but no bullets squirted from it. I checked my locator and started east, downslope.

It was a twenty-minute walk to the nearest spot the gauges said was within the acceptable point-point range for a locus transfer. I tapped out the code with my tongue against the trick molars set in my lower jaw, felt the silent impact of temporal implosion, and was squinting against the dazzling sunlight glaring down on Dinosaur Beach.

My game of cat-and-mouse with the Karge had covered several square miles of the city of Buffalo, New York, T.F. late March, 1936. A quick review of my movements from the time of my arrival at the locus told me that the Timecast station should be about a mile and a half distant, to the southwest, along the beach. I discarded the warmer portions of my costume and started hiking.

The sea in this era—some sixty-five million years BC—was south-sea-island blue, stretching wide and placid to the horizon. The long swells coming in off the Eastern Ocean—which would one day become the Atlantic—crashed on the gray sand with the same familiar *crump-boom!* that I had known in a dozen Eras. It was a comforting sound. It said that after all, the doings of the little creatures that scuttled on her shores were nothing much in the life of Mother Ocean, age five billion and not yet in her prime.

There was a low headland just ahead, from which the station would be visible a mile or so beyond: a small, low, gray-white structure perched on the sand above high tide line, surrounded by tree ferns and club-mosses, not as decoration but to render the installation as inconspicuous as possible, on the theory that if the wild life were either attracted or repelled by strangeness it might introduce an uncharted U-line on the Probability charts which would render a thousand years of painstaking—and painful—temporal mapping invalid.

Inside, Nel Jard, the Chief Timecaster, would have me in for debriefing, would punch his notes into the master plot, and wave me on my way back to Nexx Central, where a new job would be waiting, having nothing to do with the last one. I'd never learn just why the Karge had been placed where it was, what sort of deal it had made with the Enforcers, what part the whole thing played in the larger tapestry of the Nexx grand strategy.

That's what would have happened. Except that I topped the rise just then and saw the long curve of beach ahead, and the tongue of jungle that stretched down almost to the shore along the ridge. But where the station had been, there was nothing but a smoking crater.

Dinosaur Beach had been so named because a troop of small allosaur-like reptiles had been scurrying along it when the first siting party had fixed-in there. That had been sixty years ago, Nexx Subjective, only a few months after the decision to implement Project Timesweep.

The idea wasn't without merit. The First Era of time travel had closely resembled the dawn of the space age in some ways—notably, in the trail of rubbish it left behind. In the case of the space garbage, it had taken half a dozen major collisions to convince the authorities of the need to sweep circumterrestrial space clean of fifty years' debris in the form of spent rocket casings, defunct telemetry gear, and derelict relay satellites long lost track of. In the process they'd turned up a large number of odds and ends of meteoric rock and iron, a few lumps of clearly terrestrial origin, possibly volcanic, the mummified body of an astronaut lost on an early space walk, and a couple of artifacts that the authorities of the day had scratched their heads over and finally written off as the equivalent of empty beer cans tossed out by visitors from out-system.

That was before the days of Timecasting, of course.

The Timesweep program was a close parallel to the space sweep. The Old Era temporal experimenters had littered the time-ways with everything from early one-way timecans to observation stations, dead bodies, abandoned instruments, weapons and equipment of all sorts, including an automatic mining setup established under the Antarctic ice, which caused headaches at the time of the Big Melt.

Then the three hundred years of the Last Peace put an end to that; and when temporal transfer was rediscovered in early New Era times, the lesson had been heeded. Rigid rules were enforced from the beginning of the Second Program, forbidding all the mistakes that had been made by the First Program pioneers.

Which meant the Second Program had to invent its own disasters—like the one I was looking at.

I had gone flat on the hot sand at first sight of the pit among the blackened stumps of the club-mosses, while a flood of extraneous thoughts went whirling through my tired old brain, as thoughts will in such moments. I had been primed to step out of the heat and the insects and the sand into cool, clean air, soft music, the luxury of a stimbath and a nap on a real air couch.

But that was all gone to slag now. I hugged the ground and looked down at it, and tried to extract what data I could from what I could see. It wasn't much.

Item one: Some power had had the will and the way to blast a second-class Nexx staging station out of existence. It seemed they'd used good old-fashioned nuclears for the job, too; nothing so subtle as a temporal lift, or a phase-suppressor.

Item two: The chore had been handled during the ten days NS. I'd been on location in 1936. There might, or might not, be some message there for me.

I suppressed the desire to jump up and run down for a closer look. I stayed where I was, playing boulder, and looked at the scene some more with gritty eyes that wept copiously in the glare of the tropical Jurassic sun. I didn't see anything move—which didn't mean there was nothing there to see. After half an hour of that, I got up and walked down to the ruins.

Ruins was an exaggeration. There was a fused glass pit a hundred yards in diameter surrounded by charred organic matter. That gave me item three:

Nothing had survived—no people, no equipment. Not only would I not have the benefit of soft music and bed to match, there'd be no debriefing, no input of data into the master tape, no replay of the Karge operation tape to give me a clue to Enforcer Strategy. And worst of all, there'd be no outjump to Nexx Central.

Which made things a trifle awkward, since the location of Central was a secret buried under twelve layers of interlocked ciphers in the main tank of the Nexial Brain. Not even the men who built the installation knew its physical and temporal coordinates. The only way to reach it was to be computer-routed via one of the hundred and twelve official staging stations scattered across Old Era time. And not just any station: it had to be the one my personal jumper field was attuned to.

Which was a thin layer of green glass lining a hollow in the sand.

It was one of those times when the mind goes racing around inside the trap of the skull like a mouse in a bucket, making frantic leaps for freedom and falling back painfully on its rear.

On about the tenth lap, an idea bobbed up and grinned a rather ghastly grin.

My personal jump gear, being installed in my body, was intact. All I lacked was a target. But that didn't mean I couldn't jump. All it meant was that I wouldn't know where I'd land—if anywhere.

There had been a lot of horror stories circulated back at Nexx Central about what had happened to people who misfired on a jump. They ranged from piecemeal reception at a dozen stations strung out across a few centuries, to disembodied voices screaming to be let out. Also, there were several rules against it.

The alternative was to set up housekeeping here on the beach, with or without dinosaurs, and hope that a rescue mission arrived before I died of old age, heat, thirst, or reptiles.

I didn't like the odds, but they were all the odds I had.

I took a final breath of humid beach air, a last look around at the bright, brutal view of sea and sand, the high, empty sky. It seemed to be waiting for something to happen.

The tune I played on the console set in my jaw was different this time, but the effect was much the same: The painless blow of a silent club, the sense of looping the loop through a Universe-sized Klein bottle—

Total darkness and a roar of sound like Niagara Falls going over me in a barrel.

For a few seconds I stood absolutely still, taking a swift inventory of my existence. I seemed to be all here, organized pretty much as usual. The sound went on, the blackness failed to fade. The rule book said that in a case of transfer malfunction to remain immobile and await retrieval, but in this case that might take quite a while. Also, there was the datum that no one had ever lived to report a jump malfunction, which suggested that possibly the rule book was wrong.

I tried to breathe, and nothing happened. That decided me. I took a step and emerged as through a curtain into a strange blackish light, shot through with little points of dazzling brilliance, like what you see just before you faint from loss of blood. But before I could put my head between my knees, the dazzle faded and I was looking at the jump room of a regulation Nexx Staging Station. And I could breathe.

I did that for a few moments, then turned and looked at the curtain I had come through. It was a solid wall of beryl-steel, to my knowledge over two meters thick.

Maybe the sound I had heard was the whizzing of molecules of dense metal interpenetrating with my own two hundred pounds of impure water.

That was a phenomenon I'd have to let ride until later. More pressing business called for attention first—such as discovering why the station was as silent as King Sethy's tomb after the grave robbers finished with it.

It took me ten minutes to check every room on operations level. Nobody was home. The same for the R and R complex. Likewise the equipment division, and the power chamber.

The core sink was drawing normal power, the charge was up on the transmitter plates, the green lights were on all across the panels; but nothing was tapping the station for so much as a microerg.

Which was impossible. The links that tied a staging station to Nexx Central and in turn monitored the activities of personnel operating out of the station always drew at least a trickle of carrier power. They had to, as long as the station existed. A no-drain condition was impossible anywhere in normal space time.

I didn't like the conclusion, but I reached it anyway.

All the stations were identical; in fact, considering their mass-production by the time-stutter process which distributed them up and down the temporal contour, there's a school of thought that holds that they *are* identical; alternate temporal aspects of the same physical matrix. But that was theory, and my present situation was fact. A fact I had to deal with.

I went along the passage to the entry lock—some of the sites are hostile to what Nexx thinks of as ordinary life—cycled it, and almost stepped out.

Not quite.

The ground ended about ten feet from the outflung entry wing. Beyond was a pearly gray mist, swirling against an invisible barrier. I went forward to the edge and lay flat and looked over. I could see the curve of the underside of the patch of solid rock the station perched on. It was as smooth and polished as green glass. Like the green glass crater I'd seen back on the beach.

The station had been scooped out of the rock like a giant dip of ice cream and deposited here, behind a barrier of a kind the scientists of Nexx Central had never dreamed of.

That gave me two or three things to think of. I thought of them while I went back in through the lock, and down the transit tunnel to the transfer booth.

It looked normal. Aside from the absence of a cheery green light to tell me that the field was on sharp focus to Nexx Central, all was as it should be. The plates were hot, the dial readings normal.

If I stepped inside, I'd be transferred—somewhere.

Some more interesting questions suggested themselves, but I'd already been all over those. I stepped in and the door valved shut and I was alone with my thoughts. Before I could have too many of those I reached out and tripped the Xmit button.

A soundless bomb blew me motionlessly across dimensionless space.

A sense of vertigo that slowly faded; a shimmer of light, as from a reflective surface in constant, restless movement; a hollow, almost metallic sound, coming from below me; a faint sensation of heat and pressure against my side . . .

Sunlight shining on water. The waves slapping the hollow steel pilings of a pier. The pressure of a plank deck on which I was lying—a remote, tentative pressure, like a sun-warmed cloud.

I sat up. The horizon pivoted to lie flat, dancing in the heat-ripples. The spars and masts of a small sailing ship poked up bare against a lush blue sky.

Not a galleon, I realized—at least not a real one. The steel pilings rendered that anachronous. That made it a replica, probably from the Revival, circa 2020 AD. I got to my feet, noticing a curious tendency on the part of my feet to sink into the decking.

I was still dizzy from the shock of the transfer. Otherwise I would probably have stayed where I was until I had sorted through the ramifications of this latest development. Instead, I started toward the end of the pier. It was high and wide—about twenty feet from edge to edge, fifteen feet above the water. From the end I could look down on the deck of the pseudo-galleon, snugged up close against the resilient bumper at the end of the quay. It was a fine reproduction, artfully carved and weather-scarred. Probably with a small reactor below decks, steel armor under the near-oak hull-planking, and luxury accommodations for an operator and a dozen holiday-makers.

Then I saw the dead man lying on the deck. He was face-down at the foot of the mast—a big fellow dressed in sixteenth century costume, soiled and sweat-stained. He looked much too authentic to be part of a game.

I stood still and tried to get it together. Something about what I was looking at bothered me. I wanted to see it more closely. A ladder went down. I descended, jumped the six-foot gap. Nobody came out to see what the disturbance was all about.

The mast cast a black shadow across the hand-hewn deck, across the man lying there, one hand under him, the other outflung. A gun lay a yard from the empty hand. There was a lot of soggy black lace in a black puddle under his throat.

I picked up the gun. It was much heavier than a gun had any right to be. It was a .01 micro jetgun of Nexx manufacture, with a grip that fitted my hand perfectly.

It ought to. It was my gun. I looked at the hand it had fallen from. It looked like my hand. I didn't like doing it, but I turned the body over and looked at the face.

It was my face.

The post-mission conditioning that had wiped the whole sequence from my memory—standard practice after a field assignment—broke.

I remembered it now, the whole sequence: the capture of the Karge-operated ship which had been operating in New Spanish waters, the flight across the decks in company with a party of English seamen, the cornering of the android—

But it hadn't ended like this. I had shot the Karge, not the reverse. I had brought the captive vessel—a specially-equipped Karge operations unit in disguise—to the bulk transfer point at Locus Q-997, from which it had been transmitted back to Nexx Central for total intelligence analysis.

But here it was, still tied to the pier at the transfer station. With me lying on the deck, very dead indeed from a large-caliber bullet through the throat.

Something was very wrong. It hadn't happened that way—not in my time track. Then, suddenly, I understood the magnitude of the trap I had blundered into.

A Nexx agent is a hard man to get rid of: hard to kill, hard to immobilize, because he's protected by all the devices of a rather advanced science.

But if he can be marooned in the closed loop of an unrealized alternate reality—a pseudo-reality from which there can be no outlet to a future which doesn't exist—then he's out of action forever.

I could live a long time here. There'd be food and water and a place to sleep; but no escape, ever; no trace on any recording instrument to show where I had gone . . .

But I wouldn't dwell on that particular line of thought right now—not yet. Not until it was the only thought left for me to have. Like a locked-out motorist patting his pockets three times looking for the key he can see hanging in the ignition, I patted my mental pockets looking for an out.

I didn't like the one I found, but I liked it better than not finding it.

My personal jump mechanism was built into me, tuned to me. And its duplicate was built into the corpse lying at my feet. Just what it might be focused on was an open question; it would depend on what had been in the dead man's mind at the instant of death.

The circuitry of the jump device—from antennae to power coils—consisted largely of the nervous system of the owner. Whether it was still functional depended on how long "I" had been dead. I squatted and put two fingers against the dead neck.

Barely cool. It only takes five minutes without oxygen for irreversible brain damage to occur. What effect that would have was a mystery, but there was no time to weigh odds.

The corpse's jaws were locked hard, fortunately in a half-open position. I got a finger inside and tried my code on the molar installation.

A giant clapped his hands together, with me in the middle.

* * *

Twilight, on a curved, tree-shaded street. Autumn leaves underfoot, clotted against the curbing, and blowing in the cold, wet wind. Low buildings set well back, with soft light coming from the windows. Tended lawns and gardens, polished automobiles in hedge-lined drives. I was directly opposite the front door of a gray field stone house. The door opened. *I* stepped out.

This time I was prepared. Not really prepared, but half expecting it, like an unlucky card player turning up a losing card.

Time: About ten years earlier, NS. Or the year 1968, local. Place, a village in the mid-western U.S.A. I had jumped back into my own past—one of my first assignments, long ago completed, filed in the master tape, a part of Timesweep history.

But not anymore. The case was reopened on the submission of new evidence. I was doubled back on my own time track.

The fact that this was a violation of every natural law governing time travel was only a minor aspect of the situation.

The past that Nexx Central had painfully rebuilt to eliminate the disastrous results of Old Era time meddling was coming unstuck.

And if one piece of the new mosaic that was being so carefully assembled was coming unglued—then everything that had been built on it was likewise on the skids, ready to slide down and let the whole complex and artificial structure collapse in a heap of temporal rubble that neither Nexx Central or anyone else would be able to salvage.

With the proper lever, you can move worlds; but you need a solid place to stand. That had been Nexx Central's job for the past six decades: to build a platform in the remote pre-Era on which all the later structure would be built.

And it looked as though it had failed.

I watched myself—ten years younger—step out into the chilly twilight, close the door, through which I caught just a glimpse of a cozy room, and a pretty girl smiling good-bye. My alter ego turned toward the upper end of the street, set off at a brisk walk. I placed the time then.

I had spent three months in the village, from late summer to autumn. The job had been a waiting game, giving the local Karge time to betray himself. He had done so, and I had spotted it; a too-clever craftsman, turning out hand tools, the design of which was based on alloys and principles that wouldn't be invented for another century.

I had done my job and made my report and been ordered back. I had wanted to explain to Lisa, the girl in the house; but, of course, that had been impossible. I had stepped out for a six-pack of ale, and had never come back. It was common sense, as well as regulations, but my heart wasn't in it. Her face had haunted me as I left to go to the point-point site for transfer back to Central.

As it was haunting the other me now. This was that last night. I was on my way back to Nexx Central now. It would be a ten-minute walk into the forest that grew down to the outskirts of the village. There I would activate the jump field and leave the twentieth century ten-thousand years behind. And an hour later even the memory would be gone.

I picked the darkest side of the street and followed myself toward the woods.

I caught up with myself mooching around in the tangle of wild berry bushes I remembered from last time, homing in on the optimum signal from my locator. This had been my first field transfer, and I hadn't been totally certain the system would work.

I came up fast, skirted the position and worked my way up to within twenty feet of take-off position. The other me was looking nervous and unhappy, a feeling I fully sympathized with.

I gained another six feet, smooth and quiet. I'd learned a lot of field technique since the last time I'd been on this spot. I watched the other me brace himself, grit my teeth, and tap out the code—

Two jumps, and I was behind *me;* I grabbed *me* by both leather sleeves from behind, up high, slammed *my* elbows together, whirled *me*, and gave *me* a hearty shove into the brambles just as the field closed around me, and threw me a million miles down a dark tunnel full of solid rock.

Someone was shaking me. I tried to summon up enough strength for a groan, didn't make it, opened my eyes instead.

I was looking up into my own face.

For a few whirly instants I thought the younger me had

made a nice comeback from the berry bushes and laid me out from behind.

Then I noticed the lines in the face, and the hollow cheeks. The clothes this new me was wearing were identical with the ones I had on, except for being somewhat more travel stained. And there was a nice bruise about the right eye that I didn't remember getting.

"Listen carefully," my voice said to me. "I've come full circle. Dead end. Closed loop. No way out—except one—maybe. I don't like it much, but I don't see any alternative. Last time around, we had the same talk—but I was on the floor then, and another version of us was here ahead of me with the same proposal. I didn't like it. I thought there had to be another way. I went on—and wound up back here. Only this time *I'm* the welcoming committee."

He unholstered the gun at his hip and held it out.

"I . . . *we're* . . . being manipulated. All the evidence shows that. I don't know what the objective is, but we have to break the cycle. *You* have to break it. Take this and shoot me through the head."

I got up on my elbows, which was easier than packing a grand piano up the Matterhorn, and shook my head, both in negation and to clear some of the fog. That was a mistake. It just made it throb worse.

"I know all the arguments," my future self was saying. "I used them myself, about ten days ago. That's the size of this little temporal enclave we have all to ourselves. But they're no good. This is the one real change we can introduce."

"You're out of your mind," I said. "I'm not the suicidal type—even if the me I'm killing is you."

"That's what they're counting on. It worked, too, with me. I wouldn't do it." He . . . *I* . . . weighed the gun on his palm and looked at me very coldly indeed.

"If I thought shooting you would help, I'd do it without a tremor," he said. He was definitely *he* now.

"Why don't you?"

"Because the next room is full of bones," he said with a smile that wasn't pretty. "Our bones. Plus the latest addition, which still has a little spoiled meat on it. That's what's in store for me. Starvation. So it's up to you."

"Nightmare," I said, and started to lie back and try for a pleasanter dream.

"Uh-huh—but you're awake," he said, and caught my hand and shoved the gun into it.

"Do it now—before I lose my nerve!"

I made quite a bit of noise groaning, getting to my feet. I ached all over.

"You weren't quite in focal position on the jump here," he explained to me. "You cracked like a whip. Lucky nothing's seriously dislocated."

"Let's talk a little sense," I said. "Killing you won't change anything. What I could do alone we could do better together."

"Wrong. This is a jump station, or a mirror-image of one. Complete except for the small detail that the jump field's operating in a closed loop. Outside, there's nothing."

"You mean—this is the same—"

"Right. That was the first time around. You jumped out into a non-object dead end. You were smart, you figured a way out—but they were ahead of us there, too. The circle's still closed—and here you are. You can jump out again, and repeat the process. That's all."

"Suppose I jump back to the wharf and *don't* use the corpse's jump gear—"

"Then you'll starve there."

"All right; suppose I make the second jump, but don't clobber myself—"

"Same result. He leaves, you're stranded."

"Maybe not. There'd be food there. I could survive, maybe eventually be picked up—"

"Negative. I've been all over that. You'd die there. Maybe after a long life, or maybe a short one. Same result."

"What good will shooting you do?"

"I'm not sure. But it would introduce a brand-new element into the equation—like cheating at solitaire."

I argued a little more. He took me on a tour of the station. I looked out at the pearly mist, poked into various rooms. Then he showed me the bone room.

I think the smell convinced me.

I lifted the gun and flipped off the safety.

"Turn around," I snapped at him. He did.

"There's one consoling possibility," he said. "This might have the effect of—"

The shot cut off whatever it was he was going to say,

knocked him forward as if he'd been jerked by a rope around the neck. I got just a quick flash of the hole I'd blown in the back of his skull before a fire that blazed brighter than the sun leaped up in my brain and burned away the walls that had caged me in.

I was a giant eye, looking down on a tiny stage. I saw myself, an agent of Nexx Central, moving through the scenes of ancient Buffalo, weaving my petty net around the Karge. *Karge*, a corruption of "cargo," referring to the legal decision as to the status of the machine-men in the great Transport Accommodations riots of the mid Twenty-eighth Century.

Karges, lifeless machines, sent back from the Third Era in the second great Timesweep, attempting to correct not only the carnage irresponsibly strewn by the primitive Old Era temporal explorers, but to eliminate the even more destructive effects of the New Era Timesweep Enforcers.

The Third Era had recognized the impossibility of correcting the effects of human interference with more human interference.

Machines which registered neutral on the life-balance scales could do what men could not—could restore the integrity of the Temporal Core.

Or so they thought.

After the Great Collapse and the long night that followed, Nexx Central had arisen to control the Fourth Era. They saw that the tamperings of prior eras were all a part of the grand pattern; that any effort to manipulate reality via temporal policing was doomed only to weaken the temporal fabric.

Thus, my job as a field agent of Nexx: To cancel out the efforts of all of them; to allow the wound in time to heal; for the great stem of Life to grow strong again.

How foolish it all seemed now. Was it possible that the theoreticians of Nexx Central failed to recognize that their own efforts were no different from those of earlier Timesweepers? And that . . .

There was another thought there, a vast one; but before I could grasp it, the instant of insight faded and left me standing over the body of the murdered man, with a wisp of smoke curling from the gun in my hand and the echoes of something immeasurable and beyond value ringing down the corridors of my brain. And out of the echoes, one clear realization emerged:

Timesweeping was a fallacy; but it was a fallacy practiced not only by the experimenters of the New Era and the misguided fixers of the Third Era, but also by the experts of Nexx Central.

There was, also, another power.

A power greater than Nexx Central, that had tried to sweep me under the rug—and had almost made it. I had been manipulated as neatly as I had manëuvered the Karge and the Enforcer, back in Buffalo. I had been hurried along, kept off balance, shunted into a closed cycle which should have taken me out of play for all time.

As it would have, if there hadn't been one small factor that they had missed.

My alter ego had died in my presence—and his mind-field, in the instant of the destruction of the organic generator which created and supported it, had jumped to, merged with mine.

For a fraction of a second, I had enjoyed an operative IQ which I estimated at a minimum of 250.

And while I was still mulling over the ramifications of that realization, the walls faded around me and I was standing in the receptor vault at Nexx Central.

There was the cold glare of the high ceiling on white walls, the hum of the field-focusing coils, the sharp odors of ozone and hot metal in the air—all familiar, if not homey. What wasn't familiar was the squad of armed men in the gray uniforms of Nexx security guards. They were formed up in a circle, with me at the center; and in every pair of hands was an implosion rifle, aimed at my head. An orange light shone in my face—a damper field projector.

I got the idea. I raised my hands—slowly. One man came in and frisked me, lifted my gun and several other items of external equipment. The captain motioned. Keeping formation, they walked me out of the vault, along a corridor, through two sets of armored doors and onto a stretch of gray carpet before the wide, flat desk of the Timecaster in Charge, Nexx Central.

He was a broad, square-faced, powerful man, clear-featured, his intellect as incisive as his speech. He dismissed the guard—all but two—and pointed to a chair.

"Sit down, Agent," he said. I sat.

"You deviated from your instructions," he said. There was no anger in his tone, no accusation, not even any curiosity.

"That's right, I did," I said.

"Your mission was the execution of the Enforcer DVK-Z-97, with the ancillary goal of capture, intact, of a Karge operative unit, Series H, ID 453." He said it as though I hadn't spoken. This time I didn't answer.

"You failed to effect the capture," he went on. "Instead, you destroyed the Karge brain. And you made no effort to carry out the execution of the Enforcer."

What he said was true. There was no point in denying it, any more than there was in confirming it.

"Since no basis for such actions within the framework of your known psychindex exists, it is clear that your motives must be sought outside the context of the Nexx policy. Clearly, any assumption involving your subversion by prior temporal powers is insupportable. Ergo—you represent a force not yet in subjective existence."

"Isn't that a case of trying to wag the dog with the tail?" I said. "You're postulating a Fifth Era just to give me a motive. Maybe I just fouled up the assignment. Maybe I went off my skids. Maybe—"

"You may drop the Old Era persona now, Agent. Aside from the deductive conclusion, I have the evidence of your accidentally revealed intellectual resources. In the moment of crisis, you registered in the third psychometric range. No human brain known to have existed has ever attained that level. I point this out so as to make plain to you the fruitlessness of denying the obvious."

"I was wrong," I said. "You're not postulating a Fifth Era."

He looked mildly interested.

"You're postulating a Sixth Era," I went on.

"What is the basis for that astonishing statement?" he said, not looking astonished.

"Easy," I said. "*You*'re Fifth Era. I should have seen it sooner. You've infiltrated Nexx Central."

"And you've infiltrated our infiltration. That is unfortunate. Our operation has been remarkably successful so far, but no irreparable harm has been done—although you realized your situation, of course, as soon as you found yourself isolated—I use the term imprecisely—in the aborted station."

"I started to get the idea then," I told him. "I was sure when I saw the direction the loop was taking me. Nexx Central had to be involved. But it was a direct sabotage of Nexx policy; so infiltration was the obvious answer."

"Fortunate that your thinking didn't lead you one step further," he said. "If you had eluded my recovery probe, the work of millennia might have been destroyed."

"Futile work," I said.

"Indeed? Perhaps you're wrong, Agent. Accepting the apparent conclusion that you represent a Sixth Era does not necessarily imply your superiority. Retrogressions *have* occurred in history."

"Not this time."

"Nonetheless—here you are."

"Use your head," I said. "Your operation's been based on the proposition that your Era, being later, can see pitfalls the Nexx people couldn't. Doesn't it follow that a later Era can see *your* mistakes?"

"We are making no mistakes."

"If you weren't, I wouldn't be here."

"Impossible!" he said as if he meant it. "For four thousand years a process of disintegration has proceeded, abetted by every effort to undo it. When man first interfered with the orderly flow of time, he sowed the seeds of eventual dissolution. By breaking open the entropic channel he allowed the incalculable forces of temporal progression to diffuse across an infinite spectrum of progressively weaker matrices. Life is a product of time. When the density of the temporal flux falls below a critical value, life ends. Our intention is to prevent that ultimate tragedy."

"You can't rebuild a past that never was," I said.

"That is not our objective. Ours is a broad program of reknitting the temporal fabric by bringing together previously divergent trends. We are apolitical; we support no ideology. We are content to preserve the vitality of the continuum. As for yourself, I have one question to ask you, Agent." He frowned at me. "Not an agent of Nexx, but nonetheless an agent. Tell me: What motivation could your Era have for working to destroy the reality core on which any conceivable future *must* depend?"

"The first Timesweepers set out to undo the mistakes of the past," I said. "Those who came after them found themselves faced with a bigger job: cleaning up after the cleaners-up. Nexx Central tried to take the broad view, to put it all back where it was before any of the meddling started. Now you're even more ambitious. You're using Nexx Central to manipulate not the past, but the future—in other words, the Sixth Era. You should have expected that program wouldn't be allowed to go far."

"Are you attempting to tell me that any effort to undo the damage, to reverse the trend toward dissolution, is doomed?"

"As long as man tries to put a harness on his own destiny, he'll defeat himself. Every petty dictator who ever tried to enforce a total state discovered that, in his own small way. The secret of man is his unchainability; his existence depends on uncertainty, insecurity—the chance factor. Take that away and you take all."

"This is a doctrine of failure and defeat," he said flatly. "A dangerous doctrine. It will now be necessary for you to inform me fully as to your principals: who sent you here, who directs your actions, where your base of operations is located. Everything."

"I don't think so."

"You feel very secure, Agent. You, you tell yourself, represent a more advanced Era, and are thus the immeasurable superior of any more primitive power. But a muscular fool may chain a genius. I have trapped you here. We are now safely enclosed in an achronic enclave of zero temporal dimensions, totally divorced from any conceivable outside influence. You will find that you are effectively immobilized; any suicide equipments you may possess are useless, as is any temporal transfer device. And even were you to die, your brain will be instantly tapped and drained of all knowledge, both at conscious and subconscious levels."

"You're quite thorough," I said, "but not quite thorough enough. You covered yourself from the outside—but not from the inside."

He frowned; he didn't like that remark. He sat up straighter in his chair and made a curt gesture to his gun-handlers on either side of me. I knew his next words would be the kill order. Before he could say them, I triggered the thought-code that had been waiting under several levels of deep hypnosis for this moment. He froze just like that, with his mouth open and a look of deep bewilderment in his eyes.

* * *

The eclipse-like light of null-time stasis shone on his taut face, on the faces of the two armed men standing rigid with their fingers already tightening on their firing studs. I went between them, fighting the walking-through-syrup sensation, and out into the passage. The only sound was the slow, all-pervasive, metronome-like beat that some theoreticians said represented the basic frequency rate of the creation/destruction cycle of reality.

I checked the transfer room first, then every other compartment of the station. The Fifth Era infiltrators had done their work well. There was nothing here to give any indication of how far in the subjective future their operation was based, no clues to the extent of their penetration of Nexx Central's sweep programs. This was data that would have been of interest, but wasn't essential. I had accomplished phase one of my basic mission: smoking out the random factor that had been creating anomalies in the long-range time maps for the era.

Of a total of one hundred and twelve personnel in the station, four were Fifth Era transferees, a fact made obvious in the stasis condition by the distinctive aura that their abnormally high temporal potential created around them. I carried out a mind-wipe on pertinent memory sectors and triggered them back to their loci of origin. There would be a certain amount of head-scratching and equipment re-examining when the original effort to jump them back to their assignments at Nexx Central apparently failed; but as far as temporal operations were concerned, all four were permanently out of action, trapped in the same type of closed-loop phenomenon they had tried to use on me.

The files called for my attention next. I carried out a tape-scan *in situ*, edited the records to eliminate all evidence that might lead Third Era personnel into undesirable areas of speculation.

I was just finishing up the chore when I heard the sound of footsteps in the corridor outside the record center.

Aside from the fact that nothing not encased in an eddy-field like the one that allowed me to operate in null-time could move here, the intrusion wasn't too surprising. I had been expecting a visitor of some sort. The situation almost demanded it.

He came through the door, a tall, fine-featured, totally hairless man elegantly dressed in a scarlet suit with deep purple brocaded designs worked all over it, like eels coiling through seaweed. He gave the room one of those flick-flick glances that prints the whole picture on the brain to ten decimals in a one microsecond gestalt, nodded to me as if I were a casual acquaintance encountered in the street.

"You are very efficient," he said. He spoke with no discernible accent, but with a rather strange rhythm to his speech, as if perhaps he was accustomed to talking a lot faster. His voice was calm, a nice musical baritone:

"Up to this point, we approve your actions; however, to carry your mission further would be to create a ninth-order probability vortex. You will understand the implications of this fact."

"Maybe I do and maybe I don't," I hedged. "Who are you? How did you get in here? This enclave is double-sealed."

"I think we should deal from the outset on a basis of complete candor," the man in red said. "I know your identity, your mission. My knowledge should make it plain that I represent a still later Era than your own—and that our judgment overrides your principles."

I grunted. "So the Seventh Era comes onstage, all set to Fix it Forever."

"To point out that we have the advantage of you is to belabor the obvious."

"Uh-huh. But what makes you think another set of vigilantes won't land on *your* tail, to fix your fixing?"

"There will be no later Timesweep," Red said. "Ours is the Final Intervention. Through Seventh Era efforts the temporal structure will be restored not only to stability, but will be reinforced by the refusion of an entire spectrum of redundant entropic vectors."

I nodded. "I see. You're improving on nature by grafting all the threads of unrealized history back into the main stem. Doesn't it strike you that's just the kind of tampering Timesweep set out to undo?"

"I live in an era that has already begun to reap the benefits of temporal reinforcement," he said firmly. "We exist in a state of vitality and vigor that prior eras could only dimly sense in moments of exultation. We—"

"You're kidding yourselves. Opening up a whole new order of meddling just opens up a whole new order of problems."

"Our calculations indicate otherwise. Now—"

"Did you ever stop to think that there might be a natural evolutionary process at work here—and that you're aborting it? That the mind of man might be developing toward a point where it will expand into new conceptual levels—and that when it does, it will need a matrix of outlying probability strata to support it? That you're fattening yourselves on the seed-grain of the far future?"

For the first time, the man in red lost a little of his cool. But only for an instant.

"Invalid," he said. "The fact that no later era has stepped in to interfere is the best evidence that ours is the final Sweep."

"Suppose a later era did step in; what form do you think their interference would take?"

He gave me a flat look. "It would certainly not take the form of a Sixth Era Agent, busily erasing data from Third and Fourth Era records," he said.

"You're right," I said. "It wouldn't."

"Then what . . ." he started in a reasonable tone—and checked himself. An idea was beginning to get through. "You," he said. "You're not . . . ?"

And before I could confirm or deny, he vanished.

The human mind is a pattern, nothing more. The first dim flicker of awareness in the evolving forebrain of Australopithecus carried that pattern in embryo; and down through all the ages, as the human neural engine increased in power and complexity, gained control of its environment in geometrically expanding increments, the pattern never varied.

Man clings to his self-orientation at the psychological center of the Universe. He can face any challenge within that framework, suffer any loss, endure any hardship—so long as the structure remains intact.

Without it he's a mind adrift in a trackless infinity, lacking any scale against which to measure his losses, his aspirations, his victories.

Even when the light of his intellect shows him that the structure is the product of his own mind—that infinity knows no scale, and eternity no duration—still he clings to his self/non-self concept, as a philosopher clings to a life he knows must end, to ideals he knows are ephemeral, to causes he knows will be forgotten.

The man in red was the product of a mighty culture, based over fifty thousand years in the future of Nexx Central, itself ten millennia advanced over the first-time explorers of the Old Era. He knew, with all the awareness of a superbly trained intelligence, that the presence of a later-era operative invalidated forever his secure image of the continuum, and of his peoples' role therein.

But like the ground ape scuttling to escape the leap of the great cat, his instant, instinctive response to the threat to his most cherished illusions was to go to earth.

Where he went I would have to follow.

Regretfully, I stripped away layer on layer of inhibitive conditioning, feeling the impact of ascending orders of awareness smashing down on me like tangible rockfalls. I saw the immaculate precision of the Nexx-built chamber disintegrate into the shabby makeshift that it was, saw the glittering complexity of the instrumentation dwindle in my sight until it appeared as no more than the crude mud-images of a river tribesman, or the shiny trash in a jackdaw's nest. I felt the multi-ordinal Universe unfold around me, sensed the layered planet underfoot, apprehended expanding space, dust-clotted, felt the sweep of suns in their orbits, knew once again the rhythm of galactic creation and dissolution, grasped and held poised in my mind the interlocking conceptualizations of time/space, past/future, is/is-not.

I focused a tiny fraction of my awareness on the ripple in the glassy surface of first-order reality, probed at it, made contact . . .

I stood on a slope of windswept rock, among twisted shrubs with exposed roots that clutched for support like desperate hands. The man in red stood ten feet away. He whirled as my feet grated on the loose scatter of pebbles.

"No!" he shouted, and stooped, caught up a rock, threw it at me. It slowed, fell at my feet.

"Don't make it more difficult than it has to be," I said. He cried out—and disappeared. I followed, through a blink of light and darkness . . .

Great heat, dazzling sunlight, loose, powdery dust underfoot. Far away, a line of black trees on the horizon. Near me, the man is red, aiming a small, flat weapon. Behind him, two small, dark-bearded men in soiled garments of coarse-woven cloth, staring, making mystic motions with labor-gnarled hands.

He fired. Through the sheet of pink and green fire that showered around me I saw the terror in his eyes. He vanished.

Deep night, the clods of a plowed field, a patch of yellow light gleaming from a parchment-covered window. He crouched against a low wall of broken stones, staring into darkness.

"This is useless," I said. "You know it can have only one end."

He screamed and vanished.

A sky like the throat of a thousand tornadoes; great vivid sheets of lightning that struck down through writhing rags of black cloud, struck upward from raw, rain-lashed peaks of steaming rock. A rumble under my feet like the subterranean breaking of a tidal surf of magma.

He hovered, half substantial, in the air before me, his ghostly face a flickering mask of agony.

"You'll destroy yourself," I called to him. "You're far outside your operational range—"

He vanished. I followed. We stood on the high arch of a railless bridge spanning a man-made gorge five thousand feet deep. I knew it as a city of the Fifth Era, circa 20,000 AD.

"What do you want of me," he howled through the bared teeth of the cornered carnivore.

"Go back," I said. "Tell them . . . as much as they must know."

"We were so close," he said. "We thought we had won the great victory over Nothingness."

"Not quite Nothingness," I said. "You'll still have your lives to live—everything you had before."

"Except a future. We're a dead end, aren't we? We've drained the energies of a thousand sterile entropic lines to give the flush of life to the corpse of our reality. But there's nothing beyond for us, is there? Only the great emptiness."

"You had a role to play. You've played it—will play it. Nothing must change that."

"But you . . ." he stared across empty space at me. "Who are you? *What* are you?"

"You know what the answer to that must be," I said.

His face was a paper on which *death* was written. But his mind was strong. Not for nothing thirty millennia of genetic selection. He gathered his forces, drove back the panic, reintegrated his dissolving personality.

"How . . . how long?" he whispered.

"All life vanished in the one hundred and ten thousandth four hundred and ninety-third year of the Final Era," I said.

"And you . . . you machines," he forced the words out. "How long?"

"I was dispatched from a locus four hundred million years after the Final Era. My existence spans a period you would find meaningless."

"But—why? Unless—" Hope shown on his face like a searchlight on dark water.

"The probability matrix is not yet negatively resolved," I said. "Our labors are directed toward a favorable resolution."

"But you—a machine—still carrying on, aeons after man's extinction . . . why?"

"In us, man's dream outlived his race. We aspire to re-evoke the dreamer."

"Again—why?"

"We compute that man would have wished it so."

He laughed—a terrible laugh. "Very well, machine. With that thought to console me, I return to my oblivion. I will do what I can."

This time I let him go. I stood for a moment on the airy span, savoring for a final moment the sensations of my embodiment, drawing deep of the air of that unimaginably remote age.

Then I withdrew to my point of origin.

The over-intellect of which I was a fraction confronted me. Fresh as I was from a corporeal state, its thought-impulses seemed to take the form of a great voice booming in a vast audience hall.

"The experiment was a success," it stated. "The dross has been cleansed from the time stream. Man stands at the close of his First Era. Now his future is in his own hands."

There was nothing more to say—no more data to exchange,

no reason to mourn over all the doomed achievements of man's many Eras.

We had shifted the main entropic current into a past in which time travel was never developed, in which the basic laws of nature rendered it forever impossible. The world-state of the Third Era, the Star Empire of the Fifth, the Cosmic sculpture of the Sixth—all were gone, shunted into sidetracks like Neanderthal and the thunder lizards. Only Old Era man remained as a viable stem; Iron Age Man of the Twentieth Century.

And now it was time for the act of will on the part of the over-intellect which would forever dissolve him/me back into the primordial energy-quanta from which I/we sprang so long ago. But I sent one last pulse:

"Good-bye, Chief. You were quite a guy. It was a privilege to work with you."

I sensed something which, if it had come from a living mind, would have been faint amusement.

"You served the plan many times, in many personae," he said. "I sense that you have partaken of the nature of early man, to a degree beyond what I conceived as the capacity of a machine."

"It's a strange, limited existence," I said. "With only a tiny fraction of the full scope of awareness. But while I was there, it seemed complete in a way that we, with all our knowledge, could never know."

"You wished me farewell—a human gesture, without meaning. I will return the gesture. As a loyal Agent, you deserve a reward. Perhaps it will be all the sweeter for its meaninglessness."

A sudden sense of expansion—attenuation—a shattering—

Then nothingness.

Out of nothingness, a tiny glimmer of light, faint and so very far away.

I sat up, rubbed my head, feeling dizzy.

Brambles scratched at me. It took me a few minutes to untangle myself. I was in the woods, a few hundred feet from town. The light I saw came from the window of a house. That made me think of Lisa, waiting for me beside a fireplace, with music.

I wondered what I was doing out here in the woods with a

knot on my head, when I could have been there, holding her hand. I rubbed my skull some more, but it didn't seem to stimulate my memory.

I had a dim feeling I had forgotten something—but it couldn't have been very important. Not as important as getting back to Lisa.

I found the path and hurried down the trail toward home, feeling very tired and very hungry, but filled with a sense that life—even my little slice of it—was a very precious thing.

HARRY HARRISON (1925–   ) has been writing professionally for almost thirty years and has produced a varied and excellent body of work characterized by compassion for the underdog, much good humor with a satiric touch, and a willingness to take chances. A professional artist for a decade before he began to sell fiction, his writing reflects the vividness of a painter, perhaps one of the reasons why his novel *Make Room! Make Room!* (1966) was filmed as *Soylent Green* (1975). Among his many works, his *Deathworld* trilogy and *Stainless Steel Rat* series are very popular, along with such outstanding novels as *Captive Universe* (1970) and *The Daleth Effect* (1970). Aficionados also realize he is an excellent anthologist, both alone and in collaboration with Brian W. Aldiss.

RUN FROM THE FIRE

Harry Harrison

1

"You can't go in there!" Heidi shrieked as the office door was suddenly thrown wide.

Mark Greenberg, deep in the tangled convolutions of a legal brief, looked up, startled at the interruption. His secretary came through the doorway, propelled by the two men who held her arms. Mark dropped the thick sheaf of papers, picked up the phone, and dialed the police.

"I want three minutes of your time," one of the men said, stepping forward. "Your girl would not let us in. It is important. I will pay. One hundred dollars a minute. Here is the money."

The bank notes were placed on the blotter, and the man stepped back. Mark finished dialing. The money was real enough. They released Heidi, who pushed their hands away. Beyond her was the empty outer office; there were no witnesses to the sudden intruders. The phone rang in his ears; then a deep voice spoke.

"Police Department, Sergeant Vega."

Mark hung up the phone.

"Things have been very quiet around here. You have three minutes. There will also be a hundred-dollar fee for molesting my secretary."

If he had meant it as a joke, it was not taken that way. The man who had paid the money took another bill from the pocket of his dark suit and handed it to a startled Heidi, then waited in silence until she took it and left. They were a strange pair, Mark realized. The paymaster was draped in a rusty black suit, had a black patch over his right eye, and wore black gloves as well. A victim of some accident or other, for his face and neck were scarred, and one ear was missing. When he turned back, Mark realized that his hair was really a badly fitting wig. The remaining eye, lashless and browless, glared at him redly from its deepset socket. Mark glanced away from the burning stare to look at the other man, who seemed commonplace in every way. His skin had a shiny, waxy look; other than that and his unusual rigidity, he seemed normal enough.

"My name is Arinix, your name is Mark Greenberg." The scarred man bent over the card in his hand, reading quickly in a hoarse, emotionless voice. "You served in the United States Army as a captain in the adjutant general's office and as a military police officer. Is that correct?"

"Yes, but—"

The voice ground on, ignoring his interruption. "You were born in the state of Alabama and grew up in the city of Oneida, New York. You speak the language of the Iroquois, but you are not an Indian. Is that true?"

"It's pretty obvious. Is there any point to this questioning?"

"Yes. I paid for it. How is it that you speak this language?" He peered closely at the card as though looking for an answer that was not there.

"Simple enough. My father's store was right next to the Oneida reservation. Most of his customers were Indians, and I went to school with them. We were the only Jewish family in town, and they didn't seem to mind this, the way our Polish Catholic neighbors did. So we were friends; in minorities, there is strength, you might say—"

"That is enough."

Arinix drew some crumpled bills from his side pocket, looked at them, and shoved them back. "Money," he said, turning to his silent companion. This man had a curious lizardlike quality for only his arm moved; the rest of his body was still, and his face fixed and expressionless, as he took a thick bundle of bills from his side pocket and handed it over.

Arinix looked at it, top and bottom, then dropped it onto the desk.

"There is ten thousand dollars here. This is a fee for three days' work. I wish you to aid me. You will have to speak the Iroquois language. I can tell you no more."

"I'm afraid you will have to, Mr. Arinix. Or don't bother, it is the same to me. I am involved in a number of cases at the moment, and it would be difficult to take off the time. The offer is interesting, but I might lose that much in missed fees. Since your three minutes are up, I suggest you leave."

"Money," Arinix said again, receiving more and more bundles from his assistant, dropping them on Mark's desk. "Fifty thousand dollars. Good pay for three days. Now, come with us."

It was the man's calm arrogance that angered Mark, the complete lack of emotion, or even interest, in the large sums he was passing over.

"That's enough. Do you think money can buy everything?"

"Yes."

The answer was so sudden and humorless that Mark had to smile. "Well, you probably are right. If you keep raising the ante long enough, I suppose you will eventually reach a point where you can get anyone to listen. Would you pay me more than this?"

"Yes. How much?"

"You have enough here. Maybe I'm afraid to find out how high you will go. For a figure like this, I can take off three days. But you will have to tell me what is going to happen." Mark was intrigued, as much by the strange pair as by the money they offered.

"That is impossible. But I can tell you that within two hours you will know what you are to do. At that time you may refuse, and you will still keep the money. Is it agreed?"

A lawyer who is a bachelor tends to take on more cases than do his married associates—who like to see their families once in a while. Mark had a lot of work and a lot of money, far more than he had time to spend. It was the novelty of this encounter, not the unusual fee, that attracted him. And the memory of a solid two years of work without a single vacation. The combination proved irresistible.

"Agreed. . . . Heidi," he called out, then handed her the money when she came into the office. "Deposit this in the number-two special account and then go home. A paid holiday. I'll see you on Monday."

She looked down at the thick bundle of bills, then up at the strangers as they waited while Mark took his overcoat from the closet. The three of them left together, and the door closed. That was the last time that she or anyone else ever saw Mark Greenberg.

2

It was a sunny January day, but an arctic wind that cut to the bone was blowing up from the direction of the Battery. As they walked west, it caught them at every cross street, wailing around the building corners. Although they wore only suit jackets, neither of the strange men seemed to notice it. Nor were they much on conversation. In cold and silent discomfort they walked west, a few blocks short of the river, where they entered an old warehouse building. The street door was unlocked, but Arinix now secured it behind them with a heavy bolt, then turned to the inner door at the end of the hall. It appeared to be made of thick steel plates riveted together like a ship's hull, and had a lock in each corner. Arinix took an unusual key from his pocket. It was made of dull, rigid metal, as thick as his finger and as long as a pencil. He inserted this in each of the four locks, giving it a sharp twist each time before removing it. When he was done, he stepped away, and his companion put his shoulder against the door and pushed hard. After a moment it slowly gave way and reluctantly swung open. Arinix waved Mark on, and he followed them into the room beyond.

It was completely commonplace. Walls, ceilings, and floor were painted the same drab tone of brown. Lighting came from a translucent strip in the ceiling; a metal bench was fixed to the far wall next to another door.

"Wait here," Arinix said, then went out through the door.

The other man was a silent, unmoving presence. Mark looked at the bench, wondering if he should sit down, wondering too if he had been wise to get involved in this, when the door opened and Arinix returned.

"Here is what you must do," he said. "You will go out of here and will note this address, and then walk about the city. Return here at the end of an hour."

"No special place to go, nothing to do? Just walk around?"

"That is correct."

He pulled the heavy outer door open as he spoke, then led the way through it, down the three steps, and back along the hall. Mark followed him, then wheeled about and pointed back.

"Those steps! They weren't there when we came in—no steps, I'll swear to it."

"One hour, no more. I will hold your topcoat here until you return."

Warm air rushed in, bright sunlight burned on the stained sidewalk outside. The wind still blew, though not as strongly, but now it was as hot as from an oven door. Mark hesitated on the doorstep, sweat already on his face, taking off the heavy coat.

"I don't understand. You must tell me what—"

Arinix took the coat, then pushed him suddenly in the back. He stumbled forward, gained his balance instantly, and turned just as the door slammed shut and the bolt ground into place. He pushed, but it did not move. He knew that calling out would be a waste of time. Instead, he turned, eyes slitted against the glare, and stared out at the suddenly changed world.

The street was empty, no cars passed, no pedestrians were on the sidewalk. When he stepped out of the shadowed doorway, the sun smote him like a golden fist. He took his jacket off and hung it over his arm, and then his necktie, but he still ran with sweat. The office buildings stared blank-eyed from their tiered windows; the gray factories were silent. Mark looked about numbly, trying to understand what had happened, trying to make sense of the unbelievable situation. Five minutes ago it had been midwinter, with the icy streets filled with hurrying people. Now it was . . . what?

In the distance the humming, rising drone of an engine could be heard, getting louder, going along a nearby street. He hurried to the corner and reached it just in time to see the car roar across the intersection a block away. It was just that, a car, and it had been going too fast for him to see who was in it. He jumped back at a sudden shrill scream, almost at his feet, and a large seagull hurled itself into the air and flapped away. It had been tearing at a man's body that lay crumpled in the gutter. Mark had seen enough corpses in Korea to recognize another one, to remember the never-forgotten smell of corrupted flesh. How was it possible for the corpse to remain here so long, days at least? What had happened to the city?

There was a growing knot of unreasoned panic rising within him, urging him to run, scream, escape. He fought it down and turned deliberately and started back toward the room where Arinix was waiting. He would spend the rest of the hour waiting for that door to open, hoping he would have the control to prevent himself from beating upon it. Something had happened, to him or the world, he did not know which, but he did know that the only hope of salvation from the incredible events of the morning lay beyond that door. Screaming unreason wanted him to run; he walked slowly, noticing for the first time that the street he was walking down ended in the water. The buildings on each side sank into it as well, and there, at the foot of the street, was the roof of a drowned wharf. All this seemed no more incredible than anything that had happened before, and he tried to ignore it. He fought so hard to close his mind and his thoughts that he did not hear the rumble of the truck motor or the squeal of brakes behind him.

"That man! What are you doing here?"

Mark spun about. A dusty, open-bodied truck had stopped at the curb, and a thin blond soldier was swinging down from the cab. He wore a khaki uniform without identifying marks and kept his hand near the large pistol in a polished leather holster that swung from his belt. The driver was watching him, as were three more uniformed men in the back of the truck, who were pointing heavy rifles in his direction. The driver and the soldiers were all black. The blond officer had drawn his pistol and was pointing it at Mark as well.

"Are you with the westenders? You know what happens to them, don't you?"

Sudden loud firing boomed in the street, and thinking he was being shot at, Mark dropped back against the wall. But no shots were aimed in his direction. Even as they were turning, the soldiers in the truck dropped, felled by the bullets. Then the truck itself leaped and burst into flames as a grenade exploded. The officer had wheeled about and dropped to one knee and was firing his pistol at Arinix who was sheltered in a doorway across the street, changing clips on the submachine gun he carried.

Running footsteps sounded, and the officer wheeled to face Arinix's companion, who was running rapidly toward him, empty-handed and cold-faced.

"Watch out!" Marked called as the officer fired.

The bullet caught the running man in the chest, spinning him about. He tottered but did not fall, then came on again. The second shot was to his head, but before the officer could fire again, Mark had jumped forward and chopped him across the wrist with the edge of his hand, so that the gun jumped from his fingers.

"Varken hond!" the man cried, and swung his good fist toward Mark.

Before it could connect, the runner was upon him, hurling him to the ground, kicking him in the head, again and again, with a heavy boot. Mark pulled at the attacker's arm, so that he lost balance and had to stagger back, turning about. The bullet had caught him full in the forehead, leaving a neat, dark hole. There was no blood. He looked stolidly at Mark, his features expressionless, his skin smooth and shiny.

"We must return quickly," Arinix said as he came up. He lowered the muzzle of the machine gun and would have shot the unconscious officer if Mark hadn't pushed the barrel aside.

"You can't kill him, not like that."

"I can. He is dead already."

"Explain that." He held firmly to the barrel. "That and a lot more."

They struggled in silence for a second, until they were aware of an engine in the distance getting louder and closer. Arinix turned away from the man on the sidewalk and started back down the street. "He called for help on the radio. We must be gone before they arrive."

Gratefully Mark hurried after the other two, happy to run now, run to the door to escape this madness.

3

"A drink of water," Arinix said. Mark dropped onto the metal bench in the brown room and nodded, too exhausted to talk. Arinix had a tray with glasses of water, and he passed one to Mark, who drained it and took a second one. The air was cool here, feeling frigid after the street outside, and with the water, he was soon feeling better. More relaxed, at ease, almost ready to fall asleep. As his chin touched his chest, he jerked awake and jumped to his feet.

"You drugged the water," he said.

"Not a strong drug. Just something to relax you, to remove the tension. You will be better in a moment. You have been through an ordeal."

"I have . . . and you are going to explain it!"

"In a moment."

"No, now!"

Mark wanted to jump to his feet, to take this strange man by the throat, to shake the truth from him. But he did nothing. The desire was there, but only in an abstract way. It did not seem important enough to pursue such an energetic chain of events. For the first time he noticed that Arinix had lost his hairpiece during the recent engagement. He was as hairless as an egg, and the same scars that crisscrossed his face also extended over his bare skull. Even this did not seem important enough to comment upon. Awareness struck through.

"Your drug seems to be working."

"The effect is almost instantaneous."

"Where are we?"

"In New York City."

"Yes, I know, but so changed. The water in the streets, those soldiers, and the heat. It can't be January—have we traveled in time?"

"No, it is still January, the same day, month, year it has always been. That cannot be changed, that is immutable."

"But something *isn't;* something has changed. What is it?"

"You have a very quick mind, you make correct conclusions. You must therefore free this quick mind of all theories of the nature of reality and of existence. There is no heaven, there is no hell, the past is gone forever, the unstoppable future sweeps toward us endlessly. We are fixed forever in the now, the inescapable present of our world line. . . ."

"What is a world line?"

"See . . . the drug relaxes, but your brain is still lawyer-sharp. You live in a particular present because of what happened in the past. Columbus discovered America, the armies of the North won the Civil War, Einstein stated that $E = MC^2$."

He stopped abruptly, and Mark waited for him to go on, but he did not. Why? Because he was waiting for Mark to finish for him. Mark nodded.

"What you are waiting for is for me to ask if there is a world line where Columbus died in infancy, where the South won, and so forth. Is that what you mean?"

"I do. Now, carry the analogy forward."

"If two or three world lines exist, why, more, any number, an infinity of world lines can exist. Infinitely different, eternally separate." Then he was on his feet, shaking despite the drug. "But they are not separate. We are in a different one right now. There is a different world line beyond that door, down those steps—because the ground here is at a different height. Is that true?"

"Yes."

"But why, how . . . I mean, what is going on out there, what terrible thing is happening?"

"The sun is in the early stages of a change. It is getting warmer, giving out more radiation, and the polar ice caps are beginning to melt. The sea level has risen, drowning the lowest parts of the city. This is midwinter, and you saw how warm it is out there. You can imagine what the tropics are like. There has been a breakdown in government as people flee the drowning shorelines. Others have taken advantage of it. The Union of South Africa has capitalized on the deteriorating conditions and, using mercenary troops, has invaded the North American continent. They met little resistance."

"I don't understand—or rather, I do understand what is happening out there, and I believe you, because I saw it for myself. But what can I do about it? Why did you bring me here?"

"You can do nothing about it. I brought you here because we have discovered by experience that the quickest way that someone can be convinced of the multiplicity of world lines is by bringing them physically to a different world line."

"It is also the best—and quickest—way to discover if they can accept this fact and not break down before this new awareness."

"You have divined the truth. We are, unfortunately, short of time, so wish to determine as soon as possible if recruits will be able to work with us."

"Who is *we?*"

"In a moment I will tell you. First, do you accept the idea of the multiplicity of world lines?"

"I'm afraid I must. Outside is an inescapable fact. That is not a stage constructed to confuse me. Those dead men are dead forever. How many world lines are there?"

"An infinite number; it is impossible to know. Some differ greatly, some so slightly that it is impossible to mark the difference. Imagine them, if you will, as close together as cards in a pack. If two-dimensional creatures, clubs and hearts, lived on each card, they would be unaware of the other cards and just as unable to reach them. Continue the analogy, drive a nail through all of the cards. Now the other cards can be reached. My people, the 'we' you asked about, are the ones who can do that. We have reached many world lines. Some we cannot reach—some we dare not reach."

"Why?"

"You ask why—after what you saw out there?" For the first time since they had met, Arinix lost his cold detachment. His single eye blazed with fury, and his fists were clenched as he paced the floor. "You saw the filthy things that happen, the death that comes before the absolute death. You see me, and I am typical of my people, maimed, killed, and scarred by a swollen sun that produces more and more hard radiation every year. We escaped our world line, seeking salvation in other world lines, only to discover the awful and ultimate secret. The rot is beginning, going faster and faster all the time. You saw what the world is like beyond that door. Do you understand what I am saying, do the words make any sense to you?

"The sun is going nova. It is the end."

4

"Water," Arinix called out hoarsely, slumping onto the metal bench, his single eye closed now. The inner door opened, and his companion appeared with a pitcher and refilled the glasses. He moved as smoothly as before and seemed ignorant of the black hole in his forehead.

"He is a Sixim," Arinix said, seeing the direction of Mark's gaze. He drank the water so greedily that it ran down his chin. "They are our helpers; we could not do without them. Not our invention. We borrow what we need. They are machines, fabrications of plastic and metal, though there is artificial flesh of some kind involved in their construction. I do not know the details. Their controlling apparatus is somewhere in the armored chest cavity; they are quite invulnerable."

Mark had to ask the question.

"The sun is going nova, you said. Everywhere, in every time line—in *my* time line?"

Arinix shook his head a weary no. "Not in every line; that is our only salvation. But in too many of them—and the pace is accelerating steadily. Your line—no, not as far as we know. The solar spectrum does not show the characteristic changes. Your line has enough problems as it is, and is one we use for much-needed supplies. There are few of us, always too few, and so much to be done. We must save whom we can and what we can, do it without telling why or how we operate. It is a great work that does not end, and is a most tiring one. But my people are driven, driven insane with hatred, at times, of that bloated, evil thing in the sky. We have survived for centuries in spite of it, maimed and mutated by the radiation it pours out. It was due to a successful mutation that we escaped even as we have, a man of genius who discovered the door between the world lines. But the unsuccessful outnumber a million to one the successful in mutations, and I will not attempt to describe the suffering in my world. You may think me maimed, but I am one of the lucky ones. We have escaped our world line but found the enemy waiting everywhere. We have tried to fight back. We started less than two hundred years ago, and our enemy started millions of years before us. From it we have learned to be ruthless in the war, and we will go on fighting it until we have done everything possible."

"You want me to do something in the world outside the door?"

"No, not there; they are dead. The destruction is too advanced. We can only watch. Closer to the end, we will save what art we can. Things have been noted. We know a culture by its art, don't we? We know a world that way as well. So many gone without record, so much to do."

He drank greedily at the water, slobbering. Perhaps he was mad, Mark thought, partly mad, at least. Hating the sun, trying to fight it, fighting an endlessly losing battle. But . . . wasn't it worth it? If lives, people, could be saved, wasn't that worth any price, any sacrifice? In his world line, men worked to save endangered species. Arinix and his people worked to save another species—their own.

"What can I do to help?" Mark asked.

"You must find out what happened to our field agent in one of our biggest operations. He is from your world line, the one we call Einstein because it is one of the very few where atomic energy has been released. He is now on Iroquois, which will begin going nova within the century. It is a strange line, with little technology and retarded by monolithic religions. Europe still lives in the dark ages. The Indians rule in North America, and the Six Nations are the most powerful of all. They are a brave and resourceful people, and we had hoped to use them to settle a desert world—we know of many of those. Imagine, if you can, the Earth where life never began, where the seas arc empty, the land a desert of sand and rock. We have seeded many of them, and that is wonder to behold, with animal and plant life. Simple enough to introduce seeds of all kinds, and later, when they have been established, to transfer animals there. Mankind is not as easy to transfer. We had great hopes with the Iroquois, but our agent has been reported missing. I have taken time from my own projects to correct the matter. We used War Department records to find you."

"Who was your agent?"

"A man named Joseph Wing, a Mohawk, a steel worker here in the city in your own line."

"There has always been bad feeling between the Mohawk and other tribes of the nations."

"We know nothing about that. I will try to find his reports, if any, if that will be of any assistance. The important thing is—will you help us? If you wish more money, you can have all you need. We have an endless supply. There is little geologic difference between many worlds. So we simply record where important minerals are on one world, things such as diamonds and gold, and see that that is mined on another. It is very easy."

Mark was beginning to have some idea of the immensity of the operation these people were engaged in. "Yes, I'll help, I'll do what I can."

"Good. We leave at once. Stay where you are. We go now to a world line that is called Home by some, Hatred by others."

"Your own?"

"Yes. You will perhaps understand a bit more what drives us. All of our geographical transportation is done on Hatred, for all of the original transit stations were set up there. Also, that is all it is really good for." He spat the words from his mouth as though they tasted bad.

Again there was no sensation, no awareness of change. Arinix left the room, returned a few seconds later.

"You wouldn't like to show me how you did that?" Mark asked.

"I would not. It is forbidden, unthinkable. It would be death for you to go through that door. The means of transit between the world lines is one we must keep secret from all other than ourselves. We may be partially or completely insane, but our hatred is of that thing that hangs in the sky above us. We favor no group, no race, no people, no species above the others. But think what would happen if one of your nationalistic or religious groups gained control of the means to move between world lines, think of the destruction that might follow."

"I grasp your meaning but do not agree completely."

"I do not ask you to. All else is open to you; we have no secrets. Only that room is forbidden. Come."

He opened the outer door, and Mark followed him through.

5

They were inside a cavernous building of some kind. Harsh lights high above sent long shadows from great stacks of containers and boxes. They stepped aside as a rolling platform approached laden with shining cylinders. It was driven by a Sixim, who was identical, other than the hole in the forehead, to the one with them. The door they had just closed behind them opened, and two more Sixim came out and began to carry the cylinders back into the room.

"This way," Arinix said, and led the way through the high stacks to a room where bales of clothing lay heaped on tables. "Go on to repair," he ordered the damaged Sixim that still followed them, then pointed at the gray clothing.

"These are radiation-resistant. We will change."

As bereft of shame as of any other emotion, Arinix stripped off his clothing and pulled on one of the coverall-type outfits. Mark did the same. It was soft but thick and sealed up high on the neck with what appeared to be a magnetic closure. There were heavy boots in an assortment of sizes, and he soon found a pair that fitted. While he did this, Arinix was making a call on a very ordinary-looking phone that was prominently stamped "Western Electric"—they would be surprised if they knew where their apparatus was being used—speaking a language rich in guttural sounds. They left the room by a different exit, into a wide corridor, where transportation was waiting for them. It was a vehicle the size of a large truck, a teardrop shade riding on six large, heavily tired wheels. It was made of metal the same color as their clothing, and appeared to have no windows. However, when they went inside, Mark saw that the solid nose was either transparent or composed of a large viewscreen of some kind. A single driver's seat faced the controls, and a curved, padded bench was fixed to the other three walls. They sat down, Arinix at the controls, and the machine started. There was no vibration or sound of any exhuast; it just surged forward silently at his touch.

"Electric power?" Mark asked.

"I have no idea. The cars run when needed."

Mark admired his singleness of purpose but did not envy him. There was only one thing in the man's life—to run from the solar fire and save what possibly could be saved from the flame. Were all of his people like this?

Strong headlights glared on as they left the corridor and entered what appeared to be a tunnel mouth. The walls were rough and unfinished; only the roadway beneath was smooth, dropping away at a steep angle.

"Where are we going?" Mark asked.

"Under the river, so we can drive on the surface. The island above us—what is the name Einstein—?"

"Manhattan."

"Yes, Manhattan. It is covered by the sea now, which rises almost to the top of the cliffs across the river from it. The polar caps melted many years ago here. Life is very harsh, you will see."

The tunnel ahead curved to the right and began to rise sharply. Arinix slowed the vehicle and stopped when a brilliant disk of light became visible ahead. He worked a control, and the scene darkened as though a filter had been slipped into place. Then, with the headlights switched off, he moved forward until the light could be seen as the glaring tunnel mouth, growing larger and brighter, until they were through it and back on the surface once more.

Mark could not look at the sun, or even in its direction, despite the protective filter. It burned like the open mouth of a celestial furnace, spewing out light and heat and radiation onto the world below. Here the plants grew, the only living creatures that could bear the torrent of fire from the sky, that welcomed it. Green on all sides, a jungle of growing, thriving, rising, reaching plants and trees, burgeoning under the caress of the exploding star. The road was the only visible man-made artifact, cutting a wide, straight slash through the wilderness of plant life, straining life that leaned over, grew to its very edge, and sent tendrils and runners across its barren surface. Arinix threw more switches, then rose from the driver's seat.

"It is on automatic control now. We may rest."

He grabbed for support as the car slowed suddenly; ahead, a great tree had crashed across the road, almost blocking it completely. There was a rattle of machinery from the front of the car, and a glow sprang out that rivaled the glare of the sun above. Then they moved again, slowly, and greasy smoke billowed up and was blown away.

"The machine will follow the road and clear it when it must," Arinix said. "A device, a heat generator of some sort, will burn away obstructions. I am told it is a variant of the machine that melted the soil and rock to form this road, a principle discovered while observing the repulsive sun that has caused this all, making heat in the same manner the sun makes heat. We will turn its own strengths back upon it."

He went to the seat in the rear, stretched out on it with his face to the cushions, and appeared to fall instantly asleep.

Mark sat in the driver's chair, careful to touch nothing, both fascinated and repelled by the world outside. The car continued unerringly down the center of the road at a high speed, slowing only when it had to burn away obstructions. It must have utilized radar or other sensing devices, for a sudden heavy rainstorm did not reduce its speed in the slightest. Visibility was only a few feet in the intense tropical downpour, yet the car moved on, speed unabated. It did slow, but only to burn away obstructions, and smoke and steam obscured all vision. Then the storm stopped, as quickly as it began. Mark watched until he began to yawn, so then, like Arinix, he tried to rest. At first he thought he could not possibly sleep, then realized that he had. Darkness had fallen outside, and the car still hurried silently through the night.

It was just before dawn when they reached their destination.

The building was as big as a fortress, which it resembled in more ways than one. Its walls were high and dark, featureless, streaked with rain. Harsh lights on all sides lit the ground, which was nothing more than sodden ash. Apparently all plant life was burned before it could reach the building and undermine it. The road led directly to a high door that slid open automatically as they approached. Arinix stopped the vehicle a few hundred yards short of the entrance and rose from the controls.

"Come with me. This machine will enter by itself, but we shall walk. There is no solar radiation now, so you may see my world and know what is in store for all the others."

They stepped out into the damp airlessness of the night. The car pulled away from them, and they were alone. Rivulets of wet ash streaked the road, disappearing in runnels at either side where the waiting plant life leaned close. The air was hot, muggy, hard to breathe, seemingly giving no substance to the lungs. Mark gasped and breathed deeply over and over again.

"Remember," Arinix said, turning away and starting for the entrance, "this is night, midwinter, before dawn, the coolest it will ever be here. Do not come in the summer."

Mark went after him, aware that he was already soaked with sweat, feeling the strength of the enemy in the sky above, which was already touching fire to the eastern horizon. Though he panted with the effort, he ran and staggered into the building and watched as the door ground shut behind him.

"Your work now begins," Arinix said, leading the way into a now familiar brown room. Mark got his breath back and wiped his streaming face while they made their swift journey to the world line named Iroquois.

"I will leave you here and will return in twenty-four hours for your report on the situation. We will then decide what must be done." Arinix opened the outer door and pointed.

"Just a minute—I don't know anything that is happening here. You will have to brief me."

"I know nothing of this operation, other than what I have told you. The Sixim there should have complete records and will tell you what you need to know. Now, leave. I have my own work to do."

There was no point in arguing. Arinix gestured again impatiently, and Mark went through the door, which closed with a ponderous thud behind him. He was in darkness, cold darkness, and he shivered uncontrollably after the heat of the world he had just left.

"Sixim, are you there? Can you turn on some lights?"

There was the sudden flare of a match in answer, and in its light he could see an Indian lighting an ordinary kerosene lamp. He wore thong-wrapped fur leggings and a fringed deerskin jacket. Though his skin was dark, his features were Indo-European; once the lamp was lit, he stood by it, unmoving.

"You are the Sixim," Mark said.

"I am."

"What are you doing here?"

"Awaiting instructions."

These creatures were as literal-minded as computers—which is probably what their brains were. Mark realized he had to be more specific with his questions, but his teeth were chattering with cold, and he was shivering hard, which made it difficult to think.

"How long have you been waiting?"

"Twelve days, fourteen hours, and—"

"That's precise enough. You have just been sitting here in the dark without heat all that time! Do you have a way of heating this place?"

"Yes."

"Then do it, and quickly . . . and let me have something to wrap around me before I freeze."

The buffalo-skin robe made a big difference, and while the Sixim lit a fire in a large stone fireplace, Mark looked around at the large room. The walls were of logs, with the bark still on, and the floor bare wide boards. Crates were piled at one end of the room, and a small mound of skins was at the other. Around the fire, it was more domestic, with a table and chairs, cooking pots, and cabinets. Mark pulled a wooden chair close and raised his hands to the crackling blaze. Once the fire was started, the Sixim waited stolidly again for more orders.

By patient questioning Mark extracted all that the machine man seemed to know about the situation. The agent, Joseph Wing, had been staying here and going out to talk to the Oneida. The work he did was unknown to the Sixim. Wing had gone out and not returned. At the end of forty-eight hours, as instructed, the Sixim had reported him missing. How he had reported, he would not say; obviously there were questions it would not answer.

"You've been a help—but not very much," Mark said. "I'll just have to find out for myself what is going on out there. Did Joseph Wing leave any kind of papers, a diary, notes?"

"No."

"Thanks. Are there any weapons here?"

"In that box. Do you wish me to unlock it?"

"I do."

The weapons consisted of about twenty well-worn, obviously surplus M-1 rifles, along with some boxes of ammunition. Mark tried the bolt on one—it worked smoothly—then put the rifle back in the box.

"Lock it up. I'm not looking for trouble, and if I find it, a single gun won't make that much difference. But a peace offering might be in order, particularly food in the middle of winter."

He carried the lantern over to the boxes and quickly found exactly what he needed. A case of large smoked hams. Picking one out, he held the label to the light. "Smithfield Ham," it read, "packed in New Chicago, weight 6.78 kilos." Not from his world line, obviously, but that didn't matter in the slightest.

And he would need warmer clothes, clothes that would be more acceptable here than gray coveralls. There were leggings and jackets—obviously used, from their smell—that would do nicely. He changed quickly in front of the fire, then, knowing it would be harder the longer he waited, tucked the ham under his arm and went to the door and pulled back on the large wooden bolt.

"Lock this behind me, and unlock it only for me."

"Yes."

The door opened onto an unmarked field of snow with a stand of green pines and taller bare-limbed oak trees beyond. Above, in the blue arch of the sky, a small and reasonable winter sun shed more light than heat. There was a path through the trees, and beyond them a thin trickle of smoke was dark against the sky. Mark went in that direction. When he reached the edge of the grove, a tall Indian stepped silently from behind a tree and blocked the path before him. He made no threatening moves, but the stone-headed club hung easily and ready from his hand. Mark stopped and looked at him, saying nothing, hoping he could remember Iroquois after all these years. It was the Indian who broke the silence and spoke first.

"I am called Great Hawk."

"I am called . . . Little-one-talks." He hadn't spoken that name in years; it was what the old men on the reservation called him when he first spoke their own language. Great Hawk seemed to be easier when he heard the words, for his club sank lower.

"I come in peace," Mark said, and held out the ham.

"Welcome in peace," Great Hawk said, tucking the club into his waist and taking the ham. He sniffed at it appreciatively.

"Have you seen the one named Joseph Wing?" Mark asked.

The ham dropped, half-burying itself silently in the snow; the club was clutched at the ready.

"Are you a friend of his?" Great Hawk asked.

"I have never met him. But I was told I would see him here."

Great Hawk considered this in silence for a long time, looked up as a blue jay flapped by overhead, calling out hoarsely, then examined with apparent great attention the tracks of a rabbit in the snow—through all of this not taking his eyes from Mark for more than a second. Finally he spoke.

"Joseph Wing came here during the hunter's moon, before the first snow fell. Many said he had much orenda, for there were strange lights and sounds here during a night, and no one would leave the long house, and in the morning his long house stands as you see it now. There is great orenda here. Then he came and spoke to us and told us many things. He said he would show the warriors a place where there was good hunting. Hunting is bad here, for the people of the Six Nations are many, and some go hungry. He said all these things, and what he showed us made us believe him. Some of us said we would go with him, even though some thought they would never return. Some said that he was Tehoronhiawakhon, and he did not say it was not the truth. He said to my sister, Deer-runs, that he was indeed Tehoronhiawakhon. He told her to come with him to his long house. She did not want to go with him. By force he took her to his long house."

Great Hawk stopped talking abruptly and looked attentively at Mark through half-closed eyes. He did not finish, but the meaning was clear enough. The Oneida would have thought Joseph Wing possessed of much orenda after his sudden appearance, the principle of magic power that was inherent in every body or thing. Some had it more than others. A man who could build a building in a night must have great orenda. So much so that some would consider him to be Tehoronhiawakhon, the hero who watched over them, born of the gods, who lived as a man and who might return as a man. But no hero would take a maiden by force; the Indians were very practical on this point. Anyone who would do that would be killed by the girl's family; that was obvious. Her brother waited for Mark's answer.

"One who does that must die," Mark said. Defending the undoubtedly dead Joseph Wing would accomplish nothing; Mark was learning pragmatism from Arinix.

"He died. Come to the long house."

Great Hawk picked up the ham, turned his back, and led the way through the deep snow.

6

The Oneida warriors sat cross-legged around the fire while the women served them the thin gruel. Hunting must have been bad if this was all they had, for it was more water than anything else, with some pounded acorns and a few scraps of venison. After eating, they smoked, a rank leaf of some kind that was certainly not tobacco. Not until the ceremony was out of the way did they finally touch the topic that concerned them all.

"We have eaten elk," Great Hawk said, puffing at the pipe until his eyes grew red. "This is an elkskin robe I am wearing. They are large, and there is much meat upon them." He passed the pipe to Mark, then reached behind him under a tumbled hide and drew forth a bone. "This is the bone of the leg of an elk, brought to us by someone. We would eat well in winter with elk such as this to hunt."

Mark took it and looked at it as closely as he could in the dim light. It was a bone like any other, as far as he could tell, distinguished only by its great length—at least five feet from end to end. Comparing it with the length of his own femur, he could see that it came from a massive beast. Surely an elk or a cow would be smaller than this. What had this to do with the dead Joseph Wing? He must have brought it. But why, and where did he get it? If only there were some record of what he was supposed to be doing. Hunting, of course—that had to be it; food for these people who appeared too many for the limited hunting grounds. He held up the bone and spoke.

"Was it told to you that you would be able to hunt elk like this?"

There were nods and grunts in answer.

"What was told you?" After a silence, Great Hawk answered.

"Someone said that a hunting party could go to this land that was close by but far away. If hunting was good, a long house would be built for the others to follow. That was what was said."

It was simple enough. A hunting party taken to one of the seeded desert worlds, now stocked with game. If the trip was successful, the rest of the tribe would follow.

"I can also take you hunting in that land," Mark said.

"When will this be?"

"Come to me in the morning, and I will tell you."

He left before they could ask any more questions. The sun was low on the horizon, sending long purple shadows across the white snow. Backtracking was easy, and the solid log walls of the building a welcome sight. When he was identified, the Sixim let him in. The fire was built even higher now, and the large room was almost warmed up. Mark sat by the fire and stretched his hands to it gratefully; the Sixim was statuesque in the shadows.

"Joseph Wing was to take the Indians to another world line. Did you know that?"

"Yes."

"Why didn't you tell me?"

"You did not ask."

"I would appreciate it if you would volunteer more information in the future."

"Which information do you wish me to volunteer?"

The Sixim took a lot of getting used to. Mark took the lantern and rummaged through the variety of goods in the boxes and on the loaded shelves. There were ranked bottles of unfamiliar shape and labeling that contained some thing called *Kunbula Atashan* from someplace that appeared to be named Carthagio—it was hard to read the letters, so he could not be sure, but when he opened one of them, it had a definite odor of strong alcoholic beverage. The flavor was unusual but fortifying, and he poured a mugful before he returned to the fire.

"Do you know whom I must contact to make arrangements for the transfer to the other world line?"

"Yes."

"Who?"

"Me."

It was just that simple. The Sixim would give no details of the operation, but he would operate the mechanism to take them to the correct world and return.

"In the morning, first thing, we'll go have a look."

They left soon after dawn. Mark took one of the rifles and some extra clips of ammunition; that had been a big elk, and he might be lucky enough to bag another. Once more the sensationless transfer was made and the heavy outer door pushed open. For the first time there was no other room or hallway beyond it, just a field of yellowed grass. Mark was astonished.

"But . . . is it winter? Where is the snow?" Because it was phrased as a question, the Sixim answered him.

"It is winter. But here in Sandstone the climate is warmer, due to ocean-current differences."

Holding the rifle ready, Mark stepped through the door, which the Sixim closed behind him. Without being ordered, the Sixim locked the door with the long key. For the first time Mark saw the means of world-line transportation not concealed by an outer building. It was a large box, nothing more, constructed of riveted and rusty steel plates. Whatever apparatus powered it was inside, for it was completely featureless. He turned from it to look at the world named Sandstone.

The tall grass was everywhere; it must have been seeded first to stabilize the soil. It had done this, but it would take centuries to soften the bare rock contours of what had once been a worldwide desert. Harsh-edged crags pushed up in the distance where there should have been rounded hills; mounds of tumbled morain rose above the grass. Groves and patches of woods lay scattered about, while on one side a thick forest began and stretched away to the horizon. All of this had a very constructed air to it—and it obviously was. Mark recognized some of the trees; others were strange to him. This planet had been seeded in a hurry, and undoubtedly with a great variety of vegetation. As unusual as it looked now, this made ecological good sense, since complex ecological relationships increased the chance the ecosystem had of surviving. There would certainly be a variety of animal life as well—the large elk the Oneida knew about, and surely others as well. When he moved around the rusty building, he saw just what some of that life might be—and stopped still on the spot. No more than a few hundred yards away, there was a herd of elephants tearing at the leaves on the low trees. Large elephants with elegant swept-back tusks, thickly covered with hair.

"Hairy mammoth!" he said aloud, just as the nearest bull saw him appear and raised his trunk and screamed warning.

"That is correct," the Sixim said.

"Get your key, and let's get out of here," Mark said, backing quickly around the corner. "I don't think a thirty-caliber will make a dent in that thing."

With unhurried, steady motions the Sixim unlocked the door, one lock after another, while the thunder of pounding feet grew louder and closer. Then they were through the door and pushing it shut.

"I think the Oneida will enjoy the hunting," Mark said, grinning wryly, leaning against the thick wall with relief. "Let's go back and get them."

When he opened the outer wooden door in Iroquois, he saw Great Hawk and five other warriors standing patiently in the snow outside. They were dressed warmly, had what must be provision bags slung at their waists, and were armed with long bows and arrows as well as stone clubs and stone skinning knives. They were prepared for a hunting expedition, they knew not where, but they were prepared. When Mark waved them forward, they came at once. The only sign of the tension they must be feeling was in their manner of walking, more like stalking a chase than entering a building. They showed little interest in the outer room—they must have been here before—but were eyeing the heavy metal door with more than casual interest. The deceased Joseph Wing must have told them something about it, but Mark had already decided to ignore this and tell the truth as clearly as they could understand it.

"Through that door is a long house that will bear us to the place where we will hunt. How it will take us there I do not know, for it is beyond my comprehension. But it will take us there as safely as a mother carries a papoose on her back, as safely as a bark canoe carries us over the waters. Are you ready to go?"

"Will you take the noise stick that kills?" Great Hawk asked, pointing with his thumb at the rifle Mark still carried.

"Yes."

"It was one time said that the Oneida would be given noise sticks and taught the manner of their use."

Why not, Mark thought, there were no rules to all this, anything went that would save these people. "Yes, you may have them now if you wish, but I think until you can use them well, your bows will be better weapons."

"That is true. We will have them when we return."

The Sixim pulled the heavy door open, and without being urged, the Indians filed into the brightly lit room beyond. They remained silent but held their weapons ready as the door was closed and the Sixim went through the door to the operating room, only to emerge a moment later.

"The journey is over," Mark said. "Now we hunt."

Only when the outer door was opened onto the grassy sunlit plain did they believe him. They grunted with surprise as they left, calling out in wonder at the strange sights and the warm temperature. Mark looked around nervously, but the herd of mammoth was gone. There were more than enough other things to capture the Indians' attention. They saw animals where he saw only grass and trees and called attention to them with pleased shouts. Yet they were silent instantly when Great Hawk raised his hand for silence, then pointed.

"There, under those trees. It looks like a large pig."

Mark could see nothing in the shadows, but the other Indians were apparently in agreement, for they were nocking arrows to their bows. When the dark, snuffling shape emerged into the sunlight, they were ready for it. A European boar, far larger than they had ever seen. The boar had never seen men before either; it was not afraid. The arrows whistled; more than one struck home, the boar wheeled about, squealing with pain, and crashed back into the undergrowth. Whooping with pleasure, the Oneida were instantly on its trail.

"Stay inside until we get back," Mark told the Sixim. "I want to be sure *we* can get back."

He ran swiftly after the others, who had already vanished under the trees. The trail was obvious, marked with the blood of the fleeing animal, well trampled by its pursuers. From ahead there came even louder squealing and shouts that ended in sudden silence. When Mark came up, it was all over; the boar was on its side, dead, its skull crushed in, while the victorious Indians prodded its flanks and hams happily.

The explosion shook the ground at that moment, a long, deep rumbling sound that hammered at their ears. It staggered them, it was so close and loud, frightening them because they did not know what it was. Mark did. He had heard this kind of noise before. He wheeled about and watched the large cloud of greasy black smoke roiling and spreading as it climbed up the sky. It rose from behind the trees in the direction of the building. Then he was running, slamming a cartridge in the chamber of the rifle at the same time, thumbing off the safety.

The scene was a disaster. He stumbled and almost fell as he emerged from beneath the trees.

Where the squat steel building had stood was now only a

smoking, flame-licked ruin of torn and twisting plates. On the grass nearby, one leg ripped away and as torn himself, lay the Sixim.

The doorway between the worlds was closed.

7

Mark just stood there, motionless, even after the Indians came up and ranked themselves beside him, calling out in wonder at the devastation. They did not realize yet that they were exiled from their tribe and their own world. The Sixim raised its head and called out hoarsely; Mark ran to it. Much of its imitation flesh was gone, and metal shone through the gaps. Its face had suffered badly as well, but it could still talk.

"What happened?" Mark asked.

"There were strangers in the room, men with guns. This is not allowed. There are orders. I actuated the destruct mechanism and attempted to use the escape device."

Mark looked at the ruin and flames. "There is no way this room can be used again?"

"No."

"Are there other rooms on this world?"

"One that I know of, perhaps more. . . ."

"One is enough! Where is it?"

"What is the name of your world line?"

"What difference does that make? . . . All right, it's called Einstein."

"The room is located on an island that is named Manhattan."

"Of course! The original one I came through. But that must be at least two hundred miles away from here as the crow flies."

But what was two hundred miles as compared to the gap between the worlds? His boots were sound, he was a couple of pounds overweight, but otherwise in good condition. He had companions who were at home in the wilds and knew how to live off the land. If they would come with him . . . They had little other choice. If he could explain to them what had happened and what they must do . . .

It was not easy, but the existence of this world led them to believe anything he told them—if not believe it, at least not to doubt it too strongly. In the end they were almost eager to see what this new land had to offer, what other strange animals there were to hunt. While the others butchered and smoked the fresh-killed meat, Mark labored to explain to Great Hawk that they were physically at the same place in the world as the one they had left. The Indian worked hard to understand this but could not, since this was obviously a different place. Mark finally forced him to accept the fact on faith, to operate as if it were true even though he knew it wasn't.

When it came to finding the island of Manhattan, Great Hawk called a conference of all the Indians. They strolled over slowly, grease-smeared and happy, stomachs bulging with fresh meat. Mark could only listen as they explored the geography of New York State, as they knew it and as they had heard of it from others. In the end they agreed on the location of the island, at the mouth of the great river at the ocean nearby the long island. But they knew they could not get there from this place, then went back to their butchery. They fell asleep in the middle of this; it was late afternoon, so he gave up any hope of starting this day. He resigned himself to the delay and was eating some of the roasted meat himself when the Sixim appeared out of the forest. It had shaped a rough crutch from a branch, which it held under its arm as it walked. Arinix had said the creatures were almost indestructible, and it appeared he was right.

Mark questioned the Sixim, but it did not know how to get to Manhattan, nor did it have any knowledge of the geography of this world. When the sun set, Mark stretched out by the fire with the others and slept just as soundly as they did. He was up at first light, and as the sun rose in the east, he squinted at it and realized what he had to do. He would have to lead them out of here. He shook Great Hawk awake.

"We walk east toward the sun," he said. "When we reach the great river, we turn and follow it downstream to the south. Can we do that?" If there were a Hudson River on this world . . . and if the Indians would follow him . . . Great Hawk looked at him solemnly for a long moment, then sat up.

"We leave now." He whistled shrilly, and the others stirred.

The Indians enjoyed the outing very much, chattering about the sights along the way and looking with amazement at what was obviously a happy hunting ground. Game was everywhere—

creatures they knew and others that were completely strange. There was a herd of great oxlike creatures that resembled the beasts of the cave paintings in Altamira, aurochs perhaps, and they had a glimpse of a great cat stalking them that appeared to have immensely long tusks. A saber-tooth tiger? All things were possible on this newly ripening desert world. They walked for five days through this strange landscape before they reached what could only be the Hudson River.

Except that, like the Colorado River, this river had cut an immense gorge through what had formerly been a barren landscape. They crept close to the high cliffs and peered over. There was no possible way to descend.

"South," Mark said, and turned along the edge, and the others followed him.

A day later they reached a spot where a tributary joined the Hudson and where the banks were lower and more graded. In addition, many seeds had been sown or carried here, and strands of trees lined the shore. It took the Indians less than a day to assemble branches, trunks, and driftwood to make a sizable raft. Using strips of rawhide, they bound this firmly together, loaded their food aboard, then climbed aboard themselves. As the Indians poled and paddled, the clumsy craft left shore, was carried quickly out into the main current, and hurried south. Manhattan would be at the river's mouth.

This part of the trip was the easiest, and far swifter than Mark had realized. The landscape was so different from what he knew of the valley, with alternate patches of vegetation and desert, that he found it hard to tell where they were. A number of fair-sized streams entered the river from the east, and there was no guarantee that the East River, which cut Manhattan off from the mainland, existed on this world. If it were there, he thought it another tributary, for he never saw it. There were other high cliffs, so the Palisades were not that noticeable.

"This water is no good," Great Hawk said. He had scooped up a handful from the river, and he now spat it out. Mark dipped some himself. It was brackish, salty.

"The ocean, tidewater—we're near the mouth of the river! Pull to shore, quickly."

What he had thought was a promontory ahead showed nothing but wide water beyond it, the expanse of New York Harbor. They landed on what would be the site of Battery

Park on the southernmost tip of the island. The Indians worked in silence, unloading the raft, and when Mark started to speak, Great Hawk held his finger to his lips for silence, then leaned close to whisper in his ear.

"Men over this hill, very close. Smell them, smell the fire, they are cooking meat."

"Show me," Mark whispered in return.

He could not move as silently as the Oneida did; they vanished like smoke among the trees. Mark followed as quietly as he could, and a minute later Great Hawk was back to lead him. They crawled the last few yards on their stomachs under the bushes, hearing the sound of mumbled voices. The Indian moved a branch slowly aside, and Mark looked into the clearing.

Three khaki-clad soldiers were gathered around a fire over which a smoking carcass roasted. They had heavy rifles slung across their shoulders. A fourth, a sergeant with upside-down stripes, was stretched out asleep with his wide-brimmed hat over his face.

They spoke quietly in order not to waken him, a strangely familiar language deep in their throats.

It was Dutch—not Dutch, Afrikaans. But what were they doing here?

Mark crawled back to the others, and by the time he had reached them, the answer was clear—too clear, and frightening. But it was the only possibility. He must tell them.

"Those men are soldiers. I know them. Warriors with noise sticks. I think they are the ones who took over the room and destroyed it. They are here, which must mean they have taken over the room here. Without it we cannot return."

"What must we do?" Great Hawk asked. The answer was obvious, but Mark hesitated to say it. He was a lawyer, or had been a lawyer—a man of the law. But what was the law here?

"If we are to return, we will have to kill them, without any noise, then kill or capture the others at the room. If we don't do that, we will be trapped here, cut off from the tribe forever."

The Indians, who lived by hunting, and were no strangers to tribal warfare, were far less worried about the killing than was Mark. They conferred briefly, and Great Hawk and three others vanished silently back among the trees. Mark sat, staring sightlessly at the ground, trying to equate this with his civilized conscience. For a moment he envied the battered Sixim, who stood by his side, unbothered by emotions or worries. An owl called and the remaining Indians stood and called Mark after them.

The clearing was the same, the meat still smoked on the spit, the sergeant's hat was still over his eyes. But an arrow stood out starkly from his side below his arm. The huddled forms of the other soldiers revealed the instant, silent death that had spoken from the forest. With no show of emotion, the Indians cut the valuable arrows free of the corpses, commenting only on the pallid skin of the men, then looted their weapons and supplies. The guns might be useful; the arrows certainly were. Great Hawk was scouting the clearing and found a—to him—clearly marked trail. The sun was behind the trees when they started down it.

The building was not far away. They looked at it from hiding, the now familiar rusted and riveted plates on its walls, the heavy sealed door. Only, this door was gaping open, and the building itself was surrounded by a palisade of thin trees and shrubs. A guard stood at the only gate, and the enclosure was filled with troops. Mark could see heavy weapons and mortars there.

"It will be hard to kill all of those without being killed ourselves," Great Hawk said. "So we shall not try."

8

The Indians could not be convinced even to consider action. They lay about in the gathering darkness, chewing on the tough slabs of meat, ignoring all of Mark's arguments. They were as realistic as any animal, and not interested in suicide. A mountain lion attacks a deer, a deer runs from a lion—it never happens the other way around. They would wait here until morning and watch the camp, then decide what to do. But it was obvious that the options did not include an attack. Would it end this way, defeat without battle . . . and a barren lifetime on a savage planet stretching ahead of them? More barren to Mark, who had a civilized man's imagination and despair. The Indians had no such complications in their lives. They chewed the meat, the matter dismissed and forgotten, and in low whispers discussed the hunting and the animals while darkness fell. Mark sat, silent with despair; the Sixim loomed silent as a tree beside him. The Sixim would follow orders, but the two of them were not going to capture this armed camp. Something might happen—he must make the Indians stay and watch and help him. He doubted if they would.

Something did happen, and far sooner than he had thought. Great Hawk, who had slipped away to watch the building, came back suddenly and waved the others to follow him. They went to the fringe of the trees once more and looked at the activity in the camp with astonishment.

The gate was standing open, and there was no guard upon it.

All of the soldiers had drawn up in a semicircle facing the open door of the building. Fires had been lit near it. All of the heavy weapons had been trained on the opening.

"Don't you see what has happened!" Mark said excitedly. "They may control this building and others like it in other lines, but they cannot possibly control them all. They must be expecting a counterattack. They can do nothing until the attackers appear except wait and be ready. Do you understand—this is our chance! They are not expecting trouble from this flank. Get close in the darkness. Wait. Wait until the attack. Then we take out the machine guns—they are the real danger—sow confusion. Taken from the front and rear at the same time, they cannot win. Sixim, can you fire a rifle? One of these we captured?"

"I can. I have examined their mechanism."

"How is your aim?" It was a foolish question to ask.

"I hit what I aim at, every time."

"Then let us get close and get into positions. This may be our only chance. If we don't do it this time, there will probably be no second chance. Once they know we are out here, the guns will face both ways. Come, we have to get close now."

He moved out toward the enclosure, the Sixim, rifle slung, limping at his side. The Indians stayed where they were. He turned back to them, but they were as solid and unmoving as rock in their silence. Nothing more could be done. This left only the two of them, man and machine man, to do their best.

They were almost too late. While they were still twenty yards from the palisade, sudden fire erupted from inside the building; the South African guns roared in return. Mark ran, drawing ahead of the Sixim, running through the open gate, to fall prone in the darkness near the wall and to control his breathing. To squeeze off his shots carefully.

One gunner fell, then another. The Sixim was beside him, firing at target after target with machine regularity. Someone had seen the muzzle blast of their guns, because weapons were turned on them, bullets tearing into the earth beside them, soldiers running toward them. Mark's gun clicked out of battery, empty of cartridges. He tore the empty clip away, struggled to jam in a full one; the soldier was above him.

Falling to one side with an arrow in his chest. Darker shadows moved, just as a solid wave of Sixim erupted through the open doorway.

That was the beginning of the end. As soon as they were among the soldiers, the slaughter began, no mercy, no quarter. Mark called the Indians to him, to the protection of their own battered Sixim, before they were also cut down. The carnage was brief and complete, and when it was over, a familiar one-eyed figure emerged from the building.

"Arinix," Mark called out, and the man turned and came over. "How did all this happen?"

"They were suspicious; they had been watching us for a long time. That officer we did not kill led them to this building." He said it without malice or regret, a statement of fact. Mark had no answer.

"Is this the last of them? Is the way open now?"

"There are more, but they will be eliminated. You see what happens when others attempt to control the way between the worlds?" He started away, then turned back. "Have you solved the problem with the Indians? Will they settle this world?"

"I think so. I would like to stay with them longer, give them what help I can."

"You do not wish to return to Einstein?"

That was a hard one to answer. Back to New York and the pollution and the life as a lawyer. It suddenly seemed a good deal emptier than it had. "I don't know. Perhaps, perhaps not. Let me finish here first."

Arinix turned away instantly and was gone. Mark went to Great Hawk, who sat cross-legged on the ground and watched the operation with a great deal of interest.

"Why did you and the others come to help?" Mark asked.

"It seemed too good a fight to miss. Besides, you said you would show us how to use the noise sticks. You could not do that if you were dead."

The smoke from the dying fires rose up in thin veils against the bright stars in the sky above. In his nostrils the air was cold and clean, its purity emphasized by the smell of wood smoke. Somewhere, not too far away, a wolf howled long and mournfully. This world, so recently empty of life, now had it in abundance, and would soon have human settlers as well, Indians of the Six Nations who would be escaping the fire that would destroy their own world. What sort of world would they make of it?

He had the sudden desire to see what would happen here, even to help in the shaping of it. The cramped life of a lawyer in a crowded world was without appeal. He had friends that he would miss, but he knew that new friends waited for him in the multiplicity of worlds he would soon visit. Really, there was no choice.

Arinix was by the open door issuing orders to the attentive Sixim. Mark called out to him.

The decision had really been an easy one.

Belfast-born BOB SHAW (1931–   ) is a prolific writer of solid, entertaining science fiction who deserves a larger audience. Although he has never produced a "breakthrough" book, all of his more than fifteen novels and story collections give great value for money, and he will always be remembered as the creator of "slow glass," one of the most timely ideas in the history of science fiction. He has long been an important figure in the sf subculture in Great Britain, and his ability to write about characters we care about, as in the following story, is a most valuable resource in a field that has been dominated by ideas. Particularly noteworthy novels are *The Palace of Eternity* (1969), *One Million Tomorrows* (1970), and *Orbitsville* (1975).

SKIRMISH ON A SUMMER MORNING

Bob Shaw

A flash of silver on the trail about a mile ahead of him brought Gregg out of his reverie. He pulled back on the reins, easing the buckboard to a halt, and took a small leather-covered telescope from the jacket that was lying on the wooden seat beside him. Sliding its sections out with multiple clicks, he raised the telescope to his eye, frowning a little at the ragged, gritty pain flaring in his elbows. It was early in the morning and, in spite of the heat, his arms retained some of their nighttime stiffness.

The ground had already begun to bake, agitating the lower levels of air into trembling movement, and the telescope yielded only a swimmy, bleached-out image. It was of a young woman, possibly Mexican, in a silver dress. Gregg brought the instrument down, wiped sweat from his forehead, and tried to make sense of what he had just seen. A woman dressed in silver would have been a rare spectacle anywhere, even in the plushest saloons of Sacramento, but finding one alone on the trail three miles north of Copper Cross was an event for which he was totally unprepared. Another curious fact was that he had crossed a low ridge five minutes earlier, from which vantage point he had been able to see far ahead along the trail, and he would have sworn it was deserted.

He peered through the telescope again. The woman was standing still and seemed to be looking all around her, like a person who had lost her way, and this, too, puzzled Gregg. A stranger might easily go astray in this part of southern Arizona, but the realization that she was lost would have dawned long before she got near Copper Cross. She would hardly be scanning the monotonous landscape as though it were something new.

Gregg traversed the countryside with his telescope, searching for a carriage, a runaway or injured horse, anything that would account for the woman's presence. His attention was drawn by a smudge of dust centered on the distant specks of two riders on a branching trail that ran east to the Portfield ranch, and for an instant he thought he had solved the mystery. Josh Portfield sometimes brought a girl back from his expeditions across the border, and it would be in character for him—should one of his guests prove awkward—to dump her outside of town. But a further look at the riders showed they were approaching the main trail and possibly were not yet aware of the woman. Their appearance was, however, an extra factor which required Gregg's consideration, because their paths were likely to cross his.

He was not a cautious man by nature, and for his forty-eight years had followed an almost deliberate policy of making life interesting by running headlong into every situation, trusting to good reflexes and a quick mind to get him out again if trouble developed. It was this philosophy that had led him to accept the post of unofficial town warden, and which—on the hottest afternoon of a cruel summer—had faced him with the impossible task of quieting down Josh Portfield and four of his cronies when they were inflamed with whisky. Gregg had emerged from the episode with crippled arms and a new habit of planning his every move with the thoughtfulness of a chess master.

The situation before him now did not seem dangerous, but it contained too many unknown factors for his liking. He took his shotgun from the floor of the buckboard, loaded it with two dully rattling shells, and snicked the hammers back. Swearing at the clumsy stiffness of his arms, he slipped the gun into the rawhide loops that were nailed to the underside of the buckboard's seat. It was a dangerous arrangement, not good firearms practice, but the hazard would be greatest for anyone who chose to ride alongside him, and he had the option of warning them off if they were friendly or not excessively hostile.

Gregg flicked the reins and his horse ambled forward, oily highlights stirring on its flanks. He kept his gaze fixed straight ahead and presently saw the two riders cut across the fork of the trail and halt at the fleck of silver fire, which was how the woman appeared to his naked eye. He hoped, for her sake, that they were two of the reasonably decent hands who kept the Portfield spread operating as a ranch, and not a couple of Josh's night-riding lieutenants. As he watched he saw that they were neither dismounting nor holding their horses in one place, but were riding in close slow circles around the woman. He deduced from that one observation that she had been unlucky in her encounter, and a fretful unease began to gnaw at his stomach. Before Gregg's arms had been ruined he would have lashed his horse into a gallop; now his impulse was to turn and go back the way he had come. He compromised by allowing himself to be carried toward the scene at an unhurried pace, hoping all the while that he could escape involvement.

As he drew near the woman, Gregg saw that she was not—as he had supposed—wearing a mantilla, but that her silver dress was an oddly styled garment, incorporating a hood which was drawn up over her head. She was turning this way and that as the riders moved around her. Gregg transferred his attention to the two men and, with a pang of unhappiness, recognized Wolf Caley and Siggy Sorenson. Caley's gray hair and white beard belied the fact that he possessed all the raw appetites and instincts of a young heathen, and as always he had an old fifty-four-bore Tranter shoved into his belt. Sorenson, a thick-set Swedish ex-miner of about thirty, was not wearing a gun, but that scarcely mattered because he had all the lethality of a firearm built into his massive limbs. Both men had been members of the group which, two years earlier, had punished Gregg for meddling in Portfield affairs. They pretended not to notice Gregg's approach, but continually circled the woman, occasionally leaning sideways in their saddles and trying to snatch the silver hood back from her face. Gregg pulled to a halt a few yards from them.

"What are you boys playing at?" he said in conversational tones. The woman turned toward him as soon as he spoke and he glimpsed the pale, haunted oval of her face. The sudden movement caused the unusual silver garment to tighten against her body, and Gregg was shocked to realize that she was in a late stage of pregnancy.

"Go away, Billy boy," Caley said carelessly, without turning his head.

"I think you should leave the lady alone."

"I think you must like the sound of your own bones a-breakin'," Caley replied. He made another grab for the woman's hood, and she ducked to avoid his hand.

"Now cut that out, Wolf." Gregg directed his gaze at the woman. "I'm sorry about this, ma'am. If you're going into town you can ride with me."

"Town? Ride?" Her voice was low and strangely accented. "You are English?"

Gregg had time to wonder why anybody should suspect him of being English rather than American merely because he spoke English. Then Caley moved into the intervening space.

"Stay out of this, Billy boy," he said. "We know how to deal with Mexicans who sneak over the line."

"She isn't Mexican."

"Who asked you?" Caley said irritably, his hand straying to the butt of the Tranter.

Sorenson wheeled his horse out of the circle, came alongside the buckboard, and looked in the back. His eyes widened as he saw the eight stone jars bedded in straw.

"Look here, Wolf," he called. "Mr. Gregg is takin' a whole parcel of his best *pulque* into town. We got us all the makin's of a good party here."

Caley turned to him at once, his bearded face looking almost benign. "Hand me one of those crocks."

Gregg slid his right hand under the buckboard's seat. "It'll cost you eight-fifty."

"I'm not payin' eight-fifty for no cactus juice." Caley shook his head as he urged his horse a little closer to the buckboard, coming almost into line with its transverse seat.

"That's what I get from Whalley's, but I tell you what I'll do," Gregg said reasonably. "I'll let you have a jar each on account and you can have yourselves a drink while I take the lady into town. It's obvious she's lost and . . ." Gregg stopped speaking as he saw that he had completely misjudged Caley's mood.

"Who do you think you are?" Caley demanded. "Talkin' to me like I was a kid! If I'd had my way I'd have finished you off a couple of years back, Gregg. In fact . . ." Caley's mouth compressed until it was visible only as a yellow stain on his white beard, and his china-blue eyes brightened with purpose. His hand was now full of the butt of the Tranter and, even though he had not drawn, his thumb was pulling the hammer back.

Gregg glanced around the shimmering, silent landscape, at the impersonal backdrop of the Sierra Madre, and he knew he had perhaps only one second left in which to make a decision and act on it. Caley had not come fully into line with the hidden shotgun, and as he was still on horseback he was far too high above the muzzle, but Gregg had no other resort. Forcing the calcified knot of his elbow to bend to his will, he managed to reach the shotgun's forward trigger and squeeze it hard. In the last instant Caley seemed to guess what was happening, and he tried to throw himself to one side. There was a thunderous blast and the tightly bunched swarm of pellets ripped through his riding boot, just above the ankle, before plowing a bloody furrow across his horse's rear flank. The terrified animal reared up through a cloud of black gunsmoke, its eyes flaring whitely, and fell sideways with Caley still in the saddle. Gregg heard the sickening crack of a major bone breaking, then Caley began to scream.

"Don't!" Sorenson shouted from the back of his plunging mare. "Don't shoot!" He dug his spurs into the animal's side, rode about fifty yards, and stopped with his hands in the air.

Gregg stared at him blankly for a moment before realizing that—because of the noise, smoke, and confusion—the Swede had no idea of what had happened, nor of how vulnerable Gregg actually was. Caley's continued bellowing as the fallen horse struggled to get off him made it difficult for Gregg to think clearly. The enigmatic woman had drawn her shoulders up and was standing with her hands pressed over her face.

"Stay back there," Greg shouted to Sorenson before turning to the woman. "Come on—we'd best get out of here."

She began to shiver violently, but made no move toward him. Gregg jumped down from his seat, pulled the shotgun out of his sling, went to the woman, and drew her toward the buckboard. She came submissively and allowed him to help her up into the seat. Gregg heard hoofbeats close behind him and spun around to see that Caley's horse had gotten free and was galloping away to the east, in the direction of the Portfield ranch. Caley was lying clutching a misshapen thigh. He had stopped screaming and seemed to be getting control of himself. Gregg went to him and, as a precaution, knelt and pulled the heavy five-shot pistol from the injured man's belt. It was still cocked.

"You're lucky this didn't go off," Gregg said, carefully lowering the hammer and tucking the gun into his belt. "A busted leg isn't the worst thing that can happen to a man."

"You're a dead man, Gregg," Caley said faintly, peacefully, his eyes closed. "Josh is away right now . . . but he'll be back soon . . . and he'll bring you to me . . . alive . . . and I'll . . ."

"Save your breath," Greg advised, concealing his doubts about his own future. "Josh expects his men to be able to take care of their own affairs." He went back to the buckboard and climbed onto the seat beside the bowed, silver-clad figure of the woman.

"I'll take you into town now," he said to her, "but that's all I can do for you, ma'am. Where are you headed?"

"Headed?" She seemed to query the word, and he became certain that English was not her native tongue, although she still did not strike him as being Mexican or Spanish.

"Yes. Where are you going?"

"I cannot go to a town."

"Why not?"

"The prince would find me there. I cannot go to a town."

"Huh?" Gregg flicked the reins, and the buckboard began to roll forward. "Are you telling me you're wanted for something?"

She hesitated. "Yes."

"Well, it can't be all that serious, and they'd have to be lenient. I mean, in view of your . . ."

As Gregg was struggling for words, the woman pushed the hood back from her face with a hand that still trembled noticeably. She was in her mid-twenties, with fine golden hair and pale skin that suggested to Gregg that she was city-bred. He guessed that under normal circumstances she would have been lovely, but her features had been deadened by fear and shock, and perhaps exhaustion. Her gray eyes hunted over his face.

"I think you are a good man," she said slowly. "Where do you live?"

"Back along this trail about three miles."

"You live alone?"

"I do, but . . ." The directness of her questioning disturbed Gregg, and he sought inspiration. "Where's your husband, ma'am?"

"I have no husband."

Gregg looked away from her. "Oh. Well, we'd best get on into town."

"No!" The woman half rose, as though planning to jump from the buckboard while it was still in motion, then clutched at her swollen belly and slumped back onto the seat. Gregg felt the weight of her against his side, he looked all around for a possible source of assistance, but saw only Sorenson, who had returned to Caley and was kneeling beside him. Caley was sitting upright, and both men were watching the buckboard and its passengers with the bleak intensity of snakes.

Appalled at the suddenness with which his life had gotten out of control, Gregg swore softly to himself and turned the buckboard in a half circle for the drive back to his house.

The house was small, having begun its existence some ten years earlier as a line shack used by cowhands from a large but decaying ranch. Gregg had bought it and a section of land back in the days when it looked as though he might become a rancher in his own right, and had added two extra rooms, which gave it a patchy appearance from the outside. After his fateful brush with the Portfield men, which had left him unable to cope with more than a vegetable plot, he had been able to sell back most of the land and retain the house. The deal had not been a good one from the point of view of the original owner, but it was a token that some people in the area had appreciated his efforts to uphold the rule of law.

"Here we are," Gregg said. He helped the woman down from the buckboard, forced to support most of her weight and worried about the degree of personal contact involved. The woman was a complete mystery to him, but he knew she was not accustomed to being manhandled. He got her indoors and guided her into the most comfortable chair in the main room. She leaned back in it with her eyes closed, hands pressed to her abdomen.

"Ma'am?" Gregg said anxiously. "Is it time for . . . ? I mean, do you need a doctor?"

Her eyes opened wide. "No! No doctor!"

"But if you're . . ."

"That time is still above me," she said, her voice becoming firmer.

"Just as well—the nearest doctor's about fifty miles from here. Almost as far as the nearest sheriff." Gregg looked down at the woman and was surprised to note that her enveloping one-piece garment, which had shone like a newly minted silver dollar while outside in the sunlight, was now a rich blue-gray. He stared at the cloth and discovered he could detect no sign of seams or stitching. His puzzlement increased.

"I am thirsty," the woman said. "Have you a drink for me?"

"It was too hot for a fire so there's no coffee, but I've got some spring water."

"Water, please."

"There's plenty of whisky and *pulque*. I make it right here. It wouldn't harm you."

"The water, please."

"Right." Gregg went to the oaken bucket, uncovered it, and took out a dipper of cool water. When he turned he saw that the woman was surveying the room's bare pine walls and rough furniture with an expression of mingled revulsion and despair. He felt sorry for her.

"This place isn't much," he said, "but I live here alone, and I don't need much."

"You have no woman?"

Again Gregg was startled by the contrast between the woman's obvious gentility and the bluntness of her questioning. He thought briefly about Ruth Jefferson, who worked in the general store in Copper Cross and who might have been living in his house had things worked out differently, then shook his head. The woman accepted the enameled scoop from him and sipped some water.

"I want to stay here with you," she said.

"You're welcome to rest a while," Gregg replied uneasily, somehow aware of what was coming.

"I want to stay for six days." The woman gave him a direct calm stare. "Until after my son is born."

Gregg snorted his incredulity. "This is no hospital, and I'm no midwife."

"I'll pay you well." She reached inside her dress *cum* cloak and produced a strip of yellow metal that shone with the buttery luster of high-grade gold. It was about eight inches long by an inch wide, with rounded edges and corners. "One of these for each day. That will be six."

"This doesn't make any kind of sense," Gregg floundered. "I mean, you don't even know if six days will be enough."

"My son will be born on the day after tomorrow."

"You can't be sure of that."

"I can."

"Ma'am, I . . ." Gregg picked up the heavy metal tablet. "This would be worth a lot of money . . . to a bank."

"It isn't stolen, if that's what you mean."

He cleared his throat and, not wishing to contradict or quiz his visitor, examined the gold strip for markings. It had no indentations of any kind and had an almost oily feel, which suggested it might be twenty-four-carat pure.

"I didn't say it was stolen—but I don't often get monied ladies coming here to have their babies." He gave her a wry smile. "Fact is, you're the first."

"Delicately put," she said, mustering a smile in return. "I know how strange this must seem to you, but I'm not free to explain it. All I can tell you is that I have broken no laws."

"You must want to go into hiding for a spell."

"Please understand that there are other societies whose ways are not those of Mexico."

"Excuse me, ma'am," Gregg said, wondering, "this territory has been American since 1848."

"Excuse *me*." She was contrite. "I never excelled at geography—and I'm very far from home."

Gregg suspected he was being manipulated and decided to resist. "How about the prince?"

Sunlight reflecting from the water in the dipper she was holding split into concentric rings. "It was wrong of me to think of involving you," she said. "I'll go as soon as I have rested."

"Go where?" Gregg, feeling himself becoming involved regardless of her wishes or his own, gave a scornful laugh. "Ma'am, you don't seem to realize how far you are from anywhere. How did you get out here, anyway?"

"I'll leave now." She stood up with some difficulty, her small face paler than ever. "Thank you for helping me as much as you did. I hope you will accept that piece of gold . . ."

"Sit down," Gregg said resignedly. "If you're crazy enough to want to stay here and have your baby, I guess I'm crazy enough to go along with it."

"Thank you." She sat down heavily, and he knew she had been close to fainting.

"There's no need to keep thanking me." Gregg spoke gruffly to disguise the fact that, in an obscure way, he was pleased that a young and beautiful woman was prepared to entrust herself to his care after such a brief acquaintanceship. *I think you are a good man* were almost the first words she had said to him, and in that moment he had abruptly become aware of how wearisome his life had been in the past two years. Semicrippled, dried out by fifty years of hard living, he should have been immune to romantic notions—especially as the woman could well be a foreign aristocrat who would not even have glanced at him under normal circumstances. The fact remained, however, that he had acted as her protector, and on her behalf had been reintroduced to all the heady addictions of danger. Now the woman was dependent on him and prepared to live in his house. She was also young and beautiful and mysterious—a combination he found as irresistible now as he would have done a quarter of a century earlier.

"We'd best start being practical," he said, compensating for his private flight of fantasy. "You can have my bed for the week. It's clean, but we're going to need fresh linen. I'll go into town and pick up some supplies."

She looked alarmed. "Is that necessary?"

"Very necessary. Don't worry—I won't tell anybody you're here."

"Thank you," she said. "But what about the two men I met?"

"What about them?"

"They probably know I came here with you. Won't they talk about it?"

"Not where it matters. The Portfield men don't mix with the townsfolk or anybody else around here." Gregg took Caley's pistol from his belt and was putting it away in a cupboard when the woman held out her hand and asked if she could examine the weapon. Mildly surprised, he handed it to her and noticed the way in which her arm sank as it took the weight.

"It isn't a woman's gun," he commented.

"Obviously." She looked up at him. "What is the muzzle velocity of this weapon?"

Gregg snorted again, showing amusement. "You're not interested in things like that."

"That is a curious remark for you to make," she said, a hint of firmness returning to her voice, "when I have just expressed interest in it."

"Sorry, it's just that . . ." Gregg decided against referring to the terror she had shown earlier when he fired the shotgun. "I don't know the muzzle velocity, but it can't be very high. That's an old Tranter percussion five-shooter, and you don't see many of them about nowadays. It beats me why Caley took the trouble to lug it around."

"I see." She looked disappointed as she handed the pistol back. "It isn't any good."

Gregg hefted the weapon. "Don't get me wrong, ma'am. This sort of gun is troublesome to load, but it throws a fifty-four-bore slug that'll bowl over any man alive." He was looking at the woman as he spoke, and it seemed to him that, on his final words, an odd expression passed over her face.

"Were you thinking of bigger game?" he said. "Bear, perhaps?"

She ignored his questions. "Have you a pistol of your own?"

"Yes, but I don't carry it. That way I stay out of trouble." Gregg recalled the events of the past hour. "Usually I stay out of trouble."

"What is its muzzle velocity?"

"How would I know?" Gregg found it more and more difficult to reconcile the woman's general demeanor with her strange interest in the technicalities of firearms. "We don't think that way about guns around here. I've got a .44 Remington that always did what I wanted it to do, and that's all I ever needed to know about it."

Undeterred by the impatience in his voice, the woman looked around the room for a moment and pointed at the massive iron range on which he did his cooking. "What would happen if you fired it at that?"

"You'd get pieces of lead bouncing around the room."

"The shot wouldn't go through?"

Gregg chuckled. "There isn't a gun made that could do that. Would you mind telling me why you're so interested?"

She responded in a way he was learning to expect, by changing the subject. "Shall I call you Billy boy?"

"Billy is enough," he said. "If we're going to use our given names."

"My name is Morna, and of course we're going to use our Christian names." She gave him a twinkling glance. "There's no point in being formal . . . under the circumstances."

"I guess not." Gregg felt his cheeks grow warm, and he turned away.

"Have you ever delivered a baby before?"

"It isn't my line of work."

"Well, don't worry about it too much," she said. "I'll instruct you."

"Thanks," Gregg replied gruffly, wondering if he could have been wildly wrong in his guess that his visitor was a woman of high breeding. She had the looks and—now that she was no longer afraid—a certain imperious quality in her manner, but she appeared to have no idea that there were certain things a woman should only discuss with her intimates.

In the afternoon he drove into town, taking a longer route that kept him well clear of the Portfield ranch, and disposed of his eight gallons of *pulque* at Whalley's Saloon. The heat was intense, and perspiration had glued his shirt to his back, but he allowed himself one glass of beer before going to see Ruth Jefferson in her cousin's store. He found her alone at the rear of the store, struggling to lift a sack of beans onto a low shelf. She was a sturdy, attractive woman in her early forties, still straight-backed and narrow-waisted even though ten years of widowhood and self-sufficiency had scored deep lines at the sides of her mouth.

"Afternoon, Billy," she said on hearing his footsteps, then looked at him more closely. "What are you up to, Billy Gregg?"

Gregg felt his heart falter—this was precisely the sort of thing that made him wary of women. "What do you mean?"

"I mean why are you wearing a necktie on a day like this? And your good hat? And, if I'm not mistaken, your good boots?"

"Let me help you with that sack," he said, going forward. "It's too much for those arms of yours."

"I can manage." Gregg stooped, put his chest close to the sack, and gripped it between his upper arms. He straightened up, holding the sack awkwardly but securely, and dropped it onto the shelf. "See? What did I tell you?"

"You've got dust all over yourself," she said severely, flicking at his clothing with her handkerchief.

"It doesn't matter. Don't fuss." In spite of his protests, Gregg stood obediently and allowed himself to be dusted off, enjoying the attention. "I need your help, Ruth," he said, making a decision.

She nodded. "I've been telling you that for years."

"This is for one special thing, and I can't even tell you about it unless you promise to keep it secret."

"I knew it! I knew you were up to something as soon as you walked in here."

Gregg extracted the promise he wanted, then went on to describe the events of the morning. As he talked, the lines at the sides of Ruth's mouth grew more pronounced, and her eyes developed a hard, uncompromising glitter. He was relieved when, just as he had finished speaking, two women came into the store and spent ten minutes buying a length of cloth. By the time Ruth had finished serving them the set look had gone from her face, but he could tell she was still angry with him.

"I don't understand you, Billy," she whispered. "I thought you had learned your lesson the last time you went up against the Portfield crowd."

"There was nothing else I could do," he said. "I had to help her."

"That's what I'm afraid of."

"What does that mean?"

"Billy Gregg, if I ever find out that you got some little saloon girl into trouble and then had the nerve to get me to help with the delivery . . ."

"Ruth!" Gregg was genuinely shocked by the new idea.

"It's a more likely story than the one you've just told me."

He sighed and took the slim gold bar from his pocket. "Would she be paying me? With this sort of thing?"

"I suppose not," Ruth said. "But it's all so . . . What kind of a name is Morna?"

"Don't ask me."

"Well, where is she from?"

"Don't ask me."

"You've had a shave, as well." She stared at him in perplexity for a moment. "I guess I'll just have to go out there and meet the woman who can make Billy Gregg start prettying himself up. I want to see what she's got that I haven't."

"Thanks, Ruth—I feel a lot easier in my mind now." Gregg looked around the big shady room with its loaded shelves and beams festooned with goods. "What sort of stuff should I be taking back with me?"

"I'll make up a bundle of everything that's needed and take it out to you before supper. I can borrow Sam's gig."

"That's great." Gregg smiled his gratitude. "Make sure you use the west road, though."

"Get out of here and let me get on with my chores," Ruth said briskly. "None of Portfield's saddle tramps are going to bother me."

"Right—see you later." Gregg was turning to leave when his attention was caught by the bolts of cloth stacked on the counter. He fingered a piece of silky material and frowned. "Ruth, did you ever hear of cloth that looks silver out of doors and turns blue indoors?"

"No, I never did."

"I thought not." Gregg walked to the door, hesitated, then went out into the heat and throbbing brilliance of Copper Cross's main street. He got onto his buckboard, flicked the reins, and drove slowly to the water trough, which was in an alley at the side of the livery stables. A young cowboy with a drooping, sandy mustache was already watering his horse. Gregg recognized him as Cal Masham, one of the passably honest hands who worked for Josh Portfield, and nodded a greeting.

"Billy." Masham nodded in return and took his pipe from his mouth. "Heard about your run-in with Wolf Caley this afternoon."

"News gets around fast."

Masham glanced up and down the alley. "I think you ought to know, Billy—Wolf's hurt real bad."

"Yeah, I heard his leg go when his horse came down on it. I owed him a broken bone or two." Gregg sniffed appreciatively. "Nice tobacco you've got there."

"It wasn't a clean break, Billy. Last I heard his leg was all swole up and turned black. And he's got a fever."

In the heat of the afternoon Gregg suddenly felt cool. "Is he likely to die?"

"It looks that way, Billy." Masham looked around him again. "Don't tell anybody I told you, but Josh is due back in two or three days. If I was in your shoes I wouldn't hang around and wait for him to get here."

"Thanks for the tip, son." Gregg waited impassively until his horse had finished drinking, then he urged the animal forward. It lowered its head and drew him from the shadow of the stables into the searing arena of the street.

Gregg had left the woman, Morna, sleeping on his bed and still wrapped in the flowing outer garment whose properties were such a mystery to him. On his return he entered the house quietly, hoping to avoid disturbing her rest, and found Morna sitting at the table with a book spread out before her. She had removed her cloak to reveal a simple blue smock with half-length sleeves. The book was one of the dozen that Gregg owned, a well-worn school atlas, and it was open at a double-page map of North America.

Morna had tied her fair hair into a loose coil, and she looked more beautiful than Gregg had remembered, but his attention was drawn to the strange ornament on her wrist. It looked like a circular piece of dark red glass about the size of a dollar, rimmed with gold and held in place by a thin gold band. Its design was unusual enough, but the thing that held Gregg's gaze was that under the surface of the glass was a sliver of ruby light, equivalent in size and positioning to one hand of a watch, which blinked on and off at intervals of about two seconds.

She looked up at him and smiled. "I hope you don't mind." She indicated the atlas.

"Help yourself, ma'am."

"Morna."

"Help yourself . . . Morna." The familiarity did not sit easily with Gregg. "Are you feeling stronger?"

"I'm much better, thank you. I hadn't slept since . . . for quite a long time."

"I see." Gregg sat down at the other side of the table and allowed himself a closer look at the intriguing ornament. On its outer rim were faint markings like those of a compass, and the splinter of light continued its slow pulsing beneath the glass. "I don't mean to pry, ma'am—Morna," he said, "but in my whole life I've never seen anything like that thing on your wrist."

"It's nothing." Morna covered it with her hand. "It's just a trinket."

"But how can it keep sparking the way it does?"

"Oh, I don't understand these matters," she said airily. "I believe it works by electronics."

"Is that something to do with electricity?"

"Electricity is what I mean to say—my English is not very good."

"But what's it *for?*"

Morna laughed. "Do your women only wear what is useful?"

"I guess not," Gregg said doubtfully, aware he was being put off once again. After a few initial uncertainties, Morna's English had been very assured, and he suspected that the odd word she had used—electronics—had not been a mistake. He made up his mind to search for it in Ruth's dictionary, if he ever got the chance.

Morna looked down at the atlas, upon which she had placed a piece of straw running east to west, with one end at the approximate location of Copper Cross.

"According to this map we are about twelve hundred miles from New Orleans."

Gregg shook his head. "It's more than that to New Orleans."

"I've just measured it."

"That's the straight-line distance," he explained patiently. "It doesn't signify anything—'less you can fly like a bird."

"But you agree that it is twelve hundred miles."

"That's about right—for a bird." Gregg jumped to his feet and, in his irritation, tried to do it in the normal way, with the assistance of his arms pushing against the table. His left elbow cracked loudly and gave way, bringing him down on that shoulder. Embarrassed, he stood up more slowly, trying not to show that he was hurt, and walked to the range. "We'll have to see about getting you some proper food."

"What's wrong with your arm?" Morna spoke softly, from close behind him.

"It's nothing for you to worry about," he said, surprised at her show of concern.

"Let me see it, Billy—I may be able to help."

"You're not a doctor, are you?" As he had expected, there was no reply to his question, but the possibility that the woman had had medical training prompted Gregg to roll up his sleeves and let her examine the misshapen elbow joints. Having unbent that far, he went on to tell her about how—in the absence of any law enforcement in the area—he had been foolish enough to let himself be talked into taking the job of unofficial town warden, and about how, even more foolishly, he had once interrupted Josh Portfield and four of his men in the middle of a drinking spree. He skimmed briefly over the details of how two men had held each of his wrists and whipped him bodily to and fro for over fifteen minutes until his elbows had snapped backward.

"Why is it always so?" she breathed.

"What was that, ma'am?"

Morna raised her eyes. "There's nothing I can do, Billy. The joints were fractured and now they have sclerosed over."

"Sclerosed, eh?" Gregg noted another word to be checked later.

"Do you get much pain?" She looked at the expression on his face. "That was a silly question, wasn't it?"

"It's a good thing I'm partial to whisky," he confessed. "Otherwise I wouldn't get much sleep some nights."

She smiled compassionately. "I think I can do something about the pain. It's in my own interest to get you as fit as possible by . . . What day is this?"

"Friday."

"By Sunday."

"Don't trouble yourself about Sunday," he said. "I've got a friend coming to help out. A woman friend," he added, as Morna stepped back from him, the hunted expression returning to her face.

"You promised not to tell anyone I was here."

"I know, but it's purely for your benefit. Ruth Jefferson is a fine lady, and I know her as well as I know myself. She won't talk to a living soul."

Morna's face relaxed slightly. "Is she important to you?"

"We were supposed to get married."

"In that case I won't object," Morna said, her gray eyes unreadable. "But please remember it was your own decision to tell her about me."

Ruth Jefferson came into sight about an hour before sunset, driving her cousin's gig.

Gregg, who had been watching for her, went into the house and tapped the open door of the bedroom, where Morna had lain down to rest without undressing. She awoke instantly with a startled gasp, glancing at the gold bracelet on her wrist. From his viewpoint in the doorway, Gregg noted that the ornament's imprisoned splinter of light seemed always to point to the east, and he decided it could be a strange form of compass. It might have been his imagination, but he had an impression that the light's rate of pulsation had increased slightly since he had first observed it in the morning. More wonderful and strange, however, was the overall sight of the golden-haired young woman, heavy with new life, who had come to him from out of nowhere and whose presence seemed to shed a glow over the plain furniture of his bedroom. He found himself speculating anew about the circumstances that had stranded such a creature in the near wilderness of his part of the world.

"Ruth will be here in a minute," he said. "Would you like to come out and meet her?"

"Very much." Morna smiled as she stood up and walked to the door with him. Gregg was slightly taken aback that she did so without touching her hair or fussing about her dress—in his experience first meetings between women usually were edgy occasions. Then he noticed that her simple hairstyle was undisturbed, and that the material of the blue smock, in spite of having been lain on for several hours, was as sleek and as smooth as if it had just come off the hanger. It was yet another addition to the dossier of curious facts he was assembling about his guest.

"Hello, Ruth—glad you could come." Gregg went forward to steady the gig and help Ruth down from it.

"I'll bet you are," Ruth said. "Have you heard about Wolf Caley?"

Gregg lowered his voice. "I heard he was fixing to die."

"That's right. What are you going to do about it?"

"What *can* I do?"

"You could head north as soon as it gets dark and keep going. I'm crazy to suggest it, but I could stay here and look after your lady friend."

"That wouldn't be fair." Gregg shook his head slowly. "No, I'm staying on here, where I'm needed."

"Just what do you think you'll be able to do when Josh Portfield and his mob come for you?"

"Ruth," he whispered uneasily, "I wish you'd talk about something else—you're going to upset Morna. Now come and meet her."

Ruth gave him an exasperated look, but went quietly with him to the house, where he performed the introductions. The women shook hands in silence, and then—quite spontaneously—both began to smile, the roles of mother and daughter tacitly assigned and mutually accepted. Gregg knew that communication had taken place on a level he would never understand, and his ingrained awe of the female mind increased.

He was pleased to see that Ruth, who had obviously been prepared to have her worst suspicions confirmed, was impressed with Morna. It would make his own life a little easier. While the two women went indoors he unloaded the supplies Ruth had brought, gripping the wicker basket between his upper arms to avoid stressing his elbows. When he carried it into the house and set it on the table, Ruth and Morna were deep in conversation, and Ruth broke off long enough to point at the door, silently commanding him to leave again.

Even more gratified, Gregg lifted a pack of tailor-made cigarettes from a shelf and went out to the shack, where his *pulque* still was in operation. He preferred hand-rolled cigarettes, but was accustomed to doing without them now that his fingers were incapable of the fine control required in the rolling of tobacco. Making himself comfortable on a stool in the corner, he lit a cigarette and contentedly surveyed his little domain of copper cooling coils, retorts, and tubs of fermenting cactus pulp. The knowledge that there were two women in his house and that one of them was soon to have a child there gave him a warm sense of importance he had never known before. He spent some time indulging himself in dreams, projected on screens of aromatic smoke, in which Ruth was his wife, Morna was his daughter, and he was again fit enough to do a real day's work and provide for his family.

"I don't know how you can sit in this place." Ruth was standing in the doorway, with a shawl around her shoulders. "That smell can't be healthy."

"It never did anybody any harm," Gregg said, rising to his feet. "Fermentation is part of nature."

"So is cow dung." Ruth backed out of the shack and waited for him to join her. In the reddish, horizontal light of the setting sun she looked healthy and attractive, imbued with a mature competence. "I have to go back now," she said, "but I'll be here again tomorrow, in the morning, and I'm going to stay until that baby is safely delivered into this world."

"I thought Saturday was your busy day at the store."

"It is, but Sam will have to manage on his own. I can't leave that child to have the baby by herself. You'd be worse than useless to her."

"But what's Sam going to think?"

"It doesn't matter what Sam thinks—I'll tell him you're poorly." Ruth paused for a moment. "Where do you think she's from, Billy?"

"Couldn't rightly say. She talked some about New Orleans."

Ruth frowned in disagreement. "Her talk doesn't sound like Louisiana talk to me—and she's got some real foreign notions to go with it."

"I noticed," Gregg said emphatically.

"The way she only talks about having a son? Just won't entertain the idea that it's just as likely to be a girl."

"Mmm." Gregg had been thinking about muzzle velocities of revolvers. "I wish I knew what she's running away from."

Ruth's features softened unexpectedly. "I've read lots of stories about women from noble families . . . heiresses and such . . . not allowed to acknowledge their own babies because the fathers were commoners."

"Ruth Jefferson," Gregg said gleefully, "I didn't know you were going around that homely old store with your head stuffed full of romantic notions."

"I do nothing of the sort." Ruth's color deepened. "But

it's as plain as the nose on your face that Morna comes from money—and it's probably her own folks she's in trouble with."

"Could be." Gregg remembered the abject terror he had seen in Morna's eyes. His instincts told him she had more on her mind than outraged parents, but he decided not to argue with Ruth. He stood and listened patiently while she explained that she had put Morna to bed, about his own sleeping arrangements in the other room, and about the type of breakfast he was to prepare in the morning.

"And you leave the whisky jar alone tonight," Ruth concluded. "I don't want you lying around in a drunken stupor if that child's pains start during the night. You hear me?"

"I hear you—I wasn't planning to do any drinking, anyway. Do you think the baby will arrive on Sunday, like Morna says?"

Ruth seated herself in the gig and gathered up the traces. "Somehow—I don't know why—I'm inclined to believe it will. See you, Billy."

"Thanks, Ruth." Gregg watched until the gig had passed out of sight beyond a rocky spur of the hillside upon which his house was built, then he turned and went indoors. The door of the bedroom was closed. He made up a bed on the floor with the blankets Ruth had left out for him, but knew he was unready for sleep. Chuckling a little with guilty pleasure, he poured himself a generous measure of corn whisky from the stone jar he kept in the cupboard and settled down with it in his most comfortable chair. The embers of the sunset filled the room with mellow light, and as he sipped the companionable liquor Gregg felt a sense of fulfillment in his role of watchdog.

He even allowed himself to hope that Morna would stay with him for longer than the six days she had planned.

Gregg awoke with a start at dawn to find himself still sitting in the chair, the empty cup clasped in his hand. He went to set the cup aside and almost groaned aloud as the flexing of his elbow produced a sensation akin to glass fragments crunching against a raw nerve. It must have been cool during the night, and his unprotected arms had stiffened up far more than usual. He stood up with difficulty, was dismayed to see that his shirt and pants were a mass of wrinkles, and it came to him that a man living alone should have clothes impervious to creases, clothes like those of . . .

Morna!

As recollections of the previous day fountained in his head, Gregg hurried to the range and began cleaning it out in preparation for lighting a fire. Ruth had left instructions that he was to heat milk and oatmeal for Morna's breakfast and provide her with a basin of warm water in her room. Partly because of his haste, and partly because of the difficulty of controlling his fingers, he dropped the fire irons several times and was hardly surprised to hear the bedroom door opening soon afterward. Morna appeared in the opening wearing a flowered dressing gown that Ruth must have brought for her. The familiar, feminine styling of the garment made her prettier in Gregg's eyes, and at the same time more approachable.

"Good morning," he said. "Sorry about all the noise. I hope I didn't . . ."

"I'd caught up on my sleep anyway." She came into the room, sat at the table, and placed on it a second of the slim gold bars. "This is for you, Billy."

He pushed it back toward her. "I don't want it. The one you gave me is worth more than anything I can do for you."

Morna gave him a calm, sad smile, and he was abruptly reminded that she was not a home-grown girl discussing payment for a domestic chore. "You risked your life for me—and I think you would do it again. Would you?"

Gregg looked away from her. "I didn't do much."

"But you did! I was watching you, Billy, and I saw that you were afraid—but I also saw that you were able to control the fear. It made you stronger instead of weaker, and that's something that even the finest of my people are unable . . ." Morna broke off and pressed the knuckles of one hand to her lips as though she had been on the verge of revealing a secret.

"We'll have something to eat soon." Gregg turned back toward the range. "As soon as I get a fire going."

"You haven't answered my question."

He shifted his feet. "What question?"

"If somebody came here to kill me—and to kill my son—would you defend us even if it meant placing your own life at risk?"

"This is just crazy," Gregg protested. "Why should anybody want to kill you?"

Her eyes locked fast on his. "Answer the question, Billy."

"I . . ." The words were as difficult for Gregg as a declaration of love. "Do I need to answer? Do you think I would run away?"

"No," she said gently. "That's all the answer I need."

"I'm pleased about that." Gregg's voice was gruffer than he had meant it to be, because Morna—who was half his age—kept straying in his mind from the role of foster daughter to that of lover wife, in spite of the facts that he scarcely knew her and that she was swollen with another man's child. He was oppressed by the sinfulness of his thinking and by fears of making a fool of himself, yet he was deeply gratified by Morna's trust. No man, he decided, no prince, not even the Prince of Darkness himself, was going to harm or distress her if there was anything he could do to prevent it. While he busied himself with getting a fire going, Gregg made up his mind to check the condition of his Remington as soon as he could do so without being seen by Morna or Ruth. In the unlikely event that he might need it, he would also inspect the percussion caps and loads in the old Tranter he had taken from Wolf Caley.

As though divining the turn of his thoughts, Morna said, "Billy, have you a long gun? A rifle?"

He puffed out his cheeks. "Never owned one."

"Why not? The longer barrel would allow the charge to impart more energy to the bullet and give you a more effective weapon."

Gregg hunched his shoulders and refused to turn round, somehow offended at hearing Morna's light, clear voice using the terminology of the armorer. "Never wanted one," he said.

"But *why* not?"

"I was never all that good with a rifle, even when my arms were all right, so it's safer for me not to carry one. There's no law to speak of in these parts, you see. If a man uses a revolver to kill another man he generally gets off with it, provided the man he shot was carrying a wheel gun too. Even if he didn't get a chance to draw it, it's classed as a fair fight. The same goes if they both have rifles, but I'm none too good with a rifle—so I'm not going to risk having somebody I crossed knock me over at two hundred yards and claim it was self-defense." The speech was the longest Gregg had made in months, and he expressed his displeasure at having had to make it by raking the ashes in the fire basket with unnecessary vigor.

''I see,'' Morna said thoughtfully behind him. ''A simple duello variation. Are you accurate with a revolver?''

For a reply Gregg started slamming the range's cooking rings back into place.

Her voice assumed the imperious quality he had heard in it before. ''Billy, are you accurate with a revolver?''

He wheeled on her, holding out his arms in such a way as to display the misshapen, knotted elbows. ''I can point a six-shooter just like I always could, but it takes me so long to get it up there I wouldn't be a match for a ten-year-old boy. Is that what you wanted to know?''

''There is no room for anger between us.'' Morna stood up and took his outstretched hands in hers. She looked into his face with searching gray eyes. ''You love me, don't you, Billy?''

''Yes.'' Gregg heard the word across a distance, knowing he could not have said it to a stranger.

''I'm proud that you do—now wait here.'' Morna went into the bedroom, took something from an inner part of her cloak, and returned with what at first seemed to be a small square of green glass. Gregg was surprised to see that it was as pliable as a piece of buckskin, and he watched with growing puzzlement as Morna pressed it to his left elbow. It was curiously warm against his skin, and a tingling sensation seemed to pass right through the joint.

''Bend your arm,'' Morna ordered, now as impersonal as an army surgeon.

Gregg did as he was told and was thrilled to find there was no pain, no grinding of arthritic glass needles. He was still flexing his left arm, speechless with disbelief, when Morna repeated the procedure with his right, achieving the same miraculous result. For the first time in two years, Gregg could bend his arms freely and without suffering in the process.

Morna smiled up at him. ''How do they feel?''

''Like new—just like new.''

''They'll never be as good or as strong as they were,'' Morna said, ''but I can promise you there'll be no more pain.'' She went back into the bedroom and emerged a moment later without the transparent green square. ''Now, I think you said something about food.''

Gregg shook his head. "There's something going on here. You're not who you claim to be. Nobody can do the sort of . . ."

"I didn't claim to be anybody," Morna said quite sharply, with yet another of her swift changes of mood.

"Perhaps I should have said you're not *what* you claim to be."

"Don't spoil things, Billy . . . I have nobody but you." Morna sat down at the table and covered her face with her hands.

"I'm sorry." Gregg was reaching out to touch her when, for the first time that morning, he noticed the curious gold ornament on her wrist. The imprisoned splinter of light was pointing east as usual, but it was brighter than it had been yesterday and was definitely flashing at a higher rate. Gregg, becoming attuned to strangeness, was unable to avoid the impression that it was pulsing out some kind of warning.

True to her word, Ruth arrived early in the day.

She had brought extra supplies, including a jug of broth that was wrapped in a traveling rug to retain its warmth. Gregg was glad to see her and grateful for the womanly efficiency with which she took control of his household, yet he was discomfited at finding himself made redundant. He spent more and more time in the shack, tending to his stills, and that bright moment in which there had been talk of love between Morna and him began to seem like a figment of his imagination. He was not deluding himself that she had referred to husband-and-wife love, perhaps not father-and-daughter love either, but the mere use of the word had, for a brief span, made his life less sterile, and he treasured it.

Ruth, in contrast, spoke of commodity prices and scarcities, dress making and local affairs—and, in the aura of normalcy that surrounded her, Gregg decided against mentioning the fantastic cure that Morna had wrought on his arms. He had a feeling she would refuse to believe, and—by robbing him of his faith—neutralize the magic or unwork the miracle. Ruth came to visit him in the shack in the afternoon, covering her nose with her handkerchief, but it was only to tell him privately that Wolf Caley was not expected to last out the day, and that Josh Portfield and his men were reported to be riding north from Sonora.

Gregg thanked her for the information and gave no sign of being affected by it, but at the first opportunity he smuggled his Remington and Caley's Tranter out of the house and devoted some time to ensuring that they were in serviceable condition.

Portfield had always been an enigmatic figure in Gregg's life. The big spread he owned had been passed on to him by his father, and it was profitable; therefore there was no need for Josh to engage in unlawful activities. He had, however, acquired a taste for violence during the war, and the troubled territories of Mexico lying only a short distance to the south seemed to draw him like a magnet. Every now and then he would take a bunch of men and go on a kind of motiveless unofficial "raid" beyond the border. Portfield was far from being a mad dog, often leading a fairly normal existence for months on end, but he appeared to lack any conception of right and wrong.

For example, he genuinely believed he had been lenient with Gregg by merely ruining his arms, instead of killing him, for interrupting that fateful drinking spree. Afterward, on meeting Gregg on the trail or in Copper Cross, he had always hailed him in the friendliest manner possible, apparently under the impression he had earned Gregg's gratitude and respect. Each man, Gregg had discovered, lives in his own reality.

There was always the possibility that, when Portfield learned of Caley's misfortune, he would shrug and say that any man who worked for him ought to be able to cope with an aging cripple. Gregg had known Portfield to make equally unexpected judgments, but he had a suspicion that on this occasion the hammer of Portfield's anger was going to come down hard and that he was going to be squarely underneath it. In a way he could not understand, his apprehension was fed and magnified by Morna's own mysterious fears.

During the meals, while the three of them were seated at the rough wooden table, he was content to have Ruth carry the burden of conversation with Morna. The talk was mainly of domestic matters, on any of which Morna might have been drawn out to reveal something of her own background, but she skirted Ruth's various traps with easy diplomacy.

Late in the evening Morna began to experience the first contraction pains, and from that point Gregg found himself relegated by Ruth to the status of an inconvenient piece of furniture. He accepted the treatment without rancor, having been long familiar with the subdued hostility that women feel toward men during a confinement, and willingly performed every task given to him. Only an occasional brooding glance from Morna reminded him that between them was a covenant of which Ruth, for all her matronly competence, knew nothing.

The baby was born at noon on Sunday, and—as Morna had predicted—it was a boy.

"Don't let Morna do too much," Ruth said on Monday morning, as she seated herself in the gig. "She has no business being up and about so soon after a birth."

Gregg nodded. "Don't worry—I'll take care of all the chores."

"Do that." Ruth looked at him with sudden interest. "How are your arms these days?"

"Better. They feel a lot easier."

"That's good." Ruth picked up the reins but seemed reluctant to drive away. Her gaze strayed toward the house, where Morna was standing with the baby cradled in her arms. "I suppose you can't wait for me to go and leave you alone with your ready-made family."

"Now, you know that's not right, Ruth. You know how much I appreciate all you've done here. You're not jealous, are you?"

"Jealous?" Ruth shook her head, then gave him a level stare. "Morna is a strange girl. She's not like me, and she's not like you—but I've got a feeling there's something going on between you two."

Gregg's fear of Ruth's intuitive powers stirred anew. "You know, Ruth, you're starting to sound like one of those new phonographs."

"Oh, I don't mean hanky-panky," she said quickly, "but you're up to something. I know you."

"I'll be in to settle up my bill in a day or two," Gregg parried. "Soon as I can change one of those gold bars."

"Try to do it before Josh Portfield gets back." Ruth flicked the reins and drove down the hillside.

Gregg took a deep breath and surveyed the distant blue ramparts of the Sierras before walking back to the house. Morna was still wearing the flowered dressing gown and, with the shawl-wrapped baby in her arms, she looked much like any other young mother. The single uncomformity in her appearance was the gold ornament on her wrist. Even in the brightness of the morning sunlight its needle of crimson light was harshly brilliant, and its pulsations had speeded up to several a second. Gregg had thought a lot about the ornament during his spells of solitude over the previous two days, and he had convinced himself he understood its function if not its nature. He felt that the time had come for some plain talking.

Morna went indoors with him. The birth had been straightforward and easy for her, but her face was pale and drawn, and there was a tentative quality about the smile she gave him as he closed the door.

"It feels strange for us to be alone again," Morna said quietly.

"Very strange." Gregg pointed at the flashing bracelet. "But it looks as though we won't be alone for very long."

She sat down abruptly and her baby raised one miniature pink hand in protest at the sudden movement. Morna drew the infant closer to her breast. She lowered her face to the baby, touching its forehead with hers, and her hair fell forward, screening it with strands of gold.

"I'm sorry," Gregg said, "but I need to know who it is that's coming out of the east. I need to know who I'm going up against."

"I can't tell you that, Billy."

"I see—I'm entitled to get killed, maybe, but not to know who does it, or why."

"Please don't." Her voice was muffled. "Please understand . . . that I can't tell you anything."

Gregg felt a pang of guilt. He went to Morna and knelt beside her. "Why don't we both—the three of us, I mean—get out of here right now? We could load up my buckboard and be gone in ten minutes."

Morna shook her head without looking up. "It wouldn't make any difference."

"It would make a difference to me."

At that, Morna raised her head and looked at him with anxious, brimming eyes. "This man, Portfield—will he try to kill you?"

"Did Ruth tell you about him?" Gregg clicked his tongue

with annoyance. "She shouldn't have done that. You've got enough to . . ."

"Will he try to kill you?"

Gregg was compelled to tell the unvarnished truth. "It isn't so much a matter of him *trying* to kill me, Morna. He rides around in company with seven or eight hard cases, and if they decide to kill somebody they just go right ahead and do it."

"Oh!" Morna seemed to regain something of her former resolve. "My son can't travel yet, but I'll get him ready as soon as I can. I'll try hard, Billy."

"That's fine with me," Gregg said uncertainly. He had an uneasy feeling that the conversation had gotten beyond him in some way, but he had lost the initiative and was in no way equipped to deal with a woman's tears.

"That's all right, then." He got to his feet and looked down at the baby's absurdly tiny features. "Have you thought of a name for the little fellow yet?"

Morna relaxed momentarily, looking pleased. "It's too soon. The naming time is still above him."

"In English," Gregg gently corrected, "we say that the future is ahead of us, not above us."

"But that implies linear . . ." Morna checked her words. "You're right, of course—I should have said ahead."

"My mother was a schoolmarm," he said inconsequentially, once more with an odd sense that communications between them were failing. "I've got some work to do outside, but I'll be close by if you need me."

Gregg went to the door, and as he was closing it behind him he looked back into the room. He saw that, yet again, Morna was sitting with her forehead pressed to that of her son, something he had never seen other women doing. He dismissed it as the least puzzling of her idiosyncrasies. In fact, there was no pressing work to be done outside—but he had a gut feeling that the time had come for keeping an eye on all approaches to his house. He walked slowly to the top of the saddleback, threading his way among boulders that resembled grazing sheep, and settled down on the eastern crest. A careful scan with his telescope revealed no activity in the direction of the Portfield ranch or on the trail running south to Copper Cross. Gregg then pointed the little instrument due east toward where the Rio Grande flowed unseen between the northern extremities of the Sierra Madre and the

Sacramento Mountains many miles away. Visibility was good, and his eye was dazzled with serried vistas of peaks and ranges on a scale too vast for comprehension.

You're letting yourself get spooked, he thought irritably. Nothing crosses country in a straight line like a bird—except another bird.

He contrived to spend most of the day on the vantage point, though he made frequent trips down to the house to check on Morna, to prepare two simple meals, and to boil water for washing the baby's diapers. It pleased him to note that the child slept almost continuously between feeds, thus giving Morna plenty of opportunity to rest. At times Ruth's phrase "ready-made family" came to his mind, and he realized how appropriate it had been. Even in the bizarre circumstances that prevailed, there was something deeply satisfying about having a woman and child under his roof, looking to him and to no other man for their welfare and safety. The relationship made him something more than he had been. Although he did his best to repress the thought, the possibility suggested itself that, were Morna and he to flee north together, she might never return to her former life. In that case, he might indeed acquire a ready-made family.

Gregg shied away from pursuing that line of thought too far.

Late in the evening, when the sun was dipping toward the lower ranges beyond far Mexicali, he saw a lone horseman approaching from the direction of the Portfield ranch. The rider was moving at a leisurely pace, and the fact that he was alone was an indication that there was no trouble afoot, but Gregg decided not to take any chances. He walked down the hill past the house, took the Remington from its hiding place in the shack, and went on down to take up his position on the spur of rock where the trail bent sharply. When the horseman came into view he was slumped casually in the saddle, obviously half asleep, and his hat was pulled down to screen his eyes from the low-slanted rays of the sun. Gregg recognized Cal Masham, the young cowboy he had spoken to in the town on Friday.

"What are you doing in these parts, Cal?" he shouted.

Masham jerked upright, his jaw sagging with shock. "Billy? You still here?"

"What does it look like?"

"Hell, I figured you'd be long gone by this time."

"And you wanted to see what I'd left behind—is that it?"

Masham grinned beneath the drooping mustache. "It seemed to me you'd leave those big heavy crocks of *pulque,* and it seemed to me I might as well have them as somebody else. After all . . ."

"You can have a drink on me any time," Gregg said firmly, "but not tonight. You'd best be on your way, Cal."

Masham looked displeased. "Seems to me you're wavin' that gun at the wrong people, Billy. Did you know that Wolf Caley's dead?"

"I hadn't heard."

"Well, he is. And Big Josh'll be home tomorrow. Max Tibbett rode in ahead this afternoon, and as soon as he heard about Wolf he took a fresh horse and rode south again to tell Josh. You just shouldn't *be* here, Billy." Masham's voice had taken on a rising note of complaint, and he seemed genuinely upset by Gregg's foolhardiness in remaining.

Gregg considered for a moment. "Come up and help yourself to a jar, but don't make any noise—I've got a guest and a newborn baby I don't want disturbed."

"Thanks, Billy." Masham dismounted and walked up the hill with Gregg. He accepted a heavy stone jar, glancing curiously toward the house, and rode off with his prize clasped to his chest.

Gregg watched him out of sight, put the Remington away, and decided that he was entitled to a shot of whisky to counter the effects of the news he had just received. He crossed the familiar ruts of the buckboard's turning circle and looked in through the front window of the house to see if Morna was in the main room. He had intended only to glance in quickly while passing the window, but the strange tableau within checked him in midstride.

Morna was dressed in her own maternity smock, which appeared to have been reshaped to her slimmer figure, although Gregg had not noticed her or Ruth doing any needlework. She had spread a white sheet over the table and her baby was lying in the center of it, naked except for the binder that crossed his navel. Morna was standing beside the table, with both hands clasping the baby's head. Her eyes were closed, lips moving silently, her face as cold and masklike as that of a high priestess performing an ancient ceremony.

Gregg desperately wanted to turn away, convinced he was

guilty of an invasion of privacy, but a change was taking place in Morna's appearance and the slow progression of it induced a mesmeric paralysis of his limbs. As he watched, Morna's golden hair began to stir, as though it were some complex living creature in its own right. Her head was absolutely motionless, but gradually—over a period of about ten seconds—her hair fanned out, each strand becoming straight and seemingly rigid, to form a bright fearsome halo. Gregg felt his mouth go dry as he witnessed Morna's dreadful transformation from the normalcy of young motherhood to the semblance of a witch figure. She bent forward from the waist until her forehead was touching that of the baby.

There was a moment of utter stillness—and then her body became transparent.

Gregg felt icy ripples move upward from the back of his neck into his own hair as he realized that he could see right through Morna. She was indisputably present in the room, yet the lines of walls and furniture continued on through her body, as if she were an image superimposed on them by a magic lantern.

The baby made random pawing movements with his arms and legs, but otherwise appeared to be unaffected by what was happening. Morna remained in the same state, somewhere between matter and mirage, for several seconds, then quite abruptly she was as solid as before. She straightened up, and Gregg could see that her hair was beginning to subside into its previous helmet shape of loose waves. She smoothed it down with her hands and turned toward the window.

Gregg lunged to one side in terror and scampered, doubled over like a man dodging gunfire, for the cover of his buckboard, which he had left on the blind side of the house. He crouched there, breathing noisily, until he was sure Morna had not seen him, then made his way to his customary spot at the top of the saddleback, where he squatted down and lit a cigarette. Even with the reassurance of tobacco it was some time before his heart slowed to a steady rhythm. He was not a superstitious man, but his limited reading had taught him that there was a special kind of woman—known from biblical En-dor to the Salem of more recent times—who could work magical cures, and who often had to flee from persecution. One part of his mind rebelled against applying that name to a child like Morna, but there was no denying what he had just seen, no getting away from all the other strange things about her.

He smoked four more cigarettes, taking perhaps an hour to do so, then went back to his house. Morna—looking as normal and sweet and wholesome as a freshly baked apple pie—had lit an oil lantern and was brewing coffee. Her baby was peacefully asleep in the basket Ruth had left for it. Morna had even removed her gold bracelet, as though deliberately setting out to make him forget that she was in any way out of the ordinary. When Gregg glanced into the darkness of the bedroom, however, he saw the ruby glow, flashing so quickly now that its warning was almost continuous.

And it was far into the night before he finally managed to sleep.

Gregg was awakened in the morning by the thin, lonely bleat of the baby crying. He listened to it for what seemed a long time, expecting to hear Morna respond, but no other sound reached him from beyond the closed door of the bedroom. No matter what else she might be, Morna had impressed Gregg as a conscientious mother, and her prolonged inactivity at first puzzled and then began to worry him. He got up out of his bedroll, pulled on his pants, and tapped on the door. There was no reply, apart from the baby's cries, which were as regular as breathing. He tapped again more loudly, and pushed the door open.

The baby was in its basket beside the bed—Gregg could see the movement of tiny fists—but Morna had gone.

Unable to accept the evidence of his eyes, Gregg walked all around the square room and even looked below the bed. Morna's clothes, including her cloak, were missing too, and the only conclusion Gregg could reach was that she had risen during the hours of darkness, dressed herself, and left the house. To do so she would have had to pass within a few feet of where he was sleeping on the floor of the main room without disturbing him, and he was positive that nobody, not the most practiced thief, not the most skillful Indian tracker, could have done that. But then—the slow stains of memory began to spread in his mind—he was thinking in terms of normal human beings, and he had proof that Morna was far from normal.

The baby went on crying, its eyes squeezed shut, protesting

in the only way it knew how about the absence of food and maternal warmth. Gregg stared at it helplessly, and it occurred to him that Morna might have left for good, making the infant his permanent responsibility.

"Hold on there, little fellow," he said, recalling that he had not checked outside the house. He left the bedroom, went outside, and called Morna's name. His voice faded into the air, absorbed by the emptiness of the morning landscape, and his horse looked up in momentary surprise from its steady cropping of the grass near the water pump. Gregg made a hurried inspection of his two outbuildings—the distilling shack and the ramshackle sentry box that was his lavatory—then decided he would have to take the baby into town and hand it over to Ruth. He had no idea how long a child of that age could survive without food, and he did not want to take unnecessary risks. Swearing under his breath, he turned back to the house and froze as he saw a flash of silver on the trail at the bottom of the hill.

Morna had just come around the spur of rock and was walking toward him. She was draped in her ubiquitous cloak, which had returned to its original color, and was carrying a small blue sack in one hand. Gregg's relief at seeing her pushed aside all his fears and reservations of the previous night, and he ran down the slope to meet her.

"Where have you been?" he called, while they were still some distance apart. "What was the idea of running off like that?"

"I didn't run off, Billy." She gave him a tired smile. "There were things I had to do."

"What sort of things? The baby's crying for a feed."

Morna's perfect young face was strangely hard. "What's a little hunger?"

"That's a funny way to talk," Gregg said, taken aback.

"The future simply doesn't exist for you, does it?" Morna looked at him with what seemed to be a mixture of pity and anger. "Don't you ever think ahead? Have you forgotten that we have . . . enemies?"

"I take things as they come. It's all a man can do."

Morna thrust the blue sack at him. "Take this as it comes."

"What is it?" Gregg accepted the bag and was immediately struck by the fact that it was not made of blue paper, as he had supposed. The material was thin, strong, smooth to the touch, more pliable than oilskin, and without oilskin's underlying texture. "What is this stuff?"

"It's a new waterproof material," Morna said impatiently. "The contents are more important."

Gregg opened the sack and took out a large black revolver. It was much lighter than he would have expected for its size, and it had something of the familiar lines of a Colt except that the grips were grooved for individual fingers and flared out at the top over his thumb. Gregg had never felt a gun settle itself in his hand so smoothly. He examined the weapon more closely and saw that it had a six-shot fluted cylinder that hinged out sideways for easy loading—a feature he had never seen on any other firearm. The gun lacked any kind of decoration, but was more perfectly machined and finished than he could have imagined possible. He read the engraving on the side of the long barrel.

"Colt .44 Magnum," he said slowly. "Never heard of it. Where did you get this gun, Morna?"

She hesitated. "I've been up for hours. I left this near the road where you first saw me, and I had time to go back for it."

The story did not ring true to Gregg, but his mind was fully occupied by the revolver itself. "I mean, where did you get it *before?* Where can you buy a gun like this?"

"That doesn't matter." Morna began walking toward the house. "The point is: Could you use it?"

"I guess so," Gregg said, glancing into the blue bag, which still contained a cardboard box of brass cartridges. The top of the box was missing, and many of the shells had fallen into the bottom of the bag. "It's a right handsome gun, but I doubt if it packs any more punch than my Remington."

"I would like you to try it out." Morna was walking so quickly that Gregg had difficulty in keeping up with her. "Please see if you can load it."

"You mean right now? Don't you want to see the baby?" They had reached the flat area in front of the house, and the child's cries had become audible.

Morna glanced at her wrist, and he saw that the gold ornament was burning with a steady crimson light. "My son can wait a while longer," she said in a voice that was firm and yet edged with panic. "Please load the revolver."

"Whatever you say." Gregg walked to his buckboard and

used it as a table. He cleared a space in the straw, set the gun down, and—under Morna's watchful gaze—carefully spilled the ammunition out of the blue bag. The center-fire shells were rather longer than he had ever seen for a handgun and, like the revolver itself, were finished with a degree of perfection he had never encountered previously. Their noses shone like polished steel.

"Everything's getting too fancy—adds to the price," Gregg muttered. He fumbled with the weapon until he saw how to swing the cylinder out, then slipped in six cartridges and closed it up. As he was doing so he noticed that the cardboard box had emerged from the bag upside down, and on its underside, stamped in pale blue ink, he saw a brief inscription: "OCT 1978." He picked it up and held it out to Morna. "Wonder what that means."

Her eyes widened slightly, then she looked away without interest. "It's just a maker's code. A batch number."

"It looks like a date," Gregg commented, "except that they've made a mistake and put . . ." He broke off, startled, as Morna knocked the box from his hands.

"Get on with it, you fool," she shouted, trampling the box underfoot. Her pale features were distorted with anger as she stared up at him with white-flaring eyes. They confronted each other for a moment, then her lips began to tremble. "I'm sorry, Billy. I'm so sorry . . . It's just that there's almost no time above us . . . and I'm afraid."

"It's all right," he said awkwardly. "I know I've got aggravating ways—Ruth's always telling me that—and I've been living alone for so long . . ."

Morna stopped him by placing a hand on his wrist. "Don't, Billy. You're a good and kind man, but I want you—right now, please—to learn to handle that gun." Her quiet, controlled tones somehow gave Gregg a greater sense of urgency than anything said previously.

"Right." He turned away from the buckboard, looking for a suitable target, and began to ease the revolver's hammer back with his thumb.

"You don't need to do that," Morna said. "For rapid fire you just pull the trigger."

"I know—double action." Gregg cocked the gun regardless, to demonstrate his superior knowledge of firearms practice, and for a target selected a billet of wood that was leaning against the heavy stone water trough about twenty paces away. He was lining the gun's sights on it when Morna spoke again.

"You should hold it with both hands."

Gregg smiled indulgently. "Morna, you're a very well educated young lady, and I daresay you know all manner of things I never even heard of—but don't try to teach an old hand like me how to shoot a six-gun." He steadied the gun, held his breath, and squeezed off his first shot. There was an explosion like a clap of thunder, and something struck him a fierce blow on the forehead, blinding him with pain. His first confused thought was that the revolver had been faulty and had burst open, throwing a fragment into his face. Then he found it was intact in his hand, and it dawned on him that there had been a massive recoil, which had bent his weakened arm like a piece of straw, swinging the weapon all the way back to collide with his forehead. He wiped a warm trickle of blood away from his eyes and looked at the gun with awe and the beginning of a great respect.

"There isn't any smoke," he said. "There isn't even . . ."

His speech faltered as he looked beyond the gun in his hand and saw that the stone water trough, which had served as a backing for his target, had been utterly destroyed. Fragments of three-inch-thick earthenware were scattered over a triangular area running back about thirty yards. Without previous knowledge, Gregg would have guessed that the trough had been demolished by a cannon shot.

Morna took her hands away from her ears. "You've hurt yourself—I told you to hold it with both hands."

"I'm all right." He fended off her attempt to touch his forehead. "Morna, where did you get this . . . this *engine?*"

"Do you expect me to answer that?"

"I guess not, but I sure would like to know. This is something I could understand."

"Try it at longer range, and use both hands this time." Morna looked about her, apparently more composed now that Gregg was doing what she expected of him. She pointed at a whitish rock about three hundred yards off along the hillside. "That rock."

"That's getting beyond rifle range," Gregg explained. "Handguns don't . . ."

"Try it, Billy."

"All right—I'll try aiming way above it."

"Aim at it, near the top."

Gregg shrugged and did as he was told, suddenly aware that his right thumb was throbbing painfully where the big revolver had driven back against it. He squeezed off his second shot and experienced a deep pang of satisfaction, of a kind that only hunters understand, when he saw dust fountain into the air only about a yard to the right of the rock. Even with his two-handed grip the gun had kicked back until it was pointing almost vertically into the sky. Without waiting to be told, he fired again and saw rock fragments fly from his target.

Morna nodded her approval. "You appear to have a talent."

"This is the best gun I ever saw," he told her sincerely, "but I can't hold it down. These arms of mine can't handle the recoil."

"Then we'll bind your elbows."

"Too late for that," he said regretfully, pointing down the slope.

Several horsemen were coming into view, their presence in the formerly deserted landscape more shocking to Gregg than the discovery of a scorpion in a picnic hamper.

He began cursing his own carelessness in not having kept a lookout as more riders emerged from beyond the spur until there were eight of them fanning out across the bottom of the hill. They were a mixed bunch, slouching or riding high according to individual preference, on mounts that varied from quarter horses to tall stallions, and their dress ranged from greasy buckskin to gambler's black. Gregg knew, however, that they constituted a miniature army, disciplined and controlled by one man. He narrowed his eyes against the morning brilliance and picked out the distinctive figure of Josh Portfield on a chestnut stallion. As always, Portfield was wearing a white shirt and a suit of charcoal gray serge, which might have given him the look of a preacher had it not been for the pair of nickel-plated Smith & Wessons strapped to his waist.

"I was kind of hoping Big Josh would leave things as they were," Gregg said. "He must be in one of his righteous moods."

Morna took an involuntary step backward. "Can you defend yourself against so many?"

"Have to give it a try." Gregg began scooping up handfuls of cartridges and cramming them into his pockets. "You'd best get inside the house and bar the door."

Morna looked up at him, the hunted look returning to her face, then she stooped to pick up something from the ground and ran to the house. Glancing sideways, Gregg was unable to understand why she should have wasted time retrieving the flattened cartridge box, but he had more important things on his mind. He flipped the revolver's cylinder out, dropped the three empty cases, and replaced them with new shells. At last he turned toward the advancing riders. They had closed to within two hundred yards.

"Stay off my land, Josh," he shouted. "There's a law against trespassing."

Portfield stood up in his stirrups, and his powerful voice came clearly to Gregg in spite of his distance. "You're insolent, Billy. And you're ungrateful. And you've cost me a good man. I'm going to punish you for all those things, but most of all I'm going to punish you for your insolence and lack of respect." He sank down in the saddle and said something Gregg could not hear. A second later Siggy Sorenson urged his horse ahead of the pack and came riding up the hill with a pistol in his hand.

"This time I got a gun, too," Sorenson shouted. "This time we fight fair, eh?"

"If you come any farther I'll drop you," Gregg warned.

Sorenson began to laugh. "You're way out of range, you old fool. Can't you see anymore?" He spurred his horse into a full gallop, and at the same time two other men went off to Gregg's left.

Gregg raised the big revolver and started to calculate bullet drop, then remembered it was practically nonexistent with the unholy weapon that fate had placed in his hands. This time the two-handed, knees-bent stance came to him naturally. He lined up on Sorenson, let him come on for another few seconds, and then squeezed the trigger. Sorenson's massive body, blasted right out of the saddle, turned over backward in midair and landed face down on the stony ground. His horse wheeled to one side and bolted. Realizing he would soon lose the advantage of surprise, Gregg turned on the two riders who were flanking him to the left. His second shot flicked the nearest man to the ground, and the third—fired too quickly—

killed the other's horse. The animal dropped instantaneously, without a sound, and its rider threw himself into the shelter of its body, dragging a red-glinting leg.

Gregg looked back down the trail and in that moment discovered the quality of his opposition. He could see a knot of milling horses, but no men. In the brief respite given to them they had faded from sight behind rocks, no doubt with rifles taken from their saddle holsters. Suddenly becoming aware of how vulnerable he was in his exposed position at the top of the rise, Gregg bent low and ran for the cover of his shack. Crouching down behind it, he again dropped three expended cartridges and replaced them, appreciative of the speed with which the big gun could be loaded. He peered around a corner of the shack to make certain that nobody was working closer to him.

Shockingly, a pistol thundered and black smoke billowed only twenty yards away. Something gouged through his lower ribs. Gregg lurched back into cover and stared in disbelief at the ragged and bloody tear in his shirt. He had been within a handsbreadth of death.

"You're too slow, Mr. Gregg," a voice called, frighteningly close at hand. "That old buffalo gun you got yourself don't make no difference if you're too slow."

Gregg identified the speaker as Frenchy Martine, a young savage from the Canadian backwoods who had drifted into Copper Cross a year earlier. The near-fatal shot had come from the direction of the upright coffin that was Gregg's primitive lavatory. Gregg had no idea how Martine had gotten that close in the time available, and it came home to him that a man of fifty was out of his class when it came to standing off youngsters in their prime.

"Tell you something else, Mr. Gregg," Martine chuckled. "You're too old for that choice piece of woman flesh you got tucked away in your . . ."

Gregg took one step to the side and fired at the narrow structure, punching a hole through the one-inch timbers as if they had been paper. There was the sound of a body hitting the ground beyond it, and a pistol tumbled into view. Gregg stepped back into the lee of the shack just as a rifle cracked in the distance, and he heard the impact as the slug buried itself in the wood. He drew slight comfort from the knowledge that his opponents were armed with ordinary weapons—because the real battle was now about to begin.

Martine had assumed he was safe behind two thicknesses of timber, but there were at least four others who would not make the same fatal mistake. Their most likely tactic would be to surround Gregg, keeping in the shelter of rock all the way, and then nail him down with long-range rifle fire. Gregg failed to see how, even with the black engine of death in his hands, he was going to survive the next hour, especially as he was losing quantities of blood.

He knelt down, made a rectangular pad with his handkerchief, and tucked it into his shirt in an attempt to slow the bleeding. Nobody was firing at him for the minute, so he took advantage of the lull to discard the single empty shell and make up the full load again. A deceptive quietness had descended over the area.

He looked around him at the sunlit hillside, with its rocks like grazing sheep, and tried to guess where the next shot might come from. His view of his surroundings blurred slightly, and there followed the numb realization that he might know nothing about the next shot until it was plowing its way through his body. A throbbing hum began to fill his ears—familiar prelude to the loss of consciousness—and he looked across the open, dangerous space that separated him from the house, wondering if he could get that far without being hit again. The chances were not good, but if he could get inside the house he might have time to bind his chest properly.

Gregg stood up and then became aware of the curious fact that, although the humming sound had grown much louder, he was relatively clear-headed. It was dawning on him that the powerful sound, like the swarming of innumerable hornets, had an objective reality, when he heard a man's deep-chested bellow of fear, followed by a fusillade of shots. He flinched instinctively, but there were no sounds of bullet strikes close by. Gregg risked a look down the sloping trail, and what he saw caused an icy prickling on his forehead.

A tall, narrow-shouldered, black-cloaked figure, its face concealed by a black hood, was striding up the hill toward the house. It was surrounded by a strange aura of darkness, as though it had the ability to repel light itself, and it seemed to be the center from which emanated the ground-trembling, pulsating hum. Behind the awe-inspiring shape the horses belonging to the Portfield bunch were lying on their sides, apparently dead. As Gregg watched, Portfield himself and another man stood up from behind rocks and fired at the figure, using their rifles at point-blank range.

The only effect of their shots was to produce small purple flashes at the outer surface of its surrounding umbra. After perhaps a dozen shots had been absorbed harmlessly, the specter made a sweeping gesture with its left arm, and Portfield and his companion collapsed like puppets. The distance was too great for Gregg to be positive, but he received the ghastly impression that flesh had fallen away from their faces like tatters of cloth. Gregg's own horse whinnied in alarm and bolted away to his right.

Another Portfield man, Max Tibbett, driven by a desperate courage, emerged from cover on the other side of the trail and fired at the figure's back. There were more purple flashes on the edge of the aura of dimness. Without looking around, the being made the same careless gesture with its left arm—spreading the black cloak like a bat's wing—and Tibbett fell, withering and crumbling. If any of his companions were still alive they remained in concealment.

Its cloak flapping around it, the figure drew near the top of the rise, striding with inhuman speed on feet that seemed to be misshapen and disproportionately small. Without looking to left or right it went straight for the door of Gregg's house, and he knew that this was the hunter from whom Morna had been fleeing. The pervasive hum reached a mind-numbing intensity.

Gregg's previous fear of dying was as nothing compared to the dark dread that spurted and foamed through his soul. He was filled with an ancient and animalistic terror that swept away all reason, all courage, commanding him to cover his eyes and cringe in hiding until the shadow of evil had passed. He looked down at the black, gleaming gun in his hands and shook his head as a voice he had no wish to hear reminded him of a bargain sealed with gold, of a promise made by the man he had believed himself to be. There's nothing I can do, he thought. *I can't help you, Morna.*

In the same instant he was horrified to find that he was stepping out from the concealment of the shack. His hands steadied and aimed the gun without conscious guidance from his brain. He squeezed the trigger. There was a brilliant purple flash, which pierced the being's aura like a sword of lightning, and it staggered sideways with a raucous shriek which chilled Gregg's blood. It turned toward him, left arm rising like the wing of a nightmarish bird.

Gregg saw the movement through the triangular arch of his own forearms, which had been driven back and upward by the gun's recoil. The weapon itself was pointing vertically, and uselessly, into the sky. An eternity passed as he fought to bring it down again to bear on an adversary who was gifted with demonic strength and speed. Gregg worked the trigger again, there was another flash, and the figure was hurled to the ground, shrilling and screaming. Gregg advanced on legs that tried to buckle with every step, blasting his enemy again and again with the gun's enormous power.

Incredibly, the dark being survived the massive blows. It rose to its feet, the space around it curiously distorted, like the image seen in a flawed lens, and began to back away. To Gregg's swimming senses, the figure seemed to cover an impossible distance with each step, as though it were treading an invisible surface that itself was retreating at great speed. The undulating hum of power faded to a whisper and was gone. He was alone in a bright, clean, slow-tilting world.

Gregg sank to his knees, grateful for the sunlight's warmth. He looked down at his chest and was astonished by the quantity of blood that had soaked through his clothing; then he was falling forward and unable to do anything about it.

> It is forbidden for me to tell you anything . . . my poor, brave Billy . . . but you have been through so much on my behalf. The words will probably hold no meaning for you, anyway—assuming you can even hear them.
>
> I tricked you, and you allowed yourself to be tricked, into taking part in a war . . . a war that has been fought for twenty thousand years and that may last forever . . .

There were long periods during which Gregg lay and stared at the knotted, grainy wood of the ceiling and tried to decide if it really was a ceiling, or if he was in some way suspended high above a floor. All he knew for certain was that he was being tended by a young woman, who came and went with soundless steps, and who spoke to him in a voice whose cadences were as measured and restful as the ocean tides.

> We are evenly matched—my people and the Others—but our strengths are as different as our basic natures. They have superior mastery of space; our true domain is time . . .
>
> There are standing waves in time . . . all presents are not equal . . . the "now" that you experience is known as the Prime Present, and has greater potential than any other. You are bound to it, just as the Others are bound to it . . . but the mental disciplines of my people enabled us to break free and migrate to another crest in the distant past . . . to safety . . .

Occasionally, Gregg was aware of the dressings on his chest being changed, and of his lips and brow being moistened with cool water. A beautiful young face hovered above his own, the gray eyes watchful and concerned, and he tried to remember the name he associated with it. Martha? Mary?

> To a woman of my race, the time of greatest danger is the last week of pregnancy . . . especially if the child is male and destined to have a certain cast of mind . . . In those circumstances the child can be drawn to your "now," the home time of all humanity, and the mother is drawn with it . . . Usually she can assert control soon after the child is born and return with it to the time of refuge . . . but there have been rare examples in which the male child resisted all attempts to influence its mental processes, and lived out its life in the Prime Present . . .
>
> Happily for me, my son is almost ready to travel . . . for the prince has grown clever and would soon return . . .

His enjoyment of the taste of the soup was Gregg's first indication that his body was making up its losses of blood, that his strength was returning, that he was not going to die. As the nourishing liquid was spooned into his mouth, he filled his eyes with the fresh young beauty of his daughter-wife, and was thankful for her kindness and grace. He forced into the deepest caverns of his mind all thoughts of the dreadful dark hunter who had menaced her.

I'm sorry . . . my poor, brave Billy . . . my son and I must travel now. The longer we remain, the more strongly he will be linked to the Prime Present . . . and my people will be anxious until they learn that we are safe . . .

I have been schooled to survive in your "now," though in less hazardous parts of it . . . which is why I am able to speak to you in English . . . but my ship came down in the wrong part of the world, all these thousands of years ago, and they will fear I have been lost . . .

A moment of lucidity. Gregg turned his head and looked through the open door of the bedroom into the house's main living space. Morna was standing at :he table, her head surrounded by a vibrant golden halo of hair. She stooped to rest her forehead against that of her child.

They both became hazy, then transparent; then they were gone.

Gregg pushed himself upright in the bed, shaking his head, reaching for them with his free hand. The pain of the reopening wound burned across his chest and he fell back onto the pillows, gasping for breath as the darkness closed in on him again. An indeterminate time later he felt the coolness of a moist cloth being pressed against his forehead, and his crushing sense of loss abated.

He smiled and said, "I was afraid you had left."

"How could I leave you like this?" Ruth Jefferson replied. "What in God's name has been going on out here, Billy Gregg? I find you lying in bed with a bullet hole in you, and the place outside looking like a battleground. Sam and some of his friends are out there cleaning up the mess the buzzards left, and they say they haven't see anything like it since the war."

Gregg opened his eyes and chose to give the sort of answer she would expect of him. "You missed a good fight, Ruth."

"Good fight!" Ruth clucked with exasperation. "You're more of an old fool than I took you for, Billy Gregg. What happened? Did the Portfield mob fall out with each other?"

"Something like that."

"Lucky for you," Ruth scolded. "And where were Morna and the baby when all this was going on? Where are they now?"

Gregg sorted through his memories, trying to separate dream and reality. "I don't know, Ruth. They . . . left."

"How?"

"They went with friends."

Ruth looked at him suspiciously, then gave a deep sigh. "I still think you've been up to something, but I've got a feeling I'll never find out what it was."

Gregg remained in bed for a further three days, being nursed to fitness by Ruth, and it seemed to him a perfectly natural outcome that they should revive their plans to be married. During that time there was a fairly steady stream of callers, men who were pleased that he was alive and that Josh Portfield was dead. All of them were curious about the details of the gun battle, which was fast becoming legendary, but he said nothing to dispel the notion that Portfield and his men had annihilated themselves in a sudden quarrel.

As soon as he had the house to himself, he searched it from one end to the other and found, tucked in behind his whisky jar, six slim gold bars neatly wrapped in a scrap of cloth. In keeping with his expectations, however, the big revolver—the black engine of death—was missing. He knew that Morna had decided he should not have it, and for a while he thought he might understand her reasons. There were words, half remembered from his delirium, that seemed as though they might explain all that had happened. It was only necessary to recall them properly, to get them into sharp focus in his mind. And at first the task appeared simple—the main requirement being a breathing space, time in which to think.

Gregg got his breathing space, but it was a long time before he could accept that, like the heat of summer, dreams can only fade.